THEY WERE ALREADY IN THE ROOM BEFORE THEY REALIZED WHAT THEY SAW.

The company of St. Hector's, their hands hidden in the sleeves of their robes, their cowls raised obscuring their faces, lined the walls in silence. Brother Conrad closed the door and threw home an iron bolt.

"You are penitents in a Retreat at the monastery of the Order of St. Hector," Brother Martin said, his tone flat. "Penitents, you will each remove all of your clothes and put on one of these." He pointed to a heap of coarse gray robes at his feet.

One of the men blurted an obscenity.

Brother Thomas stepped from the wall, jerked the man around and drove his fist deep into the man's belly. His lungs emptied in an explosive burst. His mouth gaped and his eyes widened. He sagged to his knees.

"What are you *doing?*" another penitent shouted.

A monk moved from the wall and struck him in the kidney from behind. . . .

JERROLD MUNDIS is the author of the highly praised novel, *Gerhardt's Children*. Under the pseudonym Robert Calder, he published *The Dogs,* a best-selling horror book with over half a million copies in print.

THE RETREAT

Jerrold Mundis

POPULAR LIBRARY

An Imprint of Warner Books, Inc.

A Warner Communications Company

Popular Library books are published by
Warner Books, Inc.
666 Fifth Avenue
New York, N.Y. 10103

 A Warner Communications Company

Printed in the United States of America

First Printing: June, 1985

10 9 8 7 6 5 4 3 2 1

This is for Bob Silverberg
bis vivit qui bene vivit

Each morning remember that you may not live until evening; and in the evening, do not presume to promise yourself another day. Be ready at all times, and so live that death may never find you unprepared. Many die suddenly and unexpectedly; for at an hour that we do not know the Son of Man will come.

Thomas à Kempis
The Imitation of Christ

BOOK I

Thy Will Be Done

Chapter 1

Within his small cell in the monastery, atop a pallet of rough ticking filled with straw which rested directly on the stone floor, Brother Martin lay in fitful sleep. He had labored in the fields all day under a hot sun denying himself water and rest. Perhaps such severity had been unwise.

But that was only subterfuge: the real unraveler of his tranquility was the Retreat.

He believed he hadn't thought much about it; but it was in his mind nonetheless, seeping through like groundwater.

When he slept, Brother Martin usually did not dream. And when he did dream, his dreams were usually placid. Even serene. Tonight, they were not.

In his dream he held a straight razor, of the kind with which his father had shaved. A mother-of-pearl handle. Blade ground narrow from top to bottom in a smooth curve that was nearly sensual. He held the straight razor open, thumb pressed to the spine.

With a limber wrist and the will, the all-important will, the straight razor was murderous.

Brother Martin dreamed that he was naked, and in some dark place—an alley, a grotto, a dungeon, what—and that three men were hunting him. They wanted to kill him.

He crouched with his back to some kind of wall, sharply aware of his hanging testicles, which were shriveled with fear. Sweat slathered his skin. It stung his eyes. He tasted it on his lips.

He could see only vague shapes in the darkness. He strained to hear more than the pound of his own blood. He nearly gibbered with fear.

Where there had been nothing, a man suddenly appeared. The man slashed at him with a knife. Brother Martin leapt away, crying out in dread. The knife point slit the skin of his arm like silk from shoulder to elbow.

Panic forced him to boldness. He clamped the man's wrist as the knife completed its downstroke and arced his razor from right to left, cutting, turned his hand and brought it back from left to right, cutting, opening the throat.

Blood fountained onto Brother Martin's chest.

The man fell and thrashed on the ground with choking coughs. Brother Martin stood rigid.

He held the razor poised.

He listened.

He didn't breathe.

A quick pattering—the sound of a running cat. He spun to face it with a whimper.

But the attack came at his back. A knife plunged in below his shoulder, struck a rib. He gasped and whirled. And as he did, the last of them, the man he had heard, came at him, and he was between them, facing neither, and being cut on both sides. He screamed and lashed blindly to his right with the razor, flailed with his left hand to protect himself from that quarter. His palm was sliced open. A knife drove into his right side like fire.

He writhed, tearing the weapon from his attacker's hand. He whipped the razor around without direction, made contact with flesh, whipped it again as he fell to his knees. The man on his right slumped over him. He shrugged the dying body off and turned to his left, took a slash across his face, and on his knees he cut forth, back, forth again. A coil of gut spilled out over him, and there was no more attack.

Naked, kneeling in the dark, slick with blood that was his

and blood that was not his, he swayed in agony and murmured, "Oh my God, my God," dying.

Brother Martin woke. Suddenly. With a jerk the length of his body and a snap of his eyes.

It was totally dark in his cell, heavy clouds obscuring the waning quarter-moon, no light at all filtering through the narrow slit in the stone wall that was more a source of ventilation than a true window, even in bright sunlight.

Without, crickets were chirping, there was a distant *harumph* from a bullfrog in the pond. The faintest of breezes rustled the nearby willows, barely slipped through the window, felt chill on his moist skin.

He was free of the sanguinary theater of his dream, but the sense of it lingered, like a taste of bile.

His body knew the time: a small part past midnight.

Nearly thirty days to the stroke since Abbot Giles had died and left the Monastery of Saint Hector leaderless and without guiding hand. Had died on a hard mattress in a rough-cut wooden bed. Died in the flickering illumination of the tall candles burning around him while Brother Stewart, an ordained priest, administered the Last Rites and as the company of Saint Hector's knelt in the dark stone hall outside the abbot's cell and chanted the *Dies Irae*.

Thirty days ago, nearly to the stroke, and thirty days to the coming Retreat, nearly to the stroke.

By the end of the week a new abbot would be elected, and to him would fall that awesome responsibility.

Oh Lord, guide him and give him strength, Brother Martin prayed.

Into Thy hands I deliver my own spirit. Be merciful.

He closed his eyes.

Slowly, the dream fell away. There were moments of recollection, fortunately brief, and then a growing peace. He slipped back into sleep, thanking God, and this time he did not dream.

Outside, a great horned owl on the limb of an oak near the

livestock barn shifted its weight to one leg, flexed the long curved talons of the other, then shifted back and continued to search with its large yellow eyes for a mouse, a grain rat, a rabbit, movement of any kind. It went: *Hooooo, hooooo*.

It was hunting.

Chapter 2

Dominic Caparelli stood with his attorney before the raised desk of the judge, forced to look up, forced into the inferior position—a supplicant before the law—which was the point.

He was humiliated and furious. He wasn't used to looking up to anybody. It was the other way around.

Unconsciously, he used his anger to smother his fear. He didn't like to think himself capable of fear.

Judge Sullivan asked, the jury foreman, "On the charge of murder in the first degree, how do you find the defendant?"

"We find the defendant not guilty, your honor."

The prosecutor threw down his pen in disgust. The gallery grew so noisy that many people missed the foreman's answer to the second and third charges.

Caparelli wanted to dance in triumph. But he clamped down and remained bland. He was a man of bulky emotion, but also of control and was a fair dissembler.

Judge Sullivan rapped for silence. He looked down at Caparelli several moments before he spoke. He was clearly unhappy, but he gathered himself and rose to his responsibility. He said, "Dominic Caparelli, you have been found innocent of murder in the first degree. You have been found guilty on one count of harrassment. And you have been found guilty on one count of attempted jury-tampering. You are remanded into your attorney's custody. The court orders you to appear before this bench two weeks from today, at which time sentence will be pronounced."

Court was adjourned.

Hawthorne, Caparelli's attorney, offered his hand, but Caparelli turned instead toward the prosecutor. He smiled glitteringly, viciously, the smile that came to him at moments of triumph. The prosecutor pretended not to see and busied himself putting papers into his attaché case, but the tips of his ears burned and Caparelli was satisfied.

Now he shook Hawthorne's hand. Hawthorne was trim, in his mid-thirties. He dressed expensively, wore black-rimmed glasses and spoke in quiet measured cadences. He was married, but Caparelli still found him faggoty and didn't like him. And though Hawthorne never let it show, he knew that the lawyer didn't like him either. Caparelli was good at that sort of thing, knowing what was underneath.

"You did great," he said. "Come on, I'll buy you lunch."

Hawthorne nodded.

Orson came through the gate in the gallery railing. "I congratulate you, Uncle Dominic. The verdict was partly just."

Caparelli looked at him. The look grew harsh.

Orson beamed, his great bushy mustache rising. "Justly innocent of that first vile charge. Unjustly guilty of those slurs upon your character."

"Yeah." Caparelli laughed, pulled Orson into his shoulder and dug his fingers into the younger man's neck. He often used a display of physical strength to assert his authority or to remind people of it. "Huh," he went. "Huh. I like that, 'slurs on my character.'"

Orson was somewhat younger than Hawthorne, just past thirty. His clothes were equally as costly but much flashier—radically cut and colored. Orson danced. Orson played. Orson always knew the right place to party.

He was Caparelli's nephew. If Caparelli hadn't been in prison for breaking the knees of a furrier who was late with his payments one time too many, and who, *mala fortuna*, was connected in some obscure way no one could have foreseen with a city councilman, then Rosalia would not have married Luigi DiPalo—Orson's father. He would have seen to that. But by the time Caparelli was released, there was a baby already.

Orson. Orson DiPalo.

What kind of name was that?

Luigi, the *cretino*, had wanted to give him an American first name, so it would be easier for him in school, and later on. Jesus!

When Orson was two, Luigi discovered in a book that Orson was actually an old Latin name (and what were Italians, really, but the descendants of the Romans?) and showed Caparelli what it meant: *bear*.

What did that mean, what it meant? A name was who you were. It didn't *mean* anything.

Cretino.

Caparelli would have fitted Luigi with cement and dropped him into the river if Rosalia wouldn't have suspected him immediately.

As it was, he carried the fool for years, found him one drudge job or another within the organization and supplemented their income when he had to and paid Orson's tuition to Cornell. It had all been worth it. Orson was good. Smart. Tough. Too wild, but that'd settle down when he got older. Some of the best had been real crazies when they were kids. Caparelli had sired only a daughter and though he loved her enormously, it was nice to have Orson.

"Let's go," Orson said. "Paulie's got the car ready. You're a free man—for a while anyway."

Caparelli didn't like that part of him very much—the weird joking; he laughed at everything, even when it wasn't funny at all.

"Did he call Pomona?" Caparelli's wife didn't know why the government persecuted him. He was a good man. Sometimes during the trial he'd hear her crying in another room, but she wouldn't let him see because she knew it would send him into a rage at these people who had hurt her.

"Right away. She says her heart is yours. She's going to church with Mrs. Santini to give thanks to God. She waits for you with love."

Caparelli started out of the courtroom, flanked by Orson and Hawthorne.

The high-ceilinged hall was filled with reporters and photographers. Caparelli marched straight ahead, as if it were empty. Hawthorne fended people off on one side, continuing to earn his large fee—"Please, no questions now. Mr. Caparelli will have a statement for you tomorrow · morning"—while Orson went into action on the other, blocking and shouldering aside the more aggressive reporters, smiling with false politeness and saying, "Pardon me. Thank you. Excuse me."

The kid was good.

Television crews filmed Caparelli as he descended. A blond ABC reporter managed to slip by Hawthorne. She said into her mike, "Mr. Caparelli, a *Daily News* editorial called you a 'savage' and 'an animal' last week. How do you react to that in light of being found innocent of murdering the state's chief witness last year in that extortion case?"

Orson interposed himself quickly. He took hold of her wrist. "Hey," he said into the mike. "The man's just come through a harrowing ordeal. Ease up, will you? You'll have a statement tomorrow."

He was smiling, but Caparelli could see the woman grimace under his grip. Orson increased the pressure until a little gasp escaped her and she stepped back.

"Thanks a lot," he said, and they hurried downward past the crew while the interviewer looked after them, rubbing at her wrist.

Good kid.

It was hot. Caparelli was sweating. Paulie got out of the car and opened the rear door. Not a limousine—Caparelli didn't like to draw attention—but a solid comfortable black Lincoln sedan with smoked windows. Paulie was lumpish and middle-aged. He'd broken most of his knuckles at different times in his youth and they were outsized and misshapen. Caparelli got in, then Hawthorne. The air-conditioning was on. Paulie had been with Caparelli a long time and didn't miss much.

Orson got into the front. Paulie was back behind the wheel. "Where we going?"

"Uh, up Mulberry Street."

With his initial flush of victory subsiding, it was only now occurring to Caparelli that he'd been convicted on the two lesser charges. He hadn't paid much attention to them, dominated by the murder count. He realized suddenly that he was going to spend time in jail. And every single minute they could legally give him. The federal task force, the New York State Police *and* the New York City Police had allied themselves in one combined effort to nail him. The bastards blew the big one, but he knew they'd push for the maximum on the two they *had* won.

"How about Umberto's," Hawthorne suggested.

Caparelli came out of his unhappy reverie to glare at him. Joey Gallo had been shot dead in Umberto's. Caparelli was superstitiously fearful of eating anywhere a member of the organization had been hit. Umberto's. John and Mary's in Brooklyn, where they got Tony Galante. Tony's Place—Carmine DeSipico ice-picked in the toilet. Wee Willie Lachesa at ... It went on.

He said, "Let's go to Casa di Pietro, Paulie."

Mulberry Street was Little Italy's central thoroughfare, dotted all along with restaurants, coffee shops, pastry stores, private social clubs, cheese and butcher shops and vegetable markets. Paulie turned off onto Hester Street and parked in front of Casa di Pietro, a small storefront restaurant. The buildings here—like most in the community—were largely narrow four-, five-, and six-story affairs of gray-brown or reddish stone. Few had elevators. At intervals one had been gutted and renovated and the apartments rented out for sums ten times those being paid by families who had been in the neighborhood three-quarters of a century, whose immigrant founders were long since dead and whose onetime children now lived on Social Security.

Two youths were approaching as Caparelli got out, nineteen, twenty years old, in jeans and bodybuilders' shirts. They were squat and broadshouldered and wore small gold crucifixes on chains outside their shirts. They were smoking joints. Caparelli wrinkled up his nose at the smell. A few feet past, the taller of them bent his head to his companion. "That's Dommy Ball Bat."

Caparelli touched Orson's arm, pointed, crooked his finger.

Orson overtook them and dropped his hands on their shoulders. They turned, saw who it was, saw Caparelli looking at them, dropped their joints and became anxious. Orson walked them back.

"What's your name?" Caparelli asked the taller one.

"Guido," the boy said. "Guido Mesina."

"You?"

"T-Tommy DeNova. Sir."

"He's my cousin from Chicago," Guido said. "He's visiting this week."

"Uh-huh." Caparelli nodded. "Uh-huh."

Guido worked his lower lip. Tommy shifted his weight back and forth.

"Where do you jerkoffs get off smoking that shit on the street. My sister lives down here. My daughter. My fucking grandson, for Christ's sake. You don't dirty up the neighborhood with that shit. You don't make the streets ugly for my family to walk on. You respect these streets. You got that?"

Guido nodded. Tommy said, "Yes, sir!"

"Now what I want you to do is this. I'm going inside to eat with my friends. I don't want to have to worry about nothing. I want to enjoy a nice quiet meal. So what you're going to do for me is wait out here and watch my car until I'm done. So

I don't have to worry that nobody steals my tape player or nothing. *Capite?*"

They did.

At table, Orson said, "This is nice, Uncle, but there's much better food to be had down here."

Orson was a serious eater. He ate things Caparelli couldn't even pronounce and in places the newspapers reviewed.

"I like it." Caparelli ordered a jug of wine and a plate of antipasto to start.

Hawthorne said, "Would someone actually steal your tape player down here?"

"Naw." Caparelli tucked the cloth napkin into his collar. "I just wanted to put it to those two *Stronzi*. But it's not like it used to be. When kids had respect. The old people still walk the streets and they don't have to buy fancy locks for their doors, but it's different. Sometimes things happen." He shook his head and speared an artichoke heart.

They ate, then talked over espresso and cappucino.

"On the jury-tampering, three to five," Hawthorne said. "The harassment, we can probably force probation. They've been careful—so far we can't find any reasonable basis for appeal, though we'll file one as a matter of course."

"Three to five. That much."

"Yes."

"And I got a snowball's chance in hell of parole once I'm in."

"Right now they want blood. Things change with a little time."

"That's *my* time you're talking about, lawyer."

"It is," Hawthorne agreed.

Caparelli hadn't known him very long. Nicholas Spender, Caparelli's longtime attorney, had suffered a heart attack halfway into his defense preparation. He survived, but had to rest, couldn't work. He was worried about the murder charge—

Caparelli was guilty as hell and the government had strong position—so he recommended Hawthorne. "He's brilliant. Pay him whatever he asks. He doesn't come cheap, and sometimes he doesn't come at all, at any price." Spender didn't know why. Hawthorne defended some of the foulest, but turned down others who were no worse. He championed clients against mild charges, and didn't even bother to return calls from those in more serious trouble. He took on indigents and the rich without apparent pattern.

Spender called him for Caparelli. They sat waiting two weeks. Caparelli got angry. Spender kept him in check: he *needed* Hawthorne. In the middle of the second week, Caparelli said, "He's running a background on me. I got that from my man in the detective bureau. He's digging deep and he's going back a long way."

Hawthorne's secretary had called just in time, as Caparelli was about to blow.

Hawthorne couldn't break down the prosecutor's case, but he did succeed in puncturing it with dozens of little pinpricks that, in aggregate, *appeared* significant, and which raised enough doubt on the murder charge for acquittal and which reduced the assault charge, a felony, to harassment, a misdemeanor. Not even God could have stopped conviction on the jury-tampering charge—they had everything short of a videotape on that one.

But Caparelli still didn't like Hawthorne. There was something . . . off-center about him, something Caparelli couldn't quite put his finger on. Well, what the hell. He'd won, hadn't he?

Orson paid the check with an American Express card, a company card—*Caparelli Imports, Inc*. Olive oil and spices. Orson was secretary-treasurer.

"You got pastry crumbs on your mustache," Caparelli said.

Orson dabbed with a napkin. "Gone?"

"Yeah. You know, you look like an oldtimer with that thing.

We used to call 'em Mustache Petes. They didn't want to change from the old ways. There was a lot of trouble when the next generation grew up and wanted to do things different. Lot of trouble. Fact, you look like one I remember from when I was little—Pastore D'Amato. Some kid maybe a third his age blew him up with a shotgun right down on the next block, in Montradella's Pastry Shop."

"Terrific," Orson said. "I look like an old guy that got hit."

"Maybe you'll cut it off."

Outside, Guido and Tommy got up from the stoop where they had glumly been playing liar's poker with dollar bills. Caparelli made a circuit of his car, inspecting it.

"Okay," he said. "Come here." He lowered his voice. "You know what they call me, right?"

"Uh . . ." Guido said.

"The name you told him."

Unhappily, Guido nodded.

"I just want you to remember it. Real good." He dismissed them.

They hurried off. Caparelli smiled. He was called Dommy Ball Bat because he liked to use a bat. He'd broken a lot of legs and arms with a bat. He'd killed seven men with a bat. The last was the one for whose murder he'd been found innocent today. It was almost a year ago, one of his own people who'd turned informer. Wearing gloves and carrying a baseball bat Caparelli walked through a delivery entrance with Paulie into the garden section of a little restaurant in Brooklyn, early afternoon, where Frank was drinking from a bottle of wine and eating a plate of linguini.

He jumped up in terror and reached for his gun. Paulie's own gun was out and he slapped Frank's hand away from his weapon and shoved him back into his chair. And as Frank sat down hard Caparelli swung the bat and caught him right in the side of his head, just in front of the ear. The bat caved in Frank's temple, shot jagged bone up through his scalp and sprayed blood from his broken head and from his eyes and nose.

Caparelli dropped the bat atop the crumpled body so those for whom it was important to know *would* know and turned on his heel and walked out.

Chapter 3

It was the end of the week. Brother Martin woke. A barely discernible undertone of gray moonlight in his cell. The locusts, crickets, and pond frogs could all be heard outside; only somewhat past the midpoint of their nocturnal day. A large beetle was whirring about somewhere within the cell. It struck the wall with an audible click, like the snap of a twig, which was repeated an instant later as it fell to the floor. Several quiet moments passed. The whirring began anew.

It was nearly two-thirty. The monastery possessed but one clock, and that was in the abbot's office—for occasions on which the outside world had to be dealt with and certain time was important. The monks had no other need. The rhythm of their days scarcely varied and their bodies knew the time.

Unbidden, Brother Martin's dream of several nights ago came back to him. He lay still, with his eyes open, turning it in his mind, with little personal response, as if it were a fiction told by another. It was ugly, corrupt. That part of him still linked to the things of this world.

He was disheartened.

When, my God, shall I be free?

Immediately he repented: of all the addictions he had known, Despair was the most seductive.

Thy will be done.

The beetle struck the wall again, but this time didn't fall. It veered about erratically, the pitch of its sound wobbling up and down a moment before it settled back into a steady drone.

Brother Martin heard the rustle of robes beyond his door, the slip of sandaled feet. There was a small knock.

"It is the new day," Brother Phelan said.

"Praised be God," Brother Martin replied.

Brother Phelan moved to the next door.

Brother Martin rose and lighted a candle that stood on a little stone corbel. His sleeping chamber was only eight feet square. The beetle was at rest on a wall. He captured it with care in cupped hands and released it through the narrow window back into the night. Removing his shift he folded it and placed it on the bottom of two wooden shelves and took a fresh undergarment from the top. He stretched, loosening his sleep-stiffened muscles.

He was forty-two years old, slightly over six feet, large-handed and lean. A big, physical man, as were many at Saint Hector's—qualities often found in the kind of lives they had led before entering the order. Though not required, he wore the tonsure as a symbol of his commitment. Other than that shaven circle, his hair was full and black, graying now, and his eyebrows thick silvered ridges over dark eyes. Careful, thoughtful eyes.

He poured water from an earthenware pitcher into a bowl on his night table, washed, lathered his cheeks and shaved. The unbearded among the company shaved with straight razors, which endured and could be stropped to daily keenness; the monastery wished to be self-contained. But when the sexton made his monthly trip into Scanandaga, some thirty miles away on the edge of a cold blackwatered Adirondack lake, for those few items the monks could not produce themselves or which were more practical to purchase, he returned with blades for Brother Martin.

By dispensation, Brother Martin shaved with a safety razor.

Finished, he rinsed off the lather, put on his robe, pulled the cowl over his head and knelt before a wall niche in which a wooden crucifix was installed. He prayed, crossed himself, kissed the crucifix and went out into the hall.

He passed the Solitary's chamber. Its door was closed tight, as it had been each day of the twelve years Brother Martin had been a monk of the order.

Others were filing from their own cells into the flickering illumination of the wall-bracketed candles. They walked silently and alone to the stone stairs at the end of the hall, where they descended to the first floor and went to the chapel. There they sang in choir, recited the first of the canonical hours and heard Brother Stewart say Mass for them.

The next hour was reserved for private prayer.

Brother Martin returned to his cell and went down on his knees. The frogs and insects gradually fell into silence, and not much later the first birds began to call. The sun rose and a brilliant shaft of light plunged through the window slit to fall directly upon the crucifix. He had first seen this phenomenon the morning after he'd taken his vows and been assigned to this cell. It occurred for a few weeks each summer. Then, he had received it as a sign, and had experienced rapture: the road to salvation had been hard.

At the hour, he concluded his prayer and went to the refectory. He took his place at one of the two long trestle tables that formed, on either side of a shorter one, an inverted U. The monks waited in silence. Brother Stefan, the lector, went to a pedestal at the side of the room, whereon a large Bible rested. Brother Stefan opened it and rested his eyes on the page a moment, as if considering. Brother Stefan's face was cut by a vivid purple scar that slanted down from his right temple across the bridge of his nose and through the corner of his mouth. He looked up.

"Brothers, today's lesson is taken from the Book of Job." He read with quiet intensity, placing special emphasis, fittingly, Brother Martin thought, on one particular line: "I abhor myself and repent in dust and ashes."

Dust and ashes.

Yes.

Breakfast, during which no word was spoken, was porridge with black bread and tea.

When it was over, Prior Hilliard rose from the abbot's seat, which he had occupied since the death of Brother Giles. He surveyed them through impassive gray eyes. He was a thin angular man with a sharp nose and cheekbones. He was God's sword. The only hunger remaining him was to remove the last of himself from this mortal coil; his faith was intense and cold.

"Praise be to God," he said.

"Praise be to God," they answered.

"Blessed be His Holy Name."

"Blessed be His Holy Name."

"Brothers," he said, "our time of mourning is over. So also the careful examination of our consciences. This day we elect the one to lead and govern us. Pray that the hand of God will guide us. May His will be done." He said nothing more, simply released them with a small movement of his hand.

This was a discretionary hour.

Brother Martin went out of the monastery, as did a handful of others, each his private way. He set off across a large cleared area in which were located the livestock and storage barns toward a pasture, and the woods beyond. The sun was already bright but not yet hot and the grass was still beaded with dew. It was wet and chill against his feet. The geese gabbled at him in annoyance from their holding pen. Cows lowed within the barn, waiting to graze. The monastery's billy goat, Samson, a potent and unusually social animal, stood up, placed his sharp forehooves on the top rail of his pen and went: "Bla-ah-ah. Bla-ah-ah."

Brother Martin detoured to pat him on the head. He pushed against the goat's horns, which it liked.

"Bla-ah-ah."

Brother Martin said nothing. The monks were not vowed to strict silence, but still they avoided speech unless it was essential. Even words to an animal could distract from the inner life.

Brother Wilfred, who bore the primary responsibility for the stock, was exempt from this *de facto* rule when he was with the animals, which fared better when spoken to. He was Rhodesian and had a natural way with creatures. His voice and touch soothed them, cheered them, and he made them thrive. It was noted, and had occasionally been said, that he was spiritually impeded because of this. He walked with a bounce. Bemusement would cross his face. In forgetful moments, he was liable to whistle.

This had vexed old Abbot Giles, who had more than once ordered Brother Wilfred into irons and to acts of mortification. Brother Giles hadn't aged well. He'd grown petulant and vindictive in his last years and become a rigorous disciplinarian endlessly suspicious of infraction and laxity, of self-indulgence and considered temptation. He had ordered punishments too frequently, to Brother Martin's thinking, penances too harsh. And he'd encouraged an unhealthy burgeoning of self-abasement and self-mortification, which had been harmful, Brother Martin thought, to those already inclined in such a direction. Brother Hilliard himself, the prior, had subsisted entirely on water and gruel, with an occasional raw vegetable, for nearly a year now and wore a hair shirt beneath his robe each day.

Still, for all his mean caprice and queerness, the core of Brother Giles's intelligence remained intact: he'd managed the affairs of the monastery well until the final year and had capably, even brilliantly, directed the three Retreats which had taken place during Brother Martin's years as a monk.

And the one in which Brother Martin, then simply Martin, had participated from the other side.

Brother Martin left the goat pen, crossed the pasture and entered a forest that was hardwoods and scrub brush, spotted here and there with a pine. The sun hadn't penetrated yet and mist swirled in the low spots. The order's holdings embraced more than two hundred acres of woods, rocky mountainsides, streams, a small lake and some lower swamp, all bordering thousands of acres of state land. The hardwoods gave way to pines and the going became easier. Brother Martin followed a deer trail—the rusty pine needles scruffed up, hoof impressions in the earth, small piles of droppings—to the edge of a shallow stream. He sat on a rock and rested his back against a tree. A crow called, others answered. The water rippled over stones with a steady hiss. The first slanting shafts of sun only now pierced the thick pine branches to dapple the carpet of dead needles on the ground. It was one of his favorite times, at one of his favorite places.

He undertook a final review of the virtues and faults of those monks he thought the electors might nominate for abbot. He refused to speculate on whether they might wish him for the chair.

That was too dreadful.

He emerged from the woods at half past eight. The company assembled in the chapter room, which was off the cloister and flooded with morning light. The windows were open. A pleasant breeze carried in the scent of the cloister's flowers.

Brother Hilliard waited in the abbot's chair while they took their stools around the walls. They were fifty-six in all, including the oblates Michael and Gregory. Neither of the oblates would have a voice in the proceedings, of course, but they were still privy to it—to the extent of their comprehension. Michael sat next to Brother Harold, looking to him, as usual, for reassurance. Gregory's broad shoulders were hunched and his brow furrowed in some unfathomable contemplation. He stared at his big blunt fingers, which were twined together.

The prior said, "Brothers, we have searched our hearts and souls throughout this last month. And we have mourned for Brother Giles. Our mourning is done now, our search draws to a close. We come here to select six from among us, who, by the end of this day, shall present to us the brother who will guide and govern us henceforth. May we please the Lord."

Brother Vergil and the oblate Michael passed out pencils and slips of paper. Brother Vergil, due to some metabolic quirk, retained an endomorphic body despite the ascetic regimen that kept the rest of them in lean trim. He had a cherub's face with clear blue eyes. When he was twenty, Brother Vergil had firebombed a church in Arkansas one night, killing four black choir girls.

Brother Hilliard polled the company three times before they reached consensus. The electors were: the prior himself, Brother Martin, Brother Wilfred, Brother Leopold, Brother Thomas and Brother Peter.

Brother Hilliard thanked the company and excused them to lunch. He and the other lectors forwent the spare meal of soup and bread and retired to the conference room that adjoined the library on the second floor. They sat around a wooden table in straightbacked chairs. Brother Hilliard laid a pad and pen before him. He wasted no words. He said, "Brother Peter, whom do you wish to present?"

Brother Peter was a mostly bald man with a white beard, a steady and methodical monk. He named two monks, then said, "And yourself, Prior."

The nominations went round the table to Brother Martin, who named Brother Conrad.

The prior, the last to speak, said simply: "Brother Martin."

There were eleven candidates in all. They pared that down to five in an hour's counsel—Brothers Stefan, Martin, Hilliard, Raphael and Phelan. They recited None, the fifth canonical hour, then opened discussion on Brother Stefan.

Brother Peter said, "He's pious."

"He holds the Rule strictly," Brother Thomas said.

Brother Leopold, whose left arm ended in a stump at the wrist, said, "He spends too much time in his books. He's a dreamer. The abbot has to deal with practical matters. I don't think he's up to the responsibility."

"Yet he's intelligent," Brother Peter said, always a man of balances.

Brother Martin was uneasy. He wished the virtues of the others to prevail over any the electors might find in him, but he was constrained to say, "Every man has his special road to

God, according to his own nature. Brother Stefan's road is his studies. I worry that he would be hurt if he were kept away from them too much."

Brother Wilfred nodded vigorously. "Yes." Brother Wilfred was not very cerebral, but his intuition often applied to people as well as animals, even if he found it difficult to articulate this understanding.

They considered Brother Phelan, whose devotion to the order was exceeded only by that to his Lord.

Brother Hilliard listened to them, then said bluntly, "He's too soft. I think he'd crack under the burden of the Retreat."

This might have been overly severe, but was close enough that no one offered dispute.

The prior raised Brother Raphael. Brother Raphael had been a doctor in the outside world and had served as the monastery's infirmarer for more than twenty years.

"He's a solid man," Brother Martin said. "And truly at peace with God."

"His age is a question," said Brother Peter, who wasn't much younger himself.

"But he's still in good health," said Brother Leopold.

Brother Thomas, gaunt, redhaired and coarseskinned, said, "He's smart. He's strong. I don't care how old he is."

Brother Hilliard said, "He has compassion. That is important."

"Perhaps in troublesome amount," Brother Peter said. "You might remember that he had some difficulty in the last Retreat."

"Only at first," Brother Martin said. "As happens to many of us in the beginning, when the point is less clear, before the essential healing and restorative nature asserts itself."

"He never loses control," Brother Thomas said belligerently. "He always acts through grace."

The same—as he and the others knew—could not be said of himself. To his bitter disconsolation Brother Thomas still retained, somewhere in his center, a violence and volatility he could not root out and crush despite years of desperate attempt.

He suffered headaches of such awfulness that he could barely stand up, and at intervals he would be taken by a screaming rage in which he would strike out and destroy whatever he could get his hands on. He was weak and confused after these bouts and couldn't remember what had happened. Brother Raphael had ministered to him over the years and had managed to dampen the intensity of the seizures some and lengthen the time between them. But he couldn't eliminate them. Brother Thomas clung to him for succor, trusted him and looked to him—in some spiritual danger—almost for salvation.

"Yes, that's very much in his favor," Brother Peter said. Though consecrated to God, they were still men, mortal and fallible, and Brother James understood that God had visited a unique and terrible cross upon Brother Thomas.

Brother Martin found Brother Raphael's age not very relevant. He believed the infirmarer would be an abbot of merit, and he said so.

Brother Thomas was made happy.

The prior asked Brother Martin to leave; they would discuss him next. He wanted to say: Please, not me. He stepped from the room into the hall. He waited ten minutes.

Brother Hilliard came out. "You can go back. I'll wait now."

Brother Wilfred looked up with a hint of a smile as Brother Martin took his chair. Brother Martin knew that his candidacy had been argued well. He felt tired.

No one spoke at first. Brother Hilliard was daunting, even in his absence.

Then Brother Peter said, "He's been a good prior."

"He's strong," Brother Thomas said, striving for equity, since he was clearly championing Brother Raphael.

Brother Leopold unconsciously rubbed the stump of his wrist over the rough cloth of his robe. "He's harsh."

"He detests his responsibility," Brother Martin said. "He accepts it only because he's vowed to obedience. He yearns to be free of life and to become one with God. I think he refrains from self-murder only because it is a grievous sin."

He spoke what no one else among them had been willing to put into words. In their silence, they agreed with him. They summoned the prior back.

He seated himself. "We will vote now."

Each of the monks wrote a single name on a sheet of paper, folded it and passed it to Brother Hilliard. He opened them and read out the names. There were three votes for Brother Martin, three for Brother Raphael.

Brother Martin forced himself to maintain a neutral face. But his palms moistened, he felt lightheaded.

They voted a second time, since unanimity was required.

Again Brother Martin wrote, *Brother Raphael;* though scarcely any hope remained him.

There were four more votes, the final two tallying five for Brother Martin, one for Brother Raphael.

The prior said, "Brother Martin, it is your duty to submit to the will of the electors."

This time, resigned, Brother Martin wrote his own name.

Brother Hilliard opened the papers. He stood. He pressed his palms together and lowered his head. *"Per veros oculos Dei,"* he said. "By the true eyes of God. You are our abbot, Brother Martin."

The bells in the campanile pealed joyously, announcing the reign of a new abbot. The monks hurried in from the fields, set aside household tasks, left devotionals and studies and went directly to the chapel. Not a word was spoken as they assembled and took their places in the pews before the simple wooden altar, and no glances were exchanged, but still there was a palpable sense of tension and expectation.

When all were present, Brother Hilliard rose, sought out Brother Martin, took him by the hand and led him up to the altar to face the company. He raised Brother Martin's hand and raised also the simple but ancient gold ring of authority.

"Videat Altissiumus!" he cried. "Let the Most High look

upon us and bless His work, for today He has guided us to the election of Abbot Martin, to whom we owe unquestioning obedience. Praised be God!"

"Praised be God!" the company responded.

Brother Hilliard lowered Brother Martin's hand, slipped the ring onto his finger and knelt and kissed it. Then he withdrew, leaving Brother Martin to stand alone.

Brother Martin turned to the altar and spread his arms. His voice rang. "'Have mercy upon me, O God, according to thy loving kindness: according unto the multitude of thy tender mercies blot out my transgressions...'" He struck the fourteenth verse of the psalm he had chosen strongly. "'Deliver me from blood guiltiness, O God, thou God of my salvation—'"

A communal sigh whispered through the chapel.

"'The sacrifices of God are a broken spirit: a broken and a contrite heart, O God, thou wilt not despise...'"

When he finished he turned back to the company. He blessed them. "I am not worthy," he said. "Come forward and let me humble myself before you."

The prior, according to the dictates of ritual, was the first to step up. Brother Martin went to his knees before him. He knelt and kissed Brother Hilliard's sandaled feet. And then he kissed the feet of every other monk in turn.

There was much to do. Brother Hilliard acquainted him with the ledgers and records necessary to the maintenance of the monastery. He spent what remained of the afternoon with them in the abbot's office. He emerged to take supper with the company at six, then returned, and paused in his work only to say Compline, the last of the canonical hours.

The monastery's day ended as the evening shadows spread. By full darkness, the monks were all in their cells, preparing for sleep.

Brother Martin remained in the abbot's office, studying by candlelight. The night stillness was strange to him—he hadn't been awake at this hour in three years, since the last Retreat.

That recollection made him pause.

The Retreat was now his responsibility.

He thought of setting aside the practical, mundane material before him and bringing out the Chronicles. He hadn't known they existed until this afternoon when Brother Hilliard revealed to him the hidden vault in the office. He had thanked God with all his heart, for he sorely needed their guidance. But, he decided now, it would be best to approach them in the morning, when he was fresh and could concentrate fully.

He worked another hour on the ledgers. But the Retreat would not leave his mind. So he closed the books to rest. He rubbed his eyes.

And then he knew what was necessary.

He lit the candle in the glass lantern on the corner of his desk. He extinguished the others and left the office. The monastery was in darkness. He walked down the long west hall in a capsule of wavering light thrown by the lantern, all the way to its end, where it joined the shorter, south hall. He opened a door there, which gave onto stairs that led down to the cellar. The cellar lay beneath the cloister.

Moisture glistened on the stone walls as he descended. Not much could be stored down here in the summer because of the humidity. He went to a corner of the cellar. The lantern tossed and fluttered his shadow as he manipulated a stone. It shifted under his hand, exposing an iron ring. He turned the ring and pulled. A narrow section of wall swung outward. He picked up his lantern and started down the stone steps that were revealed.

The lower level was smaller than the cellar. And dry. Serviced by an intricate network of ventilation shafts through which air moved partly by convection and partly driven by a windmill. It was necessary to dissipate the humidity here—to prevent bone and respiratory disease.

The room was rectangular. Each of the longer walls was set with ten wooden doors. There were four in the short wall to Brother Martin's left. The doors were fitted with iron latches, which were padlocked. In the wall to his right was a single steel door.

Brother Martin unlocked and opened that one.

A stink came forth from the Chamber of Mortal Meditation, a cloying and sour stink.

Chapter 4

Five days after his acquittal, Wednesday, Caparelli slept in till nine-thirty, which was late for him. Hawthorne had telephoned the previous afternoon and asked him to come to his office this morning at eleven. Since the morning was shot, Caparelli had stayed out late Tuesday. That was his regular poker night. He played with a city councilman, a union official, an uptown restaurateur, an Italian television actor and Mattie Locasio, who ran an after-hours joint.

The restaurateur's kitchen brought over a smorgasbord, and they drank a lot, celebrating. They embraced Caparelli, there were happy tears. Caparelli had seen many of those in the past few days, and he was moved. Without friends, there was no life.

He was hung over this morning, but he didn't care. He showered. The girl who cleaned made him steak and eggs for breakfast. Pomona was already gone with their grandson Carl. It was always a treat when Carl stayed over. Pomona had left a note saying that Carl had been disappointed not to see him this morning. Caparelli felt bad. He'd make it up to the boy next week.

He knotted his tie and put on his jacket, left, walked the carpeted hall to the elevator bank and went down. The lobby was spacious and had marble floors and walls. Palms and ferns grew in cast-iron planters. There were leather couches and chairs. An armed security guard sat behind a desk where closed-circuit television monitors displayed all of the building's entrances, the elevator interiors, and random pictures of the halls, the roof garden and the interior fire stairs.

He said, "Good morning, Mr. Caparelli."

"Good morning, George."

One of the doormen touched a finger to his braided hat. "Mornin', Mr. Caparelli."

"Good morning, Rufe."

Rufe opened the glass door. "Will you want a cab, sir?"

"No thanks."

Hawthorne's office was ten blocks away, on Madison, and though the day was too warm, the humidity had abated and Caparelli, fretting over how much he had drunk and smoked last night, thought he should walk. He was worried about his heart. They don't last forever, his doctor had said. You smoke too much. You drink too much. You weigh too much. You don't get any exercise. Last month some indigestion had caused him an hour of sweaty panic. So he'd begun to make himself walk, convinced that each block would help his heart live another week. And he worried.

A long pool with fountain jets that drove plumes of water into the air lay between the sidewalk and the semicircle of the entrance drive. The misting water caught the sun in rainbow hues. At night the plumes were colored by submerged lights.

"Very good, sir," Rufe said. "Enjoy the day."

Mrs. Cadbury was waiting for her limousine. She cradled a Yorkshire terrier in her arms, which wore a silver collar set with emeralds. Mrs. Cadbury had told him the name of the breed: he'd recognized the emeralds for himself.

He said, "Good morning, Mrs. Cadbury. You're looking well. Hi, Reginald." He patted the terrier's head.

"Good morning, Mr. Caparelli. Thank you." She tickled the dog's whiskers. "Say hello like a good boy." The dog yipped. Mrs. Cadbury was happy.

A few steps away, Charles Hamilton was speaking with the Rosensteins. Hamilton used his hands when he talked, nearly as much as the Italians down on Mulberry Street, which Caparelli found a joke; a commodities trader, Hamilton had led the tenants in a fight to keep Caparelli out of the building five years ago. And he would have succeeded if Caparelli hadn't been able to force the deputy mayor's office to intervene. But at least Hamilton was a graceful loser. He'd been faultlessly civil ever since.

"Good morning," Caparelli said.

They exchanged pleasantries, Hamilton and the Rosensteins—as had nearly everyone else in the building—responding as if they'd never heard of Caparelli's trial or never read any of the lurid publicity.

"Class," Orson had said. "Money, breeding and class."

Caparelli supposed he was right.

Only the odd resident had tried to avoid him, studiously looking the other way, hurrying into an elevator before Caparelli could reach it.

He arrived at Hawthorne's promptly at eleven. It was an expensive set of rooms. Book-heavy. Thick drapes. Leather. Rosewood. Germaine brought him directly to Hawthorne's office. It was spacious, with leaded windows. Germaine had terrific tits. Her ass was too big for most tastes, but just the way Caparelli liked them, and he'd said so to Hawthorne; accommodations of that sort were frequent among the people with whom Caparelli did business.

But not with Hawthorne. He'd ignored the remark so completely that Caparelli was later uncertain if he'd made himself clear. He tried once again. And again Hawthorne ignored him. They'd both made themselves clear.

It was a shame, for Caparelli did so like to make the beast with two backs.

Hawthorne came out from behind his desk and sat in one of the leather rollback chairs opposite Caparelli. A mahogany English tea table stood between them. Germaine brought an ashtray without being asked. Hawthorne didn't smoke. The ashtray was brass.

When Germaine left, Hawthorne said, "I have something to discuss with you that might sound odd, but I think it can help us with your sentence."

"I thought we were appealing."

"We are. But you know how bad they want you. Ordinarily we could drag this out a few years and finally settle for a token. But they won't compromise on you. And they'll rush the appeal through to get you behind bars as fast as they can."

"How long can we stall?"

"Six months. Eight at the outside. Maybe only four."

"Shit."

"And they'll bird-dog you every minute looking for something else to use, seeing if they can push you into something stupid."

Germaine knocked and carried in a silver tray with two porcelain cups of espresso and a compote dish with fresh lemon slivers. She set it on the table and left.

Even the sight of her fleshy rump failed to cheer Caparelli. "So what am I supposed to do?"

Hawthorne squeezed lemon into his coffee. He sipped. "Ironically," he said, "Judge Sullivan is our best bet; in fact, our only bet."

"Jesus. He hates my guts."

"Yes. But he's a Catholic."

"Wonderful. We can ask him to show a little Christian charity."

"He's devout, very devout."

"So were the guys who torched Joan of Arc."

Hawthorne smiled. "True. However, with Sullivan, I think we can use that to our advantage. There's a monastery in the Adirondacks of which he's very fond. He—"

"A *monastery?*"

"Yes."

"Oh Jesus fucking Christ. Terrific. I can become a monk and everything'll be okay—that's the kind of choice they used to give kids who got in trouble: join the army or go to jail. Brother Ball Bat. It's got a nice ring."

Hawthorne smiled again. "It does, in a way. But you don't have to take the cloth. This monastery, Saint Hector's, is a special pet of Sullivan's. He takes a weekend there every now and then. He donates money to it. I researched this carefully. He's somewhat nutty on the subject."

"What good does that do me?"

"There's a retreat scheduled to begin three weeks from now. I think it would have large positive impact on Sullivan if you were to make that retreat..."

"Hell, man, he's gonna sentence me next week."

"I can move for a short delay. To get your affairs in order. For me to gather material with a bearing on sentence. That's no problem, almost a matter of form."

"So suddenly I get religion and just happen to do a retreat some place he's crazy about? He's an asshole, but he ain't dumb. He'd see right through us."

"We're not going to tell him about it."

"What's the goddamn point then?"

"He'll know. I'll have it leaked to him. From his point of view, you'll be a man who's gone quietly without fanfare or publicity to make his peace with God, out of the purest motives, without hope of personal advantage."

Caparelli laughed. "That's me. The way you tell it, even I'd be impressed. I don't know, though. It's pretty off the wall."

"Look, you're a violent man."

"Says who? They only got me once, fifteen years ago, for assault. The rest of the times..." His lips drew back from his teeth in his special smile, his feral smile. Caparelli had never hurt or killed capriciously—with neither cause nor gain to be had. But when he had killed he'd always *enjoyed* it.

Hawthorne said dryly, "Let us say then that he perceives

you as a violent man. Saint Hector is the patron saint of people who were once violent, or who struggle against their violence. That's one of the larger reasons Sullivan is so fond of this monastery."

"Sullivan's violent?"

"He has a temper he finds hard to control. A stay at Saint Hector's helps him."

Caparelli shook his head. "It's crazy."

"Look, if you do this we might even be able to walk away with a suspended sentence."

"You think so?" Caparelli was incredulous.

"I won't guarantee it, but I *will* guarantee that it'll help. Quite a bit."

Caparelli screwed up his face in thought.

"As it stands," Hawthorne said, "they're going to slam the door on you. You have everything to gain and absolutely nothing to lose."

Caparelli met Orson that night in the back room of the Garibaldi social club off Tribeca Square to check the count on the day's number receipts. The take had fallen in the last months—somewhere, someone was skimming, and Caparelli was going to find out who. But tonight everything was in order. He told Orson what Hawthorne had said.

"A *retreat?*"

"Yeah." Caparelli stacked the high-denomination bills into a black doctor's bag and zippered it shut.

"Christ, that's hysterical." Orson was still stuffing bundles of singles into a large canvas bag. He paused, and tapped a finger against the bridge of his nose. "But then—"

"I know. Hawthorne said he'd bet dollars to doughnuts it'll work."

"Dollars to doughnuts? Those exact words? Hawthorne?"

"Well, he would've if he knew how to say what he meant."

"I guess you have nothing to lose."

"That's what he said." Caparelli looked heavily into Orson's eyes. "In those exact words."

"It just might work." Orson laughed. He resumed stuffing the bag. "It has flair. I like it."

"You better."

"Why?"

"You're coming with me."

"I wouldn't miss it for the world. It'll be a lark."

"This is serious."

Orson's face changed. "That you are to be sentenced is serious, Don Dominic. That there is a chance to reduce your sentence is serious. But you and I on retreat in a monastery is both medieval and hilarious. And you will be better off if you can laugh about it with me."

"I don't know from that kind of shit—medieval—but I do know that sometimes I think you'd be better off if you'd spent four years in the joint instead of college."

Later, on his side in their king-size bed, with headboard of gold and white Tuscany gilt, Caparelli felt lonely, felt especially the need for solace and comfort, and he pressed his rump up against Pomona's, which was abundant, which was a kind of paragon of rumps, which put that of Hawthorne's secretary into eclipse, and its flesh, its warmth, gentled and succored him, and, unknowingly, he sighed; long, and deep, and was eased.

Caparelli had three offices in the city, one in the warehouse of C&P, Inc., which was where Hawthorne reached him two days after their meeting. *C* was Caparelli. *P* had once been Michael Pantano, Caparelli's partner. Pantano had been strangled and dumped on one of the old decaying Hudson River piers ten years ago, during their war with the Agnabeni family. The first principle of life was loyalty. Caparelli would never harm a friend or partner. Loyalty, however, did not preclude a little slip of the tongue to someone who might not feel the same way, who might wish to curry favor with the Agnabeni family, and lo, within twenty-four hours, someone found Pantano's hideaway, dispatched him and deposited his body unceremoniously on the pier, where it was first discovered, in the thin light of false dawn, by the gulls, a rank of whom were perched in a line like a grave and critical audience an hour later when various law-enforcement officials began to arrive.

After a few months, during which various thorns were removed from the sides of both parties, a truce was effected, and Caparelli was much happier with the way his business went than he had been before. The C&P warehouse contained great stacks of cartons with imported foodstuffs, and bays which held cheap repossessed furniture. At odd times the warehouse also stored, carefully boxed and mislabeled, stolen furs, contraband cigarettes, guns and an occasional $50,000 automobile.

Caparelli was playing five-card stud with two of his people when Hawthorne called. He waved them out.

"I just won a hundred bucks," he said expansively.

"Good for you," Hawthorne said. "You've also been granted a stay of sentence. Six weeks."

"It's my lucky day."

"Have you thought about the retreat? As your attorney, I have to say again that I advise you in the strongest terms to do it."

"I'm going to."

"Wonderful. This will change your life, I promise you. You haven't, as I asked, mentioned it to anyone else, have you?"

"Uh." Caparelli hesitated. "My nephew Orson."

"Damn! I told you—this has to be *absolutely* confidential. God damn it!"

"You don't talk to me that way," Caparelli said.

Hawthorne was silent a moment. "I'm sorry, Dominic. But we can succeed *only* if we convince Sullivan that you've undergone a true moral change. And that requires complete secrecy. I'll arrange to have the abbot mention it in passing to Sullivan.

But if anyone else knows where you're going—even your wife—it'll get out, it'll be in the papers and Sullivan will think you're trying to con him and we'll blow it. *No* one must know. Do you understand?"

"Yeah. But Orson already knows, and I'm taking him with me. I never go anyplace without security."

"Jesus Christ, to a fucking monastery?"

Caparelli had never heard Hawthorne swear. He was impressed. "You're really serious, aren't you?"

"Yes. We have an excellent chance to get you off without a day behind bars. I don't want to see it thrown away."

"Okay. But Orson comes."

"Can you ensure his silence?"

"Yeah."

"All right. I'll make the arrangements."

"How'd you get on to this place?" Caparelli said. "You're not a violent guy."

"No," Hawthorne said. "I'm not."

Chicago was called the Windy City because it sat out there on the flatlands with hundreds of miles of plains to the west and the flat expanse of Lake Michigan to the east and with all that great distance in which there was hardly a wrinkle in the land to impede it the wind could build to a velocity at which it would strike you like a hammer blow or fight you to a dead standstill as you leaned into it, clutching at your hat, your whipping coat, your eyes filling with tears. In winter it seemed to cut right through you like a knife of ice and even a short walk from an office to a nearby restaurant for lunch left you dazed, numbed, your cheeks flushed and the tips of your ears in pain.

But it was summer now and the wind settled for being a breeze which was coming in off the lake, fresh and zesty and cooling down the nighttime Loop, the sporting grounds, the action streets, and all the players and hustlers, the goodtimers and the lowlifes, all the freaks and badboys, the zeroes and the percenters, everyone, seemed to move a little faster, step a little higher and flash their teeth a little brighter because of it.

There was a lot of neon, a lot of music on the streets. It was the honky-tonk.

Pretty Boy was leaning up against a wall rapping with Tommy Lee Smith. Pretty Boy was dark black and glossy skinned, handsome, fast to smile, and had a goldrimmed front tooth with a little diamond chip in it. He wore a green velvet hat with a peacock feather, a tailored linen suit of lime green that fit his lean body snugly and a maroon silk shirt with long collar tips, open several buttons down his chest. To their right was the Red Revue—peep shows, live sex acts and specialty rooms for the leather and rubber crowd—and to their left a novelty shop with cheap vulgar knickknacks and a display of vicious knives with tips embedded in Styrofoam. Tommy Lee was also a pimp, but definitely not as stylish, to Pretty Boy's thinking, as he was. True, Tommy Lee's Lincoln was newer than Pretty Boy's, but it was purple, a color Pretty Boy held in contempt, and pin-striped of all things, which in itself was almost enough to make every pimp on the strip feel superior to Tommy Lee, regardless of actual stature.

Pretty Boy and Tommy Lee weren't talking about anything much in particular, just talking to make sounds and music, words, unconsciously matching their cadences to the rhythm of a doorway speaker in the record and tape shop across the street. They were both on blow and feeling good. Yes, good. And Pretty Boy was sort of waiting for Turk to show up so he could gauge how much more was necessary with the little chicken, the sweet-flesh difficult little Connie chicken he had stashed over on Wabash in the old Laketop Hotel, which hadn't been a real hotel in a long time.

Yes, Pretty Boy was up on blow, but not too up, playing it on top of the ice because he had work to do, and he didn't want to be stupid, he didn't want to get wired, he didn't want to whack himself.

Like that shirtless stone-crazy Mex in Levi's and sandals and the great build of a prison iron pumper who'd been marching up and down the street most of the early evening now, wide dark eyes staring straight ahead, saying, "Crystals, loose joints. Check 'em out, man, check 'em out. Ups, downs, reds . . ."

High as the moon, man, wired like Western Union. When a nervous pair of schoolkids tried to score from him, he didn't even see them and he marched right on past, saying, "Ups, downs, Tuies, check 'em out, man . . ."

What a crazy fuck. Another hour of eating his own shit and he'd be ready to kill somebody.

Tommy Lee was telling Pretty Boy about this new cunt he'd recruited. She was blond and Irish, had been a groupie for the Bears and sucked a cock like a vacuum cleaner. "They even smuggled her on the team bus once. She did the whole defensive line last year after they held the Cowboys to one field goal." They laughed. "And in that game with Green Bay? When the referee—"

"Excuse me."

A slightly built white man had stopped. He was round-shouldered and in a nondescript suit. He was balding and wore glasses. His shoes were scuffed. Pretty Boy sized him up. He wasn't a trick.

"Go way, ofay."

The man reached into this breast pocket and removed a photograph. "My name is Hill. Warren Hill. I'm a social worker. I'm looking for a runaway. If you could just look at this—"

Pretty Boy's eyes never left Hill's face. He took the photograph, ripped it in half and let the pieces flutter to the sidewalk. "Now can you hear better?"

Hill looked down forlornly at the torn photograph. "I'm just trying to find a little girl," he said.

Pretty Boy touched Hill's glasses with a finger. He flicked them off. They hit the sidewalk. One lens cracked.

"How 'bout now?"

"You didn't have to do that," Hill said.

"I know. I *wanted* to do it."

"Oh, shee-it," Tommy Lee said. "Ferguson."

A white squad car veered over to the side. A cop with a big belly got out, sliding his nightstick into a ring on his belt. He looked happy, and unpleasant.

"That's not nice, Pretty Boy," he said. "It's not nice to knock off a man's glasses."

Hill said, "It was, uh, it wasn't like that. It was, uh, an accident."

Ferguson looked at Hill without much more affection than he had at Pretty Boy.

Hill explained himself, which won him partly back into the policeman's favor.

"Well, Mr. Hill, you picked one of the people most likely to have grabbed up a little fifteen-year-old girl. But the thing is, you ought to have some protection if you're gonna try and talk to Pretty Boy here. Pretty Boy, see, he's one bad dude, very bad. Not because he's got balls—that would make him an honest-to-God *real* bad nigger—but because he's some kind of animal, because he *likes* to hurt people."

"Come on, man," Pretty Boy said. "What you beatin' on me for? I ain't done nothin'."

Ferguson put his arm around Pretty Boy and hugged him into himself. "Not right at the moment he hasn't," he said to Hill. "But he sure has in the past. See, Pretty Boy here is a pimp. He's other things, too, but his biggest moneymaker, and the thing he likes best, is being a pimp. Now you might say to me that whoring is the world's oldest profession, and you might say, Hey, there's no victim here, and with some you'd be right. But not with Pretty Boy. See, Pretty Boy, by my count, has wasted at least three of his girls. And cut up half a dozen more. He did a really nice job three, four months ago. Kind of a not-too-smart sixteen-year-old Polish kid down from Milwaukee. When she wanted to leave his stable, he used sulfuric acid on her. She's got this burned whole half of her face now and she can't see very much out of one eye. That's your honeybunch here. A real sweetheart. Every pimp gets tough now and then, but Pretty Boy, he *likes* to do it. He gets his rocks off that way. Fact, I wouldn't be surprised if it's the *only* way he gets 'em off. He sure does like to hurt people."

Pretty Boy shrugged free. "Fuck you, Ferguson. If you don't want to mess up your pension, then stick one of them big feet in your mouth. 'Cause if you can't prove what you're sayin', then you can find yourself a lot of trouble, an' I'm the Pretty Boy that's going to bring it to you."

"You know," Ferguson said unhappily to Hill, "in the old days, in the days of Mayor Daley, God rest his soul, I could've taken this mother out to a forest preserve and beat on his skull with my nightstick. I can't do it now, and that's a mortal shame, but I'm going to get him. Sooner or later and somehow, I'm going to get him." He looked at Pretty Boy. "You hear that, mother? Sooner or later I'm going to get you."

Pretty Boy smiled. "Ferguson, while your wife is sayin' the beads and you're wondering when you can afford a new pair of shoes, I'm layin' out more for dinner than you make in a week. That's where it's at, man, that's who I am and who you are."

Ferguson stared at him. Resting on the grip of his nightstick, his fingers opened and closed. He took a deep breath and exhaled slowly. "Mr. Hill," he said, "this isn't a good time for you to be here. It'd be best if you'd limit yourself to daytime."

"What the man means," Pretty Boy said amiably, "is that once the sun goes down, the streets belong to the players. A paddy like you, there's only two things you can be down here at night—a trick or a victim."

Hill nodded. "Could you tell me please, though, have you ever seen that girl? Her name's Cheryl. Cheryl Williams."

Pretty Boy didn't say anything.

"Answer the man," Ferguson said.

Pretty Boy hesitated. "No, I never seen her."

"Did you look at the photograph? Maybe if you—"

"I never seen her."

Hill nodded. "All right. But if you do . . . ?"

"Oh sure, man. I'll get right in touch with you."

Ferguson said, "Come on, Mr. Hill. We'll drive you out of here."

Pretty Boy watched them leave. "Dumb motherfuckers."

"The gospel," Tommy Lee said.

Pretty Boy scuffed at the torn photograph with his shoe. He blinked, squinted. "Shee-it!" he said, and then he laughed.

He and Tommy Lee went back to counting the numbers, playing the street.

Turk loped up three-quarters of an hour later, tall, head shaved, mustachioed. "My man."

"Turk."

"Tommy Lee."

"Bro."

They did the grips.

"How she doin?" Pretty Boy asked.

"I think she be cooled down now. She ain't scratchin' and fightin' no more. Marshall say she cried with him. She didn't do that with me. But she didn't do much else neither. Just kind o' laid there."

"Oh I can fix that," Pretty Boy said. "The teachin's easy. It's the breakin' that's tricky. Willie Butler had one he was breakin' jump out a window last week and kill herself naked right there on the street."

"Mmm-hm!" Turk shook his head.

"Who we got in with her now?" Pretty Boy asked.

"Dwight."

"Uh-huh. Well, it's gettin' time for the master to start his magic. I'm goin' to move on now. Catch you later, bloods."

Pretty Boy highstepped all the way to the Laketop, pausing to slap a hand, pat a bottom. The Laketop was old, the carpet in the small lobby worn through and the plastic plants gray with dust. It smelled like a closet filled with forgotten clothes.

Pretty Boy waved to the Haitian behind the desk and started up the stairs; the elevator hadn't worked in a long time.

He met Dwight on the landing of the third floor.

"Hey, Pretty Boy."

"Hey, Dwight. How was she?"

"Better'n my hand."

"She fight you any?"

"Naw, I think she done with that."

"Good. Wait till you see her in a week. She gonna be dynamite."

They parted. Pretty Boy went down the hall, stopped in front of one of the varnished wooden doors. He unlocked it with a key from his pocket.

She was lying naked on her side, knees drawn up. The sheet was rumpled beneath her.

He said softly, "Hey, Connie. Hey, little white sweetmeat. Daddy's here, Pretty Boy's here." She looked at him, but didn't say anything. He sat down beside her and stroked her hair comfortingly. "I hear you been good. I hear you been nice. Now that you over your little upset, everything's gonna be better, better'n you can imagine. You gonna be my main lady, my lady love. We gonna fly to the moon, we gonna dance on stars."

Beneath his soft voice and soothing hand, she pressed into him for comfort despite herself.

"That's right, that's right," he crooned. "The good days are comin', days so good like you can't even dream." He sighed. He stroked her hair. "There's just a few little things we got to do first."

His hand slipped from her hair to her cheek, patted her gently.

Then he seized her upper lip and twisted it hard.

She came up from the sheets with a cry, grasped at his hand but couldn't break his grip. He increased the pressure, held it, held it . . . then released her with a shove. She fell back whimpering. Tears of pain and fear rose in her eyes.

Pretty Boy became aroused. "And the first thing we got to do," he said, "is to make sure that you never lie to me, that you never lie to me about nothing."

"I never lied to you."

He punched the side of her breast, digging the knuckles under it.

"Aaaiii!" She clutched herself.

"Cheryl, Cheryl," he said in a tone of disappointment. "You're doing it again." His erection swelled and hardened.

She looked at him in terror.

"Cheryl, you have to tell me you're Cheryl Williams, not Connie Wilson."

"How . . . ?"

He shook his head sadly. "Pretty Boy knows everything. He always does. He even knows what you think."

"I was afraid at first that you'd send me back."

"No, no," he said. "You don't have to worry about that. Nobody's gonna make you go back. Pretty Boy's gonna take care of you, and part of that means to protect you. From everything and everyone. You trust me?"

She nodded. "Yes. Yes. I love you. I just don't understand."

"And I love you, little sugarcube. Here." He took a brown bottle with a tiny spoon linked to its cap from his jacket. "Now you just do a little of this and everything be brighter."

"I don't want any," she said.

"Sure you do. Everyone does."

"No," she said. "I don't feel good."

"Okay, little dove, but it's the thing that'll make you better."

She looked at the bottle. "All right," she said. "Yes. I want to feel better."

She took a spoon up each nostril.

Pretty Boy did a hit himself and put the bottle away. He opened his belt and pulled down his zipper.

"Now I'm gonna teach you how to suck cock," he said. "Because a woman that don't know how to suck good, why she ain't really no kind of woman at all."

Chapter 5

The Acapulco sky was a delicate blue scattered with billowy drifting clouds. Caparelli floated atop an air mattress in the shallows of the private pool out on the patio of his room. He floated on his back with his eyes closed while a nutbrown Mexican girl stood bent over at his head kissing him, her sleek black hair tenting his face. Reaching back, he lazily kneaded her dark-nippled breasts.

At the other end, lying partway up his legs, her breasts cushioned against his pale thighs, her legs trailing out in the water, their combined weight partly submerging the end of the raft, the heated water lapping at Caparelli's balls, a second girl, the same burnished color and with hair just as black, but a year or two younger and with smaller breasts than the first, sucked at his penis with a slow, precise rhythm.

They swore they were sisters, and for all Caparelli knew they might be. It was a nice touch. But he was happy either way.

He sighed pleasurably into the mouth of the one whose breasts he was working. She couldn't have been more than twenty-two. It was late afternoon. He'd already come twice, which cheered him enormously—the equipment was tricky and didn't work as well now as it had in the old days. So he felt happy and appreciated the girls, and it didn't matter that he was semi-soft in the mouth of the younger one, they'd already earned their money, and it just felt good to have her sucking like this and he planned to give them a big tip no matter what the outcome of her present endeavor.

Caparelli liked whores. It was one of the last honest businesses left. He loved Pomona dearly and still, after all these years, they made love together two or three times a month, which would have been enough, but whores could get him up at times he wouldn't have thought himself able, so it didn't take anything away from Pomona, rather was something that existed in addition, and so if he was going to fuck anyone but his wife, it simply made sense to have the youngest and prettiest. And with anyone but Pomona or a whore he would have had to be aware of his own body, aware, to his unhappiness, of his pale skin which had, on his legs and hands, become shiny of late, of his pudgy middle, his cheeks gone jowly, his thinning hair. This way, he didn't have to subject himself to such judgments, and he was pleased.

"Uncle Dominic."

The girl kissing him looked up in alarm. The one on his legs rolled off into the water leaving his cock to flop onto his thigh, a sad sack of a thing glistening with her spittle, half-aroused, half-deflated.

Orson stood on the patio in tailored slacks, a shortsleeve shirt and silvered sunglasses.

The girls were covering themselves with their hands.

"Don't worry, *senoritas.* Uh, no problem, uh, no *problema. Comprendo?"* Caparelli said.

Orson rattled off something in Spanish. The girls were relieved. He smiled at them. The one with the larger breasts looked at him with calculation, and beginning invitation.

"How come you talk Mex so good?" Caparelli said. He used Orson in New York when he had to deal with Puerto Ricans, but only here in the context of a Spanish-speaking country where his own English so often fell on deaf ears did it occur to him to wonder how Orson had learned the language.

Caparelli had been to Mexico before, but this was Orson's first time. Caparelli had wanted a holiday before he had to leave for the monastery. He didn't think there'd be much in the way of amusement up there.

"I studied it at Cornell."

"Yeah? Why?"

"Because a foreign language was required. It was easier than French and I figured it would be handier in New York than the others."

Caparelli thought about that. "Smart."

The girls were looking from Caparelli to Orson, assuaged but still not knowing what was expected from them.

"How'd you get in?" Caparelli said. "The door was locked."

"Not the one that connects our rooms."

Caparelli grunted. He wasn't worried here in Acapulco, but it was a dumb mistake, and dumb mistakes could get you killed. Make it once in Mexico, make it again in New York.

Orson said, "You said you'd be dressed and set at five."

"Jesus, is it five already?"

"Almost."

Caparelli heaved himself off the float and made his way to the ladder. Water dripped from his pale hairy back as he climbed up, and from his big and hairy ass.

He beckoned to the girls. "Come on along, sweethearts. Fun's over." He tracked footprints into the room on the tile floor.

Orson spoke to them again in Spanish.

They toweled quickly and imperfectly, small patches of water dampening through their cotton shifts.

Caparelli gave them twice as much as they expected, kissed them both on the cheek and patted their rumps good-bye.

"You know," he said to Orson as he dressed, "that's one of the reasons I like this country—the whores are so friendly. You don't have to worry here that some fucking revolutionary's going to split your head open with a machete or throw a fucking grenade into the dining room. Every couple of years they shoot up some commie university students, and there's some bandits in the hills—bandits for Christ's sake—but otherwise it's one of the most peaceful places on earth."

"What I saw this afternoon wasn't so peaceful."

"I told you how it was gonna be."

"On the contrary. I *loved* it."

"Yeah?" Caparelli shrugged. "Maybe if they just let the bull out against a guy with a sword it might be fair. But these guys on horseback stickin' it with spears and those other guys stickin' those other things those, what do you call 'em?"

"*Banderillos.*"

"Yeah, *banderillos* into it until the poor fucker's so chewed up it can't lift its head right, I don't see what's the point."

"It's the ritual," Orson said. "And the slow build to the kill. The kill is a climax."

"You mean like coming?"

"Not exactly. But something like it."

Caparelli shook his head. "Maybe I'm too dumb. It wouldn't look much different to me if they just chained it up out there and let a bunch of people hack it to death."

"That idea is not without merit, Uncle Dominic, but I think I prefer it the way it is."

Caparelli was buttoning his shirt. He glanced into the mirror to see Orson. His nephew was looking out through the patio doors to the sea. His expression was dreamy, a smile brushed his lips. Last year Orson had cut up a nigger who was trying to squeeze into the territory. A bloody fucking mess. Orson got a kick out of using a knife, the kid did.

Well, to each his own.

Orson drove them twenty-five kilometers out of the city in a rented car and then turned onto a narrow unpaved road that wound up the shoulder of a mountain. Vegetation grew progressively heavier and denser. Away from the cooling breezes of the seaside city, the heat intensified. It was humid. Caparelli sweated. He slapped at mosquitoes.

"Where in Christ's ass is this place? The food better be fucking fantastic."

A *bon viveur* friend of Orson's had told him he had to eat at La Cachere, outside the city, while he was there.

"Actually, we're going out of the way now. There's something else I want to show you, and to see myself, first."

Orson's friend had cited this too, had in fact insisted upon it.

Caparelli frowned. He slapped at his neck. "Fuckin' bugs!"

The road was rutted here. Orson drove with care but still the little Renault bounced crazily. Caparelli began to sulk.

"Trust me," Orson said.

Rounding a turn commanded by a towering acacia tree, they came upon three *federales*—two privates in the road and a lieutenant lounging off to the side. The privates brought their rifles to port arms and blocked the way. The lieutenant got up, buttoning his shirt and stuffing its tails into his pants. He leaned down to the driver's window and looked at them.

"You are lost, *senores*," he said affably. "This road goes nowhere."

"I thought it went to San Andros del Cuerpo." Orson said.

"Ah. Perhaps it does. It is such a little village, so easy to forget."

"May we go on ahead, then?"

"Ah. I regret to tell you that the road is unpassable. That is why we are here."

"We'll be happy to walk."

The Mexican sighed and lifted his palms toward heaven. "Such endless misfortune, *senor*. Today is the feast day of the saint for whom the village is named. Their thanksgiving is a private affair."

"Yes, I know. Still—"

The friendliness left the officer's face. "My government does not want foreigners here this day. Is that clear enough? The brush is spare behind you. You may turn your car around without much difficulty."

"Can I speak with you in privacy, lieutenant?"

The Mexican nodded. Orson got out and walked a few paces back with him. Caparelli watched in the rearview mirror. Orson reached into the breast pocket of his poplin jacket and extracted his wallet. The two privates looked on with heightened interest.

When Orson returned he said, *"La mordida,"* to Caparelli and rubbed his thumb and fingers together. "Fifty for the lieutenant, twenty-five each for his men—but I bet the real split will be eighty-twenty."

The lieutenant ordered the privates aside.

A third of a kilometer later Orson and Caparelli came upon a line of parked automobiles. Orson pulled up behind a blue Volvo. They got out to walk.

"We're a little late, but not bad," Orson said, checking his watch.

Caparelli killed a mosquito on his cheek. "What am I doing in a jungle?" he asked unhappily. "I don't know from jungles. I don't even know from *grass.*"

"It's not a jungle," Orson said. "It's just tropical plants."

"We got a gardener in the family. Wonderful."

Many of the cars were rented. "I didn't give the lieutenant his first *mordida* of the day," Orson observed. From somewhere ahead came the sound of chanting. Orson quickened his step. "The government can't stop this, but they try to keep it under wraps. They don't like tourists to see it."

Scattered among the rental cars were a number of older abused vehicles and a dented yellow bus. There were donkey-carts and mules and horses with saddles or simply striped blankets on their backs. The chanting grew louder.

They reached the outskirts of the village and saw people massed around its central square, predominantly Mexican but scattered with Europeans and North Americans. A church tower rose off to one side, and not far from it the facade of some kind of small municipal building. Within the square itself, visible only above the heads of the onlookers, a large crucifix wavered on a wooden pole.

A tanned man in a cream sports coat and a Panama hat held a 35-millimeter camera with a motor drive high up over the people in front of him. The camera went *click, shhp, click, shhp, click.* . . . He was with a blond woman who was stretched up on her toes. "I can't see," she complained. Her accent was German. "What are they doing?"

"They're still going around the square."

Click, shhp. Click, shhp.

"There." He let the camera hang from the strap around his neck. He put his hands into the woman's armpits from behind and lifted her.

"Oh," she said. "Oh. There's a little girl. She can't even be five."

The chant crested and receded in slow cycle, each crest accompanied by a many-parted slapping sound. When that occurred, the lofted crucifix twitched and the spectators audibly loosed their breath.

Orson said, *Despensame, por favor* and Excuse me, pardon, as he worked himself and Caparelli into the ranks, until they managed to break through alongside the old mortar-peeled church and gain an unoccupied corner on its top step.

Caparelli looked down. He shook his head from side to side.

A monk in brown robes carried the pole-mounted crucifix. His features were from a time before the *conquistadores*. Fifty or sixty villagers shuffled behind him in time to their chant. Men, women. Old ones, gaunt and wispy-haired. Children. Three of the very youngest were naked, a girl and two boys. Many of the men wore only pants. The women were in thin cotton dresses. At the chant's peak, they all swung leather straps up over their shoulders to strike against their backs. It was not a metaphor: they swung forcefully and shuddered at the impact.

A few eschewed straps in favor of knotted ropes fitted with little pieces of metal which, swinging, glinted in the sun, and, striking, cut into their reddened skin. A young man and one of the naked little boys lashed themselves with nettle branches. Their backs were spotted with blood. As they passed, Caparelli could see thorns which had broken off and lodged in their flesh. The child's face was beatific. His little organ was stiffly erect.

The boy couldn't have been older than Carl. His grandson Carl.

"Fuck!" Caparelli said. "What the fuck is this?"

"Flagellants," Orson said. "It's penance for their sins."

"It's crazy, is what it is."

"Do you still go to confession?"

"Yeah," Caparelli said.

He did, and was truly sorry for his sins, even the ones he didn't tell the priest, which were most—because the priest didn't know how it was, how they could happen; the priest had been taken away from real life, sheltered and taught by other priests who couldn't understand what it meant any more than he could. Caparelli didn't tell his confessor what he did, how he fucked whores, how he sold dope that turned people into animals, how much he had enjoyed, how happy it had made him, to smash Frank the fink's brains out. He didn't tell his confessor these things, although he knew they were sins, because he loved priests—the old ones anyway—and he didn't want to hurt him, to bring news of the world, to pose unanswerable questions that would challenge his simple faith and place upon his shoulders a burden he could not bear.

Caparelli was a strong man and so he took upon himself what his priests could not, because he loved them and his church, nearly as much as he loved his Pomona, nearly as much as he loved his grandson Carl, nearly as much as he loved to swing a ball bat and knock the life and blood and brains out of some asshole who needed to have his life and blood and brains knocked out.

He became angry with Orson. "Yeah, I go to confession," he said.

"Well, it's like that," Orson said. "The priest tells you to make the Stations of the Cross or say ten Our Fathers and ten Hail Marys, a penance so God will forgive you. That's what they're doing, penance for their sins."

"Even that little kid there? He's got to pay for his sins?"

Orson smiled. "For original sin, if nothing else. We're all born with it."

The penitents continued around the square to a shrine of Saint Andros that was directly across from the church. There was a round well there, and a stone cross a little taller than a man. A young man of eighteen or nineteen detached himself to join three others who already knelt before the shrine. They were shirtless. The procession made two more circuits of the square. Each time another man stepped out to join those at the shrine. The last was a muscular longfaced man of about thirty.

The chanting ceased, the marchers stopped. They formed in a thick semicircle around the shrine. The spectators pressed in behind them.

The monk spoke briefly in Spanish.

Orson translated for Caparelli. "He says these men will wash themselves in the Blood of the Lamb. They will take upon themselves and do penance for the sins of everyone in the village, for the sins of all who have come here today, of all whom Christ loves."

Caparelli watched with suspicion and distaste.

The penitents stood. An old man with a red bandana appeared before them. He carried short whips of plaited leather. Each of the penitents took one from him.

The monk raised the crucifix. *"Por el amor de Jesus Cristos!"* he cried.

The six penitents echoed him: *"Por el amor de Jesus Cristos!"*

"Por la sangre de su corrazon sancto!"

They cried out with him, For the blood of his Sacred Heart!

Silence followed. The six men arranged themselves into three pairs. *"Por el amor de Jesus Cristos!"* the monk cried.

"Por el amor de Jesus Cristos!" three of the penitents answered.

And with that, they each lashed once, savagely, at the back of his partner.

The whips left violent red tracks. On one man, an inch or two of skin split open, and blood trickled out.

The penitents reversed themselves, the men who had been lashed now poised to strike.

"*Por la sangre de su corazon sancto!*" the monk called.

"*Por la sangre de su corazon sancto!*"

Cr-rack!

"*Por el amor de Jesus Cristos!*"

"*Por el amor de Jesus Cristos!*"

Cr-rack!

It went on, it seemed, forever.

But actually, the first man fell in less than a quarter hour. He was sharpfeatured and in his middle twenties. Blood was flowing from all their ravaged backs. The whips struck with splatting sounds and drove red droplets into the air. The sharp-featured man was swaying back and forth. The crowd watched closely, holding its breath in anticipation.

He toppled, and the crowd went: "Ahhhhhhh."

Two women, of an age to be his mother and his wife, pulled him off to the side of the well. They began to wash his back and to bandage him with clean cloths.

One by one the other penitents fell. Penultimate was the oldest, who reeled under a final blow, turned in a full circle, staggered toward the onlookers and then collapsed as if his spine had been severed.

The spectators gasped.

It was the monk's duty to wield the last whip, and he cried out the litany with the remaining penitent, the boy, the youngest of them, and slashed at his ripped back, his bloody back, as the boy invited, as the boy commanded, and as they called to and answered each other:

"*Por el amor de Jesus Cristos!*"

"*Por el amor de Jesus Cristos!*"

Sluff!

"*Por la sangre de su corazon sancto!*"

"*Por la sangre de su corazon sancto!*"

Sluff!

The boy spun round. He walked drunkenly. He dropped to his knees. Blood streamed down his back. He got to his feet again. *"Por el amor de Jesus Cristos!"* he screamed.

The monk answered him, slashed the whip across his back.

The boy staggered to the stone cross. His hands clutched at its arms, got purchase, held him up.

"Démelo!" he cried hoarsely. Give it to me! *"Hágalo!"* Do it!

The monk whipped. They screamed to each other.

The boy clawed at the stone cross as he was hit, once, twice, three times more, and as he slumped down its length crying out without sense, and then fell, scraping his cheek against the rough stone, to lay bleeding and twitching upon the ground. The monk dropped the whip and lowered his head.

The square was silent.

"Well," Orson said. "Well."

Caparelli said nothing.

"I guess we should go," Orson said. "I guess it's time to eat."

"Yeah?" Caparelli said. "Eat? You really want to eat now?"

"Of course," Orson said. "That worked up an appetite. What did you think?"

Caparelli stared down into the square. He said, "I think that's the biggest bunch of dumb stupid fucking assholes I ever saw."

It was night and Pretty Boy was outside the Red Revue again, with Turk and Dwight who were sharing a joint. They didn't offer it to Pretty Boy. Pretty Boy spent his early evening setting up tricks here on the street. He never smoked or drank when he was working. You lost the edge that way, and the edge made all the difference. An occasional pinch of blow was all right—that just clarified things, even sharpened the edge— but nothing else until business was over.

"Look at what's a-comin'," Dwight said. "Wonder the simple fool ain't been mugged and dumped a dozen times already."

Pretty Boy turned. He smiled. "That's a friend o' mine. Wouldn't nobody take off a friend o' mine on this street."

The social worker, Hill, was trudging toward them. His tie was loosened and his collar button open. He was sweating and the few remaining hairs on his forehead were plastered to the skin.

Turk laughed. "You got some funny friends."

"Don' let it bother you, bro."

Hill pulled out a handkerchief as he stopped. He wiped his face and stuffed the handkerchief back in his pocket. He bobbed his head. "Uh, Mr. Pretty Boy. Hello. You—"

Pretty Boy burst into laughter. "*Mr.* Pretty Boy. Oh, I like that. I truly do. Bros, say hello to Mr. Warren Hill. He's a social worker."

"Hello," Hill said. "Mr., uh—" He winced, not knowing what other name to use and seeing that he would be derided no matter what he said. "Uh, Mr. Pretty Boy, I wonder, could you please give me just a couple minutes somewhere in private. It's important."

"Mr. Warren Hill," Pretty Boy said, "you got me t' feelin' funny and good. You are one funny honkie. Sure, old Mr. Pretty Boy'll give you a couple. Let's step down the street to one o' my private offices." He took Hill by the elbow, chuckling, and started off.

"You want a little close company?" Turk said.

Pretty Boy looked back over his shoulder. "No. I don't think Mr. Warren Hill be a dangerous man." He grinned.

Pretty Boy led Hill down the block to a narrow flight of stairs that descended to a darkened basement and service area. It stank. Pretty Boy gestured. "After you, suh. I insist. Less o' course you're afraid to go down into the dark with a bad nigger like me."

"No. No. I'm— This will do."

They went down, turned into a dimly lit corridor.

Pretty Boy said, "Now what can I do for you?"

Hill's hand shot to Pretty Boy's throat. He threw him hard against the wall. An instant later there was a revolver in his other hand. He shoved the muzzle up Pretty Boy's nostril, swelling it out and straining the flesh, the front sight tearing the inner tissue. Blood leaked out.

"Oh Jesus!" Pretty Boy cried. He was up on his toes.

Hill looked into his eyes and cocked the weapon.

"Mama."

"Right about now, my people are taking Cheryl Williams out of the Laketop."

Beneath his terror, Pretty Boy thought he saw some sense in this. "You're a cop," he said. "Let's talk. We can deal."

"I'm not a cop, and we can't deal."

"Jesus. Please! What do you want!"

"You."

Pretty Boy moaned.

"I want to kill you," Hill said. "I don't like it that you make me feel that way, that you make me want to blow you up more than anything else in my life."

The blood from Pretty Boy's nostril had run down over his lips to his chin and was dropping onto his shirt. "Don't do it, man. Please! Anything you want. Anything!"

"I want for you not to make me feel like this."

"How! Just tell me! I'll do it!"

"Oh, I know you," Hill said. "I know all about you. I've seen some of your work. When you handle runaways like I do it doesn't take long to know who's doing what to them. And you're the worst, Pretty Boy. You're the lowest shit in the whole pile. See, this one, this Cheryl Williams isn't just any runaway, she's my niece, motherfucker, my *niece!*"

He shoved the muzzle farther up Pretty Boy's nostril.

Pretty Boy gasped. He went rigid. "I didn't know, man!"

"What fucking difference does that make? Except that I want from the bottom of my feet to the top of my head and with all my heart to kill you. And I don't want to feel that. It makes me crazy to feel that."

He stopped, to let his breathing settle, and stared into Pretty Boy's eyes. Pretty Boy said nothing, didn't move. Tears rolled down his cheeks.

"We both know how things are," Hill said, "how it all works. That means we both know there's not much chance of putting you behind bars for any real time. And we both know you're a smart sonofabitch, there isn't much chance we'll catch you stupid. So, not only do I want to blow you up, but it seems the logical, maybe the only, solution to the problem that you are."

"No," Pretty Boy whispered.

"I think I'm going to make you an offer."

"Lay it out! It's yours!"

"You know what a retreat is?"

"No."

"It's a thing people do, Catholics mostly. They go away to a monastery or a big house somewhere. Usually in the country. Someplace quiet and peaceful. They look into themselves. They examine their lives and they commune—they pray and talk—with God. They try to find a way to make their lives better in His eyes."

Pretty Boy waited. When Hill remained silent, he said, "Uh-huh. Yeah. You want me to do that?" Beneath his fear was confusion.

"Yes. There's a monastery in New York. In the Adirondacks. Saint Hector's. The monastery runs retreats for men who are violent. It helps them to get over that violence, to understand it. The retreat lasts two and a half weeks."

"And you want me to go there," Pretty Boy said eagerly, seeing a way out, realizing that he wasn't about to die, that Hill was a nut, that this whole thing wasn't going to cost him much at all.

"Yes. They're having a retreat in the next couple of weeks." He explained the arrangements.

"Okay. But what's the catch?"

"There isn't any. You make this retreat, you and I are even.

That's it. It's over. You don't owe me. I don't owe you. It's like we never heard of each other."

"Hey. Sure. I can dig that. Can you take the gun out? It hurts like hell."

"In a minute."

"Yeah. Okay."

"There's just one other thing."

"Uh-huh. Right. I thought there'd be."

"You don't tell anyone where you're going."

"Okay. Sure, man. Anything you want."

"I'm serious, Pretty Boy. I want you to find God in your own heart. You won't be able to unless you keep this to yourself. And I mean just that. *No one else*. If you tell *anyone*, I'll kill you."

"Right. I understand. Hey, you know, I'm not a Catholic, man."

"God loves us all. And He loves us the same."

"Okay."

Hill kept the gun in Pretty Boy's nostril, but released his throat and patted him down. He found a flat .357 Magnum derringer holstered at the small of his back. He removed it, dropped it into his jacket pocket.

"You do all your business here, you're not going to split to another city where you don't have any weight. If you try to cop on me in any way, if you do anything except what I've told you, then I'll find you and I'll kill you. It's that simple."

"Okay, man. It's all your way. You're God."

"No, I'm not," Hill said seriously.

He withdrew the muzzle and stepped off, keeping the gun trained on Pretty Boy's head.

"It's a good deal, and you know it. So just do it. We'll both be happy—and alive. Good-bye, Pretty Boy. It'd be best for you to wait a couple of minutes before you come up to the street."

Hill turned the corner and was gone.

* * *

It was five in the afternoon in Miami. The brass sun beat down in brutal waves. People avoided the streets if they could, staying holed up in air-conditioned offices, restaurants, movie theaters, apartments and homes. Or they swarmed to the beaches, where the sun dazzled the white sand and glinted on the ocean. Yachts and sailboats plied the coast and filled the inland waterways.

Those who had to be afoot dressed as lightly as they could and even the young and strong moved slowly, with carefully regulated breathing, because anything else, even when briefly possible, would be insane in such fearsome heat. The city had been sweltering for three days and hospital emergency rooms were filled with cases of prostration, dehydration and sunstroke. The elderly were hardest hit and fatalities from respiratory failure and heart attack were mounting. So was the incidence of murder and assault as the shimmering furnace drove the marginally stable over the edge.

Wycisowicz was waiting in the rider's seat of a patrol car while Bobby Hayes, a black officer and his partner, tried to find a break in the oncoming traffic so he could make his turn into the parking lot behind the Palm Street station. The car's air-conditioning was broken and both officers were sweating heavily.

"Look at those fuckers, look at those fuckers," Wycisowicz said, glowering at the traffic. The windows of all the passing cars were rolled up tight, protecting the cooled air within. "What the fuck are we, fuckin' animals? They wouldn't make dogs go out in this heat, but *we* got to work in it. Look at those fuckers."

Hayes nodded. "Uh-huh." He wouldn't say any more—though he was angry too—because Wycisowicz had his blood up, and when that happened it was bad news for everyone around. What they had in the backseat was already trouble enough.

What they had in the backseat, behind the wire barricade, handcuffed, was a Cuban male in his early twenties. The flesh around one eye was purplish and swollen nearly shut. His nose was broken. His upper lip was split and one of his teeth snapped. There was blood on his face and on his fishnet shirt and chest.

Hayes swung into the lot and parked. Wycisowicz opened the rear door, got the Cuban by his bushy hair and pulled him out. "Come on, scumbag."

The station was long and low, two stories, dun-colored stone. Every few steps Wycisowicz shoved the Cuban, staggering him forward. "Move. Move."

"Hey," Brown said softly. "Ease back, Witz. He didn't shoot the Pope."

Wycisowicz didn't answer.

They went to the booking desk.

"Beautiful," the booking officer said. "What have we got?"

"I want my lawyer," the Cuban said angrily. He hadn't spoken since they'd busted him. "I want to see the desk sergeant. They beat me up for nothing. It's fuckin' police brutality and I'm going to sue these motherfuckers."

Wycisowicz said, "Shut up, turkey."

"Take everything out of your pockets and put it on the desk," the booking officer said.

"I want to see the duty sergeant!" the Cuban said.

"You will." To Wycisowicz, the booking officer said, "I'll have to call Murphy in."

"Sure. Do it. I don't give a fuck. This piece of shit grabbed an old lady's purse on Hyacinth and Sixth. A nice old lady, like you remember your grandmother. She screamed and tried to grab it back. Our Latin American friend here, what he did was pull a switchblade and cut her from her elbow to her wrist."

"This bastard beat me up for no reason!" the Cuban yelled. "I didn't rob no lady. I surrendered and said, 'What's the problem?' But this white cop here, he slapped cuffs on me and then he beat me up. He beat me up when I was handcuffed. I want to see the duty sergeant! I know my rights!"

"I'll bet you a dollar he does," Wycisowicz said. "And

another that when you run him, you find he's goddam *Marielito*. But he sure does know his rights. You're booking him for armed robbery, assault with a deadly weapon and resisting arrest."

"Uh-huh," said the booking officer. "You know, the way he looks, Murphy'll probably want to see you after your shift." He looked at Wycisowicz with sympathy.

"What else is new? Sure thing. Maybe we should book that old lady. She provoked the poor bastard by carrying her pocketbook on the street. It's probably entrapment or something."

He brought a fist up low, from behind the Cuban, and caught him in the kidney.

"Ahhhgg!" The Cuban fell onto the desk.

"Witz!" the booking officer yelled.

Hayes seized Wycisowicz and pulled him back.

"We'll be in at the end of the shift," Wycisowicz said. "That guy, he's a mouth, but he didn't have any problem at the desk, your desk, did he?"

"Not that I saw," the booking officer said.

Hayes said, "Thanks. We'll see you later."

When they ended their tour—sweat-soaked, weary and sullen—Sergeant Murphy was waiting. "What went on with that Cuban, the purse-snatcher, this afternoon?"

Wycisowicz shrugged. "He cut the old lady just as we were coming around the corner. We jumped out and went after him. He put up a fight. I had to knock him around before we managed to get the cuffs on."

"Hayes? Is that the way it was?"

Hayes was looking at his shoes. He glanced at Murphy, then looked at the wall. He nodded.

"You sure?"

"Yeah."

"Well, that's not the way he tells it. We got a positive ID from the victim, so there's no problem of false arrest. But she gets funny after that. She says she really doesn't know what happened, only that you saved her and that she's grateful to you."

Wycisowicz shrugged again.

"Hayes, you can take off. Witz, hang around. Lieutenant Stanley told me to get back to him after I heard what you had to say."

"Right."

Murphy went off to talk with the lieutenant.

Wycisowicz said, "Thanks, Bobby."

"That's all right. But, Witz, you got to watch yourself, man. One of these times you're going to get a shitload of trouble." He left for the lockers.

Wycisowicz slumped in a chair in the ready room and smoked. The Cuban wasn't cuffed, but he *had* given up. Wycisowicz had gone on anyhow and would have kept at it if Hayes hadn't pulled him off. He finished his second cigarette before he was summoned to Stanley's office.

He closed the door behind him and stood before the desk. "Lieutenant."

Stanley was a tall man who didn't smile very much. He frequently came in on his days off to work. He seemed never really to stop working.

"Sit down, Ed." He fooled with a pencil a moment. "You got that guy pretty good. Not near the job you did on that mugger last month, but it's a contender."

"He resisted arrest, lieutenant."

"That'll be the way the report reads—but you know that's not what happened, and the victim knows, and Hayes knows, and *I* know." The lieutenant rocked forward and slapped his hands to the desk. "Damn it, Wycisowicz, I've warned you about this!"

"Hey, if you think there was something wrong with the bust you can bring me up on charges."

"It's too late and too long past for charges. And I don't know that charges would help anyone—you, the department or the general public—anyway. Wycisowicz, you're a menace.

You've trashed too many people to count. In fact, you can hardly make an arrest without roughing someone up. You've—"

"What the hell is—"

"Shut up! You've crippled three men. And last year you beat one to death."

"Who says?"

"Yeah. He was dead when you and Drabble got there. That's why Drabble, your partner of eight years, that's why as good and dedicated a cop as Drabble was, he just ups and resigns two weeks later, and the only reason he gives is that he just can't do this kind of thing anymore. That's why he quits a job he loves, that's why he pisses away his benefits, his retirement, gives up the whole package, because he just can't do this kind of thing anymore. You owe Drabble. He saved your fucking ass—while you broke his. And all this, Wycisowicz, is just the shit I know for certain, that's happened in the four years I've been in this station. I hate to think about the rumors, the stuff I don't know, and everything that happened before I got here."

"Do I have to listen to this shit, are you ordering me to?"

"Yes, goddamn it. You've hurt people, Wycisowicz. You've killed people. It stops right now. I can't let you jeopardize the department any longer. I can't let you continue as an armed and sanctioned menace. There's something you're going to do."

"You want me to see the department shrink, or some other bullshit thing."

Stanley shook his head. "No. You're a Catholic. You know what a retreat is. There's one up in New York next month. At a monastery dedicated to working with violent men. I want you there. Do it, and the slate's clean, you start fresh."

"And if I don't?"

"It's your job."

"Not much of a choice, is there?"

"None. I'll get you medical leave and expense money."

Wycisowicz worked his jaw, but he nodded.

"Good. One further thing. I have to protect my own ass. This could come down on me if it gets out that I'm fucking with your records. So you don't tell anyone what's going on. Someone asks, you just say you've got medical leave for a couple weeks. Nothing else, not one damn word. If you tell Hayes or anyone else, anyone at all, then I fire you, I never heard of you and you're on the street and alone. All alone."

Chapter 6

The sun rose while Brother Martin was in his cell in prayer. The light fell upon and illuminated his crucifix. Would that it had never happened before, so he might take it as sign that his governing was sound: they had begun the screening process last week.

But faith based on sign and miracle was not of much worth. Only that gained through fire or wrenched from uncertainty was.

He could not help wishing the responsibility had fallen to another.

He was ashamed of the wish.

He had been abbot only half a month. No man before him had ever been elevated to the chair on the very eve of a Retreat.

It is not easy, Lord.

Nor was Calvary.

He rose up at five and left to take breakfast. In the hall, Brother Phelan was standing before the Solitary's door in consternation. Brother Phelan held a tin plate on which there was boiled cabbage and a cup of water. Each morning Brother Phelan left a little food for the Solitary and exchanged the chamber pot that the Solitary had placed outside his door in the night for a fresh one. Brother Martin raised his eyebrows in question. Brother Phelan inclined his head toward the door.

It was open a crack.

Brother Martin had never seen this before. Nor had anyone, he'd discovered in Brother Giles's logs, in seventeen years, which was how long the Solitary had remained in total isolation within his tiny cell.

Brother Martin stepped to the door. He knocked once. "Hello?"

A moment passed. Then the door banged shut and a bolt was thrown home on the other side. The Solitary cackled shrilly.

"Are you all right, brother?" the abbot asked.

There was no response.

To Brother Phelan, he said, "Notify me if this happens again or of any other change in routine."

The company assembled in the chapter room after breakfast. Ordinarily the abbot's daily comment was redundant, a simple exhortation toward continued sanctification, followed by comment on things that needed doing, reassignment of tasks. The looming Retreat changed that.

Brother Martin counseled them to rigorous preparation, to purge themselves of everything but the love of God, to become nothing but the extension of His will. "We must each," he said, "maintain our highest level of spiritual strength throughout the Retreat. If you falter, you imperil whatever hope of salvation remains those who come among us, and you place your own soul in mortal danger."

He did not feel fully balanced himself. He'd heard his own voice more in the past two weeks than he had in the past twelve years. Its unfamiliarity, disconnection, made him think he was in two parts, which was dangerous—to himself, the chapter, the penitents. *He* bore the burden of the Retreat, and if he wavered, catastrophe could follow.

He went to the abbot's office, his office now, and opened the portion of false wall that gave access to the vault. The vault was half the size of his cell and within it were safeguarded the Chronicles—all the secret records of the order that still existed, covering some two centuries. The order itself had lived the better part of a millennium, but the monks had destroyed the documents of the early centuries during the time of the great Revolution, the Terror, in France. To protect themselves from the guillotine and the stake.

From its founding in twelfth-century Italy, the Order of Saint Hector had spread through Europe, flourishing and waning according to the larger history, shrinking, finally, after the Renaissance and finally withdrawing to France. Abbot Chartesque burned the Chronicles himself. For those histories, detailing the work of the order through the centuries, would surely have meant death to them all and extinction of the order. Even so, anti-clericism was rampant and, like all the other monastic orders in France, they were persecuted—some killed, some deported to penal colonies in South America, the rest hounded from or lucky to escape the country.

The survivors of the shattered order made their way to Germany, which was predominantly Lutheran, but where they found a Catholic protector who provided the wherewithal to regroup. From Germany they went to Switzerland, in which tolerant nation they found respite. But not for long. Some of their members had been put to torture in the Terror, and in their death agonies had given depositions which were now beginning to spread as disquieting rumor. So the monks of Saint Hector rallied themselves to take ship, abandoned the old world and emigrated to Canada, and thence shortly down into America, which in time proved both hospitable and a fertile garden for their work.

There, through memory and oral tradition, they reconstituted what they could of their lost history. All the rich detail was gone forever, but they did manage to reclaim much of the essence. And they began the new Chronicles.

Brother Martin was studying the criteria used in selecting penitents. Violence, naturally, was fundamental, but there were others too. Which could influence success or failure. In a sense, there *were* no failures. But that was the least preferable sense, to be avoided if at all possible. The criteria had changed over the years, particularly in the last decades as increasingly sophisticated technology bore down ever harder on the social fabric, bringing radical alteration.

The abbot paid special attention to Brother Giles's remarks, because they were the most recent and therefore the most apropos to this new society. In a querulous tone that Brother Martin could still hear, Brother Giles had written:

All this was easier in the old days. The matter of privacy was more easily solved. Men were more closemouthed. And their wives, their lovers and their families didn't expect to be told everything. A man could say, 'I'm going away on business,' or 'I'm taking a holiday,' or 'There's something I have to do,' and let it go at that and no one would think to protest much. If you go back far enough, into the Renaissance, or better, the Middle Ages, why there was scarcely a bother at all. Religion was everywhere. And what a person did was no one else's business. It was easy to get peasants. The rising middle class wanted to imitate the nobility, and the nobility were always going off on some sort of pilgrimage or another (usually only to go through the motions, but that didn't matter to us) or cloaking themselves in beggar's rags to 'go out among the people and learn what they think' and that kind of thing. And of course religion had more impressive coin then than it did later and does today, so if we said, 'This is a private matter, between you and God. Tell no one else,' why it wasn't hard to get compliance. Even those who weren't very religious (and it's obvious that many of the kind of people we deal with aren't going to be) were still influenced by what we might call a kind of religious superstition. They might not think they believed, but they weren't going to go out of their way to tweak God's nose to see what happened. It was a lot easier to get our hands on people back then.

* * *

Well, what's gone is gone and there's no sense grumbling about the good old days. What we're faced with now is a much more secular society, and, worst of all, it's so easy to get in touch or stay in touch with someone. Instant communication and rapid travel (a world in which we learn of an assassination on another continent within minutes and in which you can hop across oceans in hours) have made the really demanding part of our task to insure that our penitents do keep their plans secret. The damned telephone alone has been a real devil to us. Regrettably, but unavoidably, we have to depend on our ability to intimidate more than anything else, which just isn't as good as the old devices (maybe it is, maybe our present intimidations just aren't as effective as our old intimidations, I'll have to research this further). What this all adds up to is greatly increased man-hours and money, heavier burdens on the screening committee and careful monitoring of the penitents in the weeks and days before they arrive to ensure that secrecy has been maintained. All this is a great bother. Sometimes when I'm tired or discouraged—and forgive me, God, but it does happen—I yearn for the very old days in which we simply dragooned some of our penitents right off the streets and spirited them away.

Brother Martin was tempted to smile. In another time and life he might have enjoyed the old man's crotchetiness.

He became aware that someone had knocked upon his door, waited, and was knocking again. "Yes?"

Brother Anthony came in to stand before the desk.

He was a compact man in his early forties with steely gray hair, long arms and an athlete's confidence of movement. There was a tattoo on the right hinge of his jaw—a death's-head with a cocked beret, pierced by a dagger.

He said, "Pardon me, my Abbot. I would like permission to see my wife tomorrow."

Brother Martin had skimmed the dossiers on the individual monks looking for aspects of character, a piece of history, anything unique that could either aid or endanger the Retreat. The name of Brother Anthony's wife was . . . Lily.

Brother Martin's wife had been Gwen. He had killed her. His stomach convulsed. He recoiled in fear—not from the event itself but from the sudden shakiness that accompanied the memory. No! Not now. He couldn't afford that now.

Lily, he thought. She lived with an order of nursing sisters in Scanandaga.

"Is that wise?" he asked. "I think it might be disruptive."

"I think it would help settle that part of my spirit. I don't want it to rise and distract me when she is here."

Brother Anthony was an estimable monk. The abbot didn't think anyone else among them could have sustained such a situation, this marriage. Certainly it had never been allowed before. Lily had been a profound help to the order in its last two Retreats. Women, Brother Martin had discovered in the Chronicles, had been used on occasion before. With some success, and some serious problems. The largest difficulty lay in finding someone suitable—not only in body, mind and spirit, but situated properly in life. Though Brother Martin had at first held deep reservations, Brother Giles had integrated Lily brilliantly into the structure of the Retreat, and he intended to follow the old abbot's direction.

Brother Martin reflected. While the use of one's wife might have broken other men, it seemed only to have strengthened Brother Anthony. "All right," he said. "But as discipline, you will walk to Scanandaga." The town was thirty miles away. "You can leave tomorrow morning after meditation. I'll expect you back by midnight. Keep your time with her brief."

"I will," Brother Anthony said. "Thank you, Abbot."

A light lunch was taken at eleven, followed in summers, when the days were long and the work grueling, by a brief respite. When the monks were back to their tasks, Brother

Martin set out with Brother Hilliard to take stock. The prior wrote in a note pad as Brother Martin made observations or asked questions that required investigation.

The larder was in good supply. The early crops, mostly leaf vegetables, were being harvested and the first tomatoes were ripening. They would slaughter meat and poultry for the penitents next week. Quartering had been planned. The monks displaced from their cells would sleep communally in the chapter room. The abbot ordered the gasoline-powered generator hooked into the monastery's primitive wiring. They used electricity only during Retreats.

He visited the infirmary. Brother Raphael, snowy-haired, incongruous laugh lines around his melancholy eyes, showed him the dispensary's inventory. They had everything they might need, except for whatever the infirmarer might find useful in the shipment now en route to him from a laboratory in New Jersey. The small surgery was in order. Stark. White tile. Stainless steel. For some, it had served as the vehicle of salvation.

They went out of the monastery. The livestock barn was a hundred yards off, the storage barns a bit farther. Brother Thomas was leading a crew who were ferrying wooden bed frames, springs and mattresses into the monastery and hanging long-unused blankets and muslin sheets to air on a line strung between poles. The sunburnt sphere of Brother Thomas's tonsure was only somewhat less red than his hair. Brother Thomas, who had once been president of the Dayton chapter of the Hell's Angels, had been working hard and his face was slicked with sweat.

"No, no," he called to the oblate Michael. "You've got to spread them all the way open."

The guileless oblate, with his perpetual look of uncertainty, turned to Brother Harold. Brother Harold was in his early thirties, fine-featured and of a gentle disposition. Michael relied upon him.

"You have to unfold them before you put them on the line,"

Brother Harold explained. "Like this, so the air can get all around them."

"Oh," Michael said. He smiled. "All right. Thank you."

Brother Harold patted him on the shoulder.

Michael set about his task happily.

Brother Thomas surveyed his crew with annoyance. "Come on. Step it up. I want to get this finished today." He wiped sweat from his brow with his sleeve in a quick jerky movement, then headed into the barn with rapid strides.

Brother Martin looked after him. "I'd like to see Brother Thomas after dinner tonight."

Brother Hilliard made a note.

They passed the livestock enclosures on the way to the workshop. The billy goat Samson bleated. The geese, a flock of twenty of the big birds, with long hard bills and sinuous muscular necks, heads on a level with a man's belly, ill-tempered even at the best of moments, were markedly peevish today. They stalked about their holding pen arguing with one another and complaining at the sky and the earth in general. The flock's dominant gander spread his wings, nearly as wide as a man's extended arms, charged the fence and hissed viciously at Brother Martin and Brother Hilliard. Ordinarily the birds spent the day in the fields picking and eating various insect pests, or were at least turned into a cow pasture to fend for and occupy and amuse themselves. But Brother Wilfred had kept them penned up yesterday and would continue to do so until the Retreat was under way, readying them.

In the workshop Brother Louis showed the abbot the devices he had prepared. Some were wood. Some were iron.

"Good," Brother Martin said, not permitting himself to feel anything.

They inspected the pond, a peaceful place around which there were many willows. Brother Lawrence and a few other monks were repairing a dike, tamping the earth with large heavy metal plates fitted to wooden shafts. Brother Lawrence reported the bass and bluegill population strong. They would seine on days when fish was to be served to the penitents.

Brother Martin and the prior walked the crop fields, where monks worked in silence. Once, they heard gunfire rolling out of a small valley to the east. Brother Anthony was there with a few other monks. First came three deep measured booms.

Brother Martin stopped to listen.

A minute later, another trio, this time sharp cracks.

"What kind are those?" he asked.

Brother Anthony had shown him the guns, but the abbot had no context in which to relate them. Many years ago, he'd carried some kind of revolver he'd stolen, but he'd never known much about it.

"Those were both rifles," Brother Hilliard said. "The first was a thirty-ought-six, a big caliber. It smashes through brush without deflection. The second was a two-seventy. Very fast, flat trajectory, long-range accuracy."

There were three thicker, mushier booms.

"Shotgun," Brother Hilliard said. "Twelve-gauge. Riot gun. We have two."

Another series of reports; ten groups, two rounds each.

"Handguns. Colt forty-five autos and Baretta nine-millimeter autos."

The firing stopped. Guns were as natural as chain saws and hammers to the inhabitants of this mountainous deeply forested land and people often took target practice and recreation with them. But despite that, and the isolation of the monastery, the monks were careful not to impress upon anyone's mind, no matter how unconsciously, the sound of repeated or unusual gunshots, which might later be recalled at an awkward moment.

Brother Martin stood ruminating as the last echoes faded. Oh my Lord, I am not strong enough for this.

Brother Hilliard waited: indifferent, cold.

"*You* are the man for the Retreat," Brother Martin said suddenly. "You are the man to be abbot."

Brother Hilliard was silent several moments. Then he said, "It's not my place to rebuke my abbot."

"I order you to."

The prior looked past Brother Martin to something unseen. "You sin by doubting yourself. You sin by denying God's wisdom in selecting you. *I* am the least qualified, less even than Brother Thomas, less even than the Solitary. I am not fully human." He looked into Brother Martin's eyes. "I wish only to be free of all this. *I want to join my God....* And in my frustration I sin against His will." He paused.

"You, my abbot, are among the most humane and the most obedient to God's will. God tries hardest those who are the strongest. They must carry heavier crosses. Forgive me: I think you are in horror of what you once were, and that you are afraid to step into that fire again. But it is not the same fire. It is brighter, and more painful, but it is *God's* fire. That you feel weak and incapable only offers you a greater opportunity of moral courage. He has called you. You must answer." Brother Hilliard went down on his knees. "Forgive my impertinence."

Brother Martin raised him. "You have shamed me to humility and obedience to the Lord. That is an act of charity. Pray for me."

Brother Hilliard said nothing more, which was proper, and Brother Martin spoke only to have him make note of a point or two, which was also proper.

The screening committee was to meet again this afternoon. Brother Martin sat in his office over a sheaf of new reports from the field agents. But he couldn't keep his mind on the words.

Unbidden, he remembered.

He was burning. His buttocks. Thighs. The backs of his calves. He was on fire. He was two years old. She was screaming at him: "Shut up! Shut up, goddamn you!" He couldn't help it, he was on fire. He was naked and she had thrust him down sitting on the fierce hot winter radiator, burning him, and held him pressed there and was slapping him again and again, screaming, "Shut up!"

He'd soiled his diaper, that was why.

Blood. God, he remembered blood. He was awash with it. His and others.

His father had left—too weak for her, unable.

He didn't know why she'd kept him.

He was hospitalized three or four times before the courts took him away from her. He'd almost lost an eye when she flailed him with a belt.

He was nine. The court sent him to live in a small town north of Minneapolis with an aunt, who wasn't actually an aunt but some distant relative who took him for the money the state paid. He never saw or heard anything about his mother again.

He fought with his aunt's sons, especially her oldest, who was a bullying hulk. He fought with his classmates and didn't do well in school, though they said he was intelligent. He ran away often.

His father came for him when he was twelve, and it was deliverance. He returned to Minneapolis to live in a shabby little house with him. His father's new wife was sluggish and bovine but no more unpleasant than pleasant and she didn't mind him. He loved his father desperately and when the man was home—he was a salesman frequently on the road—they fished and took walks and went to movies and played cards, or just sat in the same room and read books. He understood whence he had come to love books so much; his father read every day. When his father was gone, he spent a lot of time in the public library, because it was sad to read in the living room and see his father's chair empty. Sometimes he played hearts or two-handed canasta with his father's wife or they would watch the black-and-white television on its blond wood table.

He was bright, the guidance counselor told his father, but inconsistent. And he had a temper. He was a good football player but he was cut from the team because he got into too many fights. Not as many as he used to, though: he loved his father very much.

One night when he was fifteen and his father was out of town he argued with his date, left her and came home hours early and found his father's wife with her clothes in a pile on the floor naked on the couch in the drab living room with the curtains closed over the windows huffing and pumping beneath his father's boss, who still had his socks and garters on, but whose suit and shirt and tie and pants were in a pile next to the clothes of his father's wife. They looked up startled. He turned and walked out.

He sat in the blackness down the street beside a neighbor's hedge. The man left the house ten minutes later and drove away. He waited another half hour. He went back to the house.

He might have beaten her to death. But when he walked in she was in the living room, dressed, and he'd barely crossed the threshold when she said, without much emotion, "Your father knows about it. He owes his boss money. It's an arrangement he has with him. We do it when your father's gone."

He went away without a word. He lived in a friend's garage until his father returned. He came home the following afternoon. His father was sitting on the couch, just sitting there with his wrists on his knees, looking down blankly at the carpet. He raised his head and looked at Martin, sickness and weakness and misery in his eyes. Several moments passed. Then he nodded and lowered his eyes back down to the carpet.

Martin went into the bathroom, took something from the medicine chest and walked out of the house. He never saw his father again.

Three nights later, he stepped from the shadows in a deserted parking lot as his father's boss, having closed the office late, was bent probing the lock of his car door with his key. The man heard him and glanced up. He looked embarrassed and terribly uncomfortable. He opened his mouth reluctantly to speak, as if it were the last thing in all the world he wanted to do.

Martin swung the straight razor with a flick of his wrist from right to left, slashing so deep that the blade cut completely through the throat and scraped against the man's neck bones.

There was blood on Martin's shirt, but not much. He'd moved quickly out of the way. He burned the shirt down by the river, then threw the ashes into the water. He scoured the razor repeatedly.

Very late, closer to dawn than midnight, he raised a kitchen window in his father's house, slipped inside, stole silently into the living room and left his father's gleaming straight razor with the mother-of-pearl plates on its handle in the precise center of the couch's middle cushion.

Within a month, his father and his father's wife moved out of the house and away from Minneapolis.

Brother Martin opened his eyes. He could still see them all. He could see the blood. He felt it on his hands.

The *tic-douloureux* of the soul.

Strengthen me, God.

Chapter 7

With God's help, Brother Martin purged the images from his mind.

He spent a focused and productive hour on the agents' reports. With minor exceptions, everything was proceeding well.

There was a rapid knocking on the door.

"Yes?"

Brother Hilliard opened the door. He said, "Brother Thomas. A seizure."

Brother Martin left his chair. They hurried down the stone hall. "You summoned Brother Raphael?"

"Yes."

Brother Thomas was backed up against the barn holding a length of board like a club. His lips were curled back in a grimace exposing crooked yellowish teeth. His eyes were wide, face flushed. Sweat streamed down his cheeks. His robe was stained with it. He raised the board and swung it over his head.

"Ghhyaaa!"

One monk was down, legs drawn up, clasping himself with a small rocking movement. Brother Martin couldn't see who it was.

Half a dozen others had formed a cautious semicircle around Brother Thomas.

Brother Thomas shouted again and charged them. They retreated. He pulled back to the barn. The geese were in an uproar, honking and gabbling and rushing about their pen menacing one another and the fence posts.

Brother Raphael held out his liverspotted hands. He murmured steadily and soothingly to Brother Thomas. He moved closer. Brother Thomas screamed and crashed the board against the side of the barn. Brother Raphael edged back, continuing his entreaty.

The oblate Michael knelt on the ground with his face buried in his hands weeping. Brother Harold crouched beside him with an arm around his shoulder. "It's all right, Michael. It's just a game. Don't cry."

Brother Thomas howled.

"Brother Thomas!" Brother Martin shouted. "Get hold of yourself! I order you in God's name to stop!"

His words had no effect. He hadn't thought they would.

Brother Leopold was among the monks ranged around Brother Thomas. He looked to Brother Martin, his long bearded face intent and questioning. His wrist-stump, where it emerged from the sleeve of his robe, was shiny-skinned.

Brother Martin hesitated, then nodded.

Brother Leopold turned to Brother Thomas. He tensed, relaxed, and advanced with slow deliberateness. The other monks drew back.

Brother Thomas moved to meet Brother Leopold, swinging the board loosely, cagily. His eyes were bright. He snarled. Brother Leopold moved within range. Brother Thomas swung the board in a wide arc. Brother Leopold dropped to a crouch, allowing the board to slice inches over his head, then straightened immediately, threw his weight to his right leg, leaned and delivered a powerful roundhouse kick to Brother Thomas's chest with his sandaled left foot. Brother Thomas was slammed back against the barn, the board spinning from his hands. He sagged down, then slumped forward till his forehead touched the ground. Brother Leopold was on him quickly, flattened him to the ground, placed a knee in his back and twined the fingers of his right hand into his hair.

"Don't hurt him," Brother Raphael said, drawing a syringe from his robe.

Brother Leopold wore a mournful expression.

Brother Thomas was struggling for air. Weakly, he tried to gather himself up.

Brother Raphael found the vein. He depressed the plunger. In moments Brother Thomas loosened. His eyes half closed. He mumbled something.

"Bring him to the infirmary," Brother Martin said.

Brother Leopold motioned the others away. He brushed Brother Thomas's sweat-dampened hair back from his forehead, then slipped his wrist and hand beneath him and lifted him himself, cradling him tenderly in his arms.

Brother Leopold came to the office after Brother Thomas was under restraint and in Brother Raphael's solicitous hands.

He went to his knees. "My abbot, I am guilty of striking one of my brothers. I am deeply sorry. I beg God's forgiveness."

Brother Martin said, "Even though I ordered you to the act, we can violate neither our vows, nor the Rule."

"Yes."

"You will retire to your cell after supper and remain on your knees with your arms extended outward until Compline. Tomorrow you will take no sustenance except for a small piece of bread in the morning and what water you need during the day."

Brother Martin had imposed a weightier penance upon himself, since he had been the cause of Brother Leopold's transgression.

"Go," he said. "Sin no more."

The screening committee met in the conference room off the library on the second floor, the same room in which Brother Martin had been chosen abbot. It overlooked the cloister, where there were stone benches, a tiered fountain in which water ran with soft plashes, and shrubs and floral plantings amid rock arrangements. The room itself held but one ornament, a large sixteenth-century silver crucifix from Spain—the Saviour's mouth wrenched open in agony, His body twisted. It was one of the few artifacts the survivors of the order had managed to save. The oval table was oak, the chairs straight-backed and hard.

Brother Martin sat down and arranged the folders before him. The others took their places. He had selected five. Brother Stefan, who often seemed not to be of this immediate place, his great scar vivid against his pale skin, the only true mystic among them. Brother Hilliard. Brother Wilfred, in whom murderousness and joviality had once existed in equally happy proportion. Brother Jules, a pragmatic man of excellent gutter sensibilities. And Brother Conrad, keenly intelligent, schooled and analytic, who had shattered and raped women too numerous to calculate.

They were, Brother Martin thought, the finest he could have selected for this task.

He led them in prayer.

They began with Joel Ableman.

Brother Martin looked down at the open file. "He's thirty-nine. Divorced. No children. He runs the Horace Adams Home for Children in Ellis, Michigan, outside Detroit."

The child in Brother Martin shrank back from Ableman. The man in him wished to lash out and hurt. The monk had to chivvy himself to charity. The abbot was bound to remain distanced and to think only of the Retreat.

There were no marginal cases at Horace Adams. Its charges were utterly incapable, many barely more conscious than a plant.

Brother Martin said, "Ableman has killed two children intentionally in his five years as director. Two more have died later as a result of his . . . handling."

The patients at Horace Adams were so grievously afflicted that they had infused their families with horror, guilt and shame. Once relieved of them, those families wanted only to heal, *needed* to heal. That healing depended in part upon the complete excision of the children from their lives. They could bear no responsibility beyond that minimum with which their consciences could live. They would sop and balm this with a simple telephone call once or twice a year: How is Tom doing? Is Gail happy? Is he all right? Is she untroubled and content? They would be satisfied by and grateful for any mollification or reassurance. And thus relieved they could say, I've done my best, discharged my duty, now let me be free, oh God, and go their way unmolested, to try to find happiness.

No one cared about the children at Horace Adams. No one could endure thought of them.

Brother Martin circulated a typewritten profile of Ableman. Beyond the deaths, Ableman, or the morally defective goon he kept on his staff and whom he enjoyed watching work, had injured several other children.

The abbot said, "Our agent in this case is Calvin Henderson in the Michigan attorney general's office. We've accepted penitents from him twice. We were successful with one."

Ableman had slipped from under two investigations by threatening to blackball former employees from any other social-service job in the state.

"What about this girl Ableman lives with?" Brother Conrad asked.

"He disappears on her at whim," Brother Martin said. "Usually off with another woman. He never tells her anything. She puts up with it. The security's good."

Brother Jules nodded slowly. He was a ponderous man whose nose had been several times broken. "I like him."

Brother Stefan was looking out the window. "Yes," he said, abstracted.

Brother Wilfred asked, "Can we be sure he won't tell the goon?"

"He's just that, a goon," Brother Conrad said. "Not a confidant."

Brother Martin agreed.

"Is Ableman a threat to Henderson?" Brother Conrad asked.

Most penitents were forced into a Retreat by someone who'd gained power over them. They were led to believe this person was a religious lunatic who could be satisfied and neutralized by agreeing to this one idiosyncratic demand. Others were duped, such as, among those already selected, Dominic Caparelli, a hoodlum who thought he could win leniency from the court; Cesar Alvarado from Paraguay, who believed he'd be meeting in secret with certain government officials; and Gunther Hauptmann, a West German who was still in Berlin and who hadn't yet even heard of the monastery of Saint Hector. But no matter how carefully an agent worked, a penitent might come to think that his greatest security lay in killing the man. When an agent *was* murdered, which was rare, the order would respond in an appropriate manner, but that was not its business and it hurt them all morally. They preferred to drop a candidate if violence seemed possible. There were always so many more.

"No," Brother Martin said. "He's convinced that Henderson has left documentation with a friend that will be mailed to the authorities if anything happens."

"Good," Brother Conrad said. "Take him."

Brother Wilfred was smiling, because it was a sunny day and he felt good. "Yes."

Brother Hilliard moved his pencil slowly across the note pad before him. The page was marked with small, tight scribbles.

The abbot said, "Brother Hilliard?"

The prior jerked. "What?"

"Ableman."

Brother Hilliard considered. "Put him in."

The abbot could make decisions on his own discretion, but Brother Martin felt more secure with the support of the others. He closed Ableman's file and wrote *Penitent* across it.

Next was Roger Ballantine, a urological surgeon from Washington, D.C. They accepted him.

They tabled Vitek Jaretzki. Brother Martin felt they needed more information from the referral agent.

"Gregorio Rios," the abbot said. "Twenty-nine. Single. Three illegitimate children he never sees. Mexican-American. San Antonio, Texas. He smuggles illegal aliens into the country. Professionally, on a large scale. He's been arrested several times, jailed briefly twice. He has money and good lawyers. No one's been able to touch him." He passed Rio's summary out.

Rios had once thrown half a dozen Haitians overboard in chains when a coast guard cutter was closing in. He'd left a party of Salvadorans to die in the desert after robbing them.

"Recently," Brother Martin said, "he's organized a cattle-car run from Texas to New York. He fills a tractor-trailer with aliens and locks them in. They're supposed to have rest stops, but they don't. The run is straight through. There's no sanitation, little ventilation. Several people have died. Rios drives some of these trips himself. It amuses him. He's a solipsist, actually. He doesn't really believe in other people—they're just things, objects. He's casually violent. He can shake someone's hand or cut his throat. It makes little difference to him."

Brother Conrad was the last to read the summary. He returned it to Brother Martin in silence.

None of them was horrified by these candidates. Deep and riving sadness, yes, and determination, but little more. They had all known such things at one time.

They voted to take Gregorio Rios.

Brother Stefan directed their attention to the fat white clouds outside, which an erratic wind was driving like tumbling elephants.

"There is the matter at hand," Brother Martin admonished him.

"I'm sorry."

The abbot opened the file on Lee Huang, a Hong Kong immigrant. At twenty-three, Huang now led the Jade Army, a youth gang in San Francisco. While other Chinatown gangs extorted their protection money by intimidation, beatings and a rare murder, Huang's people routinely mutilated and killed.

Brother Wilfred said, "I don't feel right about this."

"Why?"

Brother Wilfred wrinkled his brow. "Because he's Chinese and the culture is strange to me? I don't know. But something bothers me."

The pencil in Brother Hilliard's hand snapped. His knuckles were white.

"Is something wrong?" Brother Martin asked.

"I . . . no. Continue. Please." He dropped his eyes under Brother Martin's gaze.

Brother Stefan and Brother Jules had no misgivings. They voted to take Huang.

"It *is* the culture," Brother Conrad said. "The Chinese are clannish and extraordinarily close. The family tradition, one of the most powerful in the world, survives, and these Chinatown gangs are surrogate families. I'd say it's nearly impossible that a man like this would withhold information of this nature from his fellow gang members. Also, I think our agent is in danger no matter how well he feels he's covered himself. We run too high a risk with this one. I don't want him."

Brother Wilfred's doubts hardened into conviction. "I vote no."

With the two men he considered the poles of judgment on this panel both opposed, Brother Martin didn't hesitate. "Lee Huang is dropped from consideration," he said. He wrote a note instructing himself to notify the agent to disengage immediately.

He took up the next file, and offered them Norman O. Marcus.

Marcus was a huge man, six-foot-six and three hundred pounds, a highly successful Hollywood producer with a ravenous appetite for drugs, flesh and pain.

"He's bisexual, to a degree, and a sadist," Brother Martin said. "His sexual proclivities don't interest us. His sadism does." The abbot included photographs with the summary sheet. "Last year he raped a fifteen-year-old boy, a street kid without any family. The boy died of a ruptured spleen. There's a young actress in a mental hospital. The list is fairly long."

Brother Jules worked his jaw as he looked at the photographs. "How can they let him get away with this? They know what's going on. They always do out there."

Brother Conrad, who had once headed a brokerage firm which had sometimes arranged financing for West Coast studios, said, "Marcus makes a lot of money for a lot of powerful people. Whatever you want, you can buy it out there—from silence to a consecrated Host. There are thousands of people all over the periphery who'd do anything to get into the center."

Brother Jules stared at the photos. "Take him," he said in a hard voice.

Brother Martin said, "This is a dangerous time to allow anger into your heart. Our role is to lead them by the hand to salvation. All that we do, we must do with unsullied hearts and out of the pure love of God and His children."

Brother Jules was chastened.

"I worry," Brother Stefan said mildly, "that with someone so well-known there might be repercussions, pressure to find answers."

"The order has never limited itself to the obscure," Brother Martin said.

"This is an age of publicity, though, and Marcus looms large in an industry whose very heartbeat is publicity."

"The point is taken," Brother Martin said.

Brother Wilfred tapped the report with his finger. "He was raised a Catholic. He's lapsed, but he *is* a superstitious man. The Retreat has an aura. He's afraid of exposure. He thinks he can get out from under if he does this. I'd say he's a good bet, security will be all right."

Brother Conrad wanted to know who the agent was.

"Herbert Foster. He's chief of surgery at the hospital where the boy died. He's given us several good penitents."

Brother Conrad thought. "Marcus and the business he's in both accept what others would find 'weird' as a matter of course. Given that, given Foster, and what Brother Wilfred rightly pointed out, I'd say yes."

"Yes," Brother Jules said.

Brother Stefan nodded.

"Brother Hilliard?"

The prior was turning a piece of the broken pencil with his fingers.

"Brother Hilliard."

He dropped the pencil. He reoriented himself. "I have not been listening," he said. "I'm sorry."

"This is a serious matter, Brother Hilliard. Your abstraction is a threat to us. I excuse you from this meeting and assign you to two hours' Mortal Meditation. I'll see you in my office after Compline."

Brother Hilliard bowed his head. "I go in shame and obedience to your rule." He left, for the chamber that lay beneath the basement.

After an awkward silence Brother Martin said, "We'll take Marcus."

He opened the last file, on Benjamin Howard, a professional arsonist responsible for eight certain deaths and possibly twice that number.

"He's not for us," Brother Conrad said after reading the summary.

"Why?" Brother Jules asked.

"He's not authentically violent. Immoral, yes, but that's all. He didn't set out to kill those people. He was just doing a job. Their deaths were incidental, not intentional."

There was further, but brief discussion. They were unanimous. Benjamin Howard, whatever else he might be, was not by nature a violent man, and therefore not a fit candidate for the Retreat.

The light was fading when Brother Martin went to the infirmary. Brother Raphael had lit kerosene lamps.

"How is he?"

"Doing well enough," Brother Raphael said.

He took the abbot into the convalescence room. Brother Thomas was sleeping fitfully in one of the four beds. A tic pulled at his acne-pitted cheek. One of his hands clenched into a fist, then relaxed slowly. His breathing was ragged.

"Has he been restless all afternoon?"

"It comes and goes. This was a heavy attack. I'll give him another injection in an hour."

"I've learned that he's been fasting on bread and water for two weeks," Brother Martin said.

Brother Raphael shook his head. "He shouldn't. He knows he shouldn't."

"Is that the answer to these attacks?"

"No. But it can trigger them. And make them more severe."

"Tell him to stop. Send him to me if he resists."

"I'd like to put him on meat, cheese and fish for at least the next week, if you'll permit."

"Yes. Will he be up to the stress of a Retreat?"

"Probably. I think it would be worse if you were to segregate him. He considers himself unworthy."

Brother Thomas lived in intense, punishing remorse for his former life and could not believe that God had accepted him.

"He sees the fits as proof," Brother Raphael said. "He thinks God sends them to him as retribution."

"There's nothing that can be done? No kind of medication?" Before, Brother Martin had simply accepted Brother Thomas's occasional seizures as something that happened. Now, as abbot, it became a responsibility.

"No. I've tested for everything I can here, we've had a complete battery run in the Scanandaga hospital. It's possibly metabolic, more likely neurological, but nothing obvious. Even the best institutions could take years to diagnose him. With steadiness, and prayer, and a reasonable diet, it's more or less manageable." Brother Raphael looked to the door. "We can care better for him here. He could be killed in the outside world."

Brother Raphael had had a son once, Brother Martin recalled from his file. A son who had died. The boy would have been about Brother Thomas's age now.

"All right," Brother Martin said. "Let me know how he is tomorrow morning."

Brother Martin took Brother Hilliard into the cloister while the rest of the company went to prayer. They sat on a stone bench near the fountain. Brother Hilliard kept his eyes on the ground. Brother Martin was still uncertain what tack to take.

The impulse was discipline—that was the cornerstone of the Rule.

Still . . .

The sound of the fountain's trickling water brought him up short.

He'd been wrong to assign Brother Hilliard to Mortal Meditation: that was precisely what was *not* called for. It could only seduce him further along the path on which he'd already embarked.

"Brother Hilliard," he said. "It's not your inattention this afternoon that disturbs me; rather, what that inattention signifies. You're losing your hold on the world. God will summon you in His own time. I fear your desire for Him is degenerating into lust."

Brother Hilliard looked up sharply.

"Yes," Brother Martin said. "That, and what I think is an indifference to the world—His world, I remind you. Indifference threatens to become contempt, even hatred. In these things you sin grievously. It is His will that you be here. You cannot withdraw from His creation simply because you wish to be at His side and He does not yet see fit to grant that."

"May I remind my abbot," Brother Hilliard said coolly, "that withdrawal from the world is precisely the nature of the monastic life."

"You are on the edge of insolence. Prostrate yourself!"

Brother Hilliard hesitated. Then he went to his face on the ground.

"We don't withdraw from the world when we enter the monastery, Brother Hilliard. We withdraw from the society of man. But we remain in the world and in the society of our brothers. And we are sworn to a special work in the service of that larger world. You sin by forgetting this. You sin by not accepting God's will. And you sin by violating your vows."

"I am sorry to have displeased my abbot."

"That is insufficient. I hear no repentance. And I hear much more unspoken."

Several beats passed. Brother Hilliard said, "I wish to become a Solitary."

"I will consider the question, but I think it would be a path of indulgence for you. Your first obligation is to God's will. Your next is to your brothers. Your immediate is to the Retreat. For now, I want you to work in the fields. You will begin with the rising sun and you will continue until the sun sets. You will take respite only when absolutely necessary, and then, briefly." A vein pulsed in Brother Martin's temple. "You will work with your hands in the dirt. You will *feel* God's earth. You will touch it, smell it. You will think about it with each beat of your heart. It will become more real to you than your own body. You will *know* that you are in the world, and that it is God's, and that it is your duty to be there. Is this clear?"

"Yes, my abbot." This time there was submission in the voice.

"Remain as you are until you have said, and truly contemplated, the Seven Joyful Mysteries. Report to Brother Stewart in the morning for your assignment."

Brother Martin strode off, leaving the prior alone on the ground, his arms outspread.

Till now, Brother Martin thought, he hadn't accomplished much more than to scrape through, to avoid doing damage.

But tonight in the cloister with Brother Hilliard he felt that for the first time as abbot he'd experienced true insight and had acted forcefully upon a problem. It gave him hope.

In his office, he removed the record of Brother Samuel from the vault and laid it upon his desk. Brother Samuel had preceded Brother Giles in the abbot's chair, an uneducated rapacious beast of a man who'd found not only repentance but a hard diamond of spirituality in his center. He'd ruled nearly thirty years and had written one of the more profound explications of the Retreat. Brother Martin opened the hand-bound volume, placed his hands flat atop the pages and closed his eyes as he prepared to concentrate.

The order had been founded in the late twelfth century by Ettore of Perugia, the son of a merchant nobleman. Ettore—Saint Hector—led an early life of privilege, was a wastrel and a sybaritic self-loving youth. At twenty, unwilling but acceding to his father's demand, he sailed to the Holy Land at the head of a troop of horse. He, who had loved the hunt, who had slaughtered hare and deer and fowl and mountain lion and wild cattle and boar in numbers beyond enumeration, who had dispatched them with arrow, sling, sword, spear, drowning net, knife and cudgel, and who had slain two other young men of the city in tavern brawls, discovered that he loved battle, that it ignited his blood as nothing ever had before. His horse was first into the line of enemy pikemen, the spearhead of clashing cavalry; he led the stormers up the scaling ladders and was first to gain the battlements. He trampled and cleaved, he maimed and beheaded. He became *il selvaggio* to his countrymen, the Savage One; and in Arabic, the Unholy One. Even his own commanders, not men of refined sensibility, grew uneasy over him—for with his valor, which was useful, they saw also a bloodmadness, which was dangerous. Nor was it confined to battle: he was also foremost in looting and pillaging, in rape, in the torture and slaughter of prisoners. Indeed, there was none who could constrain him. But he inspired the common troops. They believed him invincible and would follow him into the very heart of hell. And so, though disquieted and doubtful, the commanders did not replace him. One, however, who was himself from Perugia, did write to the youth's father expressing his concern and asked him to send a letter of counsel and guidance to his son.

But the father was in fact pleased with the boy and felt that honor was being brought to his house.

Nearly a year after he'd arrived, Hector was cut badly in the side, a scimitar slashing through his damaged armor and spilling out a rope of intestine. The surgeons did what little they could, but the wound was grievous, the loss of blood great. Every minute he continued to breathe was a boon from God. The Prince of Perugia was already in tent, by lamplight penning news of the boy's death to his father.

But the young man lived at morning, and lived still when the watch called the midnight hour. Send the letter, the chief surgeon told the Prince. If by some miracle the wound itself did not kill him, contamination was already accomplished fact, and the fever would take the boy within a day or two, a half fortnight at the most.

He burned for six weeks.

And while he burned, Christ came to him. Came with mournful eyes and a sad mouth, with eyes of pain and a heart of love. Came scourged by the lash, crowned with thorns. Came with bleeding hands and feet. Came with His side pierced by a lance. Came sweating blood.

And asked: Why, my son?

Why do you kill my creatures? Why do you shed my blood?

The boy wept while he burned. The boy raved while he burned. The boy cried out to his God while he burned.

And the surgeons ceased to marvel shortly and began to fear. The priests anointed him, and supplicated at his bedside. Wounded men begged to be placed near to his tent.

And his God enfolded him in loving arms.

And when he awakened, his side a great purple weal, his flesh shrunken and his bones the essential shape and definition of his body, a desiccated breathing cadaver, he awakened with deep mysteriously darkened and dolorous eyes.

"My child," he said hoarsely from his cot to a page who sat upon a stool drawing idly on the dirt floor with a stick.

The boy looked up startled.

"Have you been keeping vigil long?" Hector asked solicitously.

The boy sprang to his feet. "My Lord! You live!"

Hector smiled with cracked lips. "As do you."

The boy ran from the tent. He shouted.

Within minutes the tent filled with priests and surgeons and soldiers, and their excited and awe-filled voices were a babble.

Someone lifted Hector to a sitting position. Another brought him a polished brass so that he could see his reflection.

The youth had passed his twenty-first birthday in battle, and his twenty-second abed and burning with fever. But what was reflected in the brass was the lined and grizzle-bearded visage of a man twice that age, who had lived long in the sorrowful heart of the world. He pondered himself briefly and without surprise.

"Your blessing! Your blessing, my Lord!" cried a priest who flung himself to the ground before the cot.

The transformed youth turned back the cover and slowly, with effort, motioning away the hands that moved to assist him, managed to gain his feet. He stood a moment wavering.

Men were going down on their knees, others prostrating themselves. They clamored for his blessing.

"No," he said. "Rise. I am the least among you. Please."

He bent unsteadily to the priest in the dirt. He wasn't strong enough to raise the man, but pulled at his cassock until he stood.

"Up," he pled with the rest. "Please."

But the more he entreated the more among them became

convinced of his worthiness and went down before him. They demanded his blessing.

He raised his hand, faltered a moment, and then blessed them.

They took their feet. They cheered. They pressed in around him.

He raised his hands and tried to silence them. "Good people," he said. "I beg you to bless me, for I am a sinner and in mortal dread of my soul."

They cried, No! You are favored of God!

Miracolo! they cried.

He cannot be killed!

He will lead us under the Cross to trample the Turk!

These last came from the soldiers. Many were in mail or partial armor. Some wore swords. Daggers were sheathed in belts. There were archers among them with bows. Camp guards with pikes.

He looked at them sadly. "Please," he said. "Please leave your arms outside the tent."

Most, in the general uproar, did not hear him. Those closest, who did, thought it a good joke. They lifted him up to their shoulders, against his protests, and bore him out of the tent.

They carried him through the camp crying, Behold the Anointed Warrior of God who has been sent to lead us to victory against the heathen! And the pages, and the cooks, and the dark-skinned camp whores, and the hostlers, and the foot soldiers, and the farriers, and the armorers and foragers, and all the rest began to gather round in a great throng celebrating him.

No one heard his protestations.

And the commanders and the great lords came from council and their striped pavilion tents to see what the tumult was. Great billows of dust began to rise about him. Impaled on spear points, the heads of Moors wavered aloft.

The youth, who looked a man capable of being his own

father, so deeply creased and grown old was his face, his long hair and beard streaked with gray and tangled, began to roll his eyes and sway upon the jostling shoulders and begged weakly to be set down, but no one heard and he was raised even higher and celebrated ever more loudly.

He swooned, pitching over backward.

Those behind shot up their arms and caught him as he toppled, and for several moments, until the movement of the triumphal procession could be halted, he was carried aloft like a fallen hero.

"He bleeds!" cried a priest. "He carries the wounds of Christ!"

The cry swept outward, and it was twisted, magnified, and infused with hysteria. The Virgin is at hand. The Christ is come. The Archangel Michael walks among us with his flaming sword.

Into all this pushed the Prince of Perugia. The youth was lying on the dry earth with his arms outstretched and his cheek in the dust. Despite the surging press of those behind, a strong resisting circle had formed about him. And those in the fore were in fear and terror and would not be pushed nearer.

For in truth the boy—who was no longer a boy to the eye, and that was miracle enough—did have the wounds of Christ, was bleeding from his hands, was bleeding from his feet, where the nails had been hammered, and the colorless gray shift he had been abed with, which was much too large for his shrunken body, which lay about his thin self as if it had been a bolt of fabric carelessly tossed, was stained crimson on his right side, not the side in which he had been wounded, but the side, and at the place, in which his Lord, the gentle doleful visitor during the fires of his sleep, had been pierced with the soldier's lance to end His life.

The Prince himself was given pause, fear coiling within him, but he forced himself to advance, for he was a prince and it was his duty to step into the face of his fear, and he went to one knee beside the boy, though gravely unsettled in his soul, and lifted the boy's torso to rest it partly in his lap.

The boy's head lolled back. He breathed shallowly. His eyes opened and they stared, unfocused, up at the bright blue sky where the thinnest wisp of cloud floated.

The prince called a surgeon and a priest from the onlookers to help him.

They refused.

He commanded. He threatened.

Unwilling, they stepped forward.

Boiled water was sent for, clean bandaging.

The crowd went down to their knees in a slow receding wave. They began to pray, a great quiet earnest murmuring. They prayed in apprehension and trepidation.

To the disappointment of the troops, and despite the futile entreaties of the lords and commanders, he did not lead them to crush the Infidel. To the relief of the Prince of Perugia and a handful of others which included the assistant to the Vatican's emissary—who were the deepest and most insightful among them—he journeyed to the coast when he was strong enough and from there took ship back to Italy.

In Italy, word of him and his transformation preceded him by more than a month and had already been carried to the farther towns and cities. Victories were ascribed to him. Miracles. Madness. In some places the story was received with indifference or even amusement, for there was no dearth of men and women who felt themselves called, who preached the word, who took to the hills or wandered wildeyed through the cities promulgating heresy and lunacy, to whom marvels were reputed; but in others, less jaded, more credulous and hopeful, it was cause for rejoicing and expectation.

In Perugia, whence he had sprung, there was much skepticism; for he was remembered. And it was a source of embarrassment and some mercantile jeopardy for his father, whose rivals, both by noble birth and business, bruited all manner of outlandish tales and ridiculed him in private chambers.

To his father's letters, the youth had written only one answer:

> I am alive and well and in the Savior's Heart, though I am not worthy. I pray for you and our family. I shall return when my strength permits.
>
> > Your devoted son,
> > Ettore

Which letter had not reassured the father.

Perugia waited. It wished to see this miracle for itself.

Despite the multitude of people who were crowded onto the quay at Ravenna—the news of his imminent arrival reported by a vessel that made port two days earlier—the youth managed to debark anonymously. He did it with the help of the seamen, whom, to the surprise of the captain, he had calmed and strangely beguiled during the voyage. The captain himself, tough cynic that he was, had not been unmoved by this strange man. Hector did it in seamen's clothes that they had given him, walking down the gangway with them, and they did not betray him even though the crowd cried out for him and several noblemen and -women offered a prize of a gold florin to the first of the sailors to point him out.

He walked to Perugia. It took nearly a month. He ate berries and roots and accepted a little piece of cheese or bread as charity. He went undiscovered; mendicants, beggars, holy men, friars and penitents were commonplace along the road.

He knocked upon the door of his father's house at sunset one evening. His father and his father's household were astonished. It was he. Yet it was not he. It was a man of his father's age. It was a quiet soothed man wrapped in the love of his God. It was the son. It was the man who brought news of the son's death.

It was not he.

There was confusion. The father put the house under guard

and cloaked it in secrecy. But the servants could not long be prevented from carrying the news into the streets. Beset, the father entreated the bishop, who sent an aide to examine this anomalous person. The aide confirmed the tattle of the streets. Hector had indeed returned, and indeed something profound and incomprehensible had happened to him.

The general populace celebrated. The less imaginative, as well as the more sophisticated, simply accepted—like a freak summer storm, what was, was; it meant nothing other than itself.

The youth was literally held prisoner. He wished to go into the hills. He wished to surrender everything that he had and that he had been. His father thought him mad.

It was the Bishop of Perugia who broke the impasse. The bishop was a worldly man not unaware that men as well as God were responsible for his position—and the boy's father and his powerful friends were not the least among these. The prelate knew how things worked. Nonetheless, he did possess a certain integrity, even if it was not frequently consulted, and had some spiritual capacity besides. He held three extensive interviews with the youth in the father's house and could not help but conclude, in uneasy subduement, that the boy's vocation was genuine: he had been called.

The father was furious. Hector was the first child and the only son. The next three, and there would be no more, were daughters. He had arranged to marry the oldest girl into the family of another merchant, thereby substantially increasing the wealth and position of both houses; but without his son the line would die, the house would die and the father would die in name as well as flesh and all would be dust, it would be as if he had never lived.

And all this time the youth expressed his love for his father, and prayed ceaselessly for him, and asked repeatedly, and with a compassionate heart, to be released.

The father fell into a rage that stopped, just short, of murdering the boy.

Let him go, the bishop told the man. It is God's wish.

Let him go, the bishop finally commanded the man. It is God's will.

And the father verged on rebellion against God. Verged, but could not mount. And he fell back, mad because he could not surrender his crazed anger but neither could he surrender his understanding that he could not trumpet war against the heavens themselves; and so he accepted, with viciousness, and became almost as his son—became a man nearly twice his age, became dead.

Let him go.

Obedience. Because there was no other choice.

The son wished only to pray to his God.

It was done in the bishop's court.

The boy came before them all, for he understood the decorums, that it could not be done quietly. There was the family. There were those whose social position made them impossible to refuse. There were ecclesiastic witnesses. He renounced all that was his, all that had ever been promised him or that could be expected. He renounced, at his father's demand, his very name.

And he stripped himself, at his father's demand, of all that he wore, that had been provided by his father, and stood before them naked, head bowed in humility and shame.

The bishop rose from his throne and covered the youth's thin nakedness with his own robe.

"It is done," the bishop said. "This son has no father. This father has no son. This man is God's servant, as he wishes to be. Let him serve God, Who is witness and author of this, and let none molest him in any way. Go now, all of you."

The father turned and at the head of his family, some of whom, especially the mother, were weeping, exited from the bishop's chambers with a firm stride and an angry eye.

In the remainder of his life he was to see his disavowed son only once more—hair tangled, beard knotted, eyes as soft as a calf's, unshod feet calloused and grimed, voice sonorous and loving, gnarled hands open and extended as if to hold a gentle heart, preaching the renunciate's life in a public square at the side of a fountain. Some of the large group attended his words with raptness, as was not uncommon in those days, and others listened with sardonic expressions, as was also not uncommon in those days.

The bishop, who was not unafraid of this old youth, who was neither without love for him and a desire to protect him, nor without envy of his obvious calling, had him garbed in the rough robe of a friar and given a little cheese and bread. He had to force these upon the youth, who would, if he had had his way, have walked out naked and emptyhanded into the street and trusted all to God. The bishop kept him in his quarters until nightfall, sending out young priests of similar build as decoys at different times, and then finally had him smuggled out through a secret exit.

No one, for nearly a year, had any idea where he had gone.

Brother Martin read for two hours. He was interrupted by Brother Stewart, a former Dominican, a bearded man with square features, who was one of the two ordained priests in the company.

Brother Stewart apologized for intruding. "Are you familiar with Richard Higgins?"

Higgins was the order's only remaining postulant. "I remember him in the last Retreat. I know from Brother Giles's records that you've been working with him. But I'm not familiar with him, no."

"I think it's time to raise him to novitiate."

Brother Martin sat back. "On the eve of a Retreat?"

"I've spent a lot of time with him these last few months. I think he's reached a critical stage—either he makes it in the Retreat, or we lose him."

"Have you thought this through, in all its ramifications?"

"Yes. It's my considered judgment."

"Well." Brother Martin felt his confidence of a few hours

ago waver: but the question had been posed, a decision was necessary. "Prepare a written report for me. Submit it tomorrow night. I'll give you an answer in twenty-four hours."

"Thank you, my abbot."

Compline was said. The monastery closed down to sleep. Small oil lamps burned with dim little coronas along the halls and at the heads and bottoms of stairs.

Brother Martin rubbed his eyes. He hadn't slept much in the last week, and the effect was becoming cumulative. He wished to work more, but he forced himself to stop—he would need all his strength for the Retreat. He returned the Chronicles to the vault, extinguished the candles and left the office.

Carrying his small lantern, he walked down the long hall toward the cellar entrance. The night was quiet. There was no wind and even the cicadas and crickets seemed muted, the bullfrogs in the pond desultory. The monastery itself was silent save for the soft slap of his sandals and the faint rustle of his robe.

He descended to the cellar, and then down to the level below. He opened the heavy door to the Chamber of Mortal Meditation and went within. The air here was both sweet and fetid, thick, seeming nearly clotted. The rough chamber had been carved from living rock. It was somewhat higher than a man, less than a dozen feet long and only half that across. Cut into one wall were five large niches. Four were empty.

The center one was full.

Brother Martin went to his knees on the wooden prie-dieu before it and clasped his hands together. The lamplight flickered upon the contents of the niche.

The chamber was utterly still, a capsule suspended out of time and place, adrift in eternity.

Brother Martin stared unblinkingly at the object of his concentration.

And death began to flow into him.

BOOK II

Forgive Us Our Trespasses

Chapter 8

Caparelli knelt with his forearms atop the backrest of the pew in front of him and his hands folded. Pomona knelt beside him.

The big church was dim and cloyed with drifting layers of smoke from the incense smoldering within the brass censer. One of the cassocked altar boys was swinging the censer slowly on a chain. A priest in white and gold vestments was chanting the litany of High Benediction, answered in response by the altar boys. Behind the altar rose a high wall of marble carved with bas-reliefs—the Mater Dolorosa, the Scourging, the Ascension, others. There were tall candelabra. The doors of the silver tabernacle were open. A monstrance of radiant gold, with the Eucharist visible within a small glass compartment in its center, stood upon the altar. It glinted in the flickering candlelight.

"Kyrie eleison."

"Kyrie eleison."

"Christe eleison."

"Christe eleison."

"Kyrie eleison. . . ."

Soporific and fervent. The church was cavernous, ceiling high and vaulted. In wall niches and on pedestals buttressed out from fluted support columns were brightly colored statues: Moses the Lawgiver. Saint Sebastian pierced with arrows. . . . Aged men in clean, worn suits and wrinkled women in black who clutched rosaries and old holy pictures filled the first several ranks of pews. Spotted among them were a handful of younger men and women who'd come this Sunday afternoon to pray for special favors, and a few pale little boys and girls who stared with glassy eyes and whispered the response along with the altar boys.

There were churches much nearer to Caparelli's apartment, but they were all modern—glass instead of stone, pews like restaurant booths, twisty angular crucifixes that were barely recognizable for what they were and paintings that were gaudy splashes which looked like a junkie's nightmare, priests who seemed more like college students or salesmen at an expensive store.

Pomona couldn't convince herself that these were real churches and she doubted that she could fulfill her obligation to God there. She was never truly satisfied and always uneasy when she emerged from them. So at least once a week Caparelli would bring her down here into the old neighborhood, where there was a church she could believe, where God truly lived, among the shadows and in the dimness behind the burning red vigil light.

Caparelli believed in God, but that belief wasn't especially relevant to his life. Were it not for Pomona he could just as well never set foot in a church again, of any kind. But when he *was* here, or in any other traditional church, a *real* church, things changed.

He became devout.

There was peace. There was comfort. There was even bliss.

He'd been a fatherless child with a dying mother.

The Church had offered comfort.

The Church had been strong loving arms with the smell of sweat in its armpits and a day's-end stubble of beard rubbing against his child's smooth cheek. It was a snug bed, stroking hands. It was a warm apartment coming in from a winter street, filled with the smell of cooking. It was the soft delirious place under the blankets between one's mother and father on a weekend morning, a walk with one's hand in an older brother's. It was hide-and-go-seek in summer twilight. It was joy.

It was everything that had ever been good.

Caparelli loved it.

At the end of the service Pomona walked out at his side. But she didn't take his arm until they went down the stone stairs to the street and a little distance away, because she was still filled with her God, who, though reassuring, was still stern and demanding, not succoring and comforting like Caparelli's, and thus it was improper to return to her husband, the flesh, without some small interval, a transition back to the secular.

For Caparelli, the dichotomy was vastly more profound, but the change proportionally quicker, and he wasn't a moment or two out of the church when God was gone and comfort was gone and the child long since dead. He swept the street with his eyes, evaluating its life in terms of advantage and menace.

When they were home again, Pomona went to the kitchen to layer a lasagna into an oven dish, and Caparelli put *Il Barbiere di Siviglia* on the turntable and carried the bulky Sunday *Times* over to the couch. The couch was covered with plastic. As were the chairs and the love seat. The fucking furniture cost a fortune and the fabric would have made a doge jealous. But Pomona's mother had protected her own prized, hard-won couch and chair in their old walk-up apartment that way all those years ago and that's the way Pomona was going to do it till the day she died, even though Caparelli told her money didn't mean anything. That's the way Pomona was.

So he put up with the plastic, because he loved her.

He untied his shoes and propped his feet on the travertine marble coffee table. He dug through the *Times* for the financial and the sports sections, which were the only ones he ever read. But he grew bored after a quarter hour, set the paper aside, turned up the music, folded his hands over his belly, closed his eyes and leaned his head back to listen.

Caparelli was mad for opera. Father Giannini, the old priest who'd taken him into the rectory when he'd been thrown out of his third foster home, had spent most of his free time listening to opera. Caparelli first heard that glorious music and those enrapturing voices sitting at that gentle man's feet in the study, the priest's solacing hand sometimes coming to rest on his head or shoulder—always, it seemed, at precisely the moments when within the music and the smell of old leather books and pipe tobacco the boy, already tough and streetwise at eight, wanted most to crawl into the old man's lap and be held. Somehow Father Giannini's hand would be there. Now, that mostly unconscious memory, the dim churches, the opera, Pomona and his child and grandson—those were what was best in his life.

Everything else was a ball bat.

A stranger might have thought that Caparelli was asleep, so still was he on the couch and so even was his breathing. But anyone familiar with him would know that he wasn't and that his reverie was not to be disturbed for any reason less than catastrophe. Pomona touched his arm just as Count Almavia was finally revealing his true identity. He opened his eyes.

"It's Maria," she said, disturbed. "I told her you were listening, but she said she wants to talk to you."

Caparelli hadn't heard the phone ring. Ordinarily his daughter would have spoken with her mother and he would have called back to chat later.

He got up, turned the music down and went to the phone on a small Florentine writing table at the end of the room. "Hello, *cara.*"

"Hello, Daddy. I'm sorry for breaking in like this."

"What's wrong?"

"It's just . . . It's . . . This morning Mr. Gagliano said he didn't care to have our sort in the building."

Gagliano was Maria's landlord. He had connections. His connections were shit. His new Mercedes had just become six hours short of being a fireball. Gagliano was going to learn what sort he really liked.

"People wouldn't talk to us at church this morning." There was a catch in Maria's voice. "Carl was supposed to have a playmate over this afternoon, but the boy's mother canceled and said her son wouldn't be seeing Carl anymore."

"What the hell's going on?"

"You didn't hear?"

"I didn't hear what?"

"About last night."

"Tell me."

"It's . . . Orson."

"Yeah?" Maria didn't like Orson and rarely mentioned him. "What about him?" Caparelli covered the mouthpiece with his hand. Pomona was waiting, perturbed. He said to her, "It's nothing. Business."

She went back to the kitchen. Business was what her husband did. It had nothing to do with her. And business is what her husband said it was, even if it was their daughter on the phone.

"I didn't know why this was happening," Maria said. "I finally got the story out of— Well, just out of someone who could tell me."

Unlike her mother, Maria *did* know what Caparelli's business was. She and her husband Tony kept themselves far removed from it. And for her sake, Caparelli preferred it that way. He knew that she'd had to go to someone in the organization for the information, and that she hated to do that, so he understood how upset she was.

"Right," he said. "I'm listening."

"Orson picked up a girl at the Mudd Club last night. Mary Tedesco, a local girl. She lives over on Pearl Street. She's kind of flashy, but nice. Everyone likes her."

"Uh-huh."

"Orson got her high on cocaine. I know Mary doesn't do that kind of thing. But Orson, well, he can be very . . . persuasive. Let's just leave it at that."

Maria and Orson had been close when they were children, but they stopped seeing each other not long after adolescence. They encountered only infrequently now, usually at family gatherings. Maria was polite to him, but it was obvious she found him distasteful.

"Persuasive," Caparelli said.

"She did some really weird and vulgar things out there on the dance floor with him. She was very high."

"That place knows from vulgar. And it ain't a place people in your neighborhood should be."

"Yes," Maria said, wounded.

"I'm sorry, sweetheart. It's okay. Go on."

"He took her over to Gino's later. The after-hours place on Sullivan?"

"I know it." It was a spiff's joint.

"Well, they were there till eight in the morning. Orson got into a fight with a waiter. They threw him out. He had this terrible scene with Mary right out on the street while people were walking by on their way to Mass. He beat her up. He tore her dress and she was half naked right there in front of everyone. She was crying and bleeding. No one would interfere. They were afraid of him . . . of who he is." Caparelli was stung.

"It's been terrible all day," Maria said. "How people looked at us in church. The anonymous phone calls. Carl's friend. Everything." Her voice trembled.

"It's all right, baby," Caparelli said when he had a grip on his anger. "You just hang in. I'll take care of everything. What's the name of this woman who won't let her kid play with Carl?"

"No, Daddy. Please."

"Okay, we'll talk about that one later. But if anyone says or does something really bad, you call me. Because I'll hear about it anyway, so I'd rather get it from you so I get it straight."

"I just want you to talk to Orson so this doesn't happen again. Daddy . . . you're not mad at me, are you? I didn't mean to make you any trouble."

"Sweetheart, the Pope's gonna say a Black Mass before the

day comes I get mad at you. Tell Tony to take you out to a nice dinner. Give Carl a big kiss from his Grandpa. Forget about everything. It never happened."

"Thank you, Daddy. I'm sorry. I love you."

"I love you, baby."

Caparelli called Paulie. Paulie wasn't the brightest guy in the organization, but he was methodical and careful and had never gotten anything wrong in the twenty years he'd worked for Caparelli. "I want the story in half an hour," Caparelli said. "All of it."

Paulie was back to him in twenty-five minutes. It was pretty much the way Maria had told it. And the few places it differed, it was worse.

"Get the sonofabitch over here at ten tonight. You find him, wherever he is, and you bring him here at ten."

No one hurt Caparelli's daughter.

Japanese lanterns were strung all about the rolling green-sward behind the monolith that was Kirk Daley's home in Beverly Hills. The house was twenty rooms, not counting the servants' wing. There were also two smaller guest houses and a miniature Cinderella castle for his two darling children, with its own housekeeper and gardener. Kirk Daley's voice was unremarkable, but he was electric on stage. He was lean and boyish with a shock of dark wavy hair and moved with a kind of plastic sexuality that thrilled middle-aged housewives and was unobjectionable to their husbands.

Kirk Daley headlined at Las Vegas. His albums all went gold. He appeared regularly on the important talk shows and hosted his own variety special once or twice a year. He'd starred in three smash movies.

They were solid family fare. Each opened on a holiday at Radio City Music Hall. And each had been produced by Norman O. Marcus.

If you didn't know Norman O. Marcus, you didn't know Hollywood. He was six-foot-six, wore a diamond ring on each finger of his left hand and weighed three hundred pounds. When he walked, he looked like a freighter rolling through deep seas. His last seven films had all grossed over fifty million. His genius lay in combining the right writers, actors and directors into packages that resulted in family films which packed the theaters and demolished the competition.

He was golden, and Hollywood was his. People queued into long lines to kiss his enormous ass. And not only figuratively: it was common knowledge that among his bedroom idiosyncrasies, which were important to him and therefore important to those whose careers he could catapult to glory with a single nod, he liked to have his ass kissed. Kissed and then spread wide, and the dark little bud sucked.

Marcus had just commissioned a script expressly for Daley, whom he was working in a Jimmy Stewart mode. No one had ever thought to cast Daley in a film before Marcus. The public loved him. The roles nearly doubled his already impressive income. Since Daley was a man who knew on which side his bread was buttered, it was no coincidence that tonight, at his own thirty-fifth birthday party, Norman O. Marcus was the guest of honor.

Daley was standing next to Marcus on a dais under a striped pavilion. He'd called for the attention of the nearly three hundred guests and they'd emptied from the house and come in from various parts of the grounds and were now fully assembled. He put his arm around Marcus and said into a hand mike, "I have here tonight a man well known throughout the industry and indeed throughout the world of entertainment and art as a man of genius, a man of generosity, a man who has done as much for our craft and all of us who labor within it as any man who's ever lived. Ladies and gentlemen, it is my privilege to present to you my good friend—Norman O. Marcus!"

He stepped aside with a performer's grace to leave Marcus alone in the center light and he clapped and shook his shoulders, bobbed his head and shouted, "Yoweeeeee!"

The audience applauded and whistled.

Marcus raised his hands in appreciation. His thick jowls lifted with the corners of his mouth. Many of the faces below him appeared on magazine covers, in movie houses, on television, smiled out from posters and were better known than the faces of those who governed the world. These were the real heroes and gods. And right now Marcus was *primo inter pares,* first among his equals. He looked over them to the burning lanterns, to the buffets of food and liquor on linen-covered tables, the great tiled swimming pool with its statue of Kirk Daley rising from the center, the stone bathhouse set with a stained-glass window of Kirk Daley in a Harlequin costume, from *Benny and the Hobo,* their first film—and though it was all a temple to Kirk Daley and this was Kirk Daley's feast day, Kirk Daley had stepped into the background and it was all *his,* the dominion of Norman O. Marcus, and his audience knew it as well as he did and they offered him homage.

He took the mike from Daley's outstretched hand. "Thank you. Thank you. You are kind people. I've been fortunate and blessed. Despite Kirk's flattering words, I couldn't have accomplished much without you and all the other talented people in this industry. And if I can give a little back, find a way to help someone now and then—" His roaming eyes paused: on the beautiful black ingenue from Off-Broadway in New York, the young gay understudy from Houston's Alley Theater, the blond girl with the pouty mouth from the Pittsburgh comedy revue. "Well, it's the least I can do, and I'm thankful for the opportunity. God knows a lot of people helped me along the line. And one of those is our own Kirk Daley, who's going to rock the box offices with our new production. It's his birthday, his night. Come on back here, Kirk!"

Largesse. Marcus was demonstrating that he had that too.

Daley came forward shaking his head in self-effacement.

Marcus hugged the singer into him with one arm and winked broadly at the audience. "You know, friends, it's been said that Kirk gets a little too big for his britches sometimes."

Daley did an exaggerated double take.

"But that's not true. I know a bit about his britches. And I'm here to tell you that Kirk Daley is still the same down-to-earth good ol' boy he was when he was growing up out in the plains of Oklahoma." Norman O. Marcus could give, and Norman O. Marcus could take away. He was reminding them all of that. "Let me tell you a little story that happened about a year ago down in Palm Springs." He flicked his eyes to the side. A lean young man in a suit moved up and unobtrusively handed him a giftwrapped package. "Kirk and I happened to run into each other there. Well, we made a date to meet on the golf course the next morning."

Daley hunched his shoulders and began to laugh.

"Kirk showed up brighteyed as usual, but rubbing his stomach. You all know what a chili fan he is. He'd downed four bowls the night before and was still feeling it some. You couldn't tell it from the way he played the first three holes. But about the fourth he started to slow down. By the fifth he was looking a little strange. On the sixth he stopped and said, 'I don't know if I can make this one. I might have to go back to the clubhouse.' We all know what chili can do to you. About halfway to the green, ol' Kirk here yells 'Whoops!' and drops his club and takes off running. Well, folks, I'll tell you that his club wasn't the only thing he dropped. He dropped his britches too—in damn near every clump of brush all the way back to the clubhouse, leaving some mighty odd souvenirs for the groundskeepers to find that night. Well, on his last emergency stop, in a stand of trees, he threw away his shorts and just left 'em there—which was about the best thing to do with 'em."

Daley was hamming up his embarrassment.

Marcus unwrapped the package. "So what we have here is a little memento from that day, and proof positive that Kirk Daley is just plain folks and that he sure as hell is *not* too big for his britches." Marcus opened the box and raised something high. "Here are Kirk Daley's jockey shorts, bronzed just like your old baby shoes and guaranteed to last through eternity, complete in every detail, just as they were that morning he abandoned them. Happy birthday, Kirk!"

Kirk accepted his petrified shorts with a deep laugh. Because he had to. And Norman O. Marcus smiled widely. Because he was happy.

And the audience laughed and clapped and cheered because they all envied success that was not theirs and liked to see it punished and because it was none of them that Norman O. Marcus had done this to.

Dismissed, the crowd fragmented and returned to their separate activities. The actors went to mingle more or less with one another, the comics with their own kind, singers and others likewise. Drugs superseded occupation—coke freaks from various professions clustered together; hash and grass and opium smokers congregated; drinkers filled each other's glasses. A few business deals were made, many more negotiated in fantasy and lie, clients changed agents, spouses changed each other.

Marcus drifted toward the house, closely attended by his two personal aides. One was a severe young woman formerly associated with an eastern law firm, the other the young man who'd handed Marcus Kirk Daley's shorts, a Harvard MBA who had worked for the secretary of the treasury in Washington. There was also an entourage of a dozen and a half people. Its composition changed with a word or a nod from Marcus to one of his aides, who would then cut out a person in favor of a new one or reorder the nearness of someone to him. Most everyone present hoped to have at least a few words with Marcus somewhere in the evening.

Halfway to the house, Marcus stopped short. He stared. Conversation ceased. His male aide moved forward smartly and scooped up one of Daley's many cats, a solid black cat which had been about to cross Marcus's path. Marcus started off again and conversation resumed.

Daley's house was furnished predominantly in period French and Italian. He was fond of glass and there were many chandeliers and interior leaded windows. Some floors were slate, others polished wood, and those which were carpeted were done in shades of white.

In the living room a hired caricaturist was drawing rapid portraits of guests. She signed each with her name and the notation, *With thanks, Kirk Daley*. In the billiard room, a hired professional was giving lessons.

In the reception hall, a string band played slow dance music; the country-rock group was outside under the pavilion.

Marcus conferred in whispers with his male aide, who then went off. Marcus moved into the reception hall where he favored three or four women with a dance while he waited. He moved surprisingly well for a man of his bulk, though he did sweat heavily.

His aide returned, caught his eye. Marcus ambled out of the reception hall, and presently his entourage began to disperse, as if of their own accord, and then he was gone, down which of the three halls that conjoined there no one was quite sure, his female aide briefly taking hands and telling people how glad Mr. Marcus was to have had this chance to speak with them.

Marcus's male aide led him into a far wing and up the stairs to the second floor. He stopped before a closed door.

"Here, sir."

Marcus nodded. The young man left.

Marcus arranged his face into a smile and entered. He closed the door, reached behind himself surreptitiously and turned the lock.

The stunning black New York ingenue and the gay young actor from Houston stood a few feet apart from each other facing him. The room was done in floral paper and dominated by a huge four-poster bed with a matching floral canopy. It was lit softly by two table lamps. The girl's smile was stiffer than the boy's, but it was the boy whose cheek jumped when the lock clicked.

"Well," Marcus said genially. "Well, well. Thanks for coming along with Henry. Been having a good time tonight?"

They said yes.

"Good. Good. We all need to have a good time now and then, right? Puts us into a better mood, a friendlier, generous frame of mind. And we always remember the people we've had a good time with, the ones who gave it to us. We like to do things for them afterward. I know I certainly do. Sit down, sit down."

There were only two chairs, neither very comfortable, in corners facing the bed. They each took one. Marcus settled himself onto the foot of the bed. The mattress bent deeply under his weight.

"What we have here," he said, "is, ah, a kind of audition. I always have several projects under way, which means of course that I'm always in need of new talent. Talent that I can groom toward stardom. I've turned a lot of unknown names into household words, as I'm sure you're aware. A lot.

"Tina, dear, why don't you stand up and walk for me. I've read your resume and notices, and frankly, I'm impressed. But these things can be misleading sometimes and there's no substitute for seeing a person in the flesh, so to speak, to see what kind of enthusiasm they can muster, how much they can really give when they're called on. Go on, dear. Go on."

She rose awkwardly. Marcus watched closely as she crossed the room, crossed back and sat down again. He stared at her. She dropped her eyes under his continuing gaze, then managed to raise them and recompose her smile.

"Very nice. Gene, how about you? . . . Good, very nice. You both move well. Now, I don't have to tell you how important a pretty face and a pretty body are in this business. There aren't any bad-looking stars, eh? Tina, dear, why don't you slip out of your dress for us, will you please?"

Tina's smile was rigid. She stood, delicate, with sculpted light brown beauty, and began opening the buttons of her long dress.

Gene looked away.

Tina pulled her dress over her head. She wore silken green panties and bra, mildly transparent, her pubic hair and large dark nipples indefinitely visible beneath.

"Quite nice," Marcus said in the tone of a disinterested professional. "Gene, would you be so good . . . ?"

The boy rose. He looked to a bland lithograph on the wall. He divested himself of his tie, jacket, shirt, shoes, socks and slacks. He was muscled, broadchested, flatbellied and had good strong legs. Eyes on the lithograph, he flushed.

"Pleasing," Marcus said. "Indeed. Tina, love, take off your bra, won't you? . . . Ah, yes, lovely breasts, quite photogenic. And now your panties, dear. Charming, charming. But do put your shoes back on. The tall heels turn the line of your calves so nicely.

"Gene? Look at Tina, won't you? Now, isn't she a lovely creature?"

The boy's face was crimson. "Yes—Yes, she is."

The girl lowered her head.

"Come, come, child. You're not trying for a part in *Roots*. Where's that smile?"

She tried.

"Gene, I think Tina's embarrassed. Perhaps because she's the only one naked. Let's help her. Take your shorts off, please."

The boy's pubic hair was golden brown. His penis, flaccid, was still larger and weightier than most, and his balls round and healthy.

"Oh, quite nice," Marcus said. "Like a Greek statue. The Greeks were very fond of pretty young boys, did you know? But of course you did. Tina, look at Gene. Isn't he a pretty boy?"

"Yes," she said tonelessly.

"Go take his genitals in your hands and hold them out so the light strikes them better and we can see them more clearly, will you?"

The girl's mouth trembled.

For the first time, Marcus's voice was edged. "Remember, this is an audition. There are thousands of hopefuls like you out there. And very, very few are going to make it."

She did as she was told.

Marcus said, "Does that feel good, Gene?"

"It . . . feels fine."

"Good. And how does it feel to you, Tina? Tina?"

Her voice caught. "It feels good."

"Excellent. That's what we all want, don't we? For everything to feel good." He mopped his face with his handkerchief. "Now we're going to play a scene. A love scene. Because love scenes are very important to movies. And since that's true, they're very important to the three of us, aren't they? Tell me, Gene, aren't they important to you? Is this as important as anything you've ever done?"

Marcus's gaze was fierce.

"Yes."

"Tina?"

Her straightened hair hid her face. "Yes."

"Good." Marcus got off the bed and turned the covers down. "Come here, children."

Like children, they obeyed.

"Tina, sit down here on the edge. Gene, stand in front of her. Closer. Yes, that's right. Now, Tina, I want you to take Gene into your pretty little mouth. Don't look like that, child. You're an actress, remember? And you want to be a star. This is a love scene."

The girl closed her eyes. She found Gene's penis with her fingers and leaned her head forward. Her lips touched the tip. She hesitated, then opened her mouth and drew him in.

"Splendid," Marcus said. His breathing became audible as he watched. "No, Tina. More spirit. We need joie de vivre.

Élan. Suck it, girl, suck it. Go on—suck it, I said. That's it. Now harder! Faster! Good girl!"

Tina worked her head furiously, her eyes clenched shut.

Gene stared without expression at the opposing wall.

"Come on, Gene, get into it. Hold her little titties, man. They're pretty. That's it. Squeeze them. Uh-huh. Don't flag on us, Tina. Keep going, keep going."

Marcus lowered himself ponderously to the floor and lit a cigarette. He watched Tina working Gene's penis, exhaling through his nostrils in slow streams.

"This won't do, Gene. You'll have to get it up, son. Come on, now ... Gene," he said warningly.

Gene's voice cracked with misery. "I can't. I'm sorry, Mr. Marcus. But I can't!"

"Ah. It slipped my mind. How thoughtless of me. You're a faggot. Well, Gene, that's the kind of limitation a *good* actor has to overcome. Use Stanislavsky, son, go Method. Think of a plump young boy. It's a nice young boy, Gene, with yellow curls and rosy cheeks. You can do it. I have faith. Do it!"

Gene shut his eyes. He grimaced in attempted concentration.

"That's a little better, Gene. Keep at it. Put your hands on her head and help her, that is, him—think *him*—find the right rhythm. Those little titties are distracting you. I'll take care of them."

Marcus set his cigarette in an ashtray on the night table. He took the girl's breasts and dug his fingers into her flesh. She whimpered.

"That's it, Gene. Now you've got it. See? It's not so difficult."

He pinched Tina's nipples. She recoiled.

"Ah-ah," he cautioned. "A star has to be able to do anything—*anything*—and like it, or at least convince the audience that she does. Convince me, Tina. Let's hear a moan of pleasure."

She made a sound.

"That's disappointing. You can do better." Marcus crushed

her nipples between his thumbs and forefingers. She moaned. "Closer. Keep trying. You too, Gene. Let's convince that audience. Louder. Yes. That's it, children. Moan. You're in a transport, you're being taken to the heights, you know ecstasy. Ecstasy. Let me *hear* it!"

When they managed to please him, he grabbed them both and pushed them onto the bed. "Now fuck him, Tina. Fuck her, Gene. Keep your eyes closed, you pretty little fag, and pretend she's a beautiful roundassed little boy if you want, but fuck her. Fuck hell out of her. Fuck, little children, fuck!"

Tina spread herself open. She bit her lip and tried to make sounds of pleasure. Gene knelt between her legs, his eyes tightly shut, and worked himself furiously with his hand trying to stay hard.

"Get in her, Gene," Marcus said.

He tried. "I—I—"

"He can't!" Tina cried, in anguish both for herself and the boy. "I'm dry. I'm sorry, Mr. Marcus, but I can't get wet!"

Marcus sighed. "Well, you're still young and inexperienced. I suppose we have to make allowances." He opened the night-table drawer and removed a tube of K-Y Jelly, which Henry, ever efficient, had left there. He lubricated Tina with it, then Gene. "You ought to be familiar with this stuff, Gene. In you go now. . . . Good boy, I knew you could do it. Pump away. Convince me. Faster. That's a good little boy, a good little girl! Keep at it."

He picked up the stub of his cigarette and puffed on it, resuscitating the ember to a bright red.

Their drawn mouths belied the vigorousness with which Gene and Tina fucked.

Marcus leaned close to them. "Remember," he whispered harshly, "a star has to be willing to endure anything, *anything!*"

He touched the glowing end of his cigarette to the underside of Tina's breast.

"Aiiii!" She jerked. Her eyes snapped open and her face contorted in terror.

Gene looked down, horrified.

"Close your eyes!" Marcus ordered. "Perform! As if your careers depended upon it. Because they do. This is the most important audition you've ever had—and the last you'll ever get if you don't pass it!" Then, more conciliatory, he said, "There won't be much pain, dears. Not this time."

He applied the cigarette, just an instant, to Tina's other breast.

She flinched and groaned, but kept on fucking Gene. Tears forced from beneath her closed eyelids.

Marcus patted her hair. "There, there. All done." He shifted around. "Steady, Gene." He touched the cigarette to the back of Gene's testicles.

Gene threw back his head. He couldn't stifle his scream entirely.

"That's it for the more exquisite sensations, children. Keep on. I'm going to join you now."

While they fucked in dread, Marcus shrugged off his jacket. He loosened his pants and pulled them with this shorts to his knees. His belly was a great pale balloon, scraggly with sparse coiled hairs. Between his thick pocky thighs and nearly obscured by the roll of his belly were curiously small little balls and a long thin penis, hard and dark with engorging blood.

He opened the bottom buttons of his shirt, spread the tails back over his mammoth ass and knelt upon the bed. He bridged himself over Tina's head. The tip of his cock brushed against her lips. "Suck it, girl," he said. "Suck it nice. . . . Ah, good." He sighed. "No flagging, Gene. Keep at her."

Marcus began to move his pelvis slowly up and down, sliding nearly out of the girl's mouth and slipping deeply back in. He smiled serenely. In a while, he withdrew. "Very nice, Tina. It's a little too early to tell, but right now I'd say you're going to pass this audition splendidly."

He got off the bed, lubricated his already glistening shaft with jelly, then squeezed some onto his fingers and knelt on the mattress behind Gene.

"Now we'll see how *you* do in the final stages, Gene." He smeared the jelly around Gene's anus, worked some into it. Gene tightened his buttocks reflexively. "No, no. You have to relax and keep open, Gene. Nice and open." Marcus worked his crown in, then gripped Gene's hips and thrust forward, sinking all the way.

Gene groaned.

"Come now, you're used to this, my lovely. Keep going with Tina. Don't stop." Marcus dug his fingers into the muscles of Gene's thighs, mashing his belly against and around Gene's hard buttocks, pumping, and cried, "Now fuck, children. Fuck, my little children. Fuck for all you're worth. I'm your Daddy, and I want you!"

Chapter 9

A red-and-white patrol car went racing through the neon-lit darkness of Atlanta's Stewart Avenue with its roof lights flashing and siren wailing. It cut hard toward the curb, then came to a slewed stop in front of the Chinook Bar tearing rubber off the tires. The two patrolmen within threw their doors open and leaped out. They ran for the bar, drawing their service revolvers.

The people cruising the honky-tonk dropped to the sidewalk or pressed hard against walls. Two more patrol cars converged from opposite ends of the street with screaming sirens. The call was: *Man with gun. Victims down. Possible shots fired.* The two cops were both young and tense. They split right and left as they burst into the bar and dropped into combat crouches, arms extended straight out, gripping their revolvers with both hands. They scanned the room with eye movements too rapid to measure. They registered: one man sprawled unmoving on the floor, another one down and writhing, spurting blood from between his hands which were clasped to his face, patrons huddled against the bar and behind tables, and a thickset red-headed man backed up to the far wall next to the swinging doors to the kitchen. He held a double-edged fighting knife in one hand and a nickel-plated automatic pistol in the other.

"There ain't a bastard here that can take me!" he roared.

The cops clicked back the hammers of their revolvers.

The one nearest the bar shouted, "Drop it, motherfucker, or you're dead!"

"Screw you, pig." The muzzle of his revolver wavered in slow loops.

From the corner of his eye, the second cop saw his partner's finger tighten on the trigger. He whispered, "Easy, David, easy." He said to the redheaded man, "You got one second to drop that piece or I make wallpaper out of your fuckin' brains."

The man swayed. He blinked at them.

The cop said, "Bye-bye, turkey."

"Wait!" The automatic dropped to the floor with a clunk.

Four more cops crashed through the door. One carried a riot gun. They leveled their weapons.

"We got 'im, we got 'im," said David.

"Now the knife, asshole," said the second cop.

The knife fell.

"Turn around and spread yourself against the wall. Do it!"

The man complied.

One of the new cops picked up the knife and the automatic while David frisked and cuffed the man. His partner stood to the side with his pistol centered on the back of the man's head.

"That's Ryan, Matt Ryan," the bartender said to one of the other cops. "We've eighty-sixed him twice. He's been okay the last couple weeks. But tonight he gets into this argument with these four guys over some lousy song on the jukebox." He pointed at the two men on the floor and another two who were squatting by the cops attending them.

"I could o' taken you," Ryan said with drunken good humor to David and his partner.

"Call an ambulance," said a cop. "This guy's cut up pretty bad." The injured man was kicking his legs and moaning.

David's partner said, "Baby, just the tiniest hair of a second longer and you'd be on the way to the morgue right now."

"Over a lousy song," the bartender was saying. "Ryan, oh he's a tough bastard. He's going to take on four guys."

Ryan's belligerence was returning. "I killed more men than you got fingers and toes, Louie. Don't forget that."

"You have, huh?" David said with interest.

"Yeah. A lot more. And all of 'em legal. You'll find that when you run my sheet."

The bartender said, "So—bang!—out of nowhere, Ryan hauls off and chops this guy on the side of the head with some kind of karate blow. The guy goes down like his legs are cut off, boom. The other guy"—he pointed to the man who'd been cut—"he takes a swing at Ryan with a beer mug. Ryan ducks, then pulls out this big motherin' knife and slice, slice, slice, he whips it over the guy's face before anyone knows what's happenin'. The other two jerkoffs go for Ryan. Then all of a sudden he's got this gun in his hand and he's yellin', 'Come on shitsuckers, you just bought the farm.' Everybody dives for cover. The cook calls you guys from the kitchen. Ryan keeps daring someone to try him. We all make like statues, pissing our pants while we wait for you guys to get here."

The cop taking this down said, "Can you get someone to cover for you here? I need you to come and make a statement."

"Sure. Give me five minutes."

"Those peckerheads got guns!" Ryan said with sudden inspiration. "It was self-defense. They were gonna shoot me."

The cops looked at each other. One shrugged.

"Would you two gentlemen put your hands on the bar, please, and stand with your legs spread."

"Aw, come on."

"We didn't to nothin'. For Christ's sake, look what the bastard done to our buddies."

"Up against the bar!"

"Well, what do you know," said the cop who searched the taller of the two. He brandished a small .32-caliber revolver that had been stuffed into the man's waistband.

Ryan laughed maniacally.

"You got a permit for this?"

"Aw shit, man. It ain't mine. I found it in the street on the way over here. I was gonna turn it in when I left. I forgot the thing was even there."

The cop arrested him. He and Ryan were led out together but put into separate cars.

Ryan was drunkenly buoyant as he was being booked. "You know, you guys, this is all a waste of time. I mean, it's going to go self-defense. But even if it doesn't, I got protection." He winked broadly at the booking sergeant. "Heavy protection. The heaviest."

"Oh yeah?" The sergeant crossed out a mistake on the form and made the new entry with care.

"Yeah. God." Ryan bellylaughed.

"I guess He watches out for all His chillun, even the worst of 'em, Mr. Ryan."

"I mean *special* protection. The Church. The Catholic Church. It's got a special interest in me and it's going to see that nothin' happens to me."

"That's very fortunate, Mr. Ryan. But for now I'm afraid we have to lock you up. At least until we hear from the Church."

The jailer at the Detention center was an overweight middle-aged man who wore his remaining hair long and combed it over the bald crown of his head. He took Ryan into the cell block.

In another part of the building, Jules Eyler sat talking with a couple of detectives. They were old friends. Eyler was fiftyish, tall, soft-spoken and courtly. His suits were all some shade of gray, mostly dark, and whenever the temperature permitted, he wore them vested. He was an intelligent man of elaborate courtesy, and deeply spiritual.

A decade ago, he'd accepted an offer from the Atlanta *Constitution*, resigned from the *New York Times* and moved down South, where life was less harried, genteel, more suited to his temperament. He was an excellent journalist who had won a Pulitzer Prize.

Both his children were away at college now. His wife was back in school finishing her master's degree.

He was a man to whom God had been good.

Eyler was primarily a crime reporter, to the surprise of many people who would have thought it too hard on his quiet and gentle sensibilities. He was particularly adept at long in-depth pieces, and was respected by both sides of the street for his honesty.

His wife was up north visiting their daughter and he was putting in extra hours on research for a series he planned to do. He loved his wife dearly, and while he was far too integrated a man to become agitated or depressed when she was gone, he did look for ways to distract himself.

Detective-sergeant Harris was finishing an anecdote. "Somehow Copley manages to knock the door closed and lock the evidence and his service revolver in the safe. So what happens? The kid he's collared volunteers to crack it for him. 'Piece of cake,' the kid says, and zip, even with the cuffs on, the kid gives the dial a couple o' spins and's got the sucker open in about three seconds flat. He takes out the evidence bag and Copley's piece, hands them back and says, 'There you go, officer.'"

Eyler smiled. "The department lost a real classic when Copley retired."

"We might have lost the *department* if he hadn't."

Eyler stretched. "Gentlemen, it's been a pleasure. I thank you for the company and the help. I'm going to check the squad room and then I'm calling it quits. I hope it's a quiet night for you."

There wasn't much of interest downstairs in the squad room. He was about to depart when Pat Sloane, the jailer, entered and walked over to the coffee machine.

"Evenin', Jules."

"Evenin', Pat."

Sloane punched the Extra Cream button and waited while the paper cup filled. "What a night."

"Anything special?"

"Not really. Just busy. Mostly drunks and disorderly conduct. A couple o' crazies. Got this one soundin' off to the whole cell block how the Catholic Church is gonna protect him, that he can get away with anything." Sloane took his cup out and sipped. "Fact, he mentioned your name. Said you knew all about it." He looked over his coffee cup at Eyler. He might have been slow, portly and vain about his falling hair, but he wasn't dumb. "You're a Catholic, aren't you?"

"Yes," Eyler said casually. He covered a yawn with his hand.

"Guy's name is Ryan. Matt Ryan. Know him?"

Eyler nodded. "I interviewed him about half a year ago, wrote a profile on him."

"I thought the name was familiar," Sloane said.

"Not a very savory man."

"Some kind of mercenary or somethin', wasn't he?"

"Yes. He was a Green Beret. Dishonorably discharged. He freelanced a few years in Africa and the Middle East, but after a while no one would hire him anymore. He's a drunk, unreliable and very violent. Now he's a weapons trainer for right-wing groups that pass themselves off as survivalists."

"A nut case," Sloane said, interest waning. "Or drunker'n he looks. Keeps sayin' he's goin' to a retreat or somethin'. Carrying on about a monastery someplace. Says he can get away with anything." He laughed. "You ought to be choosier in your interviews, Jules—the turkey's using you as a character reference."

Eyler smiled. "It's an occupational hazard."

"I guess."

"Well, I'm going to mosey on back and turn in. Take care of my boy Ryan."

"Red carpet, seein' as how he's a friend."

"Good night, Pat."

"Night, Jules."

Eyler drove home in thoughtful silence. He lived some twenty minutes out of the city on the bend of a nice stream that adjoined a big tract of state land. It was a quiet peaceful place, good for solitude and contemplation. He took the dog out for a walk; he was as pleased as it was to be out in the crickety night, with the occasional rustle in the tall grass of a small fleeing animal, the splash of a bass breaking the calm surface of the stream to take down some hapless insect.

When he returned, he lit a pipe, put some Bach on the turntable and settled down to read awhile. The *Purgatorio*. That's what he felt like reading.

He'd probably known from the first instant what he was going to do. But he'd wanted to mull it a little to see if there was any other way. There wasn't. He shut down the house and prepared for bed. He set the alarm for four-thirty; that would be five-thirty in New York, and he knew he could get through then.

He slept well. When the alarm roused him, the light of early dawn was beginning to filter through his unshaded bedroom window. He turned on the bed lamp, knuckled his eyes. He reset the clock-radio for seven-thirty, the time at which he usually rose.

He picked up the telephone and dialed.

Half a continent away, Brother Martin answered on the second ring.

"Saint Hector's."

"Brother Martin?"

"Yes."

"This is Jules Eyler."

"Yes, Jules."

"I'm afraid you'll have to cancel Matt Ryan."

There was silence.

Eyler was momentarily disoriented. The taciturnity of the monks was alien to his own life and it always surprised him. "Security's been breached," he said.

"How badly?"

"It's a tenuous breach, but in my judgment it would be best to withdraw Ryan. There isn't any threat to the Retreat or the order."

"You're certain."

"Yes."

"Are you in any jeopardy?"

"No."

"Fine. Matthew Ryan is no longer a penitent. The order does not know he exists."

"I'm sorry."

"Why? I assume the breach wasn't your responsibility."

Eyler, an unusually capable man, now felt somehow remiss and clumsy. "I misjudged his capacity for restraint, or rather, my ability to restrain him."

"Such things have happened before and will happen again. There is no blame. Be gentle with yourself."

Eyler was humbled. "All right."

"Thank you for this notice, Jules, and for your efforts. I'll speak with you whenever contact becomes appropriate again."

"Very good, Brother Martin. May God guide you in the Retreat."

"We pray so. Good-bye, Jules."

Eyler put the receiver back in its cradle. His hand was sweating. He did not know what went on in a Retreat. He couldn't avoid certain disquieting inferences, but he didn't think that he ever truly wanted to know.

The last of the day was fading and the real blackness of night seemed to spread as quickly as a spill of crude oil over water. The Kaplan Housing Project stood on LeGrand Street on the shoulder of one of Pittsburgh's many hills overlooking the steel mills on the lower ground. Even at this distance, great clangs and bangings could be heard and the fires and spark showers of the huge furnaces were visible through the windows of the hulking mills. Plumes of steam rushed from roof vents, and soiled columns of smoke, illuminated by the many lights of the mills, rose from the tall stacks. Oakley Brown could taste the foul stuff at the back of his throat, acrid and sulfuric.

He stood motionless in the shadow formed by an angle of the building wall. It was the late dinner hour, the early TV time and there was scarcely anyone about—a couple of old winos sharing a bottle in the nearby playground and a handful of younger teenagers who were getting high and shucking to the music from a tape player. No one he couldn't handle if he had to; but they probably wouldn't give a shit if they saw anything anyway.

Oakley wanted a cigarette. But he didn't light one. A flat lusterless brown himself, and dressed all in black, even his sneakers, he was invisible, and he wanted to stay that way.

Oakley was twenty-three years old and a little under six feet tall. He didn't eat very well or take good care of himself, but he'd inherited his father's naturally powerful iron-pumper's build. That physique had been incongruous on the elder Brown. You didn't expect a minister to look and move like a professional wrestler. Oakley hadn't seen his father in ten years. Horace Brown had started Oakley preaching in a storefront church at the age of seven, had him praying on his knees on the hard floor half the day, beat the living hell out of him regularly. Oakley's mama had run off with some guy when Oakley was just a baby. That's when Horace Brown, who'd been a real drinker and a kind of street sport when he had the money, had gotten religion. And he got it with a vengeance.

Oakley ran away when he was thirteen. He lived on the streets and in abandoned buildings and sometimes in the run-down apartments of one of the few friends he occasionally had. He stayed alive by taking things—food and clothes from stores, whatever he could sell from cars and apartments, and then when he was a little older and tall enough to look mean with a knife in his hand—and later even meaner with a gun—money and jewelry from people face-to-face.

He got off on that, on scaring them and making them think he was going to kill them. He killed two people simply because they *were* so terrified.

He was picked up and questioned about the second murder, three years ago. They couldn't prove anything and they let him go, but it scared him and he holed up for a month, just being scared. When he found his nerve again he went back out on the street and his first job nearly got him killed. It was late at night in a hospital parking lot. Oakley came walking up behind this grayhaired doctor with his gun out. The guy was opening his car door. He heard the footsteps and turned. Oakley grinned at him. But the guy jammed his hand inside his coat and came out with a gun of his own and cut loose with two shots before Oakley even knew what was happening. Oakley was hit in the shoulder. He dropped his gun, staggering back, regained his balance and ran. The guy was yelling for the police. He fired twice more but missed. A dude Oakley knew who'd been a medic in Vietnam cleaned the wound and dressed it. Oakley was lucky. The slug had gone clean through without expanding and it missed the bone and major blood vessels.

Oakley gave up that shit. He wasn't afraid of dying, but he sure as hell didn't want to do it unless he had to.

Oakley wasn't scared of anything.

Well, that wasn't exactly true, but he didn't like to think about it. Churches scared him. Any kind of church. He knew where every one was in all the parts of the city he roamed, and he was careful to pick routes that would keep him away from them. If he absolutely had to go down a block with a church on it, he would cross to the opposite side of the street, keep his eyes averted and hurry past quickly.

God will damn you, God will damn you.

That's what he remembered most from his father.

He'd tried hard to forget both God and his father, but he'd never been entirely successful.

Sometimes, just because it was a high, he'd nail some guy and his chick, tie and gag the guy and make him watch while he fucked the broad or made her go down on him.

But that was personal. Just for fun.

He was a specialist now.

He did crib jobs.

Old people.

Like taking candy from a baby. Crib job.

He knew what days the welfare came, the civil service pensions, the unemployment. He was always amazed at how many old people were dumb enough to carry a wad with them. He took them on the streets, in lobbies, elevators. Hell, there were all sorts of places. Old people weren't very smart.

Best, when he could manage it—sometimes they got crafty here—he'd take 'em in hallways just as they were unlocking their doors. Fast. Push 'em in, knock 'em down, get their piss running. A lot of them had really good shit in their places, even the crazy ones who lived in dumps. Old jewelry. Gold heirlooms. Even cash. Some of the fuckin' looney tunes didn't believe in banks; they kept it all hidden away where they lived. There were some tough old cases. He'd had to peel skin off one before she told him where the money was, under a rotting floorboard by an old cook stove that hadn't worked in probably a hundred years. But the biggest score—fifteen thousand fuckin' dollars—he made just by hitting this half-blind old fart once in the stomach.

Old people's bones broke pretty easy. Jaws, arms, hips. They always made a louder sound than you'd expect.

He'd killed one for sure. An old jew ragpicker who had piles of newspaper and junk stacked up to her ceiling with only tiny little spaces to move through. God how it stank. God did she stink. She spit on him and didn't have anything worth taking. He threw her out a window.

Probably a couple more. He'd hit some of them pretty hard. He didn't know. He didn't care.

It was easy work, there wasn't much risk, and he liked it pretty much. He made good money: he lived in a jazzy apartment with great sound, bought pure Peruvian flake, had a TV with a four-foot screen and more games to play on it than he could count. He had dynamite threads and good tight pussy whenever he wanted it.

Eat shit, daddy.

Go fuck yourself, God.

He heard shuffling footsteps and realized he'd been daydreaming. He was annoyed with himself. You didn't do that while you were working. He shifted slightly, peered.

Right on.

She was five feet and a couple of inches. Slow, a little gimpy in the left leg. Whitehaired. Wrinkled-up face. Slack old body. Nice dress, though. Good-looking purse. He squinted. Was there a ring on her finger? A watch on her wrist.

She glanced around now and then, but since she didn't see anyone she wasn't worried.

Old people weren't very smart.

She was singing quietly to herself in a dry voice.

Uh-huh.

He stepped suddenly into her path and loomed over her. "Let me have the purse, mama."

Her shoulders dropped even lower. She sighed. "Oh, sweet Jesus."

He took the purse. "Give me the watch."

"Please."

He used the mass of his body to press the space against her. "Give it to me!"

She undid the clasp and handed it over.

"The ring." He saw she was wearing a thin gold chain around her neck too.

She looked up for the first time. "That's mah weddin' ring."

It was a diamond, he was pretty sure. "You got your old man. You don't need the ring, mama."

"He's dead. It be all Ah got left of him."

"If you ain't got him, you ain't married, so you don't need no ring."

"Please, child."

He grabbed her wrist. It was thin. He could have snapped it like a toothpick. He tore at the ring. She cried out in pain. He slapped her. Her head rocked back.

"Aiiiie!"

He pulled the ring from her finger, reached for the chain around her neck.

"No!" she shrilled. "Not that!"

He turned his head an instant. The teenagers were looking his way, but still moving to their music.

"Come on, you ol' bitch!" He grabbed, and missed.

She came at his face with clawed fingers. She opened flesh. One of her nails caught at the corner of his eye, hurting like hell. He bellowed and hit the side of her head. She fell and he kicked her. Hard. High in the stomach. She doubled in and gagged. He reached down and wrenched at the chain, tearing the neck of her dress. A golden crucifix was attached to the chain, lying there atop her mottled brown skin.

Light from the walkway lamp glinted upon it.

Blood gushed from the old woman's mouth. It splattered on his hand.

She looked at him through hazy eyes. "Ah curse you," she rasped. "Ah curse you in the name of God the Father, God the Son an' God the Holy Ghost." Blood seeped from her nostrils. She choked. Her head sagged back, but her eyes didn't leave his face. "Ah call on mah God t' damn you t' hell. Ah call on mah God t' burn you fo'evuh an' evuh an' evuh."

He stared at the crucifix.

She coughed blood in a spray. Drops struck his face, fell upon the golden crucified Christ. She spasmed. A gurgle began high in her throat.

Oakley cried out.

He dropped what he'd taken from her and ran away, into the night.

He didn't turn the lights on when he reached his apartment; instead went to the far corner, near the couch, and sat on the floor in the darkness. He drew up his legs and wrapped his arms around them, lay his head on his knees. He made a small mewling sound. He was terrified.

He couldn't erase the picture of the shining bloodspattered crucific from his mind. He couldn't plug his ears to her curse.

He whimpered.

He shook.

His stomach rebelled. He ran for the bathroom, tripped over an ottoman in the dark and crawled the rest of the way on his hands and knees, banging the lid of the toilet up just before his stomach spewed its contents out. As he knelt there weak and shaking, his bowels let go.

God will damn you, his father said.

Ah call on mah God t' burn you fo'evuh an' evuh an' evuh, the old lady said.

No.

No.

He got up and turned the lights on in the bathroom. He went back into the living room and turned the lights on there. He got some flake from his stash, took a hit up each nostril. He poured a big glass of Johnny Walker Red with a couple of ice cubes in and drank it down.

Eat shit, daddy.

Blow it out your ass, ol' bitch.

Fuck you, God.

He showered himself off, moving up on the coke and alcohol, padded naked and dripping water into the living room, dried his hands and wiped his nose dry with a shirt, hit the coke again and poured another big drink. Then he went back and toweled off, dressing himself in a hundred-dollar pair of slacks, a hundred-fifty-dollar pair of French shoes and a hundred-twenty-five-dollar silk shirt.

He hit the coke again. He poured more Johnny Walker.

He put the Isley Brothers on the tape deck and turned it up loud.

He drugged and boogied with himself till dawn. And then he was strung out. And the voices started again.

He took a 'lude, washed it down with a glass of Johnny Walker.

He woke up in the afternoon on the floor. He felt as if he'd been beaten by people who wanted to hurt him.

He went to the refrigerator and drank two bottles of Pepsi. He splashed water on his face. He went out and down to the corner where there was a magazine store. He bought the papers and returned to the apartment.

The *Post-Gazette* didn't have anything and he didn't see anything in the *Press* as he turned the pages, and he began to feel better. But then he found it, toward the rear, a one-column piece with a photograph.

Harelda Brooks, seventy-two years old. Killed in a mugging at the Kaplan Housing Project early last night. Beaten. Died of internal injuries.

Oakley let the paper fall. He buried his face in his hands and bent over and moaned.

You got cursed by a dying person, there wasn't any hope.

God was going to kill him and send him to Hell. His daddy had been right.

He hit the coke again, poured a Scotch. He blasted music through the speakers, trying to drive everything out of his head.

It didn't work. In an hour he was high and sick and crazy with dread.

"Thompson!" he shouted out loud. "Willie Thompson!"

Willie Thompson used to work the streets. A very bad dude, just as soon cut you as say hello. Oakley looked up to him and maybe Thompson was sort of flattered or something, because he taught the kid a few things and spent a little time rapping with him. Then one day about four years ago, Oakley had run into him coming out of a deli. Thompson wasn't himself, quiet and slow-talking, seemed like the heart had gone out of him. Oakley offered some Hawaiian he'd just scored. Thompson said no, but after a moment, real quiet, like he was sad, he said, Okay, man, okay, I'll do a little with you. They went and sat in the park and after a while, when he was drifty, Thompson talked for a little bit, all slow and blue, and Oakley couldn't really believe it, and stoned, wasn't quite sure he heard right or remembered it right later, but he'd kept quiet then because Thompson wasn't a dude you said different to.

As Oakley remembered it, Thompson had said someone

was on his ass. He'd stopped working the streets. Said, Oakley thought, he had to. Said he was gonna take a trip to a monastery, a place where there were priests or monks or something, and then things'd be straight again.

No one ever saw Thompson again.

Word was, eventually, that he'd got religion.

In his apartment, sitting on his couch rocking back and forth, hands sweating, staring intensely at nothing, Oakley began to grind his teeth. Religion. Religion. That didn't do anything one way or another. But if a bad mother like Thompson could get straight on something, then Oakley could too. These monks or priests could do it. They could get him out from under the old lady's curse. They could tell him how.

Think, motherfucker, think.

What was that place?

What?

Shit! Nothing!

The phone. He called Big Pete. No, Big Pete didn't know nothin'. He called David Johnson. Willie Thompson got religion a couple years back, that's all Dave knew. Rose Harris didn't know anything.

He called everyone he could think of.

No one knew anything.

Think!

He stalked around the apartment knocking his clenched fist against his head.

"Hector!" he shouted. "Saint Hector. All right, man!"

He screwed his face up in fierce concentration. Saint Hector. Yeah. Yeah. Now where, man? Where!

At least he had Jill.

There wasn't much else. Wycisowicz lived in a stucco house in South Miami that was more a bungalow than a real house. The grass and shrubbery were ragged, the windows dirty. The roof leaked in the kitchen. He didn't care much. He rented the house. He was lucky to have even that much with what he had to pay out in alimony and child support. For a dumb bitch and two kids he hadn't seen in three years. And now there was this shit with Stanley and this fucking retreat up north. Weird. But Stanley had his ass in a sling and there was nothing else to do. It could have been a whole lot worse, he supposed.

And he did have Jill. He'd picked her up at the Fire & Ice Club, where a lot of kinks hung out.

It was night in Miami.

Wycisowicz and Jill were in his bedroom. She was in a black bra with cutouts for her nipples. Her nipples were pierced. There were brass studs in them. He had her tied over a hassock, wrists to ankles. She wore a garter belt and black stockings, high heels. Her naked ass jutted in the air.

Two vivid red marks across it were beginning to swell.

Wycisowicz was fully dressed. He stood above her, his zipper open and his erect cock sticking out through it. He held a riding crop in his hand. He brought it down again across Jill's buttocks.

She went: "Ohhhhh." Deeply, richly.

He curled his fingers around his cock and struck her again. She jerked. "Ohhhhh."

Snap.

"Ahhhh!"

Snap.

"Jeeesus."

Snap.

He struck her half a dozen times more, harder each time. She was twisting and groaning.

"Enough, cunt?"

She moaned and moved her ass from side to side.

He hit her again.

"Mmhmm!"

And again.

"All right," she gasped. "Please. Yes. That's enough. Stop please."

He brought the crop down viciously and did what he wanted—opened her skin.

She screamed.

"That's right, bitch." He was rock-hard. He hadn't marked her permanently yet. He'd been taking his time, working up to it. It was a sweet progression. "You going to be good to me, you going to give me what I want?"

"You *hurt* me," she said in a little girl's voice.

"Uh-huh. And I'm going to do more."

"Will you?" she asked. "Will you please?"

"I might."

"I want you to."

"How much?"

"More than anything, anything." She twisted her head and looked up with pleading eyes."

"No. I don't think so. You bore me."

"I won't. I swear I won't. You'll like me. I'll make you."

He shrugged. "I guess you can try." He untied her.

She kissed his feet. "Thank you."

He put his shoe against her face and shoved. She sprawled backward. "I didn't tell you you could do that."

"I'm sorry. Don't punish me."

"Get up."

She hesitated. "Your gun?" she said.

"Yes," he said. "Yes, I like that." He opened the dresser drawer in which he kept his revolver when he was home and slipped it out of its holster.

She was lying on the floor on her back with her hands folded over her stomach and her eyes closed.

He knelt on one knee beside her. He slapped her.

"Oh!" Her eyes flew open and she looked at him in terror. "Who are you? What do you want?"

He grabbed her hair and pointed the gun at her face. "Shut up, bitch. Get onto your goddamn bed."

"No! Please! You can't do this."

He cocked back the hammer. She stared at the muzzle. Her lips parted slightly and the tip of her tongue appeared.

His cock throbbed. For an instant, the briefest instant, his finger tightened on the trigger.

Her nostrils flared. "Yes," she said softly.

His chest was strictured, breath difficult. Consciously, he eased the pressure of his finger off the trigger. "On the bed," he said hoarsely.

As she complied, he lowered the hammer back down; just a hair more, that's all it would have taken.

She lay on her back, still and passive. He aimed the gun at her again. "Not a fuckin' sound," he said.

"What are you going to do to me?" she said fearfully.

"Anything I want."

He tied her spreadeagled atop the bed. He set the gun aside and took off his clothes. He knelt between her thighs and probed her opening. She was wet. He was rigid.

"Please," she said. "My husband and my children. I've never been with any other man. Don't do this to me," she begged.

He laughed harshly. "You're all mine, cunt."

He entered her, plunged immediately, pulled back and slammed in again.

She gasped.

He drove at her.

Tears rolled down her cheeks. "Oh. Oh no, this can't be happening to me."

He took the ends of her nipple studs and pulled, elongating her nipples, coning out her breasts.

She threw her head back. Her eyes glassed. She emitted a low grating sound.

He put his hands to her throat and encircled it. She showed teeth, like a crazed animal.

He jammed himself as far into her as he could. His hands tightened around her throat. The muscles of his forearms corded.

Her mouth opened. Her face began to flush. She twitched.

He increased the pressure.

She jerked against her bonds.

He squeezed.

Her face darkened rapidly. It swelled. She thrashed beneath him. Her eyelids fluttered. Her cheek ticked.

He humped into her, squeezed.

She became spastic. She twisted and quaked, arched her back up off the bed and remained that way for a moment, shuddering, then fell back down. Her head lolled to the side and her body went limp.

Wycisowicz maintained the pressure another few moments, then released her throat; an additional thirty seconds would have been lethal.

He froze. His whole being was now centered in his pulsing cock and screamed for release, but he didn't want to come yet, and he would have if he had moved at all.

Jill's breathing was ragged at first. Her head twitched. The fingers of one hand jerked. Her eyelids trembled. They opened. She blinked, trying to orient herself.

"Hi, baby," he said.

She groaned.

"Nice trip?"

"Yes," she said, low and sated.

He petted her face, her hair. After a minute or two he tweaked one of her nipple studs.

She went: "Mhhmm," and moved her hips beneath him.

He slapped her.

"Why?" she said. "I was good, wasn't I?"

"You're never good."

He reached for her throat.

"No. Not again. I can't."

"This time," he said, "I'm going to come."

Gunther Hauptmann was belted into a window seat of the Lufthansa 747, on the left side, several rows behind the wing, which would afford him an unobstructed view.

The aircraft was poised on a runway at the Berlin International Airport, brakes locked, engines whining upward toward peak. Hauptmann could feel it tremble with restrained power, as if barely able to contain its desire to break free of the earth.

He checked his watch, an expensive Swiss instrument that was accurate to within plus or minus five seconds each year, which was a matter of occasional importance to him.

It was fourteen minutes past midnight.

He leaned his head back against the cushion, closed his eyes and breathed deeply and slowly several moments, though he was not at all tense. He was an experienced traveler and was not discomfited by flight. On the contrary, he enjoyed it quite a bit. There was a kind of quiet suspension about it, a perfect encapsulation in which he was sheltered from the vicissitudes of life, freed of responsibility and concern, granted a holiday from the universe for a few hours. When he flew at night he would push his seat back and close his eyes, aware that he hung four or five miles above the earth and its affairs, and listen to the steady drone of the engines, as soothing as the sigh of a spring wind. Or he would read; there wasn't much time in his life for reading. He liked thrillers best, or stories of the Beautiful People that spanned continents and dripped of money, power and intrigue. If it was day, he'd spend most of the time looking out the window. Clouds were best. He liked to be above them. They made him think of what he fancied the Arctic emptiness to look like—quiet, static, frozen undulations. And absolutely nothing else. It allowed him to let his mind go blank. He thought it must be similar to a successful state of Zen meditation.

Hauptmann was thirty-three, tall, darkhaired, had a face of handsome angularity and was in excellent physical condition. He could speak French, Italian and English as fluently as his native German, and could get by if he had to in another half-dozen tongues. He was traveling on a Swiss passport under the name of Michael Zuckerman. Occupation, architect.

The first officer's voice came through the intercom. He asked the attendants to take their seats for departure. They hurried up the aisles checking to see that seat belts were buckled. The one in Hauptmann's aisle was blond and had eyes as clear and blue as Lake Zurich. She was rushed and distracted, but still found a moment to touch his eyes with hers. She smiled more warmly than was necessary, as she had when he boarded.

His return smile was neutral. He had disciplined himself to avoid extremes of any kind, to seek the bland unmemorable center. He wished to remain no longer than an idle thought in the minds of those he encountered. He did not want to leave any mark of passage.

She was gone.

The pilot released the brakes. The plane surged forward.

Hauptmann looked out the window into the night. The great wings were flexing softly up and down as the plane gathered speed. Beyond, other aircraft were waiting on the parallel taxi lane, and beyond them was the terminal whose brightly lit windows revealed a bustle of activity, even at this hour.

Hauptmann felt a slight downward pull, the cabin canted, and they were airborne.

The angle steepened. They climbed into the dark sky. Hauptmann looked at his watch. It was twelve-fifteen and twenty seconds.

He put his elbow on the armrest and cupped his chin, looking out into the emptiness.

There was a brief grinding of machinery as the wheels were drawn up into the belly of the plane.

The pitch of the engines altered slightly.

The left wing dropped down and the aircraft banked into a looping turn, still climbing.

The city below was a diminishing geometry of lights. Cars flowed steadily along the ribbon of the autobahn like illuminated corpuscles in a transparent blood vessel.

The airport itself returned into Hauptmann's field of view. The runways spread out from the cluster of terminals in spokes.

He focused on the large International Terminal.

He breathed in, exhaled slowly. Again. He was as relaxed as if he'd just wakened from a long and restful sleep.

Part of the roof of the International Terminal turned a yellowish orange. Long fingers of the same color flared out through the front windows.

It was such a rich beautiful color in the night.

The front of the terminal was no longer definable. It was a billowing fireball.

Though it wasn't possible, Hauptmann imagined he could hear the deep *whumph* of the explosion and feel the distant impact of the shock wave.

He was pleased with his handiwork. His bomb. He was a professional, one of the best. He had indulged himself. He'd made this flight before and knew the route and timing of the ascent. Assuming Lufthansa was its usual precise self, he'd thought the detonation would be pretty from this vantage.

And it was.

Other passengers had been looking out their own windows.

A subdued, uncertain "Ohhh!" swept the cabin. People began to speak in several languages. They were confused and questioning at first, then some, the quicker-minded, became fearful.

The fireball had reached its farthest limit, and shrank back to a bright steady burn. Major sections of the airport were blacked out. And then it all slipped away behind them and Hauptmann could see no more.

He settled back into his seat, folded his arms across his chest and closed his eyes. He'd brought a book, but only to pass the time if, for some reason, he wasn't able to sleep. He wanted to arrive in New York refreshed and clearheaded.

Chapter 10

The early morning sky was a clear glazed blue. Light from the rising sun flooded through a gap in the low mountain range to the east and cut across the width of the valley in a golden swath to run up the slope of the western range, the bulk of which was still deeply shadowed, juts of black and speckled granite heavily forested with tall conifers.

Crows called in the distance. The cows lowed and the sheep bleated as they were led out to pasture. The pigs were grunting for food. The penned geese protested their captivity loudly.

There were steady rhythmic thunks as sledges struck post tops, and sharper *cacks* which were the sounds of hammers driving big staples into the posts.

Most of the company were at work on the fence, which was being erected along a line of flour that had been laid out fifteen yards from the monastery's walls, completely enclosing it. The fence was chain-link, to a height of four feet, though the post tops rose another two feet higher.

Thunk.

Cack-cack.

Thunk.

The monks worked in silent economy. Some were sinking posts at designated intervals. Others carried rolls of chain-link from a storage barn. Still others opened and stretched the wire, while teams came along behind them stapling it fast to the posts.

The sun topped the mountains to the east.

Someone screamed.

The scream was lost in a wild honking and gabbling.

The monks jerked their heads up.

The oblate Michael, carrying fence posts on his shoulder, had stumbled into the gate of the goose pen and knocked it open. He stood now in the midst of half a dozen of the big birds. They flared and beat their wings and lashed their long necks forward, striking at his stomach and back and into his ribs with their hard bills. The flock was in an uproar. Several more birds broke free and joined the attack, and then the rest of the wing-beating honking flock surged through the gate. Michael dropped the posts and went down under the onslaught. His hands could be seen thrashing among the leaping and striking birds, flashes of his dark robe. He was shrieking.

Monks dropped tools and rushed to help. The geese attacked the oblate frenziedly with savage hisses and loud cries. Several monks grabbed for necks and wings and tried to throw them off, but were driven back. Michael screamed in agony. Some of the birds were spattered and smeared with his blood.

"Michael! Michael!" Brother Harold rushed the birds, took violent blows and fought to break through them.

"Everybody back!" Brother Thomas roared.

A pallor, the last remnant of his seizure of a week ago, underlay his beefy complexion. He waded into the maddened geese swinging a leather harness. He struck them with it. He kicked at them. He seized and hurled them away, ignoring their powerful blows, and drove to the center. He pivoted, swung the harness in a full circle, then threw it aside and scooped up the writhing Michael as if he were a child. He raised him up out of the range of the birds that refused to break off the attack and marched out with him. A trio of geese followed, striking at him. Other monks drove them off.

Michael was sobbing. His hands had been cut, his face and neck torn. A flap of flesh hung down from beneath one eye. He bled freely. Brother Thomas set him on his feet and supported him with a brawny arm. Brother Harold was there. "It's all right, Michael," he said. "They're all gone. It's over." He took Michael into his arms. The oblate buried his face in Brother Harold's chest. He shuddered and cried.

Brother Hilliard, impassive, said, "Take him to the infirmary and have his wounds attended." He looked at Brother Thomas, whose hands were lacerated. "You should have yours looked at too."

"They're not bad. I'll wash them out under the pump." Brother Thomas was breathing heavily. The corner of his mouth twitched.

"Do you feel all right?" the prior asked.

"I'm fine," Brother Thomas snapped.

"Rest awhile before you go back to work. Take a slow walk. Down by the pond."

"I told you, I'm fine! I—" Brother Thomas stopped, breathed deeply. "All right," he said. "I will. Thank you, brother."

The geese were now making permanent their escape in noisy excitement, fleeing toward the fields and nearby woods. One bird was down, its chest caved in, a bone protruding, the white feathers bloody. Another, with a broken wing, had taken refuge near the barn. A third beat its wings and hobbled awkwardly away on a broken leg.

Brother Wilfred reported ruefully to the prior. "One definitely won't survive. There are two more I don't know if I can save. I'm going to need several brothers to round up the ones that got away."

"Take whomever you want. But catch them quickly. We want to finish the fence by nightfall."

Sunlight fell through the narrow arched windows of the hall and striped the floor with white bars. The hall itself was dim. But still the postulant Richard Higgins squeezed his eyes nearly shut and blinked repeatedly. When he came to the first bar he stopped and stood utterly still, as if it were dangerous like a coiled snake.

Brother Stewart waited patiently several moments, then placed his hand on the postulant's shoulder, not ungently. "Let's move on now, Richard."

Richard hesitated, then shuffled forward. He was gaunt and pale as a cadaver. He wore a shapeless gray gown that hung from his bony shoulders down to his shins. As he passed the first window his head turned slightly toward it, then snapped back. He lowered his eyes to the stone blocks of the floor and kept them fixed there, looking at none of the subsequent windows, nor through any of the open doors.

Brother Stewart stopped him. "In here."

The monk guided him into a room with rough wooden uprights and shelves on which were stacked the dark robes of the order, gowns similar to the postulant's, towels, washcloths and colorless undergarments. He directed him to exchange his gown for a brown monk's robe and fitted him with a pair of leather sandals. He helped the postulant tie the rope cincture and showed him how to fold the cowl so it lay flat across the back of the shoulders.

Higgins still stared down.

"Look up, Richard. God made this world and it's not right that you should cast your eyes away from it."

Alarm flickered over Higgins's face. "Yes, Brother Stewart." His voice, so long unused, was still rough.

The monk took him to the abbot's office. Brother Martin rose and walked around his desk.

"Brother Martin, this is the postulant Richard Higgins."

Higgins went down on one knee, as he had been instructed. "My abbot, you are the instrument of God's will, and I am obedient to Him in all ways. Say what I am to do. Direct me to His grace." He kissed Brother Martin's ring.

The abbot placed his hand upon Higgins's bowed head. "Is God the fullness of your heart?"

"Yes, my abbot."

"Are you willing to renounce now and forever all the things

of this world and dedicate yourself solely to the glorification of God, to have no purpose but to serve His will?"

"Yes, my abbot."

"Then we shall receive you among us with joy. Henceforth you will be known to us as the novice Brother Richard. We shall all pray for the day when we may welcome you as a full brother in truth as well as name. Rise, my son."

Higgins stood. Though it was clearly difficult for him, he met Brother Martin's eyes. This augured well to the abbot: the goal was to burn away corruption while preserving strength, so that the purified strength could be enlisted in God's service.

"You are aware that a Retreat begins in two days," Brother Martin said.

"Yes."

"Are you prepared? Are you ready to do God's work?"

"Yes."

Brother Martin nodded. "If you have any difficulty of any kind, at any moment, I want you to come to Brother Stewart or to me immediately."

"Yes. I will."

"Immediately," the abbot stressed. "Brother Stewart will familiarize you with the monastery and its grounds today. Tomorrow you will have an assigned task." He dismissed them.

He stroked his jaw after they left. There was courage in the novice, he was certain of that. But there was also shakiness.

Well, that was understandable.

Still.

The *nature* of that shakiness was the question.

Brother Martin wondered now if he'd made a mistake. The Retreat was a crucible.

Still.

He, the abbot, could not hold the Retreat intact by sheer force of his will alone. It was—and could be no other way—the undertaking of the entire community.

There was so much. It seemed that a new decision was

required of him each hour. And each decision was potentially critical.

Fear was with him always. He had trouble holding his food down. He was barely able to sleep. Sweat prickled across his back and moistened his palms.

He despaired.

He was exhilarated.

And in these oscillations he perceived the erosion of his own stability.

And sin.

Despair? Then doubt God's grace and commit the offense of Judas.

Exhilaration? Know deadly pride.

Throughout this all he had to maintain an unwavering outward composure, a steadfast serenity. He was abbot. Without him as strong keel, the Retreat could founder and shatter itself upon the shoals.

Oh, God!

For the first time in a dozen years, Brother Martin wanted a drink. Craved and was desperate for one. He thought of the infirmary, of the brandy kept there.

God, God!

He sank to his knees before the crucifix on the wall and tried to pray. But he couldn't.

And he was forlorn, alone, and damned.

Hector was forlorn, alone, and damned in the wilderness.

After the bishop had him smuggled from the palace so he would not be set upon by the waiting crowds, some of whom wanted to worship him, others of whom wanted to jeer, he had thanked his guard at the outskirts of the city and with humility and self-doubt acceded to their fervent requests and blessed them, and then turned out of the circle of their lanterns and stepped into the darkness.

He walked along a public road for some hours, taking to the brush whenever he heard the clatter of hooves or the rumbling of an approaching coach, which was not often, for people did not travel then at night unless it couldn't be avoided. And finally, an hour before dawn, he had gone into the woods and found a clearing where there was a great boulder, which had been heated by the sun all day and was now radiating that heat back, appreciably warmer than the cool night air, and he broke some boughs from a tree and pressed himself up against the rock and covered himself with the boughs and lay his head down upon his arm and went to sleep.

In the morning he ate some of his bread and cheese and went on. Still he avoided travelers and whenever a choice in the road was offered, he took the one that was more awkward, that looked less traveled.

Within two days he was following paths that were hard even for a lone rider on a horse. He no longer avoided others—most that he saw were rustics and peasants and from them he would beg a little water, a slice of sausage. In another day he was making his way up a mountainside, along footpaths that were negotiable only by a man, and with difficulty.

He passed an occasional rough cottage where he asked for water if there was no nearby stream, or whatever crust of old bread or discarded rind of cheese the occupants might be able to spare. They were little better off than he, and he was humbled by their generosity; they even offered smoked goat meat, which he declined. He heard from them of an ancient chapel a fair distance up the mountain, at the end of the waterline, just before the trees began to give way to bald rock.

He found it—little more than a large cairn of stones, only a partial wall with a low doorway still standing, and that in precarious condition. He decided this would be his work, to rebuild the chapel for God's greater glory. There was a tiny spring nearby, not much more than a trickle, but sufficient. There were a few nut trees, a patch of scraggly berry bushes, roots he could dig and eat.

He formed a crude shelter by excavating beneath a rock overhang and making walls of branches and boughs. It took him a month to repair and strengthen the existing wall, gather the fallen stones off to the side and dig flat the earth where he planned to lay a foundation. One afternoon a shepherd appeared at the site and stood some fifty paces off. He was one of those from down below who had told Hector of the ruins. Hector, bearded, wildhaired, naked save for a loincloth, his gaunt body glistening with sweat, acknowledged him with a nod and continued to work as if he were alone. The shepherd watched him in silence. When, some time later, Hector happened to turn in that direction he noticed that the man had gone. On a flat rock the man had left a small piece of cheese.

In succession over the next few weeks came half a dozen other peasants. All watched silently awhile. He continued about his business. Then two appeared together one morning. The taller stepped forward and said to him, "Holy Sir, we would like to give this day to God and help you in your labor."

"I am neither holy nor a 'sir,'" Hector answered, "but the least of God's creatures and undeserving of His or your generosity. I thank you in His name, but I must do this task myself. Return to your homes, please, and remember me in your prayers."

Twice more they came to entreat him and their numbers grew as indeed they became more certain that he was blessed of God. And each time he again begged them to forbear and told them that he would remain until the chapel was completed and God directed him to some new charge. When he left, he said, the chapel would be theirs. Subsequently, a man, a woman or sometimes an entire family would appear at the edge of the clearing and watch him labor for a time. When they left, there would be some small portion of food for him on the flat rock. Once, as winter was nearing, they left an old patched woolen blanket, for which he was grateful.

One day each month he did not work. On the night when the moon was at its slimmest, before it began to renew itself, the wounds of the crucified Christ would open in his hands and feet. He would lay a-pallet the following day, within his dark hovel, his mind inflamed with visions. Then his flesh would close again and he would resume. He came to love the birds that wheeled above him and lightened his day with their song, the chipmunks and squirrels that scratched among dry leaves on the ground for old nuts, the somber porcupines who waddled by on occasion, every creature with which God had populated His earth. He grieved at the memory of all such he had slain, and cried lamentation into the wilderness and beat his back with thorns. He came to speak to the birds and animals and to sing to them of God's goodness. He shared crumbs of bread with them and scraps of what little food he had. Many came to take up habitation near him, and they were company for him and he rejoiced.

He stayed on the mountain a year. When he came down, appearing twice his age but vigorous and strong and filled with the glory of life, all life, he did so joyfully to preach its sacredness and to carry the message of renunciation.

What he found, to his horror, as if somehow he had never known anything of men and their ways, was a world of indifference to God's lesser children, of cruelty and abuse and slaughter. He was himself beaten when he tried to dissuade a merchant from beating his draft horse. When, in a forest, he cradled the head of a fallen doe mortally wounded in a hunt and tried to stop the noblemen from finishing her, he was set upon by their dogs and sorely bitten, then whipped and hurled into a nearby river. He became known as a fool in God. Children often threw stones at him when he approached a village. He was pelted with garbage and offal.

But some listened. He was gladdened and given heart by this and he endured the suffering and vilification visited upon him in the sure knowledge that no man could suffer for Christ as greatly as Christ had suffered for man.

He traveled through Italy five years thus. And once a month, when he bled with the wounds of Christ, he took himself off in private so none could see: because he had learned that there were men who would go mad and think him a great chosen and favorite of God, or even the Messiah returned, and wish in his name to sweep all others away, or those who would call him an agent of the devil and want to see him dead. As it was, some thought him blessed and a saint, some mad or a heretic, and others an enemy of peace and the established order. He was received with welcome and his words attended; he was driven off, lashed or beaten; he was seized and taken before local magistrates and courts, banished from certain provinces under pain of dire punishment or even death.

During all this time the slow perception had been growing within him that of all God's creatures man himself was singularly the most beautiful. Paradoxically, man was also the one who inflicted the greatest pain and destruction upon all creation. And worse, the creature he abused and tormented more than any other was his own brother. Hector saw theft, cheating, lying and advantage taken. He saw treachery, calumny, fraud and false witness borne. This was troublesome and saddening, but still fathomable given the weakness of the flesh and spirit to which the creature was heir. What he could not comprehend, and could less and less abide was the outright savagery he encountered. He saw terrible beatings. Men who smiled as they wreaked torment upon the helpless. Swaggering monsters before whom everyone else cowered in dread. He was thrown to the ground, stomped and left to lie helpless while three men raped a serving girl. They pulled her skirts over her head, one sitting upon her covered face to hold her down while turns were taken on her; and when they were done the girl, who was young and had been a virgin and whose chaste white privates were torn and bloodied, was dead from suffocation. Before they left, one of them urinated on the warm body. He witnessed constables and bailiffs flog and cudgel without reason, pleasured by the cries of their victims. Finally, he saw a prince and an abbot sit laughing side by side as they watched sentence carried out upon a cobbler who'd been convicted of poaching on lands over which the abbot was suzerain. The prince could have ordered a punishment no more severe than forfeiture of half a year's wages, but at the abbot's urging, which suited his own disposition, he decreed this, the harshest sentence the law permitted. The cobbler was buried in the earth to his lower rib cage. To a plow that had never turned earth was hitched a team of untried oxen. The traces were put into the hands of a virgin boy who had never driven oxen. And while the boy, who knew the cobbler, wept, but was lashed on by the prince's retainers, and while the man's wife and young children looked on with piteous and agonized cries, Hector, restrained by the guards, his protests ignored, was forced to watch helplessly as the boy drove the oxen forward. The plow bit into the earth fifty feet from the buried cobbler, furrowing, turning the dirt in double mounds as the oxen lumbered on. Coming upon the man, they strained to either side, and a moment later the plow struck beneath his breastbone and thrust his torso back. He screamed when the point bit into his chest, then tore him, and the scream terminated in a strangled gurgle as the blade ripped into his heart and through it and out his back and then up his canted torso, cleaving out at the place where his shoulder joined the base of his neck.

Hector fell down faint. He writhed on the ground in unconsciousness, foam upon his lips, and he burned with a vision of God descending to earth in a blaze of fire, wielding the terrible sword of His anger. Those around him drew away from this poor bedraggled wretch in his affliction.

When finally he woke, it was night on the field, the stars were twinkling weakly in the sterile glare of the full moon and he was alone. Weakly, he walked the short line of the furrow to its end. The body had been removed for burial and the hole in which the unfortunate cobbler had stood filled in. But the dirt around it was still sodden with blood, a dark circular stain. Hector placed his hand upon it. It was moist and cold now to the touch. He lifted his fingers, to which some damp grains of dirt adhered. He kissed them.

Thenceforth he consecrated himself to stopping the murder and torment of his fellow man. There were times over the next few years when God granted him an eloquence that, coupled with the strength of his faith, enabled him to penetrate into the darkness of a heart and infuse it with light and repentance. Other times, failing that, he succeeded in bringing the beastliness of some person to the attention of a good burgher, constable or higher authority and had it stopped. But more commonly some human monster would laugh in his face, spit on him, beat him—twice he lay near death. Or a man's neighbors or victims were terrified and would not witness against him. Or the brute was a magistrate himself, a nobleman, even a cleric, and beyond the reach of the law. The burden weighed heavily upon Hector. He mourned. He despaired. He felt incapable of the task and unworthy of God's love.

Toward the end of this period he found himself living in an abandoned pigsty at the outskirts of a small village some miles north of Padua. There resided in that village a hulking leatherworker with a dense black beard who had terrorized the countryside, in the manner of a dread Gorgon, for some years. He had killed three men for a known fact—though the witnesses would admit to what they had seen only in hushed tones and in careful privacy, with great fear. He had taken the wives of other men nearly at will, he was suspected in the disappearance of certain travelers, he whipped his wife mercilessly and had beaten one of his own children to death.

Hector had preached patiently and gently to him for several months, whenever a situation arose in which the man could neither evade nor assault him. Even so, the leatherworker had twice beaten him badly. He had been able to make no progress with the man. And there was no one sufficiently unafraid to testify against him.

Then, a young shepherd who in a passion of love had summoned the boldness to petition the governing lord for relief against the leatherworker's unwanted attentions toward his sweetheart was found dead in a field with his skull crushed. In great distress, a fellow youth confessed to Hector, whom he considered a holy man, that unobserved from a copse of trees he had seen the leatherworker do this thing. Hector could not persuade him to take his information to the authorities. Indeed, in all good conscience, he was not certain he *should*— for the youth was perfectly correct in saying that there was no protection for him; that he too would be killed if he attempted such a thing.

Hector left the village the following day.

He traveled two days into the wilderness, and there spent the better part of a week making preparation. Then he returned, though unbeknownst to the people of the village who thought he had left them for good. He concealed himself in the outlying terrain, spying as he could, and within a fortnight his opportunity came.

The leatherworker had been off carousing with some rough fellows and was making his way home after nightfall, when the rest of the villagers were all closed into their cottages and most of the lamplights had already been extinguished. He was drunkenly leading his sturdy donkey, to which twin bundles of brushwood were lashed.

Hector left the tree line, walked quickly across the field and overtook the leatherworker a little more than a hundred paces from the nearest cottage, which was darkened.

"I thought I was rid of you," the man said. He looked around, then glowered. "Well, maybe it *is* time to be rid of you. For me to rid myself of you."

"A moment," Hector said. "I realize that I have vexed your life. I wish to atone for that. I have brought you a gift."

"A gift?" The man laughed hugely. "Let me see."

Hector extended his left hand. He opened his fingers. A small object lay in his palm.

The leatherworker bent forward, squinting in the moonlight. "I can't see."

It was a round black stone.

The man looked up, frowning. "What—"

Hector swung the club he'd concealed in his right hand behind his mendicant's robe. It caught the man atop his head with a sharp *whackk*. He sagged to his knees. Hector hit him again. He toppled over and sprawled onto the ground.

Hector loosed the bundles of firewood from the donkey. With some effort—he was strong, but the man was large and weighty—he lifted the leatherworker and laid him over the patient and unprotesting donkey, tied him hand to feet beneath the beast's belly.

He thanked God, he praised God, he assented to being God's instrument, and he led the donkey and the bound man off into the night.

Monks were putting together the runners and headboards of beds in the vacated cells, placing springs on top of the slats and mattresses on top of the springs. Brother Hiram, one of those who would sleep in the chapter room, was fitting sheets to a mattress in his own cell.

Brother Phelan appeared at the door. "Brother, we're having trouble with Gregory."

Brother Hiram followed Brother Phelan to a cell down the hall. The oblate Gregory stood next to the pieces of an unassembled bed with a surly expression. He was a heavy-boned man of about thirty with coarse skin and dense hair on the backs of his hands.

"Why isn't this bed together?" Brother Hiram demanded.

The monk who had been instrumental in a man's decision to become an oblate bore the primary responsibility for him. There were currently only two in the monastery, Gregory and Michael. Though both required supervision, Michael was quite tractable while Gregory was frequently difficult. Brother Raphael didn't know why. There were vagaries in the process.

"Why . . . should they . . . have beds and . . . I sleep on the floor?" Gregory said with slow anger.

"It's the nature of the Retreat. You know that. Now get back to work."

"No."

Brother Hiram gave Brother Phelan a barely perceptible nod, then said, "Gregory, this isn't right. You know better."

The oblate stood like a rock. "You . . . can't make . . . me."

"I can, Gregory. I hope I don't have to. Go back to work." Such suasion would never have extended so long with a monk. But oblates, of some necessity, were given more latitude.

Gregory set his jaw.

Brother Phelan returned and placed a coiled whip in Brother Hiram's hand.

"Gregory," Brother Hiram said, "go back to work."

"No."

"This is the last time, Gregory."

The oblate glared.

Brother Hiram uncoiled the whip. He waited a moment, then slashed it across Gregory's chest. The oblate showed his teeth. Brother Hiram struck him again. Still Gregory stood defiant. Brother Hiram laid into him. The whip hissed through the air and popped loudly as it struck.

Gregory balled his hands into fists and charged. Brother Hiram sidestepped and tripped him. The oblate fell, rolled and came to a halt against the opposite wall. Brother Hiram went after him, the whip a blur: *cr-rack cr-rack cr-rack.* Gregory roared in anger and tried to seize the whip, but it slashed across his hands and fell again and again too quickly to clasp. He crouched and pulled into himself, covered his head with his arms and made violent animal sounds in his throat. Brother Hiram lashed his shoulders and drew the whip back for another stroke. He hesitated. Gregory was silent. Warily, the oblate lowered his arms and looked out over them. Brother Hiram waited with the whip suspended.

"All . . . right," Gregory said. "I will."

Brother Hiram nodded. He coiled the whip. "Finish the bed. Then go outside and help with the fence."

It was necessary to make the oblate fulfill the task against which he'd rebelled; but after that, work on something else, and of a more physical nature, would probably be best for him.

Gregory got up. He walked past Brother Hiram without looking at him and went into the cell and began to assemble the bed.

Brother Wilfred was cleaning out cow stalls when he was informed that the dogs had arrived. He blinked in the bright sunlight as he emerged from the barn. A red van was parked next to the chain-link fence, which already stretched the length of the monastery's front. Block letters on the van's side read: MANHATTAN DOGS—ALL PHASES TRAINING AND CARE. A man in jeans and a denim shirt was leaning against it smoking.

"Hi, Jim," Brother Wilfred said. They shook hands. "How was the drive?"

"Hello, Brother Wilfred. A long haul." He put a hand to the small of his back and bent over at the waist. "Stiff. Hot as hell in the city, though, so it's nice to get up into the mountains. Got a couple of sweethearts for you."

He opened the vehicle's rear doors. There were two German shepherds within, each in its own wire crate. The dogs were on their feet. Their tails swished. They made small eager sounds.

Five years ago two penitents had managed to lose themselves in the woods. A day and a half passed before the monks found them, averting disaster. Abbot Giles had introduced dogs into the following Retreat. Brother Martin found the innovation valuable.

"This is Lucky," Jim said, releasing a black and silver dog. Lucky jumped from the van, went up on his hind legs and washed his tongue over Jim's face. The remaining animal, black and tan, barked its objection to Lucky's freedom while it remained caged. Jim freed it too. "Captain America. Cap," he said.

The dogs put their noses to the ground and quartered the immediate area rapidly. They lifted their legs at spots to their liking and marked the territory as their own. Jim whistled them back. They nuzzled into him for petting.

Brother Wilfred, who was secretly and guiltily pleasured to have this opportunity, held out his hands for the dogs to sniff. He knelt, scratched their chests and rubbed them behind the ears. "Hi, Cap. Hi, Lucky. Good dogs. Good boys."

The animals wagged their tails politely.

"Even though they're trained for multiple handlers, they'll still work better if you assign one man to each of them, two at the most. Cap's the better tracker. They're both good sentries."

"I'll need a brushup session," Brother Wilfred said.

"Wouldn't leave without giving you one."

"How about a sandwich and a chance to relax first?"

"I won't say no."

They walked toward the gate in the new fence. Jim snapped his fingers. The dogs followed swiftly and fell into step behind him.

Preparations were going well: the ancient form prevailed, the structure was itself. Or so Brother Martin encouraged himself to think. He needed the comfort, even if it might only be illusion that comforted him.

The penitents' quarters were in good order. The infirmary was next on the list.

Brother Raphael was seated on a stool in the dispensary before a stainless steel counter. He said, "I wish it weren't necessary to inflict this on these poor dumb creatures."

On the counter were three cages. Each held a single laboratory rat. To the left was an open wooden box stenciled *Tenafly Laboratories*. Rubber-stoppered vials were racked within it. Next to it lay a hypodermic syringe.

"Compassion is a great virtue," Brother Martin said. "There are higher ones, though. And they try us."

"Yes."

Brother Martin studied the rats. The animal in the first cage was thrashing violently. Its eyes were distended and lips curled back from its teeth. It screeched, high and continuous. The second lay on its side in stark contrast, utterly slack, unblinking. The abbot would have thought it dead were it not for the slow rise and fall of its thorax. The last one was in a state of convulsion. The cage floor was soiled with the contents of its stomach and bowels. It twisted in upon itself in repeating spasms which forced thin trickles of colorless liquid from its orifices.

Brother Raphael said, "There are other possibilities, but I'm concentrating on these three drugs now. I think they're the ones we want."

"Explain them," Brother Martin said.

Brother Raphael did.

Brother Martin forced impassivity into his voice. "Your choices are good. Thank you."

Shortly after the Angelus, Brother Cooper reported to the office, as Brother Martin had instructed him. The abbot had assigned him to keep close watch on Brother Hilliard.

He stood before the desk reluctant to speak.

"It is your duty to be truthful," Brother Martin said.

"But not my place to judge."

"You will simply describe. I will judge."

"He works hard," Brother Cooper said.

"Excessively?"

"That could be said, yes."

"Does he appear psychologically engaged, is he *present* in his work?"

Brother Cooper frowned. "Maybe not," he said, thinking. "He does everything well, but there's something . . . mechanical about it."

"What is his attitude in prayer?"

"Fervent."

"Does he make eye contact or communicate in any way with the other brothers?"

Brother Cooper pondered. "Not often."

"Go back to the fields," Brother Martin said. "Send him in to me."

When Brother Hilliard appeared, half an hour later, the abbot studied his face in silence. It was without expression, and Brother Martin could determine nothing from it. Which alarmed him. There was danger in the prior, but he could not understand its nature and was therefore uncertain of the proper course.

Reflecting, the abbot was suddenly jolted from within.

You are in horror of what you once were and you are afraid to step back into that fire.

Brother Martin had suppressed the prior's words to him. Because they were true. Could his fear of them have caused him to misperceive Brother Hilliard or, even worse, unconsciously wish to punish him?

Oh, Lord!

In a tone as neutral as the prior's face he said, "How would you account yourself to God now, after this past week?"

"I would account myself with humility and love."

"That is evasive. Bluntly, if you haven't purged yourself of this lust for Him, you are a menace to the Retreat and to the chapter. Have you?"

"I am doing so."

"Do I have your sacred word that you are not a threat to the monastery or our undertaking?"

For an instant, both rage and torment appeared in Brother Hilliard's eyes. Then were gone. "I would never willingly be so. You must know that."

"I do. Still, you have not answered."

Brother Hilliard lowered his head.

The abbot was silent. "Brother Hilliard," he said at last, "I am removing you from the priorship for the duration of the Retreat."

"Your will is my duty."

Removal was not enough.

"Further, you will not spend one minute alone until I advise you differently. Not in work, prayer or meditation. I will arrange a schedule of brothers. You will be in the company of one of them each moment of the night and day."

Brother Hilliard stiffened. "Yes, my abbot."

"You may go now."

The prior closed the door behind him.

Later that evening Brother Martin encountered Brother Harold. Brother Harold was coming from the laundry. He was carrying, on a wooden hanger, a long and filmy white gown of Grecian cut.

Lily's gown.

He held it straight out with a rigid arm. His carriage was tense. There was both anxiety and a faraway wistfulness in his face.

Brother Harold did not even notice Brother Martin.

Brother Harold was a young man.

The abbot made a mental note: it would be best to keep him distanced from Lily when she arrived.

Without realizing it, Brother Martin slowed his step and then came to a halt. He watched the gown as Brother Harold carried it down the hall. It billowed. Gently. Delicately.

He thought of Gwen, his wife.

She had been beautiful, with remarkable green eyes.

He'd cut her throat.

There was never any trouble about the murder of his father's employer. He hadn't even been questioned. It was simply filed as an unsolved killing. He was invited to live in a makeshift room in the attic of the house of a friend. Martin was on the school football team. His friend's father was big and rough and wished his own son were more rugged. He thought at first that Martin would help his son become more of a man. Martin didn't like him. But he did like the man's wife, who was good to him.

She was probably the only woman he ever truly liked in his life.

He wanted to fuck her, too. But he didn't try because he thought it would upset her.

At the end of Martin's senior year the man punched his wife during an argument. Martin jumped on him. He was smaller and not as strong as the man, but he beat him up badly. A school guidance counselor took the boy into his own home for the summer and managed to arrange a football scholarship at the University of Minnesota for him.

His coach was excited. "You got it. The killer instinct. The real stuff, baby."

That made Martin smile.

But the coach played him less and less.

Killer instinct was a sports fantasy. The authentic article was something else.

Martin started to hang around bars with townies. He drank a lot. He got into fights.

The coach rarely sent him into a game now, only when they were losing badly and a key player on the opposing team *had* to be taken out. Martin would take him out.

He impregnated a townie named Gwen. Her father forced a marriage. Martin didn't mind much because she was beautiful and they had good times drinking and smoking dope together and he liked to fuck her. She miscarried, which didn't bother either of them. They stayed married. It was fun getting stoned. He fucked her like a rutty dog. She liked it.

There were complaints in the conference about his savagery on the field. The coach cut him from the team. His scholarship was rescinded. He didn't care. He'd come mostly to play football.

He tried the pros as a free agent; they weren't as squeamish about brutality. But he was too small to crush men of the size he'd have to play against.

He and Gwen were doing a lot of drugs. He met people in

bars. They got him into robbery, some hijacking. The alcohol and drugs began to cause fights between him and Gwen. She knew enough about his childhood to strike where he was most vulnerable. He knocked her around.

One night he got into a fight at a crap game. The rest of the players grabbed their money and ran. He and the other man slugged it out in the alley. He beat the man to death. There were no witnesses.

Money was hard. He and Gwen were drunk or wasted half the time. They went at each other a lot. She said she was going to leave him. He said go ahead. She threatened him with other men: that made him a little crazy.

He was dealing dope and carrying a gun. A cop stumbled into a buy. Martin shot him. He threw the gun into a storm sewer that night. Guns had never appealed to him anyway; he liked things close and personal.

He had a real screamer with Gwen six months after the shooting. He knocked out two of her teeth. She spat her own blood at him. She grabbed her purse, jerked it open and pulled out a prophylactic. It was a used prophylactic, cold and weighted at its tip with a load of jism. She threw it in his face and told him that's what she'd been doing this afternoon, that's what she'd been doing every afternoon.

He cut her throat.

They didn't have many friends. The few there were had all heard her say over and over that she was going to leave him. Her father was dead, her mother had disowned her years ago and she had no brothers or sisters. Martin told people Gwen had walked out on him and that he didn't know where she'd gone. California maybe. No one thought to doubt him.

He worked as a goon for landlords who were clearing out old buildings and rooming houses in neighborhoods undergoing gentrification. He liked the work. He battered down doors and trashed apartments. He beat people in hallways.

People in the bars he drank at said, You're gonna kill someone sooner or later.

People didn't know shit.

Then one morning he was sitting hung over on the edge of his bed in a furnished room when a social worker knocked on his door. A frail man with glasses. One of his clients was a pensioner in a rooming house Martin was clearing. Martin had broken the old man's leg with a kick. The bone had made a sound like a wooden match snapping, up close to the ear. He could have broken the social worker's back without much more effort. It would have gone *ch-kk!* He wanted to. But the man knew too much about him, and had left a sealed letter with a friend.

All Martin had to do, he said, was make a retreat in a monastery in New York. Do that one thing and the letter got burned, Martin didn't owe him anything else and could go on with his life.

Now, nearly a decade and a half later, Brother Martin was abbot of Saint Hector's.

And the Retreat was about to begin.

Chapter 11

The intercom buzzed. Caparelli answered. The doorman said, "Your car is here, Mr. Caparelli."

"Thanks, Rufe."

Pomona came out from the living room. "So. It's time."

Making love last night she'd clasped him as tightly and rocked him as tenderly as she had when they were first married. He knew she would miss him. She always did when he was gone.

And Christ, it was going to be hard sleeping alone. He liked nestling into her broad warm back and round rump, his hand on her big nurturing breast.

"Uh-huh," he said. He picked up his suitcase, which was already at the door.

She put her hands on his shoulders. "You'll call me?"

"I'll try. I don't know if I can." Sometimes he did. When there was serious business and it was best that she didn't know where he was, he didn't.

"And you'll be back in two and a half weeks." She hadn't asked where he was going. If he'd wanted her to know, he would have told her, and she accepted that.

"Yeah. I should be able to wrap everything up by then."

She kissed him. "I hope everything goes well."

"It will. You're gonna be okay, right? You got the tickets for the musicals. You're goin' with Mrs. Santini. You got the credit cards. You got the reservations for you and Maria and Carl and Tony next week in the Poconos. You got it all, right?"

"You worry like an old man over nothing. Each time you

go away you say the same thing. Yes, I have everything. Yes, I'm going to have a good time."

"Okay. You need anything, you tell Paulie. He'll check in with you every day."

"Yes, I'll tell Paulie. You better go now, your driver's waiting."

She didn't know that Orson was behind the wheel. Just a driver. Maybe Paulie, maybe someone else. Caparelli had followed Hawthorne's instructions to the letter. It was a fruitcake deal, but better than time in the slammer.

He gave her a hug with his free arm and a loud kiss. "G'bye, *cara mia*. You take care of yourself."

"You too, Dommy."

"I do that better than anyone else in the world, except you."

She nodded, her face uncharacteristically sober. "Just, this time—take very good care."

He suppressed a smile. For the next two and a half weeks he couldn't be safer.

"I love you," he said.

"I love you," she said.

He left, went down the elevator and through the lobby.

"Good morning, Mr. Caparelli," the doorman said.

"Mornin', Rufe."

Orson was waiting in a green Plymouth sedan that Hawthorne had rented for them. He wore silvered aviator's glasses. The top buttons of his shirt were open, a gold chain around his neck. "Nice day for a drive," he said, pulling away from the misting fountains. "Though I'd rather be on the way to Atlantic City. Think maybe we can sneak over there instead?"

"Yeah. Sure. And then you can visit me in the joint."

Caparelli wasn't happy. No booze. No broads. No opera. They damn well better not object to his cigars.

"It was a joke," Orson said quietly.

Caparelli had blistered him over the Mary Tedesco incident and was still not happy with him. Orson didn't want to push. Caparelli was a nut about his daughter. Orson was always careful what he said about her. They drove across Seventy-ninth Street and got onto the West Side Highway, took the Palisades Parkway to the Thruway where they headed north, toward the Adirondacks. Caparelli asked how long a trip it was.

"About seven hours."

"Wonderful."

He slouched down, leaned his head back and closed his eyes. He slept in fits and starts, waking to rub his eyes and stare glumly out the window awhile before dozing off again. Somewhere around Utica he discovered he couldn't sleep anymore. Unhappily, he fiddled with the radio. To his delight he found a broadcast of *Il Troavatore,* still in the first act.

"Shit," he said. "All the way up here in the sticks. Can you beat that?"

He turned the volume up and listened raptly, breaking into voice with the baritone. When the station began to fade half an hour later, he told Orson to stop the car. He got out and raised the aerial as high as it would go. He was able to hold the station through most of the final act. He didn't complain about missing the end—he was cheered by what he *had* heard, and there was only another hour to drive.

He said, "'Saint Dominic.' How does that sound?"

"You can't sentence a saint to prison."

"That's what I was thinking. I'm gonna pray real hard. Sullivan gets his report, he'll think he's seen the Second Coming."

"Saint Dominic," Orson said. *"Cappo di tutti Santi."*

Caparelli laughed hugely, which relieved Orson.

The landscape became awesome. Juggernauts of variously hued mountains rose above them. They passed deep gorges where white water crashed and roared, went through hardwood forests and dense stands of pines, past cold lakes whose depth made the water seem black. Neither derived any pleasure from this. They were of the city, where a river was an oily channel with tugboats and where trees were something that grew out of a square of dirt cut into the sidewalk. They were not enchanted. They were uneasy. This was alien.

Scanandaga was a flat little town on the edge of a lake. They reached it in the late afternoon. Since it was a community largely dependent upon summer and winter vacationers, there was a preponderance of sporting goods stores, restaurants and tourist shops.

"I think maybe we better stop and eat here," Caparelli said. "Who knows what they serve at the monastery? It can't be great."

They picked the restaurant with the highest-priced menu: if you intended to gouge the tourists, you had at least to try for something that seemed worth the money. Orson had *Moules Poulette* and Caparelli ordered the Surf & Turf.

"That was almost good," Caparelli said when they left. "Maybe we'll stop here on the way back."

"If we must."

"Get a steak next time. Even the waiter couldn't pronounce what you ordered. What do you expect?"

Hawthorne had given Caparelli a hand-drawn map. They followed it out of Scanandaga down a series of backcountry roads that didn't appear on the state highway map. They wound around mountains and through dense forest.

Orson kept check on the odometer. "It should be coming up any moment. Watch for two pillars. On the right."

Shortly, as they rounded a bend, Caparelli said, "There."

The pillars weren't much higher than a man. They were made of cobblestones. Choker vines grew around them. A metal plaque bolted to one said: PRIVATE. NO ADMITTANCE. Iron rings were set into both as anchors to which some sort of barricade could be shackled. Hanging from one ring was a handlettered wooden sign that said *Saint Hector's*.

"It ain't much," Caparelli said.

"Just think about Acapulco. This is why we went."

"We might have to go again."

"A reasonable proposal."

Orson turned in between the pillars. A brownrobed monk in his forties, wearing the tonsure, sat on a wooden stool off to the side reading a devotional. He closed the book, picked up a clipboard and came to the side of the car. "Hello. I'm Brother Phelan. Can I help you?"

Orson reached through the open window and shook the monk's hand. "Orson DiPalo. This is Mr. Caparelli. We're expected for a retreat, I believe."

Brother Phelan looked down at his clipboard. "Yes. It's good to see you, gentlemen." He checked off their names. "Our road is rough going—we don't commune much with the outside world here—but it *is* passable. Just take it slowly. It's about two-thirds of a mile. We look forward to having you with us."

"Thank you," Orson said, most sincere. "It's good to be here."

The road was actually more of a firebreak, a narrow lane sliced through virgin forest and overgrown with tall grass. The grass was pressed down in two files indicating the recent passage of other vehicles. Big half-buried rocks jolted the car no matter how carefully Orson tried to ease over them. Washouts caused the undercarriage to scrape against the ground. Branches and brush scratched at the doors.

The right front wheel dropped sharply, throwing Caparelli against the door. "Umph! They don't commune much with the world? They don't even *live* in the goddamn world."

"Forgive me, Uncle, but I think it's time to watch our language. I doubt phrases such as 'goddamn world' will be appreciated here."

"Tough."

"That's not the right attitude, I fear."

"How's this?" Caparelli folded his hands and lowered his head. "Bless me, Father, for I have sinned..."

"Oh, so much better. Probation for sure."

"That's what I like to hear."

Orson patted the dashboard. "Onward, little Repentance Express."

One moment they were in dimness beneath a canopy of towering trees and pressed by the undergrowth, the next they burst into late golden sunlight to behold the cleared valley and the surrounding mountains. Orson touched the brakes reflexively.

The monastery was squat and gray, two stories high and topped with a campanile. There were barns, a handful of worksheds and animal pens. A few monks were loading cabbages from the back of a horse-drawn wagon into baskets and carrying them into the monastery. Some were tonsured, bearded. Farther off, other monks could be seen working in the fields.

"If it weren't for those cars over there and that fence," Orson said, "I'd think I went through a time machine. It could be five hundred years ago, a thousand."

"I hope they got plumbing at least."

A bearded monk left the group at the wagon and motioned Orson over to the side, where three cars were parked. Orson pulled up beside a blue Toyota. He and Caparelli got out.

The monk offered his left hand—he had no right hand. "Brother Leopold," he said.

"Orson DiPalo."

"Dominic Caparelli."

"We've been expecting you. Was your trip pleasant?"

"It was a long way," Caparelli said. "It's like you guys— you, uh, brothers, like you don't even exist. I mean, way out here in the middle of nowhere."

"Yes. Isn't it. I'll take you to your accommodations. Would you follow me, please?"

They started after him.

He paused. "Your luggage."

Caparelli was accustomed to other people picking up his bags.

"I'll get them," Orson said.

Brother Leopold resumed walking toward the monastery. Orson took the bags out of the car and hurried to catch up.

Earlier in the morning, at roughly the time Orson and Caparelli were setting off from the city, Gunther Hauptmann had been lying on his bed in the Hotel Clarenton on West Twenty-sixth Street. He was awake and fully dressed, both pillows propped behind his back, and reading a mystery novel he'd bought in the Berlin airport. The radio, as cheap and unremarkable as the hotel itself, was tuned to bland background music. Hauptmann was relaxed and comfortable.

The telephone rang.

Hauptmann folded over the corner of the page and set the book aside. He picked up the receiver. "Hello?"

"Mr. Zuckerman?"

"Yes."

"Frank Smith of United Enterprises. Good morning. Did you enjoy a good night's sleep?"

The words were the proper identification code. Hauptmann gave the appropriate response. "Yes. Except for the interruption of an occasional siren. There must be a hospital nearby."

The caller was satisfied. "You can reach your party in twenty minutes at 734-5627. Do you have that?"

"Yes. Thank you."

"You're welcome."

They hung up.

734-5627.

Hauptmann never committed anything important to paper.

He put the book in his bag, which was already packed, zippered it closed, went down to the colorless lobby and checked out, paying with cash. He walked down Twenty-sixth Street toward Second Avenue, where there was a public telephone booth.

After he'd cleared customs last evening he'd made a call from the airport to a New Jersey number. He was told how to obtain what he needed for immediate security and the name of the hotel at which he was to stay. He took the airport bus into the Manhattan terminal and walked from there to the Port Authority: taxi drivers had to keep records of their trips.

The sprawling Port Authority building had been renovated since his last trip. It was pleasing enough in an undistinguished way and certainly an improvement upon its former, seedy condition.

He went into a restroom on the main floor, entered the third toilet stall and locked the door. He knelt on one knee and probed behind the commode with his hand. He located and removed the small locker key taped to the porcelain. He washed his hands, then went to a bank of lockers on the Ninth Avenue side of the terminal. He opened the locker. Inside was a small blue nylon flight bag. He took that to another restroom and again locked himself in a toilet stall. He dropped his pants and sat down, so things would look normal to a casual eye that might strike the space at the bottom of the door, and placed the bag on his knees. Within it were a 9mm Browning automatic, a belt-clip holster, two thirteen-round magazines, full, and a box of fifty cartridges.

He fieldstripped and examined the pistol, then put it back together. He slid the first few rounds from each magazine, inspected them, held them to his ear and shook them, hearing the soft *sluff* of powder. He replaced them and checked the cartridges in the box. Satisfied, he returned the box of cartridges and one magazine to the flight bag. He stood and buckled his pants. He flushed the toilet. While the water rushed noisily, he inserted the magazine into the pistol butt, coughed loudly and quickly worked the action, jacking a shell into the chamber. He lowered the hammer carefully. He slid the pistol into the holster and clipped the holster inside his waistband. His jacket was plain, but had been custom tailored for this purpose and it concealed the gun butt without a bulge.

He left the Port Authority and went to the Hotel Clarenton. In his room, he read until it was time for the late-night news. He turned the television on. There was film from Berlin of the wreckage of the terminal. Nineteen dead. Fifty-three wounded. *Der Spiegel* had received a telephone call from an organization claiming responsibility. The caller threatened an attack of greater magnitude unless three of its members, currently imprisoned, were freed and flown to Libya immediately.

Hauptmann had no connection with the organization other than that they had paid him. He was a specialist. His only cause was himself.

Now, in the morning, walking toward the phone booth on the corner, he stopped to crumple up the blue flight bag and stuff it into a garbage can. He checked his watch when he reached the corner. He stalled a few minutes, looking about as if waiting for someone. He picked up the receiver at the precise time, got the tone and dropped in a dime.

He converted 743-5267 into 834-4358, a simple up-and-down code.

"Hello."

Hauptmann heard street noises through the receiver. His contact was also using a public phone. "This is Mr. Zuckerman," he said.

"Did Frank Jones ask you to call?"

"No," Hauptmann said. "Frank Smith."

"Good." The identification was complete. "Your safe house is upstate. You're Peter Moss. You're expected for a retreat at the monastery of Saint Hector." The man gave him the license number and location of Moss's car. "Your documents are in the glove compartment. You'll be contacted at the monastery in a few days. Oh, yes. I'm told to congratulate you. The work was excellent."

"Thank you."

The car was a tan Dodge on West Fifteenth. The keys were in a small magnetic box inside the left wheel well. Hauptmann went through the wallet in the glove compartment. There was a driver's license, credit cards and personal papers all in the name of Peter Moss. The work was good. There was also a marked highway map and a typed set of directions to follow out of the town of Scanandaga.

He started the car, put it in gear and swung into the street. He admired and was amused by the use of a monastery as a safe house.

The sculpted power of Brother Cooper's torso was mostly hidden by his loose-fitting sport shirt as he waited at Kennedy Airport. Despite the warmth of the day he wore the sleeves rolled down and the cuffs buttoned at his wrists. A great snake was tattooed in a coil around his left forearm, a horned dragon on his right. It was best for these not to be seen. The flight from Los Angeles had docked at its berth a few minutes ago and the passengers were now emerging from the connecting corridor into the terminal. Brother Cooper had photographs in the hip pocket of his slacks of each of the six men he was to meet this morning, though he didn't think he'd have to refer to them again. Certainly not for this man.

He saw him, carrying a leather briefcase, and waited until he had cleared the velvet ropes and entered the hall. Brother Cooper stepped forward and smiled politely. "Mr. Marcus?"

The man was towering, obese. He turned a sour face. "Yeah. Who are you?"

"Your driver, sir. I have to meet another gentleman here. Why don't you go to the restaurant and have a cup of coffee or some breakfast if you're hungry. I'll claim your bag for you."

"Coffee, hell. I want a drink. I couldn't sleep on the damn plane and I've been up all night."

"There's a bar next to the restaurant, sir. I'll be happy to call for you there. It should only be forty-five minutes."

"All right."

Marcus went to the bar and ordered a double Scotch. The waitress was Puerto Rican. She had great tits. He stared at them when she brought his drink. She hurried away. He laughed and took a big swallow. He didn't see why he couldn't have come in the day before and gotten a good night's sleep at the Plaza. But that fuckin' doctor had him by the *cojones*. Did the idiot really think a couple of weeks in a monastery were going to turn him into a Holy Roller? Well, boredom was a small price to pay—the asshole could destroy his career, even get him jailed.

He managed to down three doubles before the driver came for him. They walked through the terminal. "I thought you were picking up someone else," Marcus said. The alcohol had improved his mood.

"He went directly to the van, sir. We're on a tight schedule. There wasn't any use in your having to wait at his gate with me."

Marcus decided he'd tip the man well.

The van was a third of the way into the parking lot. Marcus stopped.

Pimp.

The man in the first of the vehicle's three rows of seats was black. He wore a plum suit with wide lapels, a white silk shirt with wing collar tips and a widebrim plum hat with a fluffy peacock feather fixed in the band. He was in his late twenties.

What the hell?

"I think there'll be more room if I put myself back here," Marcus said, sliding ponderously into the second rank of seats.

"As you wish, sir." Brother Cooper stowed Marcus's bag. He got into the driver's seat. "Mr. Johnson, this is Mr. Marcus. Mr. Marcus, Mr. Johnson."

Pretty Boy flashed the fat man a big wide smile, showing off his goldrimmed tooth with its little diamond chip. Oh, he knew this ofay. Money. Power. Used to making people jump. This was a motherfucker with a pig appetite who liked to do the dirty. Pretty Boy had a nose for his kind. He thrust his hand back. "How do, Mr. Mark."

"*Marcus*." Marcus gave Pretty Boy's multi-ringed hand a perfunctory shake.

"Raight."

Brother Cooper drove them out onto the access road that led to the expressway.

After several minutes, Pretty Boy turned to Marcus again. "So how's it goin', bro? Where you from?"

He knew the pig didn't like him. He also had seven grams of shiny flake stashed in his bag and two ounces of primo Hawaiian—if he was going to be stuck in the boonies he'd made damn sure he'd brought enough to keep him happy; and some extra: there was almost always business to do, no matter where you were.

"I'm from Los Angeles. I'm tired, Mr. Johnson. I've been up all night. I'm going to catch some sleep." Marcus leaned back and closed his eyes.

"Well, you sleep tight, Mr. Marky. We all'll give you a wake-up when we get there."

Pretty Boy was happy with himself.

You close your li'l eyes an' try t' tune me out, whey-face. But Pretty Boy knows what you like, an' Pretty Boy knows you goin' be layin' heavy bread on him for some o' that lovely flake before this is all over. Yas. Oh, yas.

Ten minutes onto the expressway Pretty Boy tapped Brother Cooper on the shoulder. "Hey man, can we get some sound in here?"

"Sound, sir?"

"Music, m' man."

"Oh. I'm sorry, sir. The radio isn't working."

Pretty Boy sighed. He looked out the window. They were passing what seemed to be an endless cemetery, incongruously set against the skyline of Manhattan, rank after rank of tightly packed tall thin weatherworn headstones.

Pretty Boy slapped out a rhythm on his knees, twisting his shoulders. *"Ba-*ditty-*ba-*ditty-*ba-*ditty-*boom. Ba-*ditty-*ba-*ditty-ba-ba-*boom. Boom-*ditty-*boom-*ditty..."

They drove into the city and down Ninth Avenue, to the Port Authority terminal. Brother Cooper recognized the man from his photograph. He was waiting on the sidewalk with a plastic suitcase beside him, thirtyish, blond, chubbycheeked and potbellied, wearing a tan leisure suit with a yellow shirt open at the neck.

Brother Cooper pulled to the curb, got out and raised his eyebrows in question. "Mr. Bates?"

"Yup. That's me. You the one that's gonna take me up to that monastery place?"

"Yes, sir." Brother Cooper lifted Bates's bag.

"Good t' see you. Lookin' forward t' it. Nice t' get some peace an' quiet now and then, do a little soul-searchin'."

"Yes, sir."

Bates looked at Pretty Boy, at Marcus, then opened the door to the last row of seats. He smiled widely. "How do, boys? Bates is the name. Peter T. Bates."

"Marcus."

Nigger-hater. But Pretty Boy smiled anyway, just as widely. "Floyd Johnson."

"Long bus ride," Bates said cheerfully. "But I slept most o' the way, and there was some good ol' boys t' jaw with, so I can't complain, no sir. Had me a good breakfast at that Walgreen's in there too. Ham an' eggs. Don't you people have no grits up here?"

"Oh, I expect they's some aroun'," Pretty Boy said, affecting a drawl. "But prob'ly not in the neighbo'hoods you be lahkly t' find yo'self."

Bates laughed uproariously, as if Pretty Boy had just told him a gut-funny joke. "Probably right, probably right. Woo-ee, so this is what they call the Big Apple, huh?"

Roger Ballantine debarked from the Metroliner in Pennsylvania Station beneath Madison Square Garden. Carrying a Mark Cross leather bag in his right hand, which was ornamented with a large diamond in a platinum setting, he walked down the platform toward the escalator. He was forty-three, tall, in excellent condition and had a handsome rectangular face. He was silverhaired and he wore his hair long in thick wings brushed back over his ears. Dressed in light gray slacks, a blue blazer, light blue shirt and a regimental tie, he could have passed for an actor or a statesman. He was in fact a urological surgeon.

He'd caught the early Metro out of Washington, breakfasted and read the *Times* and the *Wall Street Journal* in the club car on the way up. He was no stranger to the trip. He made it at least once a month to shop and to see theater in the company of a woman who was the former wife of an old classmate. She was an ideal companion, beautiful, stylish, and as disdainful and cold as was he. They appreciated each other. Once or twice a year they would sleep together; neatly, precisely, because it seemed the civilized thing to do. He had a somewhat similar friend in Washington. The two were quite sufficient.

Usually he would have been pleased to be in New York. But this morning, riding up the escalator, he was not. He was angry and apprehensive. Five weeks ago, when Cowley had first confronted him, he'd been terrified. Cowley had been Marian LeGarde's psychotherapist. Marian LeGarde had died in an automobile crash totally unrelated to Ballantine's treatment of her. But she'd discussed her surgery of a year earlier with Cowley. For some reason, and somehow, Cowley had then compiled a dossier on Ballantine that could ruin him, even liable him to criminal prosecution.

Astonishingly though, all Cowley seemed to want from him was that he attend a retreat in a monastery in New York. If he did, then the therapist would exit his life and everything would be forgotten. Ballantine came to believe him over the weeks, as the arrangements were made. It simply firmed his conviction that every psychotherapist was a lunatic of one kind or another.

He reached the top of the escalator. A plainfaced man in slacks and a sport shirt raised a hand. "Mr. Ballantine?"

"Yes. Are you from Saint Hector's?"

"Yes, sir. I'm your driver. Will you come with me, sir?" He took Ballantine's bag and led him over to the Information counter where two other men stood.

"Mr. Ballantine, this is Mr. Rivera and Mr. Wycisowicz. They'll be riding with us. Mr. Rivera doesn't speak much English."

They shook hands. Rivera was short and darkcomplected, with flattish features. He wore a tailored suit and dark sunglasses.

Brother Cooper said, "I'll take you to the van now, gentlemen. We'll be heading directly upstate."

A second van, identical to the first except that it was blue, was parked in the lot of the Newark airport, just across the river in New Jersey. There were five men within it. They were waiting for the driver to return with the sixth, and last.

Vitek Jaretzki sat in the second row of seats along with a big lumpenproletarian named Rauscher who rolled a toothpick back and forth from one corner of his mouth to the other while he looked blankly out the window, apparently at nothing. Jaretzki was focused internally; he was a man sensitive to the odd, the dark, the byways, the small slit of perfect skin with a dark pearl of blood; and his instincts told him that something beyond what he'd first thought was afoot here.

Jaretzki was forty-eight, a shade under six feet, knife-thin and ropily muscled. He swam, he played handball. He had a long narrow face and his features were sharp, almost pointed, as if his skin were stretched too tightly across his bones. If he stared at someone, they would often take an involuntary step back.

He'd had excellent sex with the wife of a Danish diplomat last night, and this morning had taken a fine breakfast of cheese, fruit and croissants *chocolates* in the vine-walled garden of Le Recontre. He was a stoic. Once resigned to something, it did not gnaw at him. So he was in good spirits when Jean, his waiter, informed him that his driver had arrived.

The driver was in his fifties, balding, tanned and weather-beaten, and his slacks and shortsleeved shirt didn't fit him well. He picked up Jaretzki's bag. "We're down the street, sir."

Jaretzki was introduced to the two men in the front seat.

Mr. Ableman. Mr. Sawyer.

Both appeared uninteresting.

"Are you by any chance *Vitek* Jaretzki, the photographer?" Sawyer asked. He was a young man of about thirty, with a friendly, even solicitous face.

Jaretzki smiled. His teeth were perfect. They weren't his own. His childhood in early Poland, the war years and then the DP camps, had destroyed those. "Yes, I am."

Sawyer shook his hand a second time. "It's a *pleasure* to meet you. I think your work is terrific."

Jaretzki was amused. Most of his work appeared in high-fashion magazines, with which he would doubt Sawyer had much contact, and was not of a nature he'd have thought the man would find appealing. Sawyer looked the kind of person about which people would say, He's a *nice* man.

"Thank you," Jaretzki said. "I'm flattered."

From conversation between Sawyer and Ableman while they drove downtown to pick up their next passenger, Jaretzki learned that they were both in social work, Ableman associated with a home for retarded children. That surprised him; Ableman carried himself stiffly and his eyes were hard, which didn't fit well with concern for defective children.

The driver was Lawrence—Sawyer used his name. Sawyer was Phil, and he preferred that to Mr. Sawyer. Jaretzki imagined he was a very good social worker. He had the manner.

Lawrence found a parking space a block away from Penn Station and was gone for twenty minutes.

He returned with Mr. Rauscher. Rauscher, a lumbering man with a jagged scar on one cheek, had a toothpick in his mouth. He settled into the seat across from Jaretzki without saying anything, put his elbow on the armrest, planted his big chin in his hand and stared out the window. He reacted to nothing they passed and to nothing that was said as they proceeded downtown. Jaretzki had owned an iguana once. It would remain motionless for hours, life evident only in the slow pulse of its sides and an occasional blink, its attention, Jaretzki fancied, fixed back in the Devonian age, dreaming of giant dragonflies and awesome ferns, thick heat and endless swamps.

They drove to East Sixth Street and Avenue A. Decaying buildings. Garbage. Burned-out cars. Loud music from open windows. Entropy and menace.

Jaretzki knew the neighborhood. He was equally at home in co-ops on Sutton Place and crash pads where people got hepatitis from dirty needles. One street up, behind the rundown facade of an old trucking company, was a rarefied after-hours club he enjoyed.

Lawrence pulled to the curb. An Hispanic in his late twenties was waiting on the corner. He wore skintight shirt and pants, glossy black high-heeled boots and was laden with gold—chains around his neck, a heavy bracelet on each wrist and rings on several fingers. There was a Gucci bag at his side. Most of the Hispanics in this neighborhood were Puerto Rican, with some Colombians and Ecuadorians. Jaretzki decided that this young man was Mexican, and people who knew his eye wouldn't have bet against him.

By his stance, the kid was perfectly at ease. With all that gold, in this neighborhood, that would suggest backups, protection. Jaretzki examined the street. There wasn't any. This kid didn't give a fuck. He was a badass. For real. The street people wouldn't make a mistake. Jaretzki didn't doubt that he was armed. But his clothes were so tight it was hard to decide where he kept the gun. It would be a gun; he would never go the halfway route of a knife. The boots. Of course. Most likely a nice compact .380. A small caliber, but with hollowpoints and hotloads, as this kid would use, enough to stop anybody but a tank like Rauscher; him too with a direct heart or head shot, and Jaretzki was certain the kid could do that.

Interesting.

This retreat might offer something after all.

The kid got into the seat behind Jaretzki. He was named Rios. He was haughty, sullen. He didn't say anything during the ride out to Newark Airport.

Rauscher chewed his toothpick.

Sawyer talked with Ableman.

Jaretzki mused.

At Newark, the driver had picked up their last passenger. He was introduced as Mr. Kennedy. Kennedy wore his graying black hair down to his shoulders, a black headband cinching it back from his face. He was bearded. He was Ableman's age, about forty, but the dissipation of his face made him look older. He wore solid black, shoes, socks, pants and shirt. There was a small silver hoop in each of his ears and a silver pentacle hanging from a chain around his neck. Neither his hair nor his beard had been washed recently. His eyes were bright and angry. They dismissed everyone peremptorily but Jaretzki, on whom they lingered a moment, and Rios, toward whom he curled his mouth slightly in challenge.

Rios smiled back, a slow feral display of teeth.

Jaretzki was enchanted.

When the driver entered the Palisades Parkway and headed north some fifteen minutes later, Kennedy took out a pack of cigarettes and lit one.

In the front seat Sawyer asked, "Say, would you mind holding off on that? It really bothers me."

Kennedy looked at him several moments in silence. He pulled smoke into his lungs, exhaled. "The windows are open, man. You're not going to get cancer." He leaned back, turned his eyes to the passing greenery on the median and smoked.

The first van, brown, was passing the Poughkeepsie turnoff.

Pretty Boy said to the driver, "Hey, Poughkeepsie! You remember from that movie *The French Connection?* The cop Popeye grabs guys, slams 'em up against the wall and yells,

'You from Poughkeepsie, huh? You from Poughkeepsie? Are you?' Shakes 'em all up, they don't know what's happenin'. You remember that?"

"I'm sorry, sir, I never saw the film."

Pretty Boy was incredulous. "Everyone saw *The French Connection.*"

"I'm sorry, sir."

"What's your name, man?"

"Cooper, sir."

"Well, what do you do for kicks, Coop? How d' you un-wind?"

"Oh . . . I don't know, sir. I go for walks. Things like that, I suppose."

"Coop, I'm going t' have t' have a long talk with you."

"Yes, sir."

To Wycisowicz, seated next to him, Pretty Boy said, *"You* remember."

"Sure."

"Figured you would."

"You'd o' *bet* I would."

Pretty Boy grinned. "You ever slam anybody up against the wall?"

Wycisowicz grinned back. "Never asked 'em if they were from Poughkeepsie, though."

"Gimme skin, bro."

They slapped hands.

Behind them, Ballantine was talking with Marcus about Broadway theater. He asked, "What do you do, Mr. Marcus?"

"I'm in the entertainment business."

Wycisowicz asked Pretty Boy, "And what do you do, Mr. Johnson?"

"I'm in the entertainment business too," Pretty Boy said.

"Figured you were."

"You'd o' bet I was."

"Right," said Wycisowicz.

Rivera, who was not Rivera, who was Cesar Alvarado, and

who did indeed speak English despite what the driver had said, sat silently in the rear seat across from Bates listening to his fellow passengers carefully. He had passed the journey appearing to watch the scenery or read a book.

Perhaps there was no point in this exercise and he should simply let it unfold as it would—it had all been planned—but to glean fragments of information as he could, and to try to fit them into a pattern was partly his nature, and partly his job. The other part of his job, and equally a part of his nature, was to inflict pain.

Still.

The driver, Cooper: his quiet and unassuming service could be that of a legitimate functionary, or something else entirely. The black man Johnson; again, he might be what he seemed, or he could be portraying a studied role. The man Wycisowicz was carrying a gun in a belt holster beneath his jacket. He was definitely a policeman, and just as definitely nothing more than a policeman. The banter between him and the black man was credible. Since he was too limited for subtle deception, that would argue in favor of Johnson being what he appeared to be too.

The huge sleepyeyed man with the hanging jowls, Marcus. Now here was a man of cunning and intelligence. For all his polite conversation with his seatmate Ballantine, he had revealed virtually nothing at all about himself. He had secrets. A dangerous man probably. But only where his *self* was threatened. He was interested in nothing more and he did not attach that self to any larger principle. Ballantine, Alvarado disregarded. One of this country's privileged. Confident, presumptive, arrogant. A man with little heart. Alvarado could have had him screaming within fifteen minutes.

Bates was a simple person, exactly what he'd announced himself to be—a prison guard. Alvarado knew many like him. They were useful in the police, in the army, in the prisons. Because they were strong, not burdened with intelligence, and angry that they would never achieve the position of men like

Ballantine, or even this man Johnson, and they would follow orders and do anything you wanted as long as you tossed them a piece of meat now and then.

Alvarado was perplexed. He thought he'd have seen one of his counterparts by now. And while he admired being worked into what was apparently an authentic retreat as cover, he felt that he should have been able to ferret out the common denominator in the others, who were not involved in what he was. A retreat, like any group endeavor, presupposed a community of interest on some level, and he could see none yet in these men.

This vexed him, signifying as it did lacunae in his perception. It humbled him too, because it made him realize that there were levels beyond his own and that he was truly in the hands of experts.

Brother Lawrence pulled the blue van up beside Orson and Caparelli's Plymouth just after six in the evening. Several monks appeared as the passengers got out and stretched themselves and they began to unload the baggage.

"It's beautiful," Jaretzki said to Brother Lawrence, looking from the monastery to the sunwashed valley, the mountains beyond. "Tranquil. Pastoral. An excellent setting for a retreat."

"Yes, sir. We think so."

"Do you work here?"

"I live here."

Jaretzki was surprised. "Are you a monk?"

"Yes, sir. Brother Lawrence."

Only now did Jaretzki realize that he hadn't bothered to learn the man's name.

Kennedy, who was standing next to them, said, "Where's your robe, brother?" In his mouth, "brother" described something unpleasant lying dead in the road.

"In my cell, sir. We don't always wear them when we go out from here."

"Do you go out often? Paint the town?"

"We very rarely leave, sir."

A monk a little over six feet with dark hair and silvered eyebrows was approaching with a purposeful stride. He gained the van and stopped beside Brother Lawrence.

"Gentlemen," Brother Lawrence said, "this is Brother Martin, the abbot of Saint Hector's."

Brother Martin shook each man's hand and welcomed them. He said, "These brothers will introduce themselves and take you to your rooms. We've done what we can to make them more comfortable for you, but you may still find them somewhat austere." He smiled slightly. "But then, a monastery is not a resort, and a retreat is not an occasion of frivolity, is it?"

He left.

Brother Lawrence told them they would be given towels and soap and shown the location of the lavatories so they could freshen up. Dinner would be served in an hour and a half. He assigned monks to help them. "You can relax in the library if you wish or stroll about the grounds."

He departed. The remaining monks picked up the luggage.

Brother Harold had Rauscher's bag. Rauscher directed his first words of the day to him. "Can I get a drink somewhere?" he asked.

Rios—who knew all about Catholics and monasteries from his cousin, a Capuchin monk, and who had two bottles of tequila in his bag—was behind him. He laughed.

Brother Harold said, "I'm afraid not, sir. We don't keep alcohol here. Would you come with me, please?"

The directions were excellent. Hauptmann found the two stone pillars that marked the access road without difficulty. He turned in. A monk with a clipboard approached the car.

"I'm Peter Moss," Hauptmann said. "I believe I'm expected for a retreat."

The monk checked off his name. "Yes, Mr. Moss, you are. We're happy to have you with us."

When Hauptmann emerged from the woods and saw the

monastery and valley against the surrounding mountains he was pleased. The image was aesthetically satisfying, the use of this medieval-looking monastery as a safe house an inspired idea.

He pulled his car up next to a blue van. A monk appeared within moments.

"Good afternoon. I'm Brother Conrad."

"Peter Moss."

"I'll take your bag. Was your trip pleasant?"

"Yes. Especially after I passed Albany. I've never seen the Adirondacks before. They're beautiful."

Brother Conrad nodded as they walked toward the monastery. "They are."

Hauptmann hesitated, noting the low wire fence. It was an anomaly.

He gestured. "What's that for?"

He was aware, by reflex, of the weight of his holstered gun. He was also aware that it *was* a reflex, and he suspended it momentarily.

"You'd have to ask Brother Abner, our agriculturalist. I think we're putting in a root crop—the soil isn't so rocky here—and it's to keep the rabbits out. Something like that. But I might be wrong." He touched Hauptmann's elbow unobtrusively and started him walking again. With barely a pause in his conversation he asked, "Where are you from, Mr. Moss?"

"Philadelphia."

"I was never in Philadelphia myself. Is it an interesting city?"

"I find it so."

"Ah, good. And what is your profession?"

"I'm an optics salesman. Mostly scientific."

"Aha. I understand that some truly remarkable things are being done in that field."

"Quite remarkable," Hauptmann said.

Brother Conrad had him at the monastery's entrance. He

stepped aside to allow Hauptmann to precede him. "Welcome to Saint Hector's, sir."

It was not an accident that the agile-minded Brother Conrad had been selected to greet Gunther Hauptmann.

Brother Cooper arrived in the brown van ten minutes later. Again Brother Martin emerged and greeted the penitents briefly. Monks took up their bags.

Norman O. Marcus looked around unhappily. He had napped some on the way up, but not nearly enough to compensate for last night's travel.

"Where can I get some sleep?" he asked the monk escorting him into the monastery. "I'm out on my feet."

"We'll be serving dinner in forty-five minutes, sir. Then the abbot would like to meet with you all in the chapel. After that you'll be perfectly free to retire for the night if you'd like."

"I'd like to retire for the night right now."

The monk smiled sympathetically. "It won't be long, Mr. Marcus."

A black monk, Brother William, with a tonsured head, had been assigned to Ballantine.

Pretty Boy sidled over to him. "Hey, babe. I didn't know there were bloods in this kind of place. Any more brothers here?"

"We're all brothers, sir," the monk said politely.

Pretty Boy rolled his eyes. "Right. Uh-huh. Well, carry on, bro."

Ballantine walked alongside Brother William. "This is all quite lovely."

"Thank you, sir."

"It must be a fine place for contemplation."

"It is. God has been good to us."

"Have you been a monk long?"

"Only a year, sir. But I've lived here three years. One as a postulant, then one as a novice."

"What decided you?"

"I was . . . called."

"I couldn't conceive of withdrawing from the world my-self."

"I guess none of us can—until the day we do," Brother William said.

Wycisowicz's guide was named Brother Stefan. A thick, vivid scar ran down across the monk's face. Wycisowicz had seen a lot of scars; it came with the job. This one looked like it had come from the sharp hooked point of a beer can opener. He would have liked to ask, simple professional curiosity, but he didn't know how sensitive the monk might be, or whether the question would be impolite.

Brother Gilbert was carrying Bates's plastic suitcase. Bates hadn't been quiet for more than a minute at a time all day. "This is just pretty as a picture card," he said. "Y'know, we don't have no mountains like this down home where I come from, and I don't know, I guess they make me feel kind of strange, like maybe giants lookin' over my shoulder, but they sure are impressive. An' this monastery building thing, it looks like somethin' I saw in a book when I was a kid in school, y'know? It . . ."

Brother Gilbert nodded his head slowly.

Cesar Alvarado, in the company of Brother Stewart, was the last in the file. His eyes were still hidden behind his sunglasses. He was silent. His perplexity had burgeoned into frustration. He still hadn't found the common factor among his fellow passengers.

The entrance to the monastery was double-doored. The doors were tall and thick: cross-set oak planking bound with strips of iron. Medieval doors. Doors that could have stood against a battering ram.

As Alvarado passed through and into the entrance hall, a monk stepped forward and swung them closed. They fell against their stone-and-iron casing with a deep *chunnk*, like the sound of a vault closing.

BOOK III

Deliver Us from Evil

Chapter 12

There was scarcely any conversation in the refectory. The penitents were uncertain of the decorums and therefore inhibited. They sat mostly in silence while the food was brought to the tables. There was roast beef, boiled potatoes and fresh green beans. Black bread and churned butter. Chilled water and steaming pots of coffee.

Kennedy, Bates and Rauscher reached for the platters. The monks beside them touched their arms and asked them to wait. Bates and Rauscher did. Kennedy tore off a hunk of bread, buttered it and bit into it. He chewed slowly, deliberately, moving his eyes about the table with defiance.

When the food had been set and the servers were in their seats, Brother Martin, at the head of the inverted U of tables, rose.

"My friends," he said, "we welcome you in God's name to the Monastery of Saint Hector. We take you into our hearts as our brothers in Christ. It is our hope that you will find the joy of the Lord here, that your spirits shall be cleansed and you will become new again. We will do all that we can to help you in this work.

"Though I met you all this afternoon, names are often overlooked or forgotten in the business of arrival." He smiled. "I am Brother Martin, the abbot. We'll be meeting in the chapel after dinner, at which time I'll tell you a bit about the monastery and say a few words on the nature of a retreat. Before each meal we take to ourselves a lesson. It is intended to be an inspiration, a subject of meditation and contemplation. Brother Stefan, our lector, will read this evening's lesson for us. Thank you, and again, welcome."

The abbot sat down.

Brother Stefan went to the lectern. He opened the large Bible with his thin hands and smiled out at them in a dreamlike way.

His voice was soft, but his enunciation clear. "My brothers, our lesson tonight is taken from the Holy Scriptures, the Seventh Psalm of David. Hear the words of the chosen of God."

He looked down.

"O Lord my God, in thee do I put my trust," he read. "Save me from all them that persecute me, and deliver me:

"Lest he tear my soul like a lion, rending it in pieces, while there is none to deliver.

"O Lord my God, if I have done this; if there be iniquity in my hands;

"If I have rewarded evil unto him that was at peace with me; (yea, I have delivered him that without cause is mine enemy:)

"Let the enemy persecute my soul and take it: yea, let him tread down my life upon the earth, and lay mine honor in the dust. Selah.

"Arise, O Lord, in thine anger, lift up thyself because of the rage of mine enemies: and awake for me to the judgment that thou has commanded..."

His eyes rose and drifted over them without focus. He recited the text from memory, focusing internally upon the words, only remotely aware that he was rendering them aloud.

"God judgeth the righteous, and God is angry with the wicked every day.

"If he turn not, he will whet his sword; he hath bent his bow, and made it ready.

"He hath also prepared for him the instruments of death; he ordaineth his arrows against the persecutors.

"Behold, he travaileth with iniquity, and hath conceived mischief, and brought forth falsehood.

"He made a pit, and digged it, and is fallen into the ditch which he made.

"His mischief shall return upon his own head, and his violent dealing shall come down upon his own pate.

"I will praise the Lord according to his righteousness: and will sing praise to the name of the Lord most high."

He was silent several moments. His eyes refocused. "That is our lesson for tonight, brothers. Think upon these words, for they are God's." He returned to his place at the table.

Brother Martin gave the blessing. They began to eat.

Norman O. Marcus was not happy. His three hundred pounds were the cumulative result of thousands of dollars in consort with untold hours of the best chefs in the nation. This was not fare to which he was accustomed. This was suitable only for a factory worker, as fuel in the time between a day's work and a night's bowling. He would have complained if he hadn't done so once already. Over his bed. Which, in a stone cell no bigger than a broom closet, wasn't wide enough for him and which had creaked loudly when he'd laid down to test it, threatening to come apart, and sagged so badly that he'd thought his back would break. Brother Abner, his guide, had said there were no others, they'd see what they could do to reinforce this one. Well, at least there was *enough* food, dull as it was.

Jaretzki poured himself a second cup of coffee after the meal but declined the unfrosted pound cake that was dessert. He was a disciplined eater who maintained himself in athletic trim and he was contemptuous of people like Marcus. He'd met Marcus on two or three occasions, at parties, and though the producer didn't recall him, and though he understood they had some slight commonality of taste in certain areas, he wasn't going to remind him of their acquaintance. The privileged and abstruse stratum in which Jaretzki generally moved tolerated such vulgarians only on its periphery.

Jaretzki had been dragooned into this retreat by the vice-president of a publishing conglomerate that owned a fashion magazine in which much of his work appeared. The man knew quite a bit about him, including both of the dead girls, and there had been no choice. The first girl had died of sepsis following a rectal hemorrhage. The second had committed suicide at the end of a long weekend with him. There was no danger of criminal prosecution, but he would be liable to civil action by the families of the dead girls, and all the publicity that would mean. He didn't care whether the mass mind considered him a pervert—he'd lived through the horrors of which the mass mind was capable, and he held that mind in loathing and detestation—but a scandal of such nature would force several of the designers and publications for whom he worked to shut him out. Everyone in his circle had closeted skeletons, but business was business and they would find it politic to distance themselves from him at least until the tabloids turned their gleeful attention to some new infamy. No, there hadn't been any choice.

And truth be told, his interest was piqued. By the odd lot of his fellow retreatants. By the charming medievalism. By the little details his photographer's eye had noted among the monks: the mutilated ear of one, the curiously bent finger of another, the gaudy dragon tattooed on the forearm of yet another, visible as he reached for a water pitcher. . . .

A pair of monks guided the penitents to the chapel when they were done with coffee. Bates was clasping his potbelly with satisfaction. "You fellows don't own any dogs at all?" he said to one of them. "I can't believe it. In this kind of country? Why you don't know what you're missin'. You go out at night into the woods with a couple o' good buddies and your ol' hounds an' a little somethin' t' keep your innards warm and spend a couple hours coonin', why there ain't nothin' like it atall for pure joy."

The vaulted chapel contained a simple wooden central altar, before which Brother Martin went to stand, and two smaller ones off in its short shadowed cross-arms. The guides directed the retreatants into the front pews.

The abbot waited for them to settle. "I know you're all tired from traveling, so I won't prolong this. But I do think a few words of introduction are necessary. When we make a retreat, we withdraw, we remove ourselves from the cares and demands of the outside world to a quiet and private place, a kind of refuge or sanctuary. It's a time of solitude, of contemplation and renewal. We look deeply into ourselves. We try to evaluate our lives and the state of our souls. One of the most important goals is to identify where we are in error, how we have departed from the will of God, rejecting His message of peace and love, and have therefore sinned against Him and against our fellow man. Through that knowledge, the *understanding* of our wrongness and the acceptance of our guilt, it is hoped that we will renounce our sin and pray that He will help us to cleanse our souls and emerge purified and restored into His love and on the path of righteousness.

"There are of course many ways to sin." He smiled sadly. "At least as many as there are to do good. Among what are known as the Seven Deadly Sins are Pride, Lust, Sloth and Avarice, for example. But here at Saint Hector's we're concerned with one of the Deadly Sins in particular. The one that hurts God most grievously, the one that drives love and charity from our hearts and that is especially hurtful to our fellow man. And that is the sin of Anger."

Several of the retreatants shifted uncomfortably. Kennedy snorted with disdain.

Brother Martin nodded. "I know," he said gently. "It's neither a pleasant nor a comfortable notion. And I know it not from a superior position, but from personal experience. As I'm certain we all do. What is Anger? How does it manifest itself? In its milder forms, it smolders within us turning God's grace into ashes, souring our hearts and wounding those around us. In its extreme, it is violent, murderous, catastrophic; it destroys God's children, whom He so loves."

He allowed them no time to react. "You've all taken the most important step. You're *here*. You've come because you've heard of us from friends or relatives, because you've received our literature in the mail, or however else you might have learned of us. The important thing is that you've come. We don't work miracles." He chuckled. "That's God's province. Be we *will* do everything in our power to help you purge yourselves.

"A retreat is a time to be more closely with yourself than perhaps you have ever been before. To confront yourself truly and to know that God and salvation are yours if only you desire them. We hope that you'll come to desire them. We pray that you will.

"Our schedule here is rigorous—we rise and breakfast, for example, hours before dawn—but we've modified it, particularly for the first few days, so you won't find it too demanding. Wake-up will be at eight-thirty tomorrow morning. We'll hold Mass here in the chapel at nine-fifteen. Many of you aren't Catholic, some not even Christians, and a few are atheists. That doesn't matter. God cares equally for those who accept Him and those who doubt His existence. They are all his children. There are two among our company who are ordained priests as well as monks of the order—Brother Stewart and Brother Abner. They will hear confession from any of you, regardless of your religious beliefs. Also, you are all permitted, encouraged, to receive the Eucharist tomorrow at Mass. Communion. I admonish you only thus: the Eucharist is the holiest of sacraments, the actual body and blood of Christ, and therefore, whether you are confessed or not, you should not partake of it without a repentant, open and loving heart."

He blessed them and ended the meeting.

There was a simple latch on the inside of Hauptmann's door, but no way to lock it. He removed the crock and washbasin from the small table beside the bed and set it up against the door. In the unlikely event that anyone tried to intrude without knocking, they'd have to push against the table, which would give him a second or two of latitude.

He surveyed the small cell carefully. It seemed exactly as he'd left it. He hadn't expected otherwise, but such caution had become instinct by now. He opened his suitcase and studied the careful arrangement of his clothes. Everything was in order. He dug to the bottom and took out his leather shower kit. He removed the toiletries and lifted the washcloth beneath which lay the Browning, the extra clip and the box of cartridges. He examined them, and was satisfied.

He put everything away and returned the table to its original position, replaced the crockery.

He took off his shoes and lay down on the bed, lacing his fingers beneath his head. The irony of the situation amused him. A retreat for violent men. Perhaps he might offer to guest-lecture.

Doubtless, he thought, this will be good for my soul.

He laughed out loud.

It was closing on dusk. The abbot stood by the edge of the pond. The long hanging branches of the willows along the bank undulated softly in the light breeze. The locusts had begun to chirr, even as the last songbirds were falling silent. The first bats had taken wing, swooping and darting over the pond—which was broken by surface-feeding fish—snatching up insects in their small toothed jaws. It was a quiet calm place at this time, good for solitude and meditation.

He did not hear the footfalls behind him. He was jarred from his reverie by the touch of Brother Conrad's hand upon his shoulder.

He had raised Brother Conrad to acting prior for the duration of the Retreat.

Still somewhat abstracted, he worked to focus himself. "You completed it?"

"Yes. You held them long enough. Hauptmann, DiPalo and Rios each have a handgun in their bags. There are cartridges in Wycisowicz's, but no gun. He must be carrying it. Probably habit, since he's a policeman."

Brother Martin nodded.

"Kennedy has a dagger," Brother Conrad said. "With an obscene and sacrilegious design on the handle. Rauscher has brass knuckles and a switchblade. Several of them have drugs—alcohol, cocaine and marijuana, some pills. Brother Raphael says the pills are mostly energizers and sedatives."

"All right. Thank you."

"Brother Anthony didn't have enough time in Rios's room."

"Tell him he's excused from Mass tomorrow, to do it then. Where are they now?"

"Various places. Their rooms, the library, walking around the grounds."

"Stay on top of them. Inform them that we're shutting the monastery down at—oh, give them till eleven this time. Have you selected a night watch?"

"Yes."

"Fine. I want to remain here awhile. I'll check with you before the night is over."

Brother Conrad left.

Max Rauscher stretched on his bed. He grunted. It had been a long bus ride from Indiana. He was tired. The bed was too short. Luckily the footboard wasn't high, so he could let his feet hang over. Thirty-one years old, Rauscher was six-foot-three and strong. He was carrying too much weight, but beneath the surface flesh were solid slabs of muscle.

That's what Rauscher was, muscle. Professional. He collected debts for loan sharks. He broke people into pieces.

He stared up at the ceiling, rolling a toothpick back and forth in his mouth. He wasn't thinking. He didn't often think. That was a hard, nearly painful thing to do.

But he was feeling. A heavy, clublike desire to crush something. To crush Fitzpatrick, his parole officer. Who was the reason he was stuck here now instead of out getting drunk.

He pictured Fitzpatrick. He pictured him squirming on the ground. He pictured himself kicking him, slowly, again and again.

In his cell, Brother Harold placed two pencils end to end on the floor, and then carefully knelt down upon them. He folded his hands and concentrated on the pain. He tried to see the pain as a color. He invited it to fill him.

But still the images intruded into his mind.

Out!

Pain.

It had been his task to search Gregorio Rios's room. In Rios's suitcase, beneath the bottles of tequila, had been two magazines. He'd had to riffle through them to be sure nothing was concealed within.

Women. Large color photographs of them. Lovely young breasted women. Mounded bottoms. Long legs. So lovely.

As lovely as the feel of the gown he had prepared last week. The incredible aching softness of it.

Brother Harold's knuckles whitened, so tightly did he clasp his hands. He contemplated Gethsemane, Christ sweating blood.

He prayed intensely, perspiration breaking out on his brow.

Cesar Alvarado stood smoking a cigarette some distance off from the monastery in the early night. He was looking up at the sky. There was strangeness in all of this. Even the constellations—whose names he didn't know, but with whose arrangement he was familiar—were out of place, the sky itself askew. He knew this resulted from the difference in latitude between this place and his home, but still it was one more stone on the growing edifice of his discontent.

He hadn't yet been able to determine who his contact might be, who was his protection.

And that damned abbot with his talk of God and violence. He'd like to have him for an afternoon in Security Headquarters along with some of the communist "priests" back home.

Alvarado believed in God. He went to Mass every Sunday. But God didn't have anything to do with the real world, the world you lived in. You got born, baptized, you believed, you said your prayers before you went to sleep and you went to heaven. The rest was the business of men: struggle, survival, who had their way, who did not.

Alvarado dropped his cigarette and crushed it into the grass with his heel. He was frustrated and angry.

The monks rose at their customary hour despite the lateness at which they'd retired the previous night, and completed their devotions and early tasks well before they woke the penitents. Most were roused without difficulty. Bates was sluggish and bleary and had to be reawakened twice. There was alcohol on his breath. Rios cursed when a monk knocked on his door, but was up and dressed shortly. They were directed down to the chapel.

Kennedy stopped at the chapel door. He hadn't bothered to comb his hair or pull it back with his headband. It hung long and snarled. He withdrew his silver pentacle from his pocket and hung it about his neck before he entered.

The penitents occupied the first pews again.

Roger Ballantine experienced the altar before him as a nearly tangible physical force. He was aware of the presence of the company of monks behind him. It was as if he were being pushed forward toward the altar, and he felt pressed between the two.

Brother Abner celebrated the Mass. All the monks received the Eucharist.

Caparelli and Philip Sawyer—the only ones who'd availed themselves of Confession the previous night—went forward to kneel at the rail.

After a fractional hesitation, Jaretzki followed them. He had occasionally attended a High Mass or High Benediction for the beauty of the ceremonials, the aesthetic content, but he'd never before considered taking the Sacrament. He found the idea irresistible now, especially in this milieu. He observed the others and replicated their actions. He knelt. He folded his hands. He tilted back his head as the priest approached with the ciborioum. He closed his eyes. He opened his mouth. He extended his tongue.

The thin consecrated Host came to rest upon it with eerie lightness.

Holding it in his mouth, he rose and returned to his pew. He knelt and bowed his head. He thought of the Corn King. He thought of blood sacrifice. He thought of eating one's God. He concentrated on, edged himself toward belief in, the literal flesh and blood of a god melting upon his tongue. He could not quite make the final leap, to his disappointment, but was partly successful.

He had never eaten a god before. There were elements of thrill in it.

He would have to try again, in different surroundings—a cathedral, perhaps in Barcelona, with full choir, darkness, billowing incense, brilliant robes; there, he thought, he might find ravishment.

While the company was at Mass, Brother Lawrence entered the brown van and drove it back down the rutted lane of the access road and out onto the country road. He had rented the van two days ago in Rochester. That city was only a few hours away, but he was going to spend most of the day driving, zigzagging back and forth across the state, registering additional mileage before he returned it. Much more than he would have if he'd simply driven the vehicle from Rochester to Manhattan, thence up to the monastery, and thence back to Rochester.

Shortly after Brother Lawrence departed, Brother Cooper did also, in the blue van, which had been rented in Manhattan. It had been parked in a barn overnight with the spline of its odometer cable locked in the chuck of a reversible electric drill. Its mileage, when he returned it, would indicate that it had been driven less than half the distance from the city to the monastery and back.

The interior of both vehicles had been painstakingly wiped clean, and both monks wore driving gloves.

The day was overcast and still, but not unpleasant. Most of the penitents wandered idly about the monastery lands. A few spoke superficially to one another. Ballantine and Jaretzki spent a good deal of time in the library. Marcus and Sawyer appeared there, but didn't stay long; it contained no secular books.

Brother Martin had suggested at breakfast that they select a monk with whom they thought they might feel comfortable and begin to establish a dialogue with him.

Caparelli was the only one who did. He spent an hour and a half in the cloister with Brother Leopold. They spoke a little of temper, which Caparelli admitted he often gave vent to, but mainly of the woods, the city. Brother Leopold tired to draw him out on his childhood. Caparelli gave him a bit, but not much.

Afterward, Orson said to him, "You're doing admirably, Uncle. Confession last night, communion this morning, and now a serious talk with one of the brothers. The very model of piety. Sullivan will be impressed."

"He better be."

"And what did you confess, if that's not too personal?"

"The usual shit. Yeah, I got a temper. I fuck around with broads. Sometimes I do things that aren't too honest."

"No! Uncle Dominic, *you?*"

"Maybe you could use this too, meatball. Maybe you get something out of it and learn how not to beat up broads."

Orson looked away. "Sorry."

Caparelli laughed. "At least not the wrong broads, and in public."

Orson was relieved. "Maybe."

"This might not be as bad as I expected," Caparelli said.

'The food's all right. The monks don't run around throwing holy water on you. That Brother Leopold's okay. I think he's been around, I don't think he's been a monk all his life."

"The one who's missing a hand?"

"Yeah."

"What happened to it?"

Caparelli shrugged. "An accident. He didn't want to talk about it."

"Did you notice the scar on the guy who did the reading last night?"

"No. I went blind."

"There's another one, Brother Henry, I think, with a foot that looks like it went through a meat grinder."

"I guess the quiet religious life ain't all it's cracked up to be."

"The lesson tonight," Brother Stefan said from behind the lectern, "is again taken from the Book of Psalms. Hear the word of the Lord:

"Deliver me, O Lord," he read, "from the evil man; preserve me from the violent man;

"Which imagine mischief in their heart; continually are they gathered together for war.

"They have sharpened their tongues like a serpent; adders' poison is under their lips. Selah.

"Keep me, O Lord, from the hands of the wicked; preserve me from the violent man. . . ."

He formed the verses softly, lovingly.

"Let burning coals fall upon them; let them be cast into the fire; into deep pits, that they rise not up again.

"Let not an evil speaker be established in the earth: evil shall hunt the violent man to overthrow him.

"I know that the Lord will maintain the cause of the afflicted, and the right of the poor.

"Surely the righteous shall give thanks unto thy name; the upright shall dwell in thy presence."

Brother Stefan closed the Bible. He said, "Think upon these words, my brothers, for they are God's."

Tom Kennedy muttered, "I have cried out to thee in the wilderness, but thou didst not answer. Think upon those words, friends, for they are man's."

Not many heard. Brother Abner smiled at him.

Dinner was pork chops, fried potatoes and ratatouille.

Wycisowicz was in good spirits. This was dull, but there wasn't anything hard about it, he was on medical leave and drawing full pay, so what the hell, it was a kind of vacation. He ate with gusto, helping himself several times to the pork chops. He said to the monk across from him, "You guys don't eat much, do you? You only had one chop apiece, as far as I could see."

"No, not much," Brother Phelan responded. "It's one of the sacrifices we offer to God."

Wycisowicz nodded. "Will you pass that vegetable stuff over?"

Down at the far end of the table Rios raised his voice obstreperously. "Well, I don't care. I want another drink. It's in my room. I don't bother nobody." He got up from the bench, stood blinking his eyes and wavering, then started toward the door. "Yeah," he said to no one in particular. "That's what I want."

Brother Thomas left his seat at the other table and strode to intercept him. He dropped a large hand on Rios's shoulder.

Rios shrugged violently. "Leave me alone!"

Brother Thomas's hand was not thrown off. Rios tried to move forward, but couldn't. Brother Thomas's expression was affable. He bent his head to Rios's ear, whispered to him, then turned him and walked him back to his seat. Rios sat down heavily. Brother Thomas let him go, patted him on the back and returned to his own place. Rios rubbed his shoulder and looked after Brother Thomas in fuzzy perplexity.

Gunther Hauptmann chewed thoughtfully on his bread.

Brother Thomas's blunt fingers had left indentations in Rios's silk shirt. Hauptmann poured another glass of water from the pitcher. He lifted it, turned his head, and as he sipped began to examine his fellow retreatants carefully, one by one.

The penitents were wakened half an hour earlier the following morning. There was a little grumbling, most noticeably from Norman O. Marcus, Pretty Boy and Rios, who was hung over.

At breakfast, Brother Martin told them their morning was free but requested that they assemble in the library at one-thirty that afternoon for a general meeting.

The library's windows were tall and arched, the room flooded with light. The chairs were simple but more comfortable than those in the rest of the monastery. They had arms and were thinly cushioned.

The abbot stood before them with his hands buried in the folds of his robe.

"This will be our only meeting today," he said. "There are two scheduled for tomorrow. Following that, we'll meet three times each day for the remainder of the Retreat. This afternoon Brother Leopold, Brother Stewart and I will do most of the talking. No, don't worry." He smiled. "We're not going to give you sermons. We want to keep this freeflowing and informal. We'll try to discuss some of the difficulties everyone meets in life, the things that can frustrate and eat at a man sometimes. Please be as frank and open as you can. The more participation, the better. We're all reluctant at first in this kind of situation, and it's not easy to speak of personal matters in front of strangers. We hope that as the days pass you'll come to look upon each other less and less as strangers. We're all men. We're all the same inside. We all hurt, we're all afraid, we've all known despair as well as joy, hate as well as love. Also, we'd like you to mix as much as you can with us. Do try to find a brother with whom you think you might be able to develop some sort of relationship, toward whom you feel an affinity, someone you can feel comfortable confiding in, like a sympathetic friend. That's an important part of—"

He was cut off by a shout from the hall, beyond the closed door of the library.

There was another. Then a thin high wail.

"Don't!" someone cried.

"Brother! What are you—"

"Let me help you!"

The door flew open and crashed against the wall.

A naked emaciated man with a long tangled white beard and long snarled white hair burst in. He came to an abrupt halt and stared at them with shining crazed eyes. His milky skin hung from his bony frame in slack folds. The nails of his fingers and toes were black and curled over against themselves like huge mutated snails. His penis was withered and shrunken, his testicles hung low in a roosterflesh scrotum. He opened his mouth wide, as if to bite, exposing dark gums and the stumpy remnants of teeth.

"A Retreat!" he shrieked. "A Retreat!"

Chapter 13

Hauptmann was on his feet before any of the others. His hand went to his belt buckle; he gripped it, poised his thumb.

Brother Martin moved swiftly. Brother Leopold and Brother Phelan were with him. Two other monks hurried in from the hall. The naked old man spit and kicked and scratched as they secured him. He jabbered and screamed. He was frail and it wasn't much of a struggle. The monks handled him gently.

Brother Martin took his skeletal face between his hands and said softly, "Brother, be peaceful." He kissed each of the hollow cheeks. He blessed him. "Take him to Brother Raphael," he told the monks. They removed him. The abbot closed the door. The old man's laughter sounded in the hall.

"Gentlemen, please be seated." He returned, glanced up at the ceiling, considering. "I apologize for this. I hope you weren't alarmed. That must have seemed quite bizarre to you. It did to me. That was Brother Edmund. He's a Solitary, which is an option available to us in the order. Any of us may choose to live essentially as a hermit, here, in the monastery, alone, free of all earthly connection, in total communion with God. It's rarely done. And when it is, a man will usually terminate the condition after several months, a year or so at the most. Brother Edmund is an exception. He went Solitary more than a decade and a half ago, before I arrived, and even *I* have never seen him until this moment.

"Perhaps I should give you a little background on monasticism and Saint Hector, our founder. . . ."

He sketched briefly the appearance of Christian hermits and

215

anchorites in the second and third centuries, the Desert Fathers, the rise of the communal orders. He told them of Ettore of Perugia's early life, his conversion during the Third Crusade, his eventual dedication. Then he brought himself back to general comment.

Hauptmann listened, but less to the words than to the underlying pulse. Violence. All of it. He looked again at his fellow retreatants. He summoned up images of various monks. He replayed the Solitary's garbled screeches. Then he relaxed himself and emptied his mind. He tried to *sense* the monastery.

When the abbot ended the meeting, Hauptmann went directly to his room.

He checked the Browning, clipped it into his waistband and put his sport jacket on to cover the grip. He dropped the spare magazine into his jacket pocket. He packed and locked his suitcase. He left his room and went down the hall. On the stairs, he encountered the man Wycisowicz.

"Hey. What's up?"

"A message," Hauptmann said. "A family matter. Excuse me, please. I can't talk now." He descended to the first floor and walked straight toward the open door.

Brother Anthony intercepted him. "Mr. Moss. Is something wrong?"

The tattoo at the base of the monk's jaw seemed as menacing as anything Hauptmann had ever seen. "It's a personal matter. I must leave. Please."

Brother Anthony beckoned to a passing monk. "Find the abbot and tell him Mr. Moss has some difficulty and wants to leave."

The monk nodded.

Brother Anthony took Hauptmann's arm. "Why don't you wait in the abbot's office, Mr. Moss. I'm sure he can help."

"I'd rather not." Hauptmann tried to free his arm, but Brother Anthony's grip became more forceful. The monk had his right arm, the arm he would need to draw his gun. He made himself go loose. "All right," he said. "Perhaps I am being hasty."

Brother Anthony released him. He stepped aside and indicated the hall, at the end of which lay the abbot's office.

There was no other way out from there. "I'm more comfortable here."

"All right." The monk interposed himself between Hauptmann and the door. "Is it anything I might be able to assist you with?"

"No. Thank you." Hauptmann was alert for the appearance of monks in number. His right hand came to rest unobtrusively on his hip, near the butt of his gun.

Brother Martin arrived, alone. "Mr. Moss," he said, "I'm told there's some problem. Is it our Brother Edmund? Something else? Why don't we talk about it."

Hauptmann shifted so that he had an open file to the door. "There is no problem, per se. So there is nothing to be done really. It is a matter of conscience. I'm sure that as a monk you can understand and respect that."

"Of course. I do wish that you'd sit and talk with me, though."

"Please."

"As you wish." Brother Martin extended his hand. "May God's blessing be upon you. We'll be here. We'll always be here. I hope you'll decide to come back to us someday."

Hauptmann took the abbot's hand cautiously, ready to jerk loose. It wasn't necessary. "Good-bye."

Then he was out the door, leaving the two monks to stand alone. They looked after him.

"Was there time?" Brother Anthony asked. "I wasn't sure what to do."

"There was time. You did well."

Outside, Hauptmann forced himself to walk slowly. He surveyed the immediate area as he approached his car. There were a few monks, a few retreatants about, but all at some distance and no one seemed to remark him in any special way.

He dropped his suitcase on the front seat, put the key in the ignition and turned it. The engine started immediately. He was relieved; he'd feared it might have been disabled. He backed in a half-curve, shifted and moved forward.

He entered the access road. The trees enveloped him and blotted out the sun. When he had covered three-quarters of the distance, and feeling the comforting press of his holstered gun against his flesh, he sighed, the tension leaving his shoulders. He became aware that he'd been growing increasingly fretful, that he'd been uncomfortable nearly from the moment he'd arrived. Something was wrong back there.

"There's nothing wrong," Brother Raphael told the abbot in the infirmary. "Physically, that is. At least nothing obvious. I want to give him a full exam this afternoon."

They were standing before the closed door.

Across the room, Brother Edmund sat in one of the beds, looking at them slyly.

"His mind?" the abbot asked quietly.

"We'll have to give him time and see. But..."

Brother Martin waited.

"Right now," the infirmarer said, "I'd say he's either mad, or senile, or both." He looked over at Brother Edmund in sadness. "He was a good monk, my abbot. A good man. He doesn't know me. I don't think he knows anything anymore. Anything but the Retreat."

Brother Martin went to the bed, sat down and took the Solitary's hands in his. "Brother, I am Martin. The abbot. I am glad that God has seen fit to bring us together."

The Solitary glanced to Brother Raphael, back to Brother Martin. "Retreat," he said hoarsely.

The abbot nodded. "One is under way."

"Penitents."

"Yes."

"I want one!"

Brother Martin kissed him on the cheek. "God's will will be done, brother. Rest now." He returned to the infirmarer. "He must be sequestered until the Retreat is over. See that he has everything he needs."

"I don't think he'll change. I'm afraid this is how he'll be."

"Then that is God's will for us as well as him. He is ours. We will care for him gently and with love."

"Thank you, my abbot. He was my friend."

The abbot placed his hand on Brother Raphael's shoulder. "You are still his. And he is our brother." He left.

Pretty Boy was sitting by the pond with his back up against the trunk of a willow. It was moving on toward evening and the temperature was falling off some, a little wind from the west pushing in some tall clouds. He was smoking a joint and feeling lazy and good. This wasn't too bad a gig, especially if you were stoned, which he figured to stay. He tossed another pebble into the water, liking the way it made the reflection of the clouds ripple out. The only country he'd ever seen was Lincoln Park back in Chicago. Squirrels, birds, all this shit. It was kind of neat, in a way. He took a deep hit and let the smoke out through his pursed lips in a slow stream.

"Hi."

He looked up. "'Lo, Mr . . . Sawyer?"

"Call me Phil."

"Okay, Phil."

"Mind if I join you?"

"Place don't belong to me."

Sawyer sat down, crossed his legs. "I, uh, caught a whiff of that stuff. I was wondering if I could ask you for a hit."

"We can do better'n that." Pretty Boy fished a new joint from his pocket.

"Well, thanks. Thanks a lot."

"Sure thing."

Sawyer lit up.

"You want t' be cool with that, m' man. It's primo. You go too heavy, you'll be tryin' t' walk on the water." Pretty Boy laughed. "But I guess this is the right place if you're goin' t' do it."

Sawyer laughed. He drew in smoke, exhaled. "Man, this *is* good."

Pretty Boy was feeling mellow. He didn't even mind that Sawyer was a honky and dumb. "What you do for a livin', Mr. Phil?"

"I'm a social worker. In Philadelphia. What do you do?"

"I'm a pimp. In Chicago."

Sawyer burst out laughing. "That's good. I like that."

"It is, and I do too."

"You're serious?"

"Like your mama said to your daddy the night they got you—You bet, baby."

"I'll be damned."

"Not here, you won't."

They both convulsed with laughter.

Several hundred yards back, by the barns, the geese set up a furious roar.

"Those are really mean mothers," Sawyer said.

"They ain't the only ones. You check out our civilian soulmates?"

Sawyer shook his head. "You're something, Mr. Johnson."

"Bad and glad. And Pretty Boy is who I am."

"Pretty Boy?"

"On the street."

"Wow."

Pretty Boy raised his joint. "Good shit, huh?"

"Terrific."

"And speakin' of evil—" Pretty Boy gestured. Norman O. Marcus had appeared at the shoreline and was kicking moodily at a buried stone. "I'm gonna do me some with one what is. Check you later, Phil."

He pushed up off the ground and sauntered over to Marcus. "Evenin', Mr. Marcus."

"Good evening, Mr. Johnson. Is there something I can do for you?"

"Somethin' I can do for you maybe." Pretty Boy produced a small vial of coke from his pocket.

Marcus looked at it without expression.

"Good," Pretty Boy said. "Flake."

Marcus was silent.

"Take a taste."

After several moments Marcus reached for the vial. He dabbed a bit on his fingertip, touched it to his tongue, concentrated. He took a hit up each nostril, walked a few paces off and stood looking at the pond. Pretty Boy smoked half a cigarette. He hummed to himself.

Marcus returned. "How much?"

"Two-fifty a gram. One-fifty a half."

"That's steep, Johnson."

"You know it's good. And I'm the only game in town."

"A gram."

"Whatever you say, boss."

It was late. They were all waiting for his word. No one had said anything, but he could see it in their eyes. He was sure, earlier, that Brother Conrad had been on the verge of putting the question to him.

"Yes?" he had said.

Brother Conrad had remained a moment with his mouth partly open, than had shaken his head. "Nothing, my abbot. It is nothing." He had turned away.

Now Brother Martin was at his desk, deep in the reconstructed commentaries of Brother Jean-Paul of Clichy, who had, in the late sixteenth century, written the clearest and most compelling *apologia* for the Retreat.

The sudden demented appearance of old Brother Edmund,

and Gunther Hauptmann's subsequent flight, had shaken the abbot. He'd managed it well enough, but it could just as easily have gotten out of hand.

It had to begin soon. He knew that. But he was unsure. He lacked resolve, confidence. And he was afraid.

He read Brother Jean-Paul fervently, trying to push himself to commitment.

He couldn't.

He closed the book. If there was an answer, it did not lie in the Chronicles, but rather somewhere within himself.

He left the office.

He went down to the Chamber of Mortal Meditation. There, in the flickering candlelight, he lowered himself to his knees in front of death.

The monastery hadn't yet closed down, but was about to. Joel Ableman came out of his room. The hall was quiet except for the sound of snoring that issued from Rauscher's room and Wycisowicz's. Brother Abner was sitting on a stool at the head of the stairs reading. A monk was posted there each night to help the retreatants if any problem arose.

Ableman said, "I ran out of cigarettes, Brother Abner. Can you get some for me?"

"I'm sorry. We don't keep any."

"Damn—excuse me. I've tried to quit, but I can't. I go crazy without them. I'll have to bum a pack from someone for the night."

"I think everyone's asleep already, the ones I remember who smoke, anyway."

"Well, I've got to get something. Johnson?"

"He went to sleep half an hour ago."

"DiPalo?"

"I don't know." Brother Abner went to Orson's door and knocked once, softly. There was no answer.

"Kennedy?"

They walked to Kennedy's room and knocked.

Kennedy opened the door. "Yeah?"

He was shirtless. His hair hung about his shoulders. An inverted, crucified Christ was tattooed on the left side of his chest. On the right, a naked woman on her hands and knees being mounted by a goat.

Ableman stared. "Uh, I ran out of cigarettes, Mr. Kennedy. Can I buy a pack from you?"

"You should have thought of that when you packed, man. I'm going to have to stretch myself." He shut the door.

"I never saw anything like that," Ableman said.

Brother Abner said nothing.

Bates was awake. He was down to less than a pack himself, but he gave Ableman two to get him through the night.

Ableman asked Brother Abner if anyone was going into town tomorrow.

"I don't know."

"Well, I've *got* to get some," Ableman said with a touch of anger.

"I'll see what can be done. Good night, Mr. Ableman."

Brother Martin was asleep. Someone touched his shoulder. He came bolt upright from his pallet, tense. "What is it?"

Brother Conrad was there. "We have a problem. There's an unexpected visitor. It's not simple. It requires your judgment."

"Is the Retreat in danger?"

"I don't know."

Brother Martin splashed water on his face and put on his robe. Brother Conrad told him what few details he had.

Downstairs, a young black man stood with Brother Gilbert, who was on duty at the door. The man was clenching and unclenching his hands, shifting his weight from leg to leg. He was powerfully built and dressed in jeans, a yellow T-shirt and sneakers. He sprang forward.

"Are you the guy who runs this place?"

"I'm Brother Martin, the abbot, yes."

He took Brother Martin's robe in both hands. "You got to help me. You got to. Please!"

"Let's go to my office and talk."

Brother Conrad accompanied them.

The abbot turned on the lights and went around his desk. "Sit. There."

The man took the indicated chair, bent forward and buried his face in his hands.

Brother Martin studied him. With deliberate severity he said, "Sit up!"

The man jerked straight. His eyes were teary. His mouth trembled.

"What's your name?"

"Oakley. Oakley Brown. *Please*. I'm goin' t' burn forever and ever if you don' help me."

"Why?"

"I got cursed. By a dyin' woman."

Matter-of-factly, Brother Martin asked, "Did you kill her?"

Panic seized Oakley's face.

"You *will* tell me the truth. You are in God's house. If you lie, you shall indeed burn forever. Whatever you say here will go no further. You have my word before God on that."

"I killed her," Oakley whispered.

"Louder."

"Yes! I killed her! And there was blood on her cross and she cursed me, she called God t' damn me t' hell." He hid his face and wept.

Brother Martin waited for the tears to subside. "Why did you come to us?"

"Because o' Willie Thompson. I knew him from the streets. He got stoned, tol' me he was goin' t' some monastery place. I finally remembered the name an' where it was."

"Where do you live?"

"Pittsburgh."

"With whom?"

"Myself."

"How did you get here?"

"I drove."

"In your own car?"

Oakley looked to the floor. "Mine's in the shop. I stole one."

"How did you find the monastery?"

"There was an old guy on the pumps at that all-night gas station outside town. He was half drunk. He told me the way."

Brother Martin folded his hands on his desk. Though outwardly calm, he was confused and in turmoil.

"You *got* t' take the curse off me!" Oakley cried.

"Silence!"

Oakley cowered back.

After several moments the abbot told Brother Conrad to bring Brother Stewart and Brother William to him. Brother Conrad left.

"You'll speak with Brother William," Brother Martin said, "then you'll make confession to Brother Stewart."

Oakley was alarmed.

"This is a *religious* confession. It cannot go further than Brother Stewart's ears. After that, I'll make my decision."

"You *got* to take me in. I seen it in a movie. Sa— Sac— Sanctuary. That thing."

"I do not. No such rule exists."

"I won't leave!"

Coldly, Brother Martin said, "That choice is not yours, Mr. Brown."

There were hard footsteps in the stone hall; sandals were exchanged for sturdy field shoes during a Retreat. Brother Conrad entered with the other two monks.

"Willie!" Oakley lunged from his chair and threw his arms around the black Brother William. "Willie, help me, for God's sake, help me!"

Brother William was startled. He looked to Brother Martin.

"We'll leave you alone with him for ten minutes," the abbot said.

He went into the hall with Brother Conrad and Brother Stewart, shutting the door.

When Brother William emerged, Brother Stewart put the purple stole of the confessional around his neck and went in.

"Explain," Brother Martin said.

Brother William was fearful. "He says I was stoned. I swear I don't remember ever telling anyone anything. I followed my instructions to the letter. I was too afraid not to."

"That's not relevant now. Is he who he says he is?"

"Yes."

"Does anyone know he's here?"

"I don't think so. He's a real loner. And he's been crazy ever since he killed that woman, all he's been able to think about is getting here."

"Tell me everything you know about him."

There wasn't much. It didn't take long. Brother Martin dismissed Brother William.

Brother Stewart came out of the office a few minutes later.

The abbot struggled to find the right words, that would not violate the rules of the confessional. "Is he . . . an appropriate person for a Retreat?"

Brother Stewart examined the question for the same danger. He was satisfied. "Yes," he said.

"Thank you. You may go."

"I think," Brother Martin said to Brother Conrad, "that we can take him in. He's a suitable penitent. He has no ties to anyone. The only person who saw him was a drunk who probably won't remember anyway. In the improbable event of an inquiry, simple denial should be sufficient."

"I agree. I also think it would be dangerous not to. He's obsessed. If we turn him out, he could cause trouble."

Brother Martin winced internally. He too should have seen that. "It's done, then. Get him settled into a cell for the night. I'm returning to my own."

He did not sleep well. He had to be their rock, and he was crumbling.

Wake-up the next morning was advanced yet another half-hour. Several of the penitents grumbled and complained. Joel Ableman was feeling the effects of nicotine withdrawal and was querulous as they trooped down the stairs for breakfast. Kennedy turned him down again. Orson had left his back in his room. Bates said, "Tell you, friend, I really don't have enough left. But I'll split one with you after we-all chow down. How's that?"

"Goddamn it, I need a fucking cigarette and I need it now. Come on!"

He reached for Bates's pocket.

Bates swatted his hand away. "Hey. After breakfast, ol' buddy."

Ableman shoved him against the wall. He jerked the pack from his pocket. The pocket ripped.

The gaunt novice Brother Richard was three steps above them. "What are you doing?" he screamed. He rushed down and hit Ableman in the face.

Ableman was knocked down. Shock registered on his face, then anger. He balled his hands into fists and started to rise.

Brother Richard hit him again. "No! You can't do this. No violence! No violence!" He struck repeatedly at Ableman.

Brother Cooper grabbed the novice. "Brother Richard, stop!"

Brother Richard began to shake. He stared down at Ableman through wide eyes, high spots of color rising on his pallid cheeks.

The other penitents looked on with astonishment.

"I'm sorry, Mr. Ableman," Brother Cooper said. "Brother Richard is recovering from an illness. He's been under strain." To the novice he said, "Come. Let's go outside and take some air." He led Brother Richard down the stairs.

"Sorry about that," Ableman said to Bates, with some difficulty. "I don't know what happened. I just went off the handle."

"Yeah," Bates said. "Sure. Well, here." He gave Ableman a cigarette. "We'll have 'em get us some this afternoon."

Several steps above them, Vitek Jaretzki smiled. He was truly beginning to enjoy all this.

Several steps below, Roger Ballantine was repelled. He abhorred florid displays of emotion.

Brother Conrad reported the incident to the abbot before Brother Martin entered the refectory.

Brother Martin said, "Have Brother Richard taken to Brother Raphael. I want his evaluation. Get Ableman some cigarettes. Tell everyone we're sending someone to town tomorrow morning, that we'll get them whatever they need. I don't want anyone acting up now."

Brother Martin was anguished. It was compounding. Time was closing. He couldn't bring himself to it.

At breakfast, he introduced Oakley Brown to the others as a latecomer.

Oakley looked about fearfully.

In the early afternoon, under a sky that was slowly filling with dark clouds, Caparelli and Orson set off for a brief constitutional before the meeting in the library. Some five minutes after they were out, Caparelli stopped in mid-step and reached suddenly for Orson's arm. He placed his foot down slowly. He was staring straight ahead.

"Uncle? What is it?"

Caparelli grunted. The color drained from his face. He placed his hand to his chest. "I don't feel so good."

Orson looked around. There was a big wood-splitting block nearby, its flat surface scored with ax cuts. Orson led him over to it and helped him sit.

"Pain," Caparelli said. "In my chest."

"What kind."

"Sharp. Right up the middle."

"Anything else?"

"Down my left arm. Fingers kind of numb and tingly." Perspiration beaded his face.

Orson called to a monk who was working outside the nearest barn. The monk came to them. It was Brother Phelan.

"Mr. Caparelli doesn't feel well," Orson said.

"My heart. It's my heart."

"We need a doctor," Orson said.

"We have a doctor among us. Brother Raphael. Our infirmary is fully equipped."

"Can you walk, Uncle?"

Caparelli nodded. "Yeah ... slow."

They helped him up, supported him.

Brother Phelan said, "Easy now, Mr. Caparelli. Don't worry. Brother Raphael's a fine doctor. I'm sure everything's all right, but we'll take you to the hospital in Scanandaga if it's necessary."

That, of course, was a lie, but there was nothing else the monk could say.

"It was only indigestion," Brother Raphael told Brother Martin. "You can never be absolutely sure, but he had none of the other symptoms. I examined him thoroughly and took a pretty good medical history. My diagnosis is, he's phobic about his heart and that his own doctor has played some on that in an attempt to get him to drop weight and give up cigars. I gave him a sedative. He's resting easily now."

The abbot saw in Brother Raphael's eyes the same question that increasingly appeared in the eyes of the rest of the company: When?

"That phobia might be useful," he said. "Hawthorne didn't know about it. It's not in the profile." He dismissed Brother Raphael.

When?

* * *

In the late afternoon Brother Martin was in the chapel deep in prayer.

A cough from the rear caused him to raise his head. Brother Conrad was there.

The abbot crossed himself and stood.

Brother Conrad said, "Brother Henry is ready to prepare dinner. He asked me if . . ."

Brother Martin waited.

"It is the third full day already," Brother Conrad said.

"It's not your place to remind me of that!"

"Forgive me, my abbot." Brother Conrad knelt and kissed his ring.

"Tell Brother Henry to reduce the portions. Also . . . you may attend to the beds. Do it during dinner."

Brother Conrad looked at him expectantly.

"That is all."

When?

The hour seemed much later than it was. The sky was dark with clouds. A strong wind was gusting, and through the refectory windows the trees on the nearby mountainsides could be seen swaying in waves. Several of the company were absent from the table. The few penitents who thought to comment on this were told they were on a work detail.

"What's this?" Bates asked with a grin. "Appetizers?"

There were few platters on the table, and they were sparsely filled. Some chicken. Rice. Peas. A little bread. No butter.

Beside him, Brother Wilfred said, "This is dinner. There isn't any more."

"You're kidding."

"No."

"Hell, this ain't enough even to get my appetite up."

A few places down, Orson objected.

At the next table, Ballantine said, "Really, this is quite insufficient."

Norman O. Marcus banged his hand on the planking and rose to his feet. "Brother Martin," he called. "'Christian charity' prevents me from commenting on the quality of the fare here, but the least you can do is give us enough to keep us alive."

"We normally eat even less than this, Mr. Marcus, and we are all healthy men who work long days."

"Well, I'm not a member of your goddamn order."

Brother Hilliard, who was seated across from Marcus, smiled up at him. "Someday you might be."

"Not on your life."

"True, not on *my* life. But who can tell? God works in mysterious ways."

"Brother Hilliard," the abbot said, "that is enough."

Marcus locked eyes with Brother Hilliard. "I want more, damn it. What are you going to do about that?"

Brother Hilliard stood. His hands began to rise as if of their own volition. "Oh, you have no idea what I'm going to do about it."

"Brother Hilliard!" The abbot's voice was a whipcrack.

Brother Hilliard jerked.

"Sit down."

Reluctantly, he did. He folded his hands before him and stared at them.

"You too, Mr. Marcus.... *I said sit down, Mr. Marcus.*"

Marcus glared at the abbot, but lowered himself back to the bench.

"This is a retreat," Brother Martin said with some anger, his eyes moving across the penitents. "A time of renewal and rebirth. Discipline and self-denial are valuable tools in effecting that. A retreat is not a vacation. It isn't easy on you, I know. But nor is it easy on us, who live solitary lives of silence, meditation and work. But we *will*, with God's grace, bring this to a successful conclusion, and all of us, we as well as you, will emerge stronger men and better servants of the Lord for that. I am imposing a rule of silence for the duration of this meal. Make use of the opportunity to reflect upon the state of your souls."

Sawyer said, "Brother Martin, is this—"

"I said there shall be *silence!*"

And there was silence.

The penitents broke into pairs and little groups according to their developing affinities as they filed out of the refectory. They were, in varying degrees, curious, bewildered or angry.

Brother Martin brushed past the few who tried to speak with him. He went directly to his office and closed the door.

Several minutes later, on the second floor, Joel Ableman shouted furiously, "What the fuck happened to my bed!"

He stood in the doorway, staring into his cell. The frame and springs were gone. The mattress rested directly on the stone floor.

Pretty Boy went to his own door and opened it. "Shee-it."

Farther down the hall, Marcus bellowed in rage and charged back out into the hall.

The penitents who had remained in the monastery instead of going outside after dinner—about half—gathered together in confusion and fury.

"What the hell is going on here?" Ableman demanded of Brother Stefan, who was passing en route to the library.

"I don't know, Mr. Ableman. You'll have to ask the abbot."

"There's a goddamn accounting due here," Marcus said.

He led them down the stairs and to the abbot's closed door, before which Brother Thomas and Brother Leopold stood side by side, large grave men with their arms folded across their chests.

"I want to see the abbot."

Brother Leopold said, "I'm sorry, Mr. Marcus. He's in conference now."

"I don't care if he's face-to-face with Jesus Christ. I want to see him, and I want to see him *now.*"

"That's not possible. There's no reason to be upset. Why don't you go for a walk. I'll notify you when he's free."

Even if he'd tried, Marcus wouldn't have been able to remember the last time anyone had said no to him. He moved his bulk forward.

Brother Thomas stepped from the door and planted himself like a granite column directly in his path. "Brother Leopold said that's not possible."

Less than a foot separated them. Marcus clenched and unclenched his hands. Brother Thomas looked steadily into his eyes.

Marcus exhaled, eased back. "I want to know what the hell happened to our beds."

"I don't know," Brother Leopold said. "I suggest you wait in the chapter room. I'll ask the abbot to meet with you there as soon as he's free."

"That better be soon. And tell him he better have a damn good answer."

Neither monk responded.

Marcus swung around. The penitents pressed aside so he could pass through them. They fell in behind him as he stalked off to the chapter room, his great size, anger and clear air of authority having thrust him into the position of leadership.

A light rain began to fall. The penitents who'd been outside returned to the monastery. They learned what had happened, and joined with the others in the chapter room.

Brother Martin kept them waiting an hour.

When he arrived, striding in briskly, he was flanked by Brother Leopold and Brother Thomas. He went to the front of the room. Brother Anthony and Brother Louis entered unobtrusively and took up positions in the rear.

"You wanted to see me," the abbot said.

"What happened to our beds?" Marcus demanded. He was controlling his anger, but it was large and obvious.

"We removed them."

"And just why in hell did you do that?"

"As I said earlier, this is a retreat, Mr. Marcus. And as I also said, denial and discipline enable us to concentrate on our spiritual selves more freely. The mattresses are sufficiently comfortable. You can all get a good night's sleep on them."

Roger Ballantine said, "This is outrageous."

"What about my uncle?" Orson asked with temper. "He's sick. You expect him to sleep on the goddamn floor?"

"He's resting easily. He'll sleep in the infirmary tonight."

Marcus said, "Just who in the hell do you think you are?"

"The abbot."

"This isn't the way a retreat is run," Kennedy said. "And you know it, man."

"It's the way it's run at Saint Hector's."

Sawyer said, "Brother Martin—"

The abbot lifted his hand. "I have pressing business. I'll be available to anyone who wants to speak with me tomorrow morning. Incidentally, we're shutting the monastery down at ten tonight. Good night, gentlemen."

He was out the door, Brother Thomas and Brother Leopold on either side of him.

Brother Anthony and Brother Louis waited another few moments, watching the penitents, before they withdrew too.

It was midnight. Brother Martin rose from his knees in the candlelit Chamber of Mortal Meditation. He looked one final moment at fate and at destiny, at God's will, at the liquefying corruption, and then turned and went out.

He locked the door behind him. He climbed the steps slowly.

Brother Henry was posted at the door in the entrance hall. Thunder boomed heavily without, muffled by the thick stone walls.

Brother Martin went to the door, gestured for Brother Henry to open it.

"It's storming out there," Brother Henry said.

"Yes."

Brother Henry unlocked and pulled open the iron-bound door. The wind drove large drops of rain into the hall.

Brother Martin stepped into the night. Brother Henry closed the door behind him.

The rain beat down upon the abbot. A finger of lightning lanced down, whitening the night, and struck the mountaintop to the west. An instant later a second one—forked—struck the neighboring peak. Two crashes of thunder sounded one atop the other. Brother Martin felt them in his chest and stomach.

He stood several minutes thus. The rain pelted him. It matted his hair to his head and streamed down his face. Lightning illuminated the night in flashes and thunder reverberated off the mountains. His robe became sodden.

He turned and went back into the monastery.

"Bring Brother Conrad," he said.

Brother Henry left.

Brother Martin stood by the door. He thought of nothing. Water dripped from his robe and pooled around his feet.

Brother Conrad appeared.

The abbot looked at him several beats. "Do it," he said.

Chapter 14

There were only half a dozen monks present at Mass the next morning.

"Where is everybody?" Bates asked.

Brother Lawrence said, "They attended an earlier Mass."

Resentment simmered among the penitents. There was a sense of solidarity and determination in them.

When the service was over, Marcus said to Brother Conrad, "Where's the abbot? He said he'd be available this morning. It's morning. We want to see him."

"If you'll go to chapter room, please. I'm sure he'll clear things up."

Marcus led the penitents to the chapter room. The few monks who'd been with them in the chapel followed behind. Orson and Joel Ableman, who had emerged as Marcus's unofficial but *de facto* seconds, were directly behind him. Marcus yanked open the door and marched in, Orson and Ableman following by half a step. They were several paces in before they were able to register what they saw. They faltered. They were jostled by the other penitents, who in turn were shouldered forward by the monks in the rear.

The room was dim, most of the morning sun blocked out by the closed shutters. The company of Saint Hector's, their hands hidden in the sleeves of their robes, their cowls raised obscuring their faces, lined the walls in silence.

Brother Martin stood apart from them, before the abbot's chair.

"Jesus Christ!" Bates said.

Alvarado spun back toward the door.

Brother Conrad closed it and threw home an iron bolt. He raised his cowl and stood before the door with the other monks who had brought up the rear.

"You are penitents in a Retreat at the monastery of the Order of Saint Hector," Brother Martin said, his tone flat. "Penitents, you will each remove all of your clothes and put on one of these." He pointed to a heap of coarse gray robes at his feet.

Marcus said: *"Fuck you."*

Brother Thomas stepped from the wall, jerked Marcus around and drove his fist deep into the man's great belly. Marcus's lungs emptied in a plosive burst. His mouth gaped and his eyes widened. He sagged to his knees. He reached for his gut, gaping up at Brother Thomas.

Brother Thomas took a step, swung his leg and kicked Marcus in the mouth. Marcus's lip split with a spray of blood. Two teeth snapped off. He was hurled backward. He rolled like a wounded animal, struggling for breath. Blood from his mouth smeared on the stone floor.

"What are you *doing?*" Ableman shouted.

A monk moved from the wall and struck him in the kidney from behind.

"Ahhhg!" Ableman fell. He writhed.

"You sonsofbitches are crazy," Orson said. "This shit stops right now!"

Brother Wilfred slashed a knotted cord across Orson's face. A bright red weal rose instantly. The skin over the cheekbone was cut. Orson touched his hand to his cheek. He blinked at Brother Wilfred incredulously. He opened his mouth to speak. Brother Wilfred poised the cord. Orson closed his mouth.

"Oh, mama," Pretty Boy said. He moved to the robes, unbuttoned his shirt and dropped it from his shoulders. He took off his shoes and socks, undid his belt.

Caparelli turned his head slowly, surveying the whole of the room. His face was glum.

He said, "Uh-huh." He nodded to himself. "Uh-huh."
He walked forward and began unbuttoning his shirt.

A key turned in the lock and the door opened. There were two of them. Their cowls were up. Hauptmann couldn't see their faces. The light behind them was dim, but still it hurt his eyes; he had been imprisoned in total darkness these last two days.

As he'd neared the end of the pocked and rutted access road, he had begun to think that he'd probably been unduly wary—and that he was going to have some difficulty reestablishing contact with his people since he'd bolted from the place they expected him to be. But he wasn't remonstrating with himself. His instincts had kept him alive and free in the past, and if they were to make a mistake, he'd rather that it was a mistake on the side of caution.

Almost to the stone pillars and the macadam county road, he had to brake and stop. A dead tree had fallen. It canted across the rough lane, top caught in the lower branches of another tree on the opposite side. It wasn't very big, only three or four inches in diameter. It wouldn't be hard to clear.

He shifted to neutral and set the hand brake, letting the engine idle. He got out. He went to the butt of the fallen tree.

Two monks stepped from the brush.

Instantly, Hauptmann threw control to his reflexes: his right hand dipped to the butt of the holstered Browning. His fingers closed around it, his thumb hit the release, then pushed the safety down even as he was drawing the pistol, and his index finger slid into the trigger guard. He dropped into a crouch. His left hand rose to curl around the right, he locked his arms, centered the muzzle on the chest of the closest monk, thumbed back the hammer and applied light, preliminary pressure to the trigger.

All this happened in less than a full second from his first sight of them.

"Freeze or you're dead," he said.

The muzzle was sighted on the chest of Brother Louis, a burly monk with a skewed nose. The other one was the young fairhaired monk, Brother Harold.

The problem: What to do with them. The question: What lay behind all this.

It was difficult to resolve the problem without knowing the answer to the question.

"Move to the back of the car," he said. Escape was paramount now. Lock them in the trunk. Work through the rest later.

Brother Harold smiled. A genuine, friendly smile. He stepped forward. "Mr. Moss, I'd like your gun, please."

"Stop. I will kill you if you make it necessary. Believe me."

"I do believe you, Mr. Moss."

The monks advanced. Brother Harold's smile turned sympathetic.

Hauptmann gauged the distance. Seven yards. At four, they would be close enough to try a rush and he'd have no choice but to kill them.

"You're committing suicide," he said.

Brother Harold extended his hand. "The gun, please."

Five yards.

Four.

Hauptmann pulled the trigger.

Clack.

Misfire. He jerked and released the slide, chambering a new round.

Clack.

He straightened, knowing there was no use trying again. The gun had been tampered with.

He laid it in Brother Harold's palm. "When?"

"The first night. During dinner and orientation. Our Brother Anthony is quite good at this sort of thing. I don't know much about handguns, but I think he removed the firing pin."

"Why didn't you just take it? You already had me."

"It wasn't time."

"But it is now."

"No. We would have preferred not having to do this."

"What is going on? Who are you?"

"It isn't time yet."

The room in which they'd held him was tiny, its walls stone. The locked door was solid and unmovable. There was utter silence. Twice each day, a small panel in the bottom of the door was slid back and a plate of food pushed in, the slop jar replaced. Not a word was said to him.

Now they had come.

The taller one handed him a folded piece of coarse cloth. "Strip naked and put this on."

Hauptmann turned his back, in the semblance of modesty. Actually, he did so to conceal his manipulation of his belt. He freed the buckle, which was the handle of a slim three-and-a-half-inch dagger, blade sheathed within the belt itself. He palmed the dagger, stripped, and fussed with the garment, feigning difficulty getting his arms into the sleeves while he snagged the small hook at the butt into the fabric of the left armpit.

The garment was a simple collarless robe with loose-fitting sleeves. It dropped shapelessly down his body to a hem a few inches above his ankles.

"Come," said one of the monks.

At breakfast, the monks took their usual places on the long benches. Interspersed between them, the penitents were made to kneel on the stone floor and use the empty space on the bench before them as their table. They were each given a tin plate of gruel.

Joel Ableman knelt with his hands braced on the bench and his head lowered. The entire lower quadrant of his back was a dull ache. He was nauseated. His face was covered with sweat.

Brother Hiram said, "What's the matter, Mr. Ableman? You haven't touched your food. Not hungry this morning?"

Ableman started to answer, then stopped himself, not knowing what was expected or forbidden, fearing another blow.

Brother Hiram tore off a piece of bread, covered it with butter and preserves. "Well, what the hell, we all have days like that." He began a conversation with the monk across the table.

Ableman became very afraid.

Up the table, Sawyer was halfway through his gruel. He put his spoon down. Brother Raphael, the monk to his right, an older man, had been pleasant to him before. He took a chance. "Brother Raphael," he said. "What's going on here?"

Brother Raphael ignored him.

Sawyer turned to the monk on his other side. "Brother Gilbert, please. Will you explain this?"

Brother Gilbert said nothing.

Sawyer looked across the table. "Brother—I'm sorry, I don't know your name—will *you* tell me. Please."

The monk continued to eat, as if Sawyer did not exist at all.

At the opposite table, Brother Henry said to Peter Bates, "I understand you raise hunting dogs, Mr. Bates. What is it that you hunt with them?"

Bates was greatly relieved. "Coons and rabbits," he said eagerly. "They—"

Seated on the other side, Brother Thomas backhanded him. The blow sprawled him to the floor, banging his head. He got slowly to his hands and knees.

"Get back to your place!" Brother Thomas said.

"What did I *do?*"

"You talked."

"But he asked me a question."

"*I* didn't."

Brother Henry poured himself a cup of coffee. "How does that work, Mr. Bates? Do they catch them themselves, or do they lead you to them, or what?"

Bates looked fearfully to Brother Thomas.

Brother Henry hit him in the face. "Answer when you're spoken to, Mr. Bates!"

"A little air, a little sun will do us all good," Brother Martin said after breakfast. "We have a strenuous time ahead of us."

The monks took the penitents outside.

The rain had ended half an hour ago. The early morning sun dazzled the high lingering moisture into a rainbow that arched from a mountain peak in the east across the valley to another in the west. The sun also glinted off a coil of fearsome metal that had been mounted atop the fence during the night. It spiraled tightly from post to post, raising the height of the fence to well over six feet. The monastery was now a sealed compound.

"Ah, yes," Brother Martin said. "That. It's razor wire. Developed, I believe, by the Israelis. You can't touch it anywhere without getting slashed. The fence encloses the monastery entirely. It's a uniform fifteen yards out from the walls, quite an adequate area for exercise and taking air. You are not permitted beyond it."

"This is insane!" Ballantine said. "Just what are you doing?"

Brother Martin left.

"Brother Conrad," Ballantine said. "You're a rational man. Has your abbot gone mad?"

Brother Conrad looked at him in silence.

Ballantine said to Kennedy, "Are you going to put up with this?"

"Not fucking much more."

A monk hit Kennedy in the back of the head, staggering him forward.

"Mr. Jaretzki," Ballantine appealed. "Surely you're a man of too much intelligence to accept this."

Jaretzki said, "It appears that—"

Brother Abner stepped in and kneed him in the groin. Jaretzki fell. He doubled up and groaned.

"Brother Stewart," Ballantine said with desperation. "You're a priest. How can you accept this?"

Brother Stewart said nothing.

Ballantine went to Sawyer. "Help me."

Sawyer looked apprehensively at the closest monks. He shook his head and backed away.

Ballantine kept trying. The monks all ignored him. The other penitents retreated from him.

He became hysterical. "You can't do this! I'm getting out of here!"

He ran for the gate and jerked at the lock that secured the latch.

A cowled monk walked up behind him and gave him a mild shove. Ballantine was propelled forward. He put out his hands to brace himself. He fell against the razor wire. He jerked back, screaming.

His palms were slashed and his cheek sliced open. Dark red blood welled from his hands, ran down his face, fell in thick drops.

He held his hands up, staring at them, and screamed again.

He fell to his knees. "Oh my God. Oh my God in heaven. Help me!"

"That is a good start," the monk said.

Benches had been brought into the chapter room. The penitents occupied the first rows. The company sat behind them. Brother Martin stood before them at a lectern.

"You are now truly going to begin to know one another," he said to the penitents. "Each of you in turn will tell the others who you are. Not where you grew up or went to school and such things, but who you *are*. What kind of man you are, what the state of your soul is. We'll begin with, oh, let's say you, Sawyer. Come up here."

There was no more honorific "Mister."

Sawyer ran his tongue over his lips. He stood and approached the lectern reluctantly. Brother Martin took a chair to the side.

"What do you want me to say?"

Brother Martin didn't answer.

After a moment Sawyer said, "I—I'm a social worker. In Philadelphia. A caseworker. I handle people who are mostly on some sort of welfare. I watch for cheating, but my primary job is to get them the help they need, cut through red tape, arrange special services, that sort of thing." He lifted his hands helplessly. "I—I don't know. I'm a quiet man. I try to help people." He glanced at the abbot, looked back to the penitents. "I guess I lose my temper sometimes. I was reprimanded for, for punching a woman. She'd spent her welfare check on drugs and had neglected her children. She spit at me." He looked at Brother Martin again. "Is that what you want me to say?"

The abbot was silent.

"I can't think of anything else."

"Sit down," Brother Martin. "You, Hauptmann."

Hauptmann had no idea what he was involved in, but given what had already happened, he wasn't surprised that they knew his name. Nevertheless, he didn't respond.

"Hauptmann!" The abbot pointed to him. "You!"

Hauptmann complied. He kept his face neutral. "I don't know this 'Hauptmann,'" he said to them. "My name is Peter Moss. I am an optics salesman from Philadelphia. I do not know anything about myself that would make others think I am much different from any other man. I don't understand what is going on here. I am confused and I admit to being afraid." He returned to his seat and looked straight forward, at the wall.

"Caparelli," the abbot said.

Caparelli went to the lectern, put his hands on it, looked out and worked his tongue against his cheek, thinking. He rarely gave anything to anyone unless there was advantage for him in it, but he'd never had much trouble figuring out what people wanted from him; he held others in contempt because they so often lacked what seemed to him such a simple ability.

"My name is Dominic Caparelli," he said. "Last month I was convicted of harassment and jury-tampering. I was found not guilty on a murder charge. I'm a businessman. I let my lawyers worry about whether my businesses are legal or not. I'm no kind of saint. I busted a lot of chops on the way up, and when someone wouldn't get out of the way, I knocked 'im over." He paused, appearing to think. "Maybe that's why I'm here. I never asked any favors from anybody and I'm not askin' now. I don't bullshit. I took knocks, and I handed 'em out. Maybe I got to take some now."

Orson stood at the podium next. He protested that he was a decent man. So did Ableman. Rauscher hulked over the lectern. He told them his name, said he was an unskilled laborer and sat down. Bates said he was a guard in a state prison in Alabama. He was really upset about this and wouldn't someone tell him what was going on, please?

Pretty Boy, with cockiness, but tempered, he hoped it would appear, with some humility, told them, "I'm a pimp. I sell chicks, I sell some drugs. I cut a few people. On the street, I'm a dude everybody knows not to mess with." He moved his eyes over the penitents. "I got me a feelin' all of you be some kind of mean mother. I got me another feelin' that we all gonna have some real problems 'less we get down to it."

Jaretzki, who was called next, decided that Pretty Boy was one of the brightest of the lot. Who knew what he could have done with his life if he'd had a chance? Not that Jaretzki felt much sympathy; his own early life had been a horror. He said, "I'm a high-fashion photographer. I photograph women who are largely naked and I juxtapose them with leather, chains, wild animals. That is a reflection of my own psyche. I like sex in a variety of forms. I like drugs. I like wealth, privilege and power. I have probably hurt people. People have hurt me."

Rios said he was a chicano. "You anglos been on me all my life. Just like you are now. I do what I have to. I don't roll over and kiss anybody's ass. I bring illegals into the country for money. Maybe somebody gets hurt sometimes. Maybe we all fall into the sun tomorrow."

Marcus identified himself as a film producer and said nothing more. Wycisowicz told them he was a police officer.

The abbot said, "Kennedy."

Kennedy folded his arms and didn't move from the bench. Several moments passed. Then he leapt from his seat with a shout.

Behind him, Brother William sat with Kennedy's dagger in his hand. The double-edged blade was tapered to a needle point. Brother William had pricked Kennedy's back with it.

Kennedy went to the lectern. A small red stain appeared around the slit in his robe. He turned. His voice was taut with anger. "I'm Tom Kennedy. I live on a commune in the hills outside Los Angeles. I run it, and I run it the way I like, which means I live the way I want and don't follow anyone else's rules." His lips curled. "You might say that I'm kind of like the abbot of the place."

Oakley Brown sobbed at the lectern. He managed to say, "I hurt some people. I'm cursed. Please don't hurt me!" He stumbled back to his seat in tears. Brother Martin said, "Alvarado."

Alvarado walked up smartly. "My name is not Rivera, as you were told. And I *do* speak English. I am an official of the Paraguayan government. There has been a mistake. I should not be here. A powerful sector of your own government will be looking for me. There will be serious consequences. I am traveling under diplomatic immunity at the invitation of your government. I have nothing more to say."

Ballantine was the last. He was drawn and his face and hands were bandaged. But he stood erectly and looked the penitents and monks directly in their eyes. "I am a urologist and a surgeon. I practice in Washington, D.C., and am a respected member of the community. I am deeply disturbed about this. I hope for everyone's sake"—he looked over at

Brother Martin—"that whatever is afoot here comes to a quick conclusion and that proper explanations are made."

Brother Martin waited several moments after Ballantine had returned to his bench. He stood. He said, "Penitents, return to your rooms."

Chapter 15

Joel Ableman didn't know what time it was.

He didn't know what day it was.

He didn't know where he was.

He had some ideas about these things, if what he thought could accurately be termed ideas. If what was happening in his mind could accurately be called thought. It was a cumulation of senses, graspings, murky confabulations, an occasional bright image, a word or string of words, which would then slip away and leave him baffled, yearning, and with a vague sense of loss.

He cried. Sometimes he was happy. Sometimes he hurt. He drooled. There were lights and sounds. There was nothing. He made gurgling sounds in his throat and felt good. He spit up. He played with his toes.

There were three big brown things now. One lowered itself near to him and made a crooning noise. He felt good on his face, his chest.

Then suddenly he felt a terrible burning pain. He screamed. "Aaahheeeee!"

He tried to roll away but he couldn't.

"Aaahheeeee! Aaahheeeee!"

It left him. But some of the hurt was still there.

He slobbered.

In the cell were Brother Martin, Brother Raphael and Brother Andrew. They had entered together. Ableman was lolling slackly atop his mattress staring up through unfocused eyes. Brother Andrew had knelt down next to him.

Ableman had made a small barely audible sound in his throat.

"Hi there," Brother Andrew said gently. "How are you today?" He stroked Ableman's face, rubbed his chest.

Ableman made a sound that approximated happiness.

"That's a good boy," Brother Andrew said.

He lifted the collar of Ableman's tunic. He held a stiff wire brush in his other hand. He pressed the brush to Ableman's skin and scraped hard across his chest.

Ableman screamed.

Brother Andrew scraped again.

Ableman screamed and screamed. He flailed ineffectually.

"Enough," Brother Martin had said.

Brother Andrew had stopped.

"He's too far down," the abbot said to Brother Raphael. "He's barely functioning. We want him with the motor control of a ten-month-old and the mental faculties of a two-year-old. Can you do it?"

"It'll take some tinkering, but I think so."

"Good. How soon?"

"There are half a dozen drugs involved. If I adjust one, I have to refigure all the others. Twenty-four to forty-eight hours."

"Keep me apprised."

They left Ableman. He lay on his back with his limbs slack, staring glassily, his tongue protruding from his mouth, his chin covered with spittle.

It was two days since Marcus's teeth had been kicked out. The gum was still tender, but at least the throbbing had stopped. The split in his swollen lip hadn't scabbed yet and it oozed a viscous fluid. They'd given him an antibiotic ointment, but they hadn't stitched it, as they had Ballantine's face and hands. They should have. He was going to need cosmetic surgery if it healed in this fashion.

He was barefoot, as were the other penitents trooping from

the chapel to the refectory for breakfast. His great bulk had flattened his arches years ago. He had orthotics custom-built into all his shoes. Deprived of them, his ankles folded in. There were now great blisters on his big toes and the balls of his feet, which bore the brunt of his weight. Last night he'd been made to stand for hours without respite in the library watched over by Brother Stefan, who passed the time in study.

His ankles ached, his knees, his hips. He was tired. He hurt all over. He'd lost maybe fifteen pounds already and he was weak. But that didn't blunt his anger. He was safeguarding and nurturing that, carefully, almost lovingly.

As he entered the refectory a monk dropped a hand on his shoulder and motioned him out of the file of penitents. "Stay here."

The monk wasn't very large. Marcus could have crushed him like a slug. He wanted to.

The rest of the company were standing by their places. They prevented the penitents from kneeling at their own, turned them instead to face the hollow center between the tables.

Brother Lawrence placed a tin bowl of gruel on the floor.

The monk with Marcus said, "Get down on your belly. Crawl to it."

Marcus set his jaw. He stood rigid.

The monk clipped him behind his legs, dropping him to his knees with jarring pain. Then the monk placed a foot against his back and shoved. He sprawled forward. He lay with his arms outstretched, eyes wide and mouth tight with rage.

The monk kicked him in the side.

He gasped with pain.

He crawled toward the plate under all the watching eyes, pulling his bulk along the stone floor clumsily and with difficulty.

Only his rage enabled him to do this, to submit to this humiliation. It was the source of his strength and his will. He blotted everything else from his mind and concentrated upon it.

He was nearly breathless when he gained the plate, more from emotion than effort.

"Now lap it up," the monk said. "Like a dog."

Marcus trembled in his rage. He lowered his head. He dipped his tongue into the gruel.

He ate, tasting nothing. Images of slaughter ran like a wild river through his mind. Destruction. Blood. Murder. He had the power. He could find the means. He was going to have them butchered to the last man. There would be nothing left of them. Nothing.

Pretty Boy watched Marcus through dulled eyes, swaying on his feet. He was exhausted. They weren't allowing him to sleep.

The fat man was left to lie on the floor when he finished, gruel sticking to his nose, his jowls, his chin.

Pretty Boy felt only relief. He groaned when he knelt down. It felt that good. God, if only he could sleep. He rested his arms on the bench. He leaned forward. His head sagged. His eyes closed. He snapped them open and forced himself upright. That saved him a blow from Brother Gilbert who was seated beside him.

On his plate were an apple and a chunk of bread. The apple was soft and discolored. There was mold on the bread. He looked up at Brother Gilbert in appeal. Brother Gilbert ignored him, as did the others to whom he turned. He was afraid to speak.

His stomach growled. There hadn't been much to eat.

He picked up the apple. He turned it to find the part that was least brown, least cidery-smelling. Gingerly, he bit into it. It was doughy and sickly sweet. Chewing only made it worse. He swallowed a few small bites whole, then set the apple aside and took up the bread. He picked off the mold, tasted the bread. It was sour, but he could get it down. He ate some of it. Then he stopped, staring at the remainder in his hand. There were holes in it, and in one the severed body of a white worm was thrashing.

He gagged and spat out the piece in his mouth. There, glistening with his saliva and partly crushed by his molars, writhed the other half of the worm. Bile rose to his throat.

He put his hands to the bench to steady himself. Easy, baby. Easy now.

Brother Andrew said, "How is your breakfast, Brother Gilbert?"

The monks were eating cantaloupe, sausages and dark bread with butter and jam.

"Fine, thank you. And yours?"

"Excellent."

The fragrance of the melons and savory odor of the sausages brought saliva to Pretty Boy's mouth. Sharp hunger merged with his nausea. He was afraid he would faint.

He bit into the apple. He tore the bread into tiny pieces. He found four more worms. He pushed them to the side of his plate. He ate all of the bread.

"Would you pass the sausages, please," Brother Gilbert said.

"Certainly," Brother Andrew replied.

Pretty Boy hung his head and began to cry.

Closing on noon, a station wagon driven by a man, with a woman in the front seat beside him and three children in the rear, slowed on the county road, then came to a stop abreast the two stone pillars that marked the entrance to the monastery. The car's bumper sported a sticker depicting a scenic gorge and another from an exotic animal park. The woman craned her head to read the simple plaque.

She said, "It says, 'Saint Hector's Monastery.'"

A heavy rusty chain hung between the pillars blocking access.

"What's a monastery, Daddy?" one of the children asked.

"A place where monks live. Monks are sort of like priests or ministers."

"Dullsville," said the oldest child, a girl.

"Shame it's blocked off," the man said. "It might be interesting."

"About as interesting as a dead cat," said the girl.

"Maybe we could walk in."

The children were unanimously opposed.

"It looks like it's been abandoned for years," the woman said. "There's probably nothing left of it anyway."

"Daddy," the girl said impatiently. "You promised we could go water-skiing this afternoon."

"All right. All right. But someday you're going to have to learn something about culture."

"Not today."

"Right. Today is water-skiing," the man said.

He put the car back in gear and pulled away.

Not far from the pillars, masked from the road by brush, Brother Hiram was sitting on a stool. In his lap was a book. Beside him was a walkie-talkie. He had observed the family quietly.

The monks had blocked the long access road with three separate deadfalls. Brother Hiram's post had been and would continue to be manned around the clock until the Retreat came to conclusion.

There were no mirrors in the monastery, but the flesh beneath Hauptmann's left eye was swollen and tender and he knew it was discolored. There were bruises on his body. His nose was sensitive and enlarged. He'd probed it carefully. He didn't think it was broken.

They'd set upon him at various arbitrary moments over the last three days—a blow, a trip, a kick. Sudden, brief assaults without pattern, which followed no act nor failure to act on his part. Completely random. And from that very senselessness he deduced the sense of it: they wished him to understand that he could neither please nor displease them, that he was utterly helpless to influence his fate not only in its larger dimension but even moment-by-moment.

He was not unfamiliar with the system. His own people had originated it and used it in the *Konzentrationslager*.

It could hardly fail to break a man.

But it would not break him.

First: the Jews had not understood what was being done to them and were therefore doomed to the destruction of their personality and character.

He did understand, and could use that comprehension to anchor himself.

Second: these people wanted something from him. If not, he wouldn't be in their hands now and they wouldn't be working on him thus. Since he possessed whatever it was that they wanted, it followed then that he occupied the superior position regardless of what they wished him to think, that there were self-imposed limits to their power, that he could still manipulate the situation.

Brother Louis and Brother Wilfred had brought him to the abbot's office. They stood on either side of his chair. Brother Martin was leaning against his desk with his arms folded.

Hauptmann repeated, "My name is Peter Moss. I am an optics salesman from Philadelphia. I don't know why I am here. I don't know what is happening. I am afraid. Please tell me what is going on, what you want from me."

"Your name is Gunther Hauptmann," Brother Martin said without emotion. "You were born in Stuttgart in 1948. Your parents are dead. You have a sister who lives in Heidelberg with her husband and two children. You attended the University of Tubingen. You were apolitical, but you knew people in the Bader-Meinhoff Gang. You assassinated Eberhard Brunning, chairman of Schenkendorff Steel for the underground in 1969, which was your first personal murder. You had, of course, helped plan and execute three early bombings which resulted in four fatalities.

"While we might have missed the odd detail here and there, believe me—I can give you a litany of your acts of murder and destruction that is probably more complete than you could reconstruct from memory yourself.

"It compounds to this: you are, as you sit here today, the most feared professional terrorist in the western hemisphere, excepting Carlos the Jackal, with whom, incidentally, you have a professional rivalry, and of whom you are personally jealous."

Hauptmann sat back, stunned. Instantly he realized his mistake and drew himself forward again. "That's insane," he said. "My God, please believe me. I don't have any idea what you're talking about. There has been some terrible mistake."

"There has," Brother Martin agreed. "But we are not the ones who have made it."

Hauptmann shook his head in apparent disbelief and confusion.

"A week and a half ago thirteen people were killed and nearly fifty more mutilated and injured in an explosion in the West Berlin airport."

Hauptmann frowned. "Yes . . . I think I read something about that."

"I'm sure you did. A craftsman is always interested in the results of his work."

"This doesn't make any sense. Even if I were this person, this Hauptmann"—he shuddered, as if at the unthinkable— "what would you want from him? What would a religious order . . ." He filtered surprise into his face. "Are you . . . something . . . else?"

"We are precisely what we appear to be, monks of the Order of Saint Hector."

"Then what would you want from a terrorist?"

Brother Martin smiled. "We don't want anything from you. There is nothing you can give us. Nothing at all."

The man had to be lying. Hauptmann decided to switch tacks. "If you are monks, wouldn't you have been morally bound to stop that bombing?"

"We did not know it was planned. Only that you were coming to this country on a certain date."

Hauptmann injected the smallest note of confidence into his voice. "And if I were this terrorist, wouldn't I be connected with an organization that would know where I was, that would protect me, that would even now be working to rescue me? And I would think an organization of terrorists would be vastly more efficient in such matters than an order of religious solitaries. I would think it would exact fearsome retribution."

Brother Martin smiled. "Herr Hauptmann, your organization is good, but ours is so very much better. You see, we've been at it for eight centuries now."

"Have been at what?"

"Our work," the abbot said quietly.

Hauptmann was unnerved. The information was contradictory, anarchic. He couldn't synthesize it. He tried to empty his mind. He had to start fresh.

To Brother Louis and Brother Wilfred, the abbot said, "Proceed."

They strapped Hauptmann to the chair—chest, wrist and ankles. He didn't resist. There was no point. All he could think to do was to appear frightened, as Peter Moss would be.

Brother Martin took a length of cord from his desk, about the thickness of a pencil. He gave it to Brother Louis who tied it in a slack circle around Hauptmann's arm, a few inches above the elbow.

"This is the *fidicula*," the abbot said. "A simple device with a very long history, dating back to the Romans, but I think you'll find it effective."

Brother Louis slipped a short pipe beneath the cord. There was still a good deal of slack. Brother Louis grasped both ends of the pipe and began to turn it.

"You know," the abbot said conversationally, "one of the dead at the air terminal was a six-year-old girl. She was decapitated by a piece of plate glass."

Brother Louis turned the pipe, twisting up the slack until the cord was snug around Hauptmann's arm.

Hauptmann tried to regulate his breathing, tried to relax.

Brother Louis turned the pipe a full revolution. The cord tightened around Hauptmann's bicep, bunching the fabric of the loose sleeve of his robe.

Brother Martin looked dispassionately into Hauptmann's eyes.

Brother Louis turned the pipe again.

Hauptmann felt the first discomfort, like the determined grip of a strong man. "Brother Martin, in the name of Jesus, tell me what's going on!"

Brother Martin was silent.

Brother Louis turned the pipe.

"You can't do this," Hauptmann said.

Brother Louis turned the pipe.

Hauptmann exhaled involuntarily.

Brother Louis turned the pipe.

Hauptmann set his jaw.

Brother Louis turned the pipe.

The cord bit in, constricting Hauptmann's blood vessels. He could feel his blood begin to hammer at the blockage. His forearm began to tingle.

Brother Louis turned the pipe.

The cord compressed flesh and muscle into the bone, became a band of pain.

Brother Louis turned the pipe.

Hauptmann gasped. Perspiration sprang out on his forehead.

Brother Louis gave the pipe a slow half-turn.

"Oh *Jesus!*" Hauptmann's heart drove his blood up against the blockage in smashing waves of pain. The meat of his arm felt as if it were being crushed to jelly.

Slowly, Brother Louis completed another half-revolution.

Hauptmann's eyes bulged. His mouth gaped. He strained against his bonds.

Brother Louis administered a quarter-turn.

Hauptmann screamed. "Stop it! Please! Anything! Stop!"

Another quarter-turn.

"Aiieeeee!"

Brother Wilfred had him by the shoulders, but still Hauptmann threw himself about, rocking the legs of the chair. His feet slapped up and down on the floor.

Brother Louis turned the pipe.

Hauptmann's eyes flooded with tears. He banged his head against the back of the chair. He bit his tongue and drew blood. A long ululating wail escaped him.

He didn't see Brother Martin nod.

Brother Louis jerked the pipe free. The tight twist sprang open and the *fidicula* went slack.

The sudden release of pressure was a shearing pain in itself, as terrible as that which had preceded it, and then the pent-up blood slammed through the unimpeded vessels with the force of a blow and Hauptmann's forearm felt awash with molten metal.

He screamed, rigid against his bonds, then slumped back, limp, head hanging, and shook uncontrollably.

"The little girl's mother wasn't killed in the blast," Brother Martin said. "But her face was cut to pieces and she lost an eye and three fingers."

The day was temperate and bucolic. The afternoon sun was pleasant on Jaretzki's back, the cultivated earth comfortingly warm to the soles of his bare feet. Periodically a drifting cloud would cover him with shadow and he found the contrast between that coolness and the warm earth pleasing. When the shadow passed, he would be momentarily startled by the sudden brightness, as if an encroaching evening had decided to reverse itself to day in an instant.

He was working in a bean field. Brother Phelan was crouched on the opposite side of this particular row of low plants. Jaretzki enjoyed the slightly pungent odor of the snap-bean bushes. The long green beans hung from them in clusters and the work wasn't hard. He would stand and stretch when he moved the bushel basket to a new section. When the basket was full he'd carry it down the row and set it in the wagon at the end and return with an empty one. He was, to his bemusement, enjoying the day.

Yesterday a monk he didn't know had struck him across the face with a leather strap—his cheek was still tender—and on the previous day Brother Cooper had spat full in his face and then walked away without a word. These were inexplicable, but certainly not egregious. He was baffled by the retreat, but also rather taken with it.

Jaretzki snapped a bean in half, inhaled its fresh smell, then popped it into his mouth and chewed it. It was crunchy and a little tart. He liked it.

"How long is it since you've been in the country?" Brother Phelan asked.

"I don't remember. Several years."

"You don't enjoy the outdoors, being around nature?"

Brother Phelan did. He had been convivial company in the bean field, recounting his boyhood in Missouri, on the banks of the Mississippi.

"I play polo, but being in a ring isn't being in the outdoors. I ski, but running a slope doesn't really bring you very close to nature."

"Did you have any experience of it when you were a boy?"

"Some."

"You didn't find it pleasant?"

"No." Jaretzki had tried to excise that part of his history from his life. It had never happened.

"Where did you grow up?"

"In Poland. If you don't mind, brother, I'd rather not talk about it."

"The things we'd rather not talk about are often precisely the things we *should* talk about."

"This isn't." Jaretzki shifted down the row, pulling the basket behind him.

"I ask you, I urge you," Brother Phelan said. "Tell me about it."

Jaretzki looked across the bushes. "Do I have a choice?"

"Man always has a choice. His will is free."

"And if I choose silence, what will be the consequence?"

Brother Phelan smiled enigmatically.

"All right," Jaretzki said. "I was brought up in Warsaw. But when I was seven, in 1941, my parents sent me south to live with the cousin of a man who worked for my father. I am a Polish Jew. You might recall that those were not particularly good days for Jews in Europe."

He looked away, to the shadows that moved over the sunlit slopes of the mountains. After several moments he said, "I was lucky. My parents, my brother and my sister died at Auschwitz. All the rest—my grandparents, uncles, aunts, cousins—died too. In Auschwitz, Teblinka and Belsec. I survived."

"Were you lucky?"

"I'm here, aren't I?"

"You survived. But were you lucky?"

Jaretzki didn't answer.

"What happened to you?"

"You're not going to leave it alone, are you?"

"No."

"The man with whom I was sent to live wasn't a Jew. He threw me out after a month. He kept the money my father had sent with me, of course. Understand that rural Poland hadn't changed much then since the Middle Ages. They were rough meanspirited peasants. I lived in the forest. I ate roots and nuts, tree bark to keep my stomach quiet when I couldn't find food. Sometimes I was taken in for a while. And *taken* is the appropriate word. They couldn't prove I was a Jew, but they knew there weren't many other reasons a boy would be alone in that wilderness, without family, friends, people who knew him, a village he'd come from. Along the way I was made a house slave, beaten, tortured and sodomized. Toward the end, a couple of drunken savages dragged me to the edge of town where there was a big maggot pit. People used to dump dead animals in there, rotten food. These men thought it would be a good joke to throw me in." A tic pulled at Jaretzki's eye. "I wasn't a very big child. Do you know what it's like to sink into a pit of maggots and rotting filth? To have your mouth fill with maggots when you try to scream? To have them in your ears, across your eyes, to think you're going to *drown* in that? I managed to reach the side, claw my way up and pull myself out. The men were already walking away. They were laughing and pounding each other on the shoulder. I was struck mute. I lost the power to speak. And I didn't regain it until three years later, in a DP camp."

He sat back on his heels and looked at the ground; then he reached for the bushes and resumed working.

"No. You were not lucky," Brother Phelan said quietly. He stood and lifted his basket, which was only partly full. "Come, Jaretzki. We have picked enough beans for the day. I want to hear more of this, but let us go down to the pond. It is prettier and more peaceful there."

Oakley Brown shuffled toward his room. His hands were swollen and they hurt. He was overwhelmed by despair, but grateful that the day was over and they were letting him go to bed.

Oh, sweet Mama, what was happening to him?

He didn't understand any of it. The monks hadn't done anything to him like they had to the fat man, making him crawl and eat off the floor like that. Or given him shitty food like the other blood. Or worked him over bad like that big guy Rauscher. Or any of the other stuff.

But what they had done was, for three days now, made him spend nearly every hour in the library reading the Bible. He didn't read so good and it was hard to get through all the pages that they told him he had to. His head would be pounding and his eyes hurt by the time he could finally close the book.

Then they would question him for an hour on what he'd read. Each time he gave a wrong answer or couldn't remember, they hit him across the hand with a ruler. Not too hard, only enough, ordinarily, to have stung a bit. But over three days of it, his hands had become so puffy and tender that he couldn't touch anything or even move them without pain.

He opened the door to his room carefully, protecting his hands. He closed it. He moved wearily to his sleeping board. There wasn't even a mattress anymore, just a board on the floor. Something fixed to the far wall caught the edge of his vision. He lifted his eyes.

He screamed.

He staggered back and came up hard against the door. He fumbled behind himself to open it, unmindful of the pain, not able to tear his eyes from the object on the wall, as if it might leap to attack him.

He backed into the hall with his hands shielding his face. "No!"

Brother Cooper and Brother George were on him immediately. They seized him by the shoulders. Brother Cooper twisted his arm up behind his back.

"Go on. Inside," Brother Cooper said.

"No! Don't make me!"

They wrestled him forward. He caught the sides of the door frame and tried to brace against them.

"Please!" he wailed.

They forced him through.

He stared transfixed with horror. A large gold crucifix had been mounted on the wall. It was spattered with blood, dark blood that glistened in the lamplight and dripped down the wall to form a little pool on the floor.

He moaned.

The monks released him. He shrank back against the wall.

Brother Cooper produced a wineskin from his robe and un-screwed the cap. Brother George took hold of Oakley's wrists. Brother Cooper poured blood from the skin onto Oakley's hands. The blood was warm.

Oakley shrieked.

Brother George held him firmly while Brother Cooper emp-tied what remained in the skin over Oakley's head. It ran down his face.

"No!"

Brother George let him go.

"If you take that crucifix down," Brother Cooper said, "then at dawn I will break your legs."

The monks left, shutting the door behind them.

Oakley held his bloodied hands away from his body. Blood ran down his cheeks and neck and dampened his tunic. He half crouched, and edged along the wall in terror toward the lamp on the end table. He reached his hand out, staring at the crucifix, and switched off the lamp. The room plunged into blackness.

He scuttled back along the wall. He sank down in the corner and put his arms up over his head, squeezed his eyes tightly shut. But still he saw the bloody crucifix in his mind. He whimpered.

At breakfast the following morning, the monks on either side of Cesar Alvarado rose suddenly, took him by the arms and pulled him upright.

"What are you doing?"

Some of the penitents looked up in alarm. Others carefully kept their eyes on their tin plates. The rest of the company paid no attention.

Alvarado was half dragged, half pulled out of the refectory.

"Don't let them take me," he appealed as he passed through the door, without effect.

The two monks marched him down the hall with long quick strides. Alvarado had been part of this kind of thing many times in Paraguayan prisons, but always from the other side.

"Where are we going? *Por favor*, tell me what is happening."

Images of the possibilities, the devices, the pain that he inflicted on a daily basis in his homeland tumbled through his mind and terrified him.

They brought him into a dispensary, through it and into a surgery. Brother Raphael was standing there beside a steel operating table, his fine white hair slightly ruffled, his face impassive.

"No!"

Alvarado tried to break free. But the monks were strong. They lifted him to the table and forced him down on his back. He struggled futilely as Brother Raphael secured him with straps. The infirmarer switched on the hooded surgery lamp and adjusted it so that it shone on an area somewhat lower than Alvarado's hips.

Alvarado's breath was quick and shallow. "I am an official of the Paraguayan government," he managed to say. "You are already involved in an international incident. Do not make it any worse."

Brother Raphael pulled Alvarado's robe up around his waist, exposing his groin. He picked up a scalpel.

"Por el amor del Cristo!" Alvarado shrieked. "What are you going to do?"

Brother Raphael bent forward. "Hold him."

Alvarado craned his head up and stared down the length of his torso in horror, his mouth a rictus, the cords in his neck swollen. He cried out when the scalpel touched him—as much in relief as in pain, for the blade fell upon his thigh, not his genitals.

Brother Raphael drew the scalpel across the thigh with delicate precision, slitting only the skin.

Alvarado gritted his teeth. Mostly to force himself to keep silent. He wanted to rage against them, to tell them they were calling the wrath of two governments down upon their heads, to tell them—and how sweet that would be—precisely what he would do to them if he had them in his own theater, to what heights of ecstasy he would rise. But whatever else he was, he was not mad. One does not say such things to men with knives who have you at their mercy.

Alvarado could make no sense of the monk's work, which was done in only a minute. Brother Raphael had slit the skin in a square, roughly five inches by five inches. The monk leaned closer, squinting. He pressed the scalpel in. Alvarado grunted and clenched his jaw. Brother Raphael separated the top edge of the square of skin from the underlying flesh.

He straightened and set the scalpel aside. He picked up a broad-bladed clamp. And then Alvarado understood; he had done the same thing himself.

He twisted against his bonds.

Brother Raphael applied the clamp along the length of the narrow flap he had created. He gripped the handle in both hands and exerted a slow steady pressure.

The skin was pulled off Alvarado's living flesh.

He screamed. His screams resonated down the stone hall into the refectory where the kneeling penitents froze, or twitched or jerked their heads up, which was why the door to the surgery had been left open.

Alvarado lay sweating and panting upon the table. The large patch of raw flesh was searingly painful. He groaned.

Brother Raphael held the square of living skin up to examine it. It was wet and grayish red on one side; the other was pale, with a few hairs growing from it.

"Very good," he said.

That evening, the penitents were told to sit at their places on the benches rather than to kneel. They were reluctant and apprehensive. Glasses were set before them, a dry white wine poured. They were served pork chops with a light orange sauce, parsleyed rice and creamed asparagus.

The monks didn't speak, but they did respond with a friendly smile if addressed. Some of the penitents picked dully at their food, others ate with furtive glances to the side and a few gobbled theirs down as quickly as they could. Fruit tarts were served for dessert, and after that the penitents were each given a snifter with a generous portion of cognac.

Brother Martin rose. He smiled out at them, exuding bon-homie and good cheer. "I hope you enjoyed your dinner," he said. "It's moments like this that remind us that life can be good, eh? It *is* good, because it is God's life. It only goes bad when man, when *we* pervert it. And we're quite adept at that, as all of you well know. God has given each of us a choice. But there's no sense laboring the point now—we've been over it before, we'll be going over it again.

"I trust that you've all found the Retreat to be, at the least, interesting, thus far. It is also effective, though many of you probably wouldn't agree with me now. I know that I didn't when I was wearing the gray robe of a penitent. Yes, I underwent my own Retreat once. As did every brother in this monastery. You see, we were each of us once men just like you. Not simply civilians or lay persons out in the world, but: men . . . just . . . like . . . you.

"That is the reason we are so good at this sort of thing. We *understand*."

Chapter 16

The respite continued through the evening. The Retreat began anew at midnight when two monks entered Peter Bates's cell and beat him with lengths of rubber hose.

Behind the lectern in the chapter room the next morning Alvarado told them, "I am an officer in the security branch of my government. There is much trouble in my country. It is my job to counteract the assassinations, murders and attacks upon legitimate authority. Our history and our society are different from yours. We must use stronger measures. I am forced to resort to physical persuasion sometimes. Sometimes the prisoners get hurt."

He sat down.

Brother Martin leaned back in his chair. He said, "Alvarado's official title is Chief Deputy of Education. What he is, is chief torturer. He's a skilled man and he likes his work. Close to a hundred men, women and children have died in agony under his hands; several hundred more have prayed that they would die." He summoned Oakley Brown.

Oakley's eyes were bloodshot. He stood hunched over the lectern. His ironpumper's body seemed to be collapsing in on itself. "I killed a old lady," he said. "I rip people off, that's what I do for bread. This old lady was about two weeks ago. She cursed me t' hell when she was dyin'. I'm gonna burn. There ain't no hope."

He returned to his seat. Brother Martin made no comment.

* * *

The afternoon was humid. Sweat stained Caparelli's robe. It ran in rivulets down his face, stung his eyes and was salty in his mouth. It rolled down his body and slicked his buttocks and thighs, chafing his skin as he worked. His hands were blistered. The sweat and dirt between his fingers were rubbing the skin raw.

He stood before the big pile of rocks with a heaving chest and aching arms and shoulders. The pile was his own height and perhaps fifteen feet in diameter, variously shaped rocks of between twenty and fifty pounds. He had been lifting and carrying them one at a time to another pile thirty yards away, which had not existed at all when he'd begun this morning. It seemed that he had moved half a mountain already, but the new pile was still only a small heap. He was beyond exhaustion. He could not lift one more stone. He sucked breath raspily, terrified that his pounding heart would clench in upon itself like a brutal fist and crush out his life.

Stitching a harness nearby, Brother Andrew asked, "What's the matter?"

Caparelli waited till he had enough breath. "My heart. I told you . . . weak heart. I got to . . . rest."

"What you have to do is make that one pile into the other."

"You're . . . gonna kill me!"

"Move the rocks." Brother Andrew set down the harness and picked up a whip.

Caparelli had been lashed twice already. He held up his hand. "No. I'll . . . do it."

He bent and took hold of a moderate rock, groaned with the strain to his back as he straightened. He stumbled toward the other pile. He'd picked the smallest rock at hand, but it felt as heavy as any he'd moved so far. His arms began to shake. Two-thirds of the distance, he lost control of them altogether. The rock fell to the ground with a thud. He sank dumbly to his knees, then down to all fours, struggling for breath.

Cr-rack!

The whip slashed across his back.

He threw back his head. "Ghhaaa!"

"Pick it up," Brother Andrew said.

"All right. I am . . . I am."

He struggled to lift the stone. He staggered the remaining distance like a drunk, near blinded by sweat.

He prayed without even knowing that he was doing so: Hail Mary, full of grace, the Lord is with thee. Blessed art thou amongst women and blessed is the fruit of thy womb, Jesus. Holy Mary, mother of God, pray for us sinners now and at the hour of our death. Amen.

Kennedy was outside in the fenced exercise area. Jaretzki was there too, and Pretty Boy, Bates, Wycisowicz. Kennedy didn't know where the other penitents were—they were a whole group only at the sessions in the chapter room now and sometimes at meals—and he didn't give a damn. He wasn't thinking of anything. That was the best way to get through this, he'd decided. Just go blank. He was walking slowly without purpose, looking down so he could avoid the goose droppings. Each night the flock of ill-tempered birds were released into the enclosure to serve, as they had in ancient times, as guards.

"Ummph!"

He was seized suddenly from behind, spun around and thrown to the ground. Brother Thomas and Brother George were on him immediately. They pinned him and ripped his robe down from the neck.

"What the fuck!"

Brother Thomas stunned him with an openhanded blow. They tore his tunic to either side, baring his chest.

Pretty Boy and Bates hurried away. Wycisowicz moved back, but didn't leave. Jaretzki, who was sitting nearby with his back against the monastery wall, looked on with interest.

Brother Hiram knelt down beside the pinioned Kennedy. He wore rubber gloves and held a sponge in one hand, a glass bottle in the other. He opened the bottle.

"This is a place of God. Those tattoos of yours are an abomination, Father."

He sloshed liquid from the bottle over the sponge, then pressed the sodden sponge onto the inverted crucified Christ tattooed on the left side of Kennedy's chest. Kennedy's skin began to sizzle and little wisps of smoke rose from it as the sulfuric acid ate its way in.

He twisted and screamed.

Brother Hiram loaded the sponge again. It was smoking and falling apart in liqueous shreds. He pressed it to the tattoo of the goat and naked woman on the right side of Kennedy's chest.

Kennedy's eyes were bulbous, his mouth a screaming hole in his bearded face.

Brother Hiram loaded what remained of the disintegrating sponge once more and squeezed the acid out in equal portions onto the tattoos.

Kennedy shrieked. His flesh bubbled and cooked.

Brother Hiram waited several moments, watching, then took up a bucket of clear water and sloshed it over Kennedy's chest.

The monks released him and left.

He lay on the ground hugging himself with his eyes squeezed shut, rolling from side to side, moaning.

The committee was the same that had served Brother Martin in selecting the penitents, except that he had replaced Brother Hilliard with Brother Cooper. The meeting was drawing to a close.

"So with several of them," the abbot said, "it's too early for a meaningful reading. I agree with Brother Cooper that Brother Phelan is indeed winning Jaretzki's trust, opening him up, and that though it's unusual, we should continue with this relatively soft tack. Caparelli is coming along well. Marcus is difficult. I think we might see some movement in Kennedy over the next day or two. We may have a serious and unforeseen problem with Rauscher. I'd like you there when I speak with him tonight, Brother Conrad. Ballantine's using his intelligence against us with some success, but I think we can break through in the next few days. That's about it, as far as I can see. Does anyone wish to add anything?"

None did. He dismissed them. He remained alone in the room a few minutes reviewing his notes. When he emerged, Brother Hiram was waiting in the hall.

"May I speak with you, abbot?"

Brother Martin motioned him inside and closed the door.

Brother Hiram's face was troubled. "I, I took Kennedy down this afternoon."

"Was there a problem?"

"No, no. That went well enough, but . . . I liked doing it. I liked inflicting the pain."

Brother Martin reflected several moments. "I'm not going to take you out of it. You have to face it, and vanquish it. You will wear a hair shirt for the rest of the Retreat to keep you aware of this."

Brother Hiram nodded.

"Was this feeling intense?"

"Yes."

"Did you welcome it?"

"Yes."

The problem was serious; it demanded strong response. "You must make amends. You will remove the nail from one finger tonight. Tear it out with a pliers. Offer your pain to God and beg His forgiveness."

Brother Hiram set his shoulders. "I am obedient to your will."

"Go now. Make your confession. Spend the remainder of the day in prayer."

Brother Martin made a mental note. He would monitor Brother Hiram closely over the next few days.

* * *

It was late night. The door to Pretty Boy's cell burst open. The light went on. He was shaken by the shoulder.

"Wha?" he cried, deep in murky exhaustion.

"Wake up. Up!"

The struggle to consciousness was awful. Even his *mind* hurt.

"No," he begged. *"Please*. I *got* t' sleep."

He was pulled to his feet. He trembled. A leg buckled. He caught himself against the wall. He couldn't open his eyes.

"I'll do anything," he mumbled. "Just let me sleep."

He couldn't calculate how long it had been since he'd rested. All his life. He couldn't think. He was coming apart.

"Stand up."

He swayed on his feet. He was sick—with exhaustion, hunger and thirst.

The novice, Brother Richard, watched the haggard black man rock back and forth, catch himself with a jerk as he started to slump. Pretty Boy was Brother Richard's responsibility tonight. Wake him at random intervals. No more than forty minutes uninterrupted sleep. They'd been at the man four days now.

"Tell me your address," Brother Richard said. "Tell me where you were born. What do you eat for lunch?" The questions were meaningless, no more than a device to prevent the darkness of sleep the man so desperately wanted.

Pretty Boy slurred incoherently.

Brother Richard kept it up several minutes. Then he took a flask of water and a lump of meat from his robe. The meat was turning. It was a slick greenish brown. It smelled bad. He gave it to Pretty Boy.

The penitent looked at it a moment. Then he ate it. He gagged, but he ate it.

Brother Richard offered the flask.

Pretty Boy unscrewed the cap and put it to his lips. He

drank, then retched and spat the water out. It was laced with vinegar.

Tears rose in his eyes. "Why you doin' this? Why you give me rotten food an' water?"

The novice should have kept his silence. But he said, "Because that's what you do. People come to you for things they think will make them happy, and you give them poison. Poison!"

Pretty Boy stared at him without comprehension. Shakily, he lifted the flask, poured a little of the fouled water into his mouth, held it, then forced himself to swallow.

Brother Richard took back the flask. "Go to sleep," he said.

He went out into the hall. There he stood quietly a moment. His own hands were trembling. He was disoriented. He was in the hall, but he was in the cell too. He was a novice in the Order of Saint Hector. He was a penitent. He was afraid. He was afraid of God.

A hand fell on his shoulder. He was startled and he dropped the flask.

Brother Stewart, his sponsor, said, "Is everything all right?"

"Yes. Yes, it is." He stooped and retrieved the flask. He shook his head. "No. I don't know. It brings back all the memories."

"Your own Retreat is over, brother. It was over three years ago. Let's talk. It will be all right."

They went down the hall, Brother Stewart's hand laying comfortingly on the novice's shoulder.

Roger Ballantine was manacled naked atop a low bench alone in the basement. His lower torso was completely immobilized by straps across his pelvis and thighs. A jerry can was suspended from the ceiling above him. It had been tapped and fitted with a spigot. A slow pearl of water was forming at the end of the spigot.

Ballantine stared at it through pain-shot eyes. It weighted into a teardrop, elongated, hung for a long moment by a thinning strand, then fell.

Splat. It struck his right testicle, exploding into tiny droplets across his wet thigh and belly.

Ballantine closed his eyes and groaned. A long, deep, sickened groan.

He lay in water that overran the bench and formed a small pool on the floor.

His testicle was bright red and distended to the size of an egg.

Every twenty seconds a thick, globular drop of water plunged down. Every twenty seconds for the last thirty-six hours.

A few of the penitents were absent from the chapter room. No one commented. Kennedy stood behind the lectern. A swath of gauze bandaging secured by adhesive tape was visible above the neck of his robe. Pinpoints of black and red burn marks freckled the base of his throat.

"I was a priest once," he said in a distanced voice. "A parish priest. I abused my office, especially the confessional. I used it to get what I wanted. With women. Mostly for sex. We had a school. I slapped a couple of nuns around. There was a big tough kid, fifteen, still in the eighth grade, who caused a lot of trouble. I beat him up. He spent two weeks in the hospital. The diocese sent me to a rest home for treatment. After a week I beat up my psychiatrist, broke his jaw, some ribs, and split and never went back. I live in the hills outside of Los Angeles, in a commune. There's a lot of sex, a lot of drugs."

He walked back to his place on the bench.

"It's a cult rather than a commune," Brother Martin said. "A Satanic cult, and Kennedy is its leader. He preys upon his own followers. He's been arrested twice for murder. In one case, charges were dropped after two of his 'wives' retracted their testimony. In the other, the state's witness disappeared." The abbot looked at Kennedy. "Did you kill him?"

Kennedy's hand drifted unconsciously to his chest. After several moments he said, "Yes."

"And were you guilty of the other two murders?"

"Yes."

Brother Martin allowed silence to gather in the room. Then he said, "Jaretzki."

From the lectern, Jaretzki searched out Brother Phelan with his eyes. "Some of you know my work. It's fashion photography. Its foundation is sado-masochistic—leather, chains, vicious animals, weapons, the spectrum of accoutrements. This isn't a conceit. It is organic to me, it's how I lead my own personal life. There are many willing partners in this kind of thing. But best, and most exciting, are those who aren't willing. The modeling profession is very competitive, the ego-gratification seductive and the rewards, at the top, enormous. Most models will do or submit to anything if it will help them. I am in a position of power, and I use that power constantly. I use it to coerce young women to satisfy my appetites. The more they hold out, the more the activities revolt them, then that much more exciting it is for me.

"There is a lovely blond young woman who is now identified as the mother in advertisements for a baby shampoo. She is depicted as the very ideal of sweetness and wholesomeness. And she is very much that way in reality. It was six months before I could force her into my bed and another three before I could make her degrade herself. The campaign was exquisite, her humiliation thrilling."

He faltered, rubbed at his mouth.

"Sometimes I've gone too far. Last month a woman was hospitalized with a vaginal wound that required suturing. It is less the physical abuse that pleases me than the subjugation and humiliation of . . . I suppose you could call them my victims." He worked his jaw. "I am also responsible for two deaths. One died from an infection following a hemorrhage, the other cut her wrists after I had had her for the weekend."

He went back to his place.

Brother Martin said nothing.

* * *

The morning was cheery and bright. Sunlight spilled in through the open windows and songbirds were in chorus. Brother Martin and Brother Anthony walked across the entrance hall toward the stairs.

They climbed to the second floor.

Ableman was sitting crosslegged on his mattress in a diaper and T-shirt. He had a big rubber ball. One hemisphere was a blue field with red stars, the other a red field with blue stars, separated by a white band. He was rolling the ball a few inches to his right, then back again to the left. There were a rolypoly clown, a jack-in-the-box and other toys scattered about. Ableman was babbling to himself when the monks entered.

He looked up with an uncertain smile. "Ba?"

Brother Martin said, "Hi there, little fellow. How are you this morning?"

"Gavoo. Beeta. Mobuh."

"Sure." The abbot knelt on the mattress. "Let's see if we were a good boy last night." The drugs made that impossible.

"Buh?"

And indeed Ableman had soiled his diaper. Brother Martin tore it off and held it up before Ableman's eyes.

"What did you do?" He slapped Ableman. "Bad boy! Shame on you! You're a bad boy!"

Ableman fell over and tried to shield himself with his arms, which were weak and not well-coordinated.

Brother Martin ranted and flailed at him.

Ableman was crying bitterly.

The abbot ceased. He stood. He looked down at the man-baby and felt sick to his stomach. He needed urgently to be gone from here.

"Finish it," he said to Brother Anthony.

He left. He walked down the hall to a study nook, braced his hands on the sill of the open window and leaned forward.

He looked out to the stolid and imperturbable mountains. Tears rose to his eyes. He remembered how much it hurt—the bewilderment, the horror, the pain, the bitter helpless tears. For a moment he was that baby again, confused and tormented. He curled his hands, digging his nails into his palms, and offered the pain up to God. He prayed for strength.

In the cell, Brother Anthony crooned to Ableman. "There, there, it's all right now. Everything's fine, little fellow, everything's fine."

Brother Anthony maintained the reassuring patter while he cleaned Ableman up with soap and warm water. Ableman finally quieted under the gentle touch and voice. Tentatively, he smiled. He began to coo. He was a gurgling baby a little under six feet tall, lying on his back while someone washed his nether parts—the full wrinkled scrotum and the thick stub of his penis, encouched in a tangle of dense pubic hair—patted them dry with a towel and powdered them.

"Ah-gah," he said, with pleasure.

Brother Anthony smiled. "That's right, little fellow. And ah-gah-gah to *you*." He made a blubbery sound with his breath and flapping lips.

Ableman laughed delightedly.

Brother Anthony rubbed the powder on softly. Ableman's penis began to grow.

"Ah-by-ba . . . ?" A look of happiness and inner focus spread over his face. "Ay?"

Brother Anthony took the lengthening penis into his hand. Slowly, he began to stroke it up and down.

"Ghuh," Ableman said.

"Good. Feels good," Brother Anthony said. He detached from himself. He pictured the Scourging. He tried to become one with the mortal body of Christ, tied to the pillar.

"Gah-woo."

"Buh."

"Maa-ba-gha."

Brother Anthony increased the pace. The lash fell steadily on Christ's back.

"Eh."

"By-ba?"

"Oooooooooooo."

The infant Ableman came in thick spurts, with a slack glassy and beatific expression.

He sighed.

"Bad!" Brother Anthony shouted. He slapped Ableman's testicles. "That's dirty, disgusting!" He punched Ableman in the stomach. He needed will to do this, to overcome his compassion for the child; for it was a child now, despite the appearance of its body. He struck Ableman across the face. Again. "That's filthy. You're a rotten stinking piece of shit." He hit him.

And then anger burgeoned within him. Not at this helpless guise, but at Ableman the man, who regularly tortured the helpless.

The blows struck more forcefully. "You son of a fucking bitch!"

He hit Ableman all over his body. Ableman cried and whimpered and screamed and waved his arms and legs in terror.

And then Brother Anthony *wanted* to beat him. And the instant he realized that, he stopped. He gripped his hands in prayer and pressed his forehead to his knuckles.

Ableman rolled about on his mattress, squalling.

The moment passed. Brother Anthony was delivered. He offered thanksgiving from the depths of his soul.

Ableman collapsed. He sobbed.

Brother Anthony wished to comfort him, wished to comfort his own child, who was dead. God was wise. He would not have been a fit father; he had not even been a fit human being. But to comfort the man now would be to undo what had been done. So he diapered him quickly and efficiently and walked out of the room.

The hall was empty. Birds were singing in the branches of

the cloister trees. Brother Anthony wondered what his child would have been like. He thought of Lily, missing her, which was wrong. But he could not help wondering to which of the penitents she would be offered.

Gregorio Rios was pure, disembodied, hysterical consciousness.

He was dead.

He shrieked without sound.

There was nothing.

No breath. No heart. No eyes, ears, touch. Nothing.

He was frenzied. Thought was only a thing of fragmented instants. The rest was raw mad panic.

In the objective world he was limp on his back in a bed in the infirmary.

Brother Hilliard stood beside him and looked down lovingly, enviously at his slack corpselike face. The prior imposed upon it a state of serenity, and oh how he yearned for that serenity.

Brother Raphael entered. He raised his eyebrows. "Yes?"

"How long has he been like that?"

"Going on fifteen hours."

"What's it like?"

"Like being in hell."

"How does it work?"

"Basically it blocks sensory input to the brain. The involuntary nervous system keeps functioning, but nothing else. You could shout at him, stick him with a pin, shine a light in his eyes and he wouldn't know it. Nothing reaches him. It's as if his *being*, his consciousness, perhaps even his soul, if you will, were suspended in a vacuum, isolated in an utterly empty universe."

"He looks so peaceful," Brother Hilliard mused.

"He isn't. Depending upon the individual, hallucination begins somewhere between two and three hours. Mental integrity deteriorates steadily. He's living in unadulterated nightmare now."

And I too, thought Brother Hilliard.

How he had once fled from the ever-patient Hound of Heaven. He recalled from Thompson's poem:

> Up vistaed hopes I sped;
> And shot, precipitated,
> Adown Titanic glooms of chasmed fears,
> From those strong Feet that followed, followed after.

But he'd been caught finally, snatched up by adamantine jaws in the dark cave of Saint Hector's. But then the Hound had dropped him and in turn fled itself. Now it was he who followed, followed after. With the ravening hunger of a starveling.

From the same poem he remembered, and spoke silently, as a prayer: Naked I wait Thy love's uplifted stroke!

Brother Raphael shattered his abstraction. "Is there something you want?"

"No. No, nothing you can give me." Brother Hilliard turned and walked out.

Caparelli stood at the lectern in the chapter room. He was pale and his unshaven cheeks were stubbled gray and black. "I made my bones when I was nineteen," he said. "They told me, 'You look good, kid. You want to work for us, you take care of this guy.' They gave me a gun. I just walked up behind him in the street, put the barrel about an inch from his head and pulled the trigger. I don't know how many guys I killed. A lot. And I busted up a lot more. Even when I could give the orders, I still liked to do it myself. The last guy was the job they just found me not guilty for. I knocked his brains out and left him ass over heels in the garden of this restaurant out in Brooklyn. I done a lotta people and I had fun doin' 'em all."

Sitting with the other penitents, Orson winced to hear him say this.

When Caparelli was back at his place, Brother Martin called up Pretty Boy. Pretty Boy kept his eyes focused at a point somewhere level with their knees. His voice was flat.

"I hustle runaways. They don't have no place to stay, no way to live. I turn 'em into hookers. Sometimes you got t' break 'em before they'll do it. You lock 'em up and get about ten guys t' fuck 'em round the clock, every way someone can get fucked, for a week. Mostly I turn 'em into junkies too. That keeps 'em needin' me. Now and then one gets out of line and I cut her or burn her to make sure the others don't get no ideas. I wasted two guys and three chicks in my life. This one chick was mine, but she was tryin' t' swing my whole string to this other dude. I tied her to a bed and gagged her. I shoved a curling iron up her cunt, turned it on and left her there. Let her cook t' death."

The penitents were all present in the refectory on the evening of the thirteenth day. This engendered hope in some, caused new alarm in others.

Brother Stefan went to the lectern. He said, "Tonight's lesson is from the Book of Numbers. Take heed and meditate upon it for it is the Word of God." He opened the Bible.

He read: "And if he smite him with an instrument of iron, so that he die, he is a murderer: the murderer shall surely be put to death.

"And if he smite him with a stone, wherewith he may die, and he die, he is a murderer; the murderer shall surely be put to death.

"Or if he smite him with a hand weapon of wood, wherewith he may die, and he die, he is a murderer: the murderer shall surely be put to death.

"The revenger of blood himself shall slay the murderer: when he meeteth him, he shall slay him. . . .

"Moreover ye shall take no satisfaction for the life of a

murderer, which is guilty of death: but he shall surely be put to death. . . .

"So ye shall not pollute the land wherein ye are: for blood it defileth the land: and the land cannot be cleansed of the blood that is shed therein, but by the blood of him that shed it."

Brother Stefan stood with his hands upon the Bible. His eyes wandered over the penitents. "So it is written," he said. "So shall it be."

Oakley Brown collapsed and began to sob.

At midnight the penitents were roused from sleep and brought to the chapter room. The company was already assembled there.

Brother Martin walked slowly back and forth before them. He stopped at midpoint and gazed at them several moments.

"None of you," he said, "is here of your own free will. You each know that *you* were either duped or forced into coming to us. Be assured that the same is true of your fellows. You were *all* manipulated into this Retreat."

He paused, allowing them to absorb this.

"You are violent and destructive men. You have murdered, mutilated and in other ways hurt a large number of people. You have done this willfully and happily. Violence is the very core of your lives. You are a plague upon the earth and a living scourge to God's children.

"You are not alone. You and your kind roam the world killing and tormenting like ravening beasts. By 'your kind' I mean men about whom one additional thing can be said— for one reason or another, the normal institutions of society have not been able to stop you. Law, peer pressure, religion, all of society's devices and functions, have failed against you. You are too powerful, too clever, too quick, you have outwitted or in some other way neutralized sanction and restraint and remained free to continue your depredations. In so doing, not only have you inflicted agony, but you have imperiled your own immortal souls."

The abbot gazed at them, and love suffused his face. "All that, my brothers in Christ, is no longer true."

He was silent a beat.

"Our primary concern is the salvation of your souls. Everything we are and everything we do is in the service of that cause. Our secondary goal, which is less important, but still of concern, is to prevent you from continuing to prey upon your fellow man. If we can help you to achieve the first, then the second automatically follows. If we fail in the first, we shall be deeply grieved, but still, we will not be deterred in accomplishing the second.

"You will probably not believe me at this point, but we have no desire to exact retribution from you or to act as surrogate for your victims and bring vengeance upon you in their behalf. But there must be punishment. Punishment which will enable you to reach a point where you can offer it up to God as penance. For there can be no forgiveness of sin without the sacrament of Penance.

"Soon you will be asked to name for us some particular penance that you believe is fitting in light of your individual sins. You will be judged by God—and us—on the appropriateness of the penance you choose. That will indicate your sincerity or lack of it, the truth of your contrition.

"And finally, I stand here to tell you, my beloved brothers in Christ, that you have passed through the most profoundly significant door of your lives. It is a one-way door. There is no going back.

"None of you is ever going to get out of here. Ever."

Chapter 17

Hector guided the occasionally stubborn but in general agreeable donkey two days into the wilderness, to the place he had prepared. They traveled where there were no trails, through woods and across stony dry hills, where they would not encounter anyone. The leatherworker, who was bound tightly over the back of the donkey, demanded to know what Hector thought he was doing, detailed the many and horrible things he would do to the mendicant if he were not set free at once. Hector made no answer. The leatherworker bellowed. He threatened. He cajoled. He offered bribes and roared himself hoarse. To no effect. When it became too dark to travel at the end of the first day, Hector pulled him from the donkey and tied him sitting up to the bole of a tree.

In the morning, wakened by Hector at dawn, he blinked, oriented himself, then started in again. Hector cut a long switch from a tree and whipped him until he held his tongue. He used the switch four more times that morning. The correlation finally clarified itself to the leatherworker, who kept his silence for the rest of the journey.

The place Hector had prepared was on the side of a harsh mountain, where there were patches of scraggly woods and infrequent trickles of water. He had built a little hovel there. Not far from the hovel was a sturdy twisted tree to which he had attached a six-foot length of chain. From his hovel he brought forth two sets of iron shackles. He secured them with bolts to the leatherworker's wrists and ankles and peened the bolts closed. He attached the short chain between the ankle shackles to the length secured to the tree. Then he lay down on the ground to rest.

When he woke, an hour later, the leatherworker was sitting glowering at him and chewing on his beard in fury. He shook his chains and demanded to be released.

Hector went into his hovel and returned with the staff he had cut and shaped. He beat the man with it. He beat him methodically and for a long time, careful of where and how hard he struck so that he wouldn't break a bone or grievously injure an organ.

The hours became days, which became weeks, which became months. The leatherworker's clothes rotted away and he was left naked in the elements. Hector starved him. He beat him. He read to him from the Bible. He pelted him whole days with small stones. He burned his feet and hands with glowing coals. He tormented and bedeviled him in every way his mind could devise. And he prayed ceaselessly over him and poured out his love to him. When the leatherworker became sick, he built him a small shelter, gave him his own blanket and food, nursed him and lay down beside him and held him to give him warmth.

In time, over the passage of three seasons, it was done. The leatherworker, whose name was Joseph, was delivered of his evil at last. Gaunt, scarred and stricken, he embraced Hector in the name of their Savior and they became as brothers.

They passed an entire month together in prayer and meditation, laboring silently through the days with Christ burning in their hearts. They built a small but more solid habitation for themselves of stone. Then, when they felt ready, they went down from the mountain, leading the phlegmatic little donkey behind them.

When they returned, a short pockfaced man was lashed over the donkey's back. His name was Carlo. He was a potter. Carlo was easier than Joseph had been. The process required only three months. By the following spring, they were four. The next man, a bailiff who had held his community in terrified thrall, was much more difficult than any of them could have imagined. After fourteen months he would still lunge at them if they happened, abstracted and unawares, within the little striking range his chain allowed. He would begin to growl and snarl again whenever, in testing respites, they allowed him to rebuild his strength, and at night he continued to mutter to himself all the dire vengeance he planned to wreak on them.

Hector was troubled. He left his brothers to climb higher on the mountain, and there he fasted and meditated for three days. When he returned it was late evening, almost fully dark, and a fire was burning outside the cramped little stone shelter. He called them to his side. "Brothers," he said with a disquieted face, "there is something we must discuss."

The penitents were told in the morning to remove their gray robes. They were each given a tunic of stiff woven horsehair. The tunics fell to mid-thigh, the sleeves fit closely. The morning was warm, and thickening with humidity. At breakfast, the penitents were sweating. Angry rashes began to spread across their skin.

In a chair beside one of the infirmary beds, Brother Raphael made an entry in his log. DiPalo's blood pressure was down, his respiration quick and shallow and his pulse rate high, but all within acceptable limits.

He was strapped naked atop the bed. Sometimes he screamed, and sometimes he moaned, but he was gagged and the sounds were muffled. In the beginning he'd wrenched himself about violently. But the two-hour session had exhausted him and now he simply lay quivering, bathed in sweat, staring up through pain-bright eyes.

So far, Brother Raphael was pleased with the drug, one of the new ones. On a tray at the bedside were two additional syringes as safety precaution—one charged with an antidote, the other with a heart stimulant—and an oxygen tank and mask stood against the wall. It seemed, however, that these would not be necessary.

The clandestine drug was a third-generation derivative of cobra venom, which attacked the central nervous system. One effect of the natural venom was hypersensitivity of the skin. Legitimate research was targeted on certain nervous disorders. This particular, unauthorized, version heightened skin sensitivity to the point where it was if there were no skin at all, as if the entire body surface were raw flesh; even the caress of a mild breeze resulted in undiluted and excruciating pain.

Brother Raphael felt some sorrow, some reluctance over this, but it was his moral duty, required by his love of mankind, and he was obligated to do all that he could to aid in the salvation of this particular man's immortal soul. That, and his clinical, professional curiosity about the drug were enough to sustain him.

"DiPalo," he said. "Can you see me?"

Orson simply lay there trembling, bathed in his own sweat.

"Can you hear me?"

Again, there was no discernible response.

It was possible, Brother Raphael thought, that the unwavering reception of pain had pushed the man over a threshold, blocking out any stimuli but itself. He was uncertain whether this would be a desirable effect. He would have to discuss it with Brother Conrad, who had the most acute psychological insight among them, and with Brother Stefan, who would reflect upon the spiritual implications.

The infirmarer took up a piece of steel wool and ran it down the length of Orson's body. Orson threw himself against the restraints like a man engulfed in flame. Beneath the gag, he screamed.

Half an hour more, Brother Raphael decided. Then he'd bring him out, give him an hour to recover and put him under again.

* * *

"The *picquet*," Brother Cooper had said. "A French innovation of several centuries ago. Not nearly so elaborate or
stylish as most of their constructs, but not without a certain
simple elegance, and conducive of meditation on a specific
level."

Three hours ago.

Sweat ran down Sawyer's forehead, stung his eyes and
blurred his vision. He'd chewed his lips raw. The taste of sweat
and blood intermingled in his mouth. The first pain, of course,
had originated in his shoulder and the pad of his great toe.
Now it inhabited most of his body, expressed in diverse modes:
a biting constriction round his wrist, pounding ache, strain
and the sensation of imminent separation in his shoulder; which
bled torturously down his side through his twisted musculature,
a pulling of his joints; the ball of his toe was pulsing torment,
pierced ever more deeply, and from it each beat of his heart
shot charges of pain up his leg and into his groin; this in the
right side of his body, now sympathetically mimicked by the
left, which of its own accord, wrenched out of alignment, had
formulated its unique complex of misery, overflowing into the
right.

There behind the monastery Sawyer hung alone and agonized from the limb of an oak, suspended by a carefully measured length of rope. The rope was knotted to a leather strap
around his right wrist. His body stretched down to the swollen
and inflamed pad of his big toe. The toe had been secured with
thongs in such a way that, in the beginning, he could just lift
the flesh away from the tip of the sharp wooden stake beneath
it if he flexed the muscles of his back and arm and pulled
himself up a little.

His capacity to exercise that option had ended quite some
time ago.

The stake was striated with dark red lines of his blood.

The pain was ceaseless, and Sawyer could think of nothing
else. Nothing at all.

* * *

Roger Ballantine stood at the lectern in the chapter room. The hair tunic was in stark contrast to his pallidity, looking like some dark beast that had clamped itself around his body.

He said to them: "I have performed unnecessary surgeries. Every surgeon has. The large fees are tempting. Maybe I've done more than others. My surgery has also been . . . sloppy at times." He glanced at the abbot. He didn't know the extent of the monks' information. It would be madness to reveal more than the minimum required to satisfy them. He decided to test by tossing them a sop—they knew about Marian LeGarde anyway. "And once," he said, "I, I was angry with a patient and purposely botched the job. I scarred her urethra, which resulted in pain whenever she urinated and in recurring infection."

He hung his head, as if in shame, stood silent a moment, then started back to the bench.

Brother Martin's voice caught him up short.

"Dr. Ballantine recounts his career too modestly. He's performed several dozens of unnecessary surgeries. And the fees aren't much relevant. Dr. Ballantine has very little sexual appetite. And he finds the sexual lives of others repugnant. He dislikes people for their sexuality. He feels that they should be punished. He's in a position to do that. He does, frequently, and he enjoys it. He has removed testicles, ovaries, prostates and uteruses without cause or when a less radical procedure would have sufficed. He has mutilated genitals and performed surgery in such fashion that the patients are condemned to pain whenever they attempt a sexual act for the rest of their lives."

Arrested in midstride, standing still with his back to the abbot, Ballantine was horrified and frightened.

Brother Martin said, "Sit down, Doctor Ballantine."

Rios was called up. He looked drained to the point of collapse. "I've done a lot," he said. "I've murdered people, I've starved them, I've left them to die." He spoke with his eyes cast down, barely audible, as if to himself. He was only partly coherent, his mind still reeling from his time under the drug. Brother Martin let him ramble until he began to repeat himself and wander down odd little byways of memory.

The abbot said, "That is enough. Sit down now, Rios."

Rios blinked. He nodded several times. He went back slowly to his place.

They came for Alvarado late at night, three of them, bursting into his room and jerking him up from his sleeping board. They pulled his arms behind his back and were tying his wrists before he was fully awake. A gag went over his mouth, was knotted tight behind his head.

"What are you doing?" he tried to cry. The gag allowed only a sound of garbled panic.

They rushed him out into the hall and down the stairs. They went through the door out of the monastery into the night. There were no geese. The fence gate was open. Far ahead, somewhere behind the barn, torchlight flickered in the darkness, illuminating part of the nearby forest line.

Alvarado tried to brace against the monks, but it was useless. He half stumbled, was half dragged between them.

He heard the low chant of massed voices, which grew louder as he neared the barn. The monks bulled him around the corner, came to a halt.

The chant stopped abruptly.

Alvarado's eyes widened. His legs collapsed. The monks caught him under the armpits and dragged him forward.

A great pile of brushwood and logs, some fifteen feet in diameter and nearly the height of a man, rose in the clearing behind the barn. And standing at the center was a tall wooden post fitted with chains. The monks of the order were ringed around the pyre, cowls drawn up, with burning brands in hand.

Brother Martin appeared before Alvarado. "A decision has been made," he said. He raised a crucifix. *"In Nomine Patri et Filii et Spiritu Sancti. Amen."* He stepped back.

A ramp led up the sloping pyre. Alvarado was dragged up it to the top, held pressed against the post and chained tightly to it. He twisted and tried to scream.

The ramp was withdrawn.

"Pray for the salvation of your soul," Brother Martin said below him. "May God welcome you into his heart." He touched a torch to the edge of the pyre.

The brushwood caught. It crackled. The other monks lowered their torches to the wood.

The fire began to eat its way upward.

Alvarado threw himself against the taut chains. He screamed, to no effect. The fire advanced on him from all sides. It snapped and hissed. Smoke billowed, burning his lungs. The flames leaped higher, shimmering the air. He could feel the heat beating at him now.

He was engulfed by thick plumes of smoke, which, colored by the reaching fire, appeared to him as sheets of flame. He choked beneath the gag. Tears streamed from his stung eyes. He fought the chains. The metal links bit into his flesh.

No! he tried to shriek.

A blast of superheated air hit him. His body hair sizzled. Flames licked at his legs.

He fainted, sagging limply in his chains.

Brother Martin said, "Go!"

Brother Vergil had been chewing the inside of his cheek with mounting force. Images of the church he had firebombed in Alabama clicked in and out of his mind. He saw the flames roar through the shattered windows, race up the walls toward the roof. He heard the screams of the choir girls burning to death within.

God, oh God, the screams!

Then, finally, Brother Martin said, "Go!"

Brother Vergil grabbed up the ramp with Brother Abner. They heaved it atop the pyre. It fell short of Alvarado by a couple of feet. They shoved it from the bottom, thrusting up to him. Brother Vergil leaped on it and ran up its length, disregarding the flames that licked at his robe, the popping sparks that burned his legs.

Around the pyre, three more ramps were thrown up. Monks with watersoaked blankets made their way up them beating at the flames on either side. Two other monks approached with hoses connected to the water line in the barn, opened the nozzles and played streams of water over the burning wood, most of which they had soaked earlier, layering only a thin cover of dry pieces over the top.

The hem of Brother Vergil's robe caught fire. He ignored it, fumbling with the locks on Alvarado's chains.

Brother Abner was behind him, beating the burning wood with a sodden blanket. "Up here!" he shouted. "Get a hose on us!"

A jet of water was directed at them. Brother Abner struck at Brother Vergil's burning robe with his blanket.

"Ah!" Brother Vergil freed the last lock. Alvarado fell into his arms. He caught the man up. "Give me room," he said urgently.

Brother Abner edged aside. Brother Vergil ran down the ramp. He carried Alvarado several yards away from the pyre. He laid him down carefully. Brother Raphael knelt stiffly on one knee. He raised Alvarado's eyelid. He checked the man's respiration and pulse. "He's fine."

"Precipitant," Brother Martin said to Brother Vergil. "But bravely done."

"It was in God's name."

Brother Raphael pronounced the burns on Alvarado's legs superficial. He examined Brother Vergil's legs, inspected his hands. "You took as much damage as he did. I want you in the infirmary too. I'll salve you both down. There's a nasty one on your calf."

Brother Martin remained at the pyre until the last ember was extinguished. The smell of wet charred wood hung heavily in the humid night. Alone, he played his flashlight across the blackened pile and up to the post with its hanging chains.

He heard in his mind the screams of thousands, down through the centuries.

Hauptmann recognized it instantly. Cylindrical, gray, half an inch long, about the diameter of a pencil.

A blasting cap.

They had him outside, near the ice house at the rear of the monastery. Brother Anthony held his shoulders pinned to the ground. The monk's face was as dispassionate as the Death's-Head tattooed at the base of his jaw.

Brother Gilbert held the blasting cap in one hand, a roll of duct tape in the other.

Hauptmann knew what was going to happen. The question was: where? Sweat prickled out on his body. Brother Gilbert knelt. Hauptmann sucked in breath.

The monk taped the cap to his outer thigh.

Hauptmann's relief was the thing of an instant. He steeled himself.

Brother Gilbert attached two wires to the cap, stepped off and fixed the other ends to the terminals of a small hand switch. He nodded to Brother Anthony.

Brother Anthony turned his head away.

Hauptmann shut his eyes and clenched his jaw. The tendons in his throat rose into relief.

Brother Gilbert threw the switch.

Buumph!

The heavy duct tape had a tamping effect. It was blown apart, but still it directed the larger part of the force into Hauptmann's thigh.

"Yhhhaaa!" Hauptmann arched up violently, then dropped back down.

The cap had blown a crater into his flesh larger than a silver dollar and nearly three quarters of an inch deep. It was a mix of seeping blood and black charred meat; specks of unconsumed powder smoldered within it.

* * *

Max Rauscher hunched over the lectern in the chapter room. His eyes were blackened, his nose swollen, his lower lip split. His hairy hands gripped the corners of the lectern hard. He glowered out at monks and penitents alike.

He said: "Eat shit."

There was silence.

Brother Martin said, "Rauscher is what's known as 'muscle.' A goon. He works for loan sharks, extortionists, anyone who wants someone else hurt. He breaks bones. He fractures skulls. He's stomped half a dozen people to death. He enjoys his work. If he can't get paid, he'll go out and do it just for the pleasure. Sit down, Rauscher."

The abbot summoned Orson.

A sickly pallor underlay Orson's dark complexion. He stood several moments collecting his thoughts. "'I like to toy with people," he said slowly. "Especially women. I like the added sexual kick. But anybody'll do. I like to spin them around and fuck up their minds. And I like to cut people. I like to slice them and see that smooth skin open up and the blood pour out, the shock on their faces—the disbelief at first, and then the horror."

When he finished several minutes later, Brother Martin dismissed him without comment. "Sawyer," the abbot said.

Sawyer limped to the lectern. His fine brown hair was unwashed and tangled. His boyish handsomeness had become a distorted mirror image of itself. He spoke about his welfare clients.

". . . and I force them to make phony claims. I approve the claims. I keep most of the money. You see, I have all this power over them, they're dependent on me. If I cut them off the list, there's nowhere else to go. I get them to wash my clothes, clean my apartment. I make them shoplift for me. I get them off if they're caught. Once I couldn't swing it. The woman had too long a record. She told the court I made her do it. It was her word against mine, which was no contest. They put her away.

"It's the power," he said. "All that power. I can make them do anything I want. Sometimes, with a pretty one, I'll beat her with a belt. She can't do anything. It gets me high. But for most sex . . ." He stopped. "For most sex, I like the young ones best. Twelve, thirteen. Sometimes the girls just go along because that's what their life is like. That's okay, but what's better is when they don't want to and I make their mamas talk them into it, I make their mamas *make* them do it. Mama always does because she knows that's the way it has to be. Sometimes, when they just won't and they cry and get hysterical, I make their mamas hold them down while I do it to 'em."

Brother Martin said nothing when Sawyer finished.

"Please," Wycisowicz begged. "Not again. I can't take any more. Please, no."

Brother Raphael was drawing light amber liquid from a stoppered bottle up through the needle into the cartridge of a syringe.

Wycisowicz was weak. He could barely struggle up to a sitting position. He tried to swing his legs off the infirmary bed. Brother Raphael put a hand on his shoulder and gave him the lightest of shoves. Wycisowicz fell back down to the rubber sheet. The sheet was foul with urine, vomit and excrement.

Brother Raphael dabbed Wycisowicz's arm with a cotton ball wetted with alcohol. There were already two needle marks in this arm; six in the other. Drug-antidote. Drug-antidote. A two-hour session thus far, fifteen minutes under, fifteen minutes to recover. Brother Raphael slipped the needle into the vein and slowly depressed the plunger.

Wycisowicz wept.

The first convulsion struck ninety seconds later. It twisted him into a ball and forced a grating rasp from his throat. Then it threw him onto his side. His legs drew up, shot straight again. An arm pulled hard into his diaphragm. He jerked. Frothy bile spilled from his lips. A trickle of liquid escaped his clenched buttocks, all that was left in him. He flipped onto his back. His knees locked almost to his chin. His arms shook.

Brother Raphael decided this would be the final dose. The penitent was strong and in good condition, but not even the healthiest heart could stand against this kind of strain much longer.

Five monks were required to wrestle Rauscher down into the basement. They were sweating and breathing hard by the time they managed to strap him to the table. They had taken several hard blows and one had been bitten badly on the arm. Three of them withdrew, leaving Brother James and the novice Brother Richard behind.

"You fuckin' freaks. You fuckin' assholes," Rauscher said from the table. "You fuckin' think you're gonna beat me down? Fuck you, jerkoffs."

Neither Brother James nor Brother Richard responded.

Rauscher lay back, his big chest pumping. He alternately balled his hands into fists, then relaxed them. He uttered low growling sounds to himself. He blinked, then scowled up at the thin haze of smoke undulating near the ceiling. He sniffed, and frowned.

Brother Richard wheeled over from the corner a brazier that stood upon a tripod. A wavering aura of heat and wispy smoke rose from it. Projecting out from the bowl was a thick iron bar some two and a half feet long.

Brother James donned heavy leather welder's gloves. He removed the bar from the brazier. It glowed white-red at its tip. He advanced on the table. "'And call ye on the name of your gods, I will call on the name of the Lord: and the God that answereth by fire, let him be God.'"

Rauscher bared his teeth in feral menace.

Beside the table, Brother Richard pulled into himself. It felt as if his soul were shriveling. "Wait..."

Brother James pressed the tip down across Rauscher's forehead.

"Ghhyaahhh!"

The iron burned in. Rauscher's flesh crackled and smoked.

"Ghhyahhh! Ghhyahhh!"

The sound filled Brother Richard's mind and shattered him. Brother James withdrew the rod.

Rauscher kept screaming. He heaved against the straps.

"Oh no. Oh no," Brother Richard said. Tears rose in his eyes. He loosed the strap across Rauscher's ankles.

"What are you doing?" Brother James shouted over Rauscher's cries. He moved to stop the novice.

Brother Richard pushed him away. "Oh no. We mustn't hurt him." He freed the strap across Rauscher's waist.

Brother James dropped the bar. It fell with a clang. He seized Brother Richard. "Don't do that!"

Brother Richard threw him off. Brother James stumbled backward and fell.

Brother Richard fumbled open the chest strap, then went to the wrist straps. "It's all right," he said, tears slicking his cheeks. "It'll be all right. I'm so sorry."

"Yaaah!"

Rauscher lunged up from the table. He grabbed Brother Richard by the throat and drove his great fist into the novice's face. Brother Richard's cheekbone cracked. He went spinning away and fell to his hands and knees. He knelt there dazed.

Brother James was on his feet. A man of size and strength himself, he hurled himself at Rauscher from behind and clubbed the back of his head with his fist. Rauscher whirled and backhanded him across the face. Brother James grunted. He aimed a kick at Rauscher's groin. Rauscher dodged it and almost caught his foot. They closed and hammered at each other. One of Brother James's ribs cracked with stabbing pain. He broke off and was able to grab up the iron bar before Rauscher could reach him. He swung it in a short vicious arc. Rauscher evaded it.

The penitent's face was twisted with rage. His mouth was open. He was growling far back in his throat.

They circled, feinting. Brother James swung and missed. And again, but at least he was keeping Rauscher at bay. Brother Richard crawled to the wall and worked his way upright. He held his head in his hands. Brother James swung at Rauscher's knee. Rauscher pulled back. The tip of the bar had faded to a dull gray-red. The penitent threw a punch straight from the shoulder. Brother James moved to block it with the bar. Rauscher pulled the punch, came in fast behind the bar and wrenched it away from Brother James.

He bellowed in triumph, pivoted and swung the bar. It arced into Brother James's side, breaking three more ribs and knocking out his breath. The monk went to his knees with his mouth agape.

Rauscher kicked him in the face.

Brother James's jaw broke and he was flung backward.

Rauscher threw the bar aside and went for the stairs.

Brother Richard staggered from the wall. He held his hands out. "Please. Stop. I'll help you. I'll make it better "

Rauscher drove his fist into the novice's stomach. Brother Richard gagged and doubled over. Rauscher threw him against the wall and hit him hard, fast, in the upper body, then smashed his fist into his face, crushing his nose and splattering blood out the nostrils. He grabbed the novice's hair and cracked his head back against the stone wall, again.

There was the sound of an egg breaking, but louder, duller.

The novice's weight hung slack from Rauscher's hand. Rauscher released him. Brother Richard slid down the wall and crumpled limply. The wall was marked with a starburst of blood where his head had struck.

Brother Phelan was startled as the door to the basement crashed open at the end of the hall and Max Rauscher burst out. Rauscher looked at him wildly, then shouted and charged.

The monk dropped his books and raised his hands, braced to meet Rauscher. Rauscher threw him down without breaking stride.

Brother Hiram had just come down the stairs from the second floor. He turned at Brother Phelan's cry, read the situation in an instant and called to the monk posted at the door, "Brother Lawrence, guard yourself!" He ran to intercept Rauscher.

An instant before they collided, Brother Hiram left his feet and threw himself against Rauscher in a cross-body block. They went down in a tangle of legs and arms. They grappled with each other trying to rise. Rauscher hit Brother Hiram in the mouth, breaking teeth and knocking him back down. The penitent was up and running again.

Brother Lawrence had drawn a hickory club from his robe and set himself. Rauscher didn't falter. Brother Lawrence swung the club. Rauscher hunched, took the blow on his muscled arm, then smashed a fist directly to Brother Lawrence's heart. The monk sagged. Rauscher tore at the door bolt.

"Stop! Sonbitch!" The hulking oblate Gregory stood in the refectory door with a wet mop in his hands.

Rauscher bolted out of the monastery. He ran to the fence, seized the frame of the locked gate and jerked at it, cursing.

Gregory came running up behind him. The oblate speared him in the kidney with the blunt end of the mop handle. Rauscher shouted in pain and dropped to his knees grabbing at his back. Gregory kicked him, knocking him over. Rauscher rolled, caught the oblate's ankle and pulled him down. They wrestled on the ground. Rauscher got his hands on Gregory's throat. The oblate couldn't break the grip. He clawed for Rauscher's eyes.

Brother Hiram and Brother Phelan reached them. The monks hammered at Rauscher. He released Gregory and surged up. Towering over the two monks, he went at them like a maddened bear set upon by dogs, roaring his fury.

Brother Phelan went down.

Brother Hiram fell.

Gregory was on his feet. He closed with Rauscher, his own growls echoing the penitent's. They battered each other, grunting with the impact of the blows, but neither giving ground.

Brother Leopold and Brother Andrew ran from the monastery.

Gregory and Rauscher stood sweating and growling and pounding steadily at each other.

Brother Leopold stepped up behind Rauscher. His arm flashed up and down and he landed the hard edge of his left hand, his only hand, on the back of Rauscher's neck. Rauscher staggered but didn't fall. Brother Leopold hit him again. Rauscher dropped to his knees, then collapsed.

Gregory's teeth were bared. His chest heaved. There was fury in his eyes. "Was mine," he said to Brother Leopold. "Could've done it!"

"You did, Gregory," Brother Leopold said. "No one else could have stopped him like that."

"Huh!" Gregory said with satisfaction.

Brother Hiram was getting to his feet. Gregory helped him. The oblate touched the monk's bloody mouth. "You hurt," he said with concern.

"Not badly," Brother Hiram said. "Are you all right?"

"Fine."

"You did well, Gregory. Very well."

Gregory smiled. Then he frowned at Brother Hiram's face again. He turned. "Sonbitch!" He kicked Rauscher.

Brother Martin stood silently in the basement while Brother Raphael examined Brother James, who was still unconscious. The infirmarer motioned to two other monks who were waiting off to the side with a stretcher. "Tell Brother Walter to give him one thousand milligrams of ampicillin and start an IV drip. Tell him I'll be there directly."

The monks shifted Brother James onto the stretcher and removed him.

Brother Martin said, "How bad?"

"His jaw is broken. There are four, possibly five fractured ribs. He's in mild shock, but his vital signs are good."

"Does he need hospitalization?"

"Not unless the ribs punctured an organ, which I doubt. I'll watch him carefully."

They returned to Brother Richard. The novice lay on his stomach with his cheek flat against the floor, his eyes open. The hair on the back of his head was matted with blood. A portion of the skull was flattened. A fragment of bone stuck out through the clotted hair.

"You can see what did it," Brother Raphael said.

The abbot nodded. "Have Brother Conrad sent to me. Then attend to Brother James. Notify me when he's conscious. I want to know what happened here."

Brother Raphael left.

Brother Conrad came down the stairs five minutes later. He stopped short, looking at Brother Richard. "Dead?"

"Yes. I want a guard posted at the basement entrance. No one is to enter until I order differently. Rauscher is being held in my office. Isolate and secure him from the population, penitents *and* brothers. Brother Gilbert and Brother Peter were down here. They may or may not have realized that Brother Richard was dead. Instruct them that they are to say nothing to anyone about this. It is to go no further than those who already know. Report back to me. I'll instruct you then on the disposition of Brother Richard's body."

"Yes, my abbot."

Alone, Brother Martin put his hands to his face and closed his eyes. Brother Richard's death hung heavily over him. He did not know what to do.

Chapter 18

While Brother Richard's corpse lay in the cellar above him, Brother Martin knelt in the soundless Chamber of Mortal Meditation. A small candle burned at his side. His stomach spasmed reflexively against the fetid air.

He knew that somehow the novice had been instrumental in his own death, but still, the final responsibility was his, the abbot's, and his alone.

Rauscher's profile, he understood in retrospect, contained the signs.

He should have recognized them.

To have raised a postulant to novice at the very opening of a Retreat was folly, no matter the advocating arguments.

He should have known better.

The indications had all appeared in Brother Richard over the last two weeks.

He should have seen them.

I like to cut people, DiPalo had said. *I like to see that smooth skin open up and the blood come pouring out.*

Brother Martin was fifteen. He saw the bewildered face of his father's employer. Saw his own arm loop, his wrist flick, the keen edge of the razor sink into the man's throat, pass through, and the blood geyser out.

He had killed Brother Richard. As surely as he had killed that man in the parking lot.

My abbot, he prayed, *look down upon me with mercy and guide me now as you did in life.*

Slumped, liquefying and collapsing now, the remains of his

predecessor sagged to the wall of the niche, where they had been brought directly from the deathbed and placed there sitting naked and crosslegged, leaning back, hands folded in an attitude of prayer and sightless eyes open. The eyes no longer remained. They had jellied and seeped back into the head. The skin was black. It had separated over Brother Giles's left cheekbone, which was now prominent in its naked hardness. The left jowl had sagged, and finally fallen away to expose the jaw. As the right side of his face had rotted and loosened, its hanging weight had gradually pulled the scalp and what remained of the left temple across Brother Giles's skull and sliding downward. The fine white hair that once crowned the old abbot's head now rested where his right cheek had been.

The skin had parted in several other places too and hung from left to right across his torso like shreds of ripped fabric. Sections of his rib cage were visible. As was the bone of one of his shoulders, and both his kneecaps. The left kneecap hung down from a length of tendon and was twisted, exposing its underside to view. The thigh and shin bones had separated at the join. Brother Giles's belly had swollen and burst early on, spilling bloated intestines into his lap. The intestines were now a dark pudding. The candlelight glinted off strings and drops of moisture. Brother Giles was melting, slowly, thickly, and as he did the viscosity that had once been his flesh seeped down into the concave stone seat and thence through a drain hole into a large amphora.

"Guide me," Brother Martin said aloud.

Brother Giles, of course, said nothing.

When Brother Martin went up to the cellar, he knelt to pray several moments over Brother Richard. He bent forward and kissed the novice's forehead. "I'm sorry," he said. "Forgive me."

Brother Abner was posted at the cellar door.

"Remain here until Brother Conrad dismisses you," the abbot said.

Brother Conrad was waiting for him in the office. Brother Martin told him what to do with the novice. "Then wash the blood from the wall and floor, put everything right. Again, no one is to know of this."

He sent for Kennedy. He had planned to see him this afternoon, and he thought it important now to maintain the established schedule.

Kennedy was haggard. But his eyes were clear, and his earlier contempt had been replaced by apprehension. Brother Martin let him sit in silence several minutes, allowing tension to build.

Then, in a friendly, solicitous tone he said, "Why did you leave the priesthood, Tom?"

Kennedy loosened, precisely the effect the abbot had intended.

"If you were all really like me, like you said, then you understand."

"We were. And we do. That is, we understand your nature. But why did you renounce your vows and turn away from God?"

"You really believe in God?"

"Yes."

Kennedy shook his head, as if confronted with some impossible task.

"I take it you don't," Brother Martin said.

"No."

"Why?"

"Oh, man. Look around you. This world is shit. It's people who eat and people who get eaten. They're murdering each other all over the fucking globe. Where's this all-powerful, all-loving God of yours? He gonna come down today and hold one soldier in His arms who just got his guts blown out? Put food in the belly of one kid who's gonna starve to death by nightfall? I never saw the motherfucker. Not once. I— Ah," he said wearily. "What's the use?"

"Maybe you were looking through a filter. Maybe all you could see was the shit."

Kennedy didn't say anything.

"You had faith once."

"Once."

"You lost it."

"I learned there weren't any little people in the television set either."

"What *do* you believe in?"

"Myself. For whatever that's worth."

"What is it worth?"

"Loose shoes, tight pussy and a warm place to shit."

"I hope we can help you regain your faith."

"Uh-huh."

Brother Martin steepled his fingers. "What punishment do you think appropriate for yourself?"

"Being here."

"That is a joy, not a punishment."

"*De gustibus.*"

"*De fide.*"

"For you."

"And I hope for you someday. You may go now."

Kennedy got up from his chair.

Brother Martin stopped him at the door. "Tom?"

Kennedy turned.

"Think of another punishment."

Later in the afternoon the abbot met again with his committee in the conference room. They evaluated the penitents to date, reserving the more difficult for last.

"Bates is a problem," Brother Louis said. "He has a high pain threshold. His psychology is simple and well integrated. I can't find a way in. He's holding strongly to his good ol' boy persona."

Brother Martin made a note. "Ableman?"

"Trouble," Brother Cooper said. "He looked good for a while after the drug regression, but he's hardening up again. He wanted to take a swing at me this morning. I could see it in his eyes."

Brother Martin nodded. "He's one of the most vicious. Ballantine?"

"He hates our guts," Brother Cooper said. "He's not going to be easy. He's used everything we've done to him simply to fuel his anger."

The abbot wrote on his pad.

"You know," Brother Louis said suddenly. "we didn't mention Kennedy before. He's doing pretty well."

"Yes," Brother Cooper said. "One of the better ones."

"So it seems," Brother Martin said. "But I have misgivings. That's why I didn't bring him up earlier. My instincts tell me something's wrong. He's intelligent and he's a dissembler. It's no accident that he leads a cult. I'd like you to watch him carefully, Brother Conrad. And you, Brother Wilfred. I want your impressions."

They went to Marcus.

Brother Cooper shook his head. "I don't know that he can ever be humbled."

"I think perhaps it's a mistake to try to humble him," Brother Martin said. "I think that if we're to succeed we have to *humiliate* him. We'll hit him hard tomorrow. We're going for broke. I think we have to."

He had held Jaretzki for last. There was much enthusiasm in the company for the man. Brother Phelan felt that he was their finest prospect. "You're aware," Brother Martin said to them, "that we've given him minimal abuse. He's responded so well to our reaching out that that seemed unnecessary and possibly even counterproductive. I still feel it's the right tack, but there is something I worry about. He's a passionate, intense man. Those qualities have heightened and reinforced his negative aspects in the past. They're serving us now and could eventually lead him into a deep spirituality. But I fear that before the process is complete, he might, while living among us as a novice or even a brother, remember his past, begin to dwell on the outside world, that his animal appetites could return. If we're to save him, I think we have to take radical action. Something that will in effect cut him off from the outside world and give him the time he needs to solidify."

He laid his proposal before them.

They gave him consensus.

"Good. That's all then, brothers. You are excused."

"What about Rauscher?" Brother Cooper said. "We didn't cover him."

"No," the abbot said. "We didn't. You are excused, brothers."

The cloister was awash with sunlight the following day. The afternoon was tranquil. The fountain bubbled gently. The flowers swayed in a light breeze. A flock of finches were bathing in the fountain, shaking themselves and splashing water.

The company was formed into a large square around one of the benches. The penitents were interspersed among the monks. They were apprehensive. They cast surreptitious glances about. No one spoke, no one moved for several minutes.

Then Brother Thomas and Brother Conrad, who were on either side of Marcus, took him by the arms, drew him out of the line and walked him to the bench. His face was set in anger.

"Strip," Brother Conrad said.

Marcus snorted down in contempt at the monk.

Behind Marcus, Brother Gilbert drew a cat-o'-nine-tails from his robe and left the line. He slashed the leather thongs against the back of Marcus's calves. Marcus threw his head back and cried out through clenched teeth. He took hold of his tunic, hesitated, then released it and folded his arms across his chest. Brother Gilbert scourged him again. Skin split; blood welled out.

"You fuckers!"

Marcus pulled the tunic over his head and threw it to the ground. He was covered with angry rashes where the coarse horsehair had rubbed against his sweaty skin. He'd lost nearly thirty pounds—his skin was ribboned in slack folds—but he was still huge, pulpous and blubbery. His sparse body hair was like a delicate fungus on his bulk.

Brother Thomas and Brother Conrad bent him forward over the bench. Brother Gilbert tied him with rope, legs spread-eagled wide, gross rump high in the golden sunlight, his head hanging down on the other side, his wrists secured.

"You stinking bastards," he said, hoarse with rage.

A monk handed Brother Gilbert a wooden dowel and a ceramic bowl. The dowel was a foot long and an inch in diameter, one end sanded to a blunt cone. He dipped his hand into the bowl and smeared lard from it liberally over the dowel. He leaned over Marcus, braced himself with one hand on the man's huge buttock and positioned the dowel. . . .

Bates looked on stricken and petrified.

Marcus was screaming, as much in shock and horror as in pain.

Brother Gilbert worked the dowel.

Marcus writhed and screamed in his debasement.

Brother Martin signaled.

Brother Thomas and Brother Conrad pulled Bates out of the line and rushed him forward.

"No!" Bates shrieked. "Oh my God, *no!*"

They forced him to the ground on his back, hips below Marcus's flushed and stupefied face, and jerked his tunic up to his navel.

Marcus stared down aghast at Bates's organ. He moaned.

Bates screamed in terror. "Oh Jesus, you can't do this!"

"No," Marcus gasped.

"Take him!" Brother Thomas commanded.

Marcus shook his head.

Brother Thomas picked up the cat and laid into the fat man until, sobbing, he opened his mouth, lowered his head and closed his lips around Bates.

"Do it," Brother James ordered. "Faster!"

Marcus did.

Holding down Bates, who was screaming in mortal dread, and while tears squeezed from Marcus's closed eyes as he moved his head, Brother Conrad tried to neutralize himself. He was revolted by this. The disgust, horror and totally devastating fear in the two penitents triggered in him vivid memories of the women he had so brutally taken all those years ago, out in the world. He was odious and unworthy.

That was not me, he told himself. That was someone else. Oh please, let this be over.

Verging on panic, he struggled for control. He forced himself to rationality, to cool intellectual analysis, a barrier against his emotions.

The function. Consider the function.

While Marcus had done to others what Brother Gilbert was now doing to him, and had forced done to him what he was now doing to Bates, he had never permitted this to be done to himself or had he done this to someone else. Those proscriptions were integral to the structure of his dominance. *He* was master; *they* were chattel.

Bates. He possessed a phobic hatred and dread of such contact. Which was in some measure responsible for his savage treatment of the helpless prisoners in his purview.

The strategy was sound. It struck to the center of both penitents.

Brother Conrad offered up his own suffering as a sacrifice.

Nothing was required of the penitents for the rest of the afternoon. They kept strictly to themselves. Most went to their rooms. Caparelli walked about the exercise area. He found a grassy area that was free of geese droppings and lay down on his back with his hands under his head and looked up at the sky. He didn't think about anything. He wanted not to think about anything.

He fell asleep. He dreamed of his wedding. Pomona was a Madonna in her gown. She broke his heart with her beauty. He danced the tarantella for hours. He danced, and he knew he would dance forever.

A hand touched his shoulder.

He woke smiling. He was twenty-one and it was the happiest day of his life.

He opened his eyes to see the monastery looming over him. The music ended. Pomona died. The smile faded from his lips.

Brother Raphael was leaning over him. "Come."

Caparelli followed him. He felt no fear. He hadn't in several days. There was nothing to be done.

Brother Raphael led him inside, to the chapel. "Sit."

The sun pierced the narrow stained-glass windows of the west wall and threw dazzles of color on the pews and the stone floor, but still the chapel was dim, almost dark. A red vigil light burned beside the tabernacle on the altar, proclaiming the living presence of the Eucharist, of God.

"What is the state of your soul?" Brother Raphael asked. With his white hair and the prominent blue veins on his long-fingered hands he reminded Caparelli somewhat of old Father Gianini. "'I don't know."

"I think," Brother Raphael said, "that there is more grace in it now than when you arrived."

"Maybe. I'm tired. I don't know. I can't think so well."

"Do you want to kill me?"

"You? No."

"Do you want to kill anyone here?"

"I don't know. I don't think so."

"I don't think so either."

"Sometimes I've wanted to."

"That's not surprising. But there's no profit in dwelling on it now. Here." He gave Caparelli a small cardboard box.

Within was a cassette player with a set of headphones.

Caparelli turned it over in his hands, as if it were some astonishing and incomprehensible device.

"Go ahead," Brother Raphael said. "While you listen, I will pray." He lowered himself to the kneeler.

Caparelli opened the tape compartment. There was a cassette inside.

Puccini. *Sour Angelica.*

Caparelli's vision blurred. His mouth trembled.

Opera was so long ago. Everything was.

He put the headphones on.

The opening voice chorus was as clear and pure as spring water.

Angelica conceived a child illegitimately. She gave it away. She entered a convent to atone for her sin. The separation from her baby was agony, but gradually, as she found God, she was given comfort. In a final rapturous aria, with God flooding into her heart, she was exalted in the Lord and mystically reunited with her lost child.

Caparelli buried his face in his hands. He was ravished by the gorgeousness of the music and voices, ravished by the glory of Sister Angelica's transmogrification, and ravished by Brother Raphael's love and generosity. He wept, and could not stop.

Brother Raphael drew him into his chest and held him. Gently, he patted Caparelli's head. "There, there. It's all right now."

And Caparelli, the child, wept against him with great wracking sobs, as he had never been able to weep within the offered comfort of old Father Gianini.

At dinner Marcus knelt before his plate with his head hanging and his eyes closed. The food remained untouched. Farther down, Bates was hugging himself and shuddering. Sometimes he would sob.

The silence was broken only by the occasional clink of a

utensil against a tin plate. The monks ate calmly and steadily.

Halfway through the meal Brother Martin set his fork down and called out: "Ableman."

Ableman was kneeling at the far end of the table to the abbot's right. There was a piece of bread in his hand. He turned his head.

"Stand up," Brother Martin said.

Ableman raised the bread to his mouth and tore off a chunk with his teeth. He got to his feet. He folded his arms over his chest. He chewed slowly and deliberately.

"What punishment do you think appropriate as penance for yourself?"

Ableman continued to chew. He swallowed. "Oh, I don't know. I'm really a bad guy. Why don't you just execute me?"

Brother Martin looked to Brother Anthony, who was seated near the end of the opposite table. The abbot lifted his index finger up from the table.

Brother Anthony reached within his robe. He withdrew a 9mm automatic. He pulled back the slide and let it snap forward, throwing a cartridge into the chamber. He brought the pistol to bear, hesitated a fractional moment, then fired.

The report was deafening.

The slug caught Ableman in the bridge of his nose, exited high at the rear of his skull with a gout of blood. He was knocked off his feet. He landed in a heap several paces back and didn't move.

Brother Anthony returned the pistol to his robe.

Brother Martin picked up his fork and directed his attention back down to his plate.

When Hector had returned from his period of fast and meditation high up the mountain, he called his three companions away from the fire outside their little stone shelter and, saddened and troubled, said, "Brothers, there is something we must discuss."

They drew out of earshot of the bailiff who was secured

naked and draggled to the twisted old tree in the center of the clearing. He was gnawing on a charred goat rib and he paid them no attention.

Hector spoke with his brothers. They had held the man fourteen months now and hadn't been able to make any spiritual progress with him; indeed, he would have killed them all if he could get his hands on them. Hector told them of his contemplation on the crags. He laid his proposal before them. Two agreed. Joseph, the former leatherworker and Hector's first brother in this work, was unsettled and disturbed. Hector spoke with him until the moon was high. And at last Joseph nodded and said, "Yes, it is right."

Hector had released the other two brothers to sleep hours ago. He told Joseph, "You may absent yourself if you wish."

"I think it would be better if I shared it with you."

"I will be grateful for that."

The bailiff was curled up on his bed of leaves asleep. Hector found a heavy stone and worked it free of the earth. He approached from the rear, placing his feet with care and silence. He stopped, raised the stone high above the sleeping man, then sent it crashing down upon his head. The bailiff's legs kicked out. He quivered violently a moment. He stilled. Hector knelt beside him and felt with his hands. He looked up to Joseph, his brother.

"It is done." To the dead man he said softly, "Go with God's love."

The air was chill at dawn. Fog swirled about the ground, obscuring the bailiff's body.

The brothers put fresh wood on the firebed, poked at the ashes to expose the embers and blew upon them until the fire caught. They warmed themselves and broke morning bread together, took a little cheese and some water with it. The rising sun began to burn the fog off, gradually exposing the dark hump of the bailiff's body.

"I admonish you once again, my brothers," Hector said.

"Our primary concern is to secure the salvation of the immortal souls of men who live as we once did. Our secondary purpose is to remove from the general world those who are ravening beasts and a scourge to God's children. Whenever we achieve the first, the second will necessarily follow. If we fail in the first"—he gestured toward the dead man—"we will be deeply grieved, as we are now, but we shall not be deterred from accomplishing the second."

He blessed them, and asked their blessing in turn.

They unshackled the dead man and carried him to a place some three hundred yards off that Hector had selected. It was a huge jut of mossy rock that humped out from the slope of the mountain like the shoulder of a giant. It was marked with a vertical fissure partly concealed by a boulder. The fissure was roughly seven feet high and just wide enough so that a man could squeeze through if he was determined. It opened into a small chamber with a kind of natural ledge at the rear. They placed the dead man in this chamber, seating him upon the ledge and leaning him back against the wall. They folded his hands into an attitude of prayer.

They remained on the mountain another six weeks. They worked. They prayed. They maintained silence except for the evening meal when Hector, who alone among them was lettered, would read aloud some special lesson from the scriptures. The Bible had been a gift from a noblewoman whose retinue Hector had encountered on a public road the previous year. It was their most cherished possession, and indeed the only thing they possessed that was neither a tool nor a garment to wear.

Each day, singly and at a separate time, they went into the chamber in which they had placed the corpse and where it was now decaying, to look upon it and to meditate.

When Hector felt that he and his brethren had strengthened and prepared themselves sufficiently, they divided their meager store of provisions into two equal parts and they went down from the mountain in pairs, Hector and Carlo together, and

Joseph with the fourth brother. They went down and back out into the world, each pair to find and secure a proper penitent and to return with him to their little shelter before two more lunar cycles had passed.

Such were the humble beginnings of the Order of Saint Hector. . . .

It was nearly one in the morning. The monastery was quiet. The knock Brother Martin had been expecting sounded on the door to his office. He closed his log. "Enter."

Brother Henry opened the door. He stood aside to permit a slight figure in a light gray cloak, hood raised up over the head, to pass through. He closed the door.

Brother Martin came around his desk.

Slim delicate hands rose to the hood and pushed it back to reveal the narrow fine-featured face of a young woman of patrician beauty.

Brother Martin took both her hands. She wore a wedding band. "Lily," he said. "How are you?"

She knelt and kissed the ring of his authority. "Your blessing, please."

He gave it to her.

She stood. "I'm well, thank you."

"We met briefly at the last Retreat. I'm Brother Martin. Brother Giles died some three months ago. I serve as abbot now."

She nodded. "My husband informed me."

Lily was the wife of Brother Anthony. Their marriage was no longer of this plane. It was a marriage in Christ.

Brother Martin hung her cloak from a peg on the wall. She shook her dark hair out. It hung sheened and with light wave to her shoulders, pitchblende against her snowy skin. Her eyes were large and nearly as dark, her cheeks high and her skin finegrained. Her mouth was sculpted, lips light pink. She was slim. The graceful curve of her breasts and hips were apparent despite the loose and unremarkable blue dress she wore.

Brother Martin experienced a flicker of longing. But only a flicker, and he was scarcely aware of even that. Celibacy was not simply habit now but a physical fact of his life, as much as were the fingers of his hand.

"Please sit," he said. He took his own chair. "You had no difficulty arranging a leave?"

She lived in a convent in Scanandaga, was a lay sister in an order of nursing nuns who served in the town's hospital.

"No. I'm visiting an old friend in Rochester whose husband has just died."

"Good. Are you spiritually balanced and prepared for this, sure that it won't harm you?"

"Yes."

"All right. We're grateful to you. If you should have any difficulty, at any point, I want you to come to me immediately."

"I will," she said.

"There will be two of them, possibly three. I'm not certain yet." He told her about them. "Do you have any questions?"

"No. It's all clear. Thank you."

He brought her to her quarters, a storage room they had cleared for her with a window off the cloister. They had brought in a bed, a small chest for her things, a sitting chair, and had set up a wooden table and a mirror to serve as her vanity. Cosmetics and perfumes stood on the table. The window itself had been fitted with an iron grill and shutters that she could close.

Her gown was on a hanger hooked over a peg.

She looked at it only for a moment.

She asked again for Brother Martin's blessing before he took leave of her.

Brother Hilliard sat reading on a stool beneath the wall torch at the south end of the hall. At the opposite end, at the head of the stairs, the oblate Michael sat on another stool, his arms folded over his chest, looking at the empty wall. There were two more hours till dawn. Brother Hilliard turned a page.

Across from him, movement caught his eye and he looked up.

The door to Hauptmann's cell was opening. The penitent appeared, leaning against the frame and holding his side. "Help," he whispered in a pained voice.

Brother Hilliard set aside his book. He went to the door. "What's the matter?"

Hauptmann's arm shot from his side straight to Brother Hilliard's chest.

The monk felt as if he'd been punched hard. There was a small flare of pain too, but he was more surprised than anything else.

What? he tried to say.

Curiously, no sound passed his lips.

He tasted blood in his mouth. Then the pain struck. He clutched both hands to his chest. Blood pumped heavily around his fingers. He began to jump up and down.

Hauptmann jerked him in and threw him to the floor. Brother Hilliard spasmed there. He saw the short triangular knife in the penitent's hand.

In the hall, the oblate Michael frowned. From the corner of his eye he'd noticed Brother Hilliard rise. He'd turned his head to look. Brother Hilliard was standing at a penitent's door. He had appeared to snap back, then spring forward into the room. He still hadn't come out. Michael pondered this.

He stood and started down the hall. Behind him, two doors opened simultaneously. Kennedy and Alvarado stepped silently from their rooms. Kennedy lunged, looped an arm around Michael's throat and clapped his other hand tight over the oblate's mouth. They dragged him into Kennedy's room.

The hall was empty and silent.

Brother Hilliard's chest was on fire. He choked on his blood. He couldn't control the spastic violence of his body.

Hauptmann leaned and peered cautiously into the hall.

Brother Hilliard struggled to focus his will, which was formidable. With great effort, he took control of his body. He seized Hauptmann's ankle and sank his teeth into it, ground them, tried to bite through the Achilles tendon. Hauptmann grunted in pain. He braced against the wall and kicked at Brother Hilliard's head until he jarred the monk loose.

"*Aschloch!*" He went out.

Brother Hilliard, his grasp weakening, but still holding his purpose, crawled into the hall.

Hauptmann was poised before another penitent's door. He looked back over his shoulder. A kind of fascinated horror took his face as he saw the dying monk.

Brother Hilliard's head fell. But still he clawed and pushed himself on, leaving a crimson trail of blood behind him.

And then he could sustain it no longer. His will disintegrated, he was wracked by convulsions. In the last moment of his graying consciousness, he formed the words: *Thank you, my Lord, for summoning me to you.*

He went still. His body loosened.

Hauptmann stared at him a moment longer, then entered Kennedy's room. Kennedy and Alvarado had Michael down on the floor, gagged, hands tied behind his back. The penitents exchanged no words. Hauptmann knelt and cut strips from the oblate's robe. He kept some for himself and gave the rest to Kennedy and Alvarado. He rose and checked the hall. Brother Hilliard was still. He signed to the others. Bringing the bound oblate, they slipped quietly from the room. Alvarado padded silently down the hall and picked up Brother Hilliard's stool. Kennedy took up Michael's.

They stood poised, listening. They heard nothing but the sough of wind outside the monastery.

They crept down the stairs nearly to the bottom. They paused to listen again. Hauptmann nodded to Kennedy and Alvarado. They readied themselves. The oblate's eyes were wide with fear.

Hauptmann went to his hands and knees and crawled down the last two steps to the entrance hall. His head was hanging, he was breathing rapidly and shallowly. He collapsed. Through slitted eyes he saw Brother Gilbert moving from his post by the door.

"Hauptmann? What's the matter?" The monk bent over him.

Alvarado sprang from the stairwell and swung his stool. The edge of the seat caught the monk on his temple and laid his scalp open. He went down as if his spine had been severed.

Hauptmann went through the man's robe rapidly and thoroughly. "Shit!" He'd expected the guard to be armed. He'd wanted a gun. Well. So. It would have to be done without one.

They went to the door. Hauptmann extinguished the torch there. Carefully, he slid the iron bolts free and edged the door open. The three-quarter moon was muddied by a thin wisp of cloud, but still provided sufficient light. The geese were off in some other area. There had to be a guard somewhere outside the fence, but Hauptmann couldn't see him. He had no doubt that this one would be armed.

He looked at the other two penitents. They took the oblate by the shoulders.

Hauptmann yanked the door fully open. "Now!"

They rushed out, jumped the steps down from the pad to the ground and ran for the fence. The coiled razor wire was sheened like water by the moonlight.

A goose honked off to the side, then the entire flock broke into a squall. They came out of the shadows and bore down on the penitents with a drunken rolling gait.

Some distance to the left, beyond the fence, a furious barking sounded.

Hauptmann cursed. A goddamn dog.

The first of the big birds hit him when they were still fifteen paces from the fence, driving its bill hard into his buttock. He swung the stool and cracked its chest. He turned to face the geese, moving backward toward the fence, serving as rear guard for Kennedy and Alvarado. The next two came in. He hit one in the head, missed the other, which struck dead center into the wound from the blasting cap. The bandage didn't soften the blow. He grunted in pain. The birds jostled and beat at each other in their frenzy to reach him. A stabbing bill tore open his thumb. He kicked at them and swung the stool.

Kennedy and Alvarado gained the fence. Without breaking stride they lifted the oblate and heaved him up onto the wire. He came down on his midsection, torso hanging over, legs dangling back. The wire bowed down beneath his weight.

He tried to scream around his gag. He twisted like a gigged fish. His legs thrashed.

"Hauptmann!" Kennedy yelled.

Hauptmann spun, tossed his stool over the fence and locked hands with Alvarado. The caterwauling geese lashed at them. Kennedy stepped into the stirrup of their hands. They boosted him up. He sprawled onto the oblate's back, slid over and off. He leaned his chest onto the oblate, reached for Alvarado's hands and pulled him up the oblate and over. Michael was twisting atop the wire. His cries were muffled. Kennedy and Alvarado pulled Hauptmann over him.

"Stop!" A monk and a leashed German shepherd came running toward them.

Kennedy grabbed up the stool.

"Spread out!" Hauptmann shouted. He tightened his fingers around his knife.

The monk pulled an automatic from his robe.

The dog leaped high for Kennedy's arm. It's driving weight pulled the monk off balance just as he was bringing the gun to level. The tightened leash stumbled him forward.

Hauptmann went in fast, locking the monk's gun hand and driving the knife into his side. The monk fell, dropping the gun.

Alvarado was on it in an instant, and Hauptmann was on Alvarado just as quickly. He pressed the blade of his knife to the Paraguayan's throat. "Don't make me kill you."

Alvarado froze.

"I don't care what happens to you," Hauptmann said. "But my own chances are better if you're alive."

Alvarado let loose of the gun. Hauptmann took it. He withdrew the knife. "Club that dog off."

"Shoot it," Alvarado said.

"The geese will have everyone up in minutes. A shot would wake them at once."

Alvarado picked up the fallen stool and attacked the dog, which was savaging Kennedy. The dog turned from Kennedy to Alvarado. It got into Alvarado's leg and pulled him down. Alvarado lost the stool. Hauptmann retrieved it and landed a solid blow to the top of the animal's skull. It released its bite, wobbled toward Hauptmann with a growl, then fell over on its side.

"Oh Jesus!" Kennedy said, holding himself. "It hurts like a motherfucker!"

"You're alive," Hauptmann said flatly. "Now go." He pointed north. "You," he said to Alvarado. "That way." He pointed east.

"Fuck you," Kennedy said. "The road is due west."

"I know which way it is." Hauptmann leveled the pistol. "Run."

Alvarado turned in the direction he'd been told. After a moment's hesitation, Kennedy did too.

Hauptmann stood only long enough to see that neither man tried to veer off. Then he struck out west, toward the county highway at the end of the access road.

At the tree line, he paused to tie a folded piece of robe to each of his bare feet. Lights were beginning to go on in the monastery.

It wasn't much of a lead, but it was the best he was going to get. They would send a party down the road at once and he knew they'd overtake him before he could reach the end. So he angled off it into the woods, heading west by northwest.

Chapter 19

Brother Martin looked down at Brother Hilliard's body. He moved his eyes back along the wide trail of blood that led from Hauptmann's room. Brother Stewart, purple stole around his shoulders, knelt next to Brother Hilliard. He anointed the dead man's forehead and lips with oil, murmuring the Latin words of Conditional Absolution.

Did you provoke it? Brother Martin wondered. Did you invite it? I hope not, for the sake of your soul.

Somehow, he didn't think the prior had. And that gladdened him.

Receive this man into the joy of your Sacred Heart, oh Lord. For he was your good and faithful servant.

Go in peace, my brother.

Monks were in the hall, checking each of the penitent's rooms.

Brother Stefan approached. "Brother Gilbert's been hurt. Brother Raphael says a concussion, a possible skull fracture. The door was open. Brother Conrad's checking outside."

Brother Martin dispatched him to Lily's room. "If she's all right, don't alarm her. Just tell her there was a small problem and I wanted to be sure she was secure and comfortable."

Brother Andrew touched the abbot's arm. "I think you should come with me."

Brother Martin followed him to Bates's room. The monk opened the door and stepped back for the abbot to precede him, closed the door behind them.

Bates was naked, against the wall beneath the window. His legs were bent, his ankles flat against the floor. His neck was grotesquely long. One sleeve of his tunic was tied tight beneath his chin, the other around a hinge of the shutter. His face was mottled and his thick tongue protruded from his mouth.

"He garroted himself," Brother Andrew said.

"Seal the room."

The abbot went back to the hall.

Brother Phelan had the tally. "Hauptmann, Alvarado and Kennedy are missing."

"Tell Brother Anthony to arm five men as he sees fit. Send them directly down the road to the highway. If the penitents are found, they are to be brought back alive if possible. Dead, if not. Have all the company been roused?"

"Yes."

"I'll have orders soon. Tell them the penitents are not to leave their rooms." He looked down at the corpse several moments. "Remove Brother Hilliard to the chapel. Wash the blood away."

The abbot went down the stairs. The door was open. The geese were still in an uproar, but Brother Wilfred and several others, using blankets and sticks, had them bunched against the fence. Lanterns bobbed in the night. Brother Conrad and three other monks were carrying a limp figure toward the monastery. There were monks beyond the fence, lifting someone else.

The first one was the oblate Michael. Brother Conrad and Brother Harold had their hands locked beneath his shoulders. The other two supported his thighs. The front of Michael's robe was shredded and drenched with blood. His living intestines were visible. Blood dripped in thick drops onto the floor. The oblate was unconscious.

There were tears in Brother Harold's eyes. "They used him like a mattress," he said to the abbot in a cracked voice. "They threw him on top of the wire and went over him like he was a mattress."

"Hurry," Brother Martin said, nodding toward the infirmary. There was nothing else to do that would comfort the young monk now.

Brother Edward was brought in next. His eyes were slitted with pain. There was a large circle of blood on the right side of his robe. He reached out and grasped Brother Martin's finger tightly.

"I'm—sorry, my abbot." He grimaced. "I—"

"Hush. Conserve your strength."

Brother Martin walked alongside as they carried him to the surgery. Michael was lying on the single operating table. A few feet away from it, monks were setting planks atop a pair of sawhorses. One was swabbing the planks with alcohol. Brother Raphael was already in his surgical gown.

He took Brother Martin to the side while Brother Edward was placed on the plank-table. "I could use experienced help. Ballantine's a specialist, but at least he's a surgeon. Is there any chance . . . ?"

Please, my Lord! the abbot cried silently.

He was holding himself intact by will alone. If he broke, it would all collapse.

And if I sweated blood for you at Gethsemane, do you quail under this trifle?

He put his hand to his forehead. He found a moment's calm, and he praised God for it. "No. I don't trust him. And further, he'd feel in a strengthened position, that we owed him something, which would make our work all the more difficult, maybe even impossible."

Brother Raphael accepted the judgment with a nod.

Brother Walter, the infirmarer's assistant, had cut away Brother Edward's robe. There was a stab wound in the monk's lower rib cage.

"Are you strong enough to tell me what happened?" the abbot asked him.

"Was fast," Brother Edward said, short-breathed. "Three, I think. The dog . . . uhhn! . . . pulled me. Lost my gun. Couldn't stop them. One was Kennedy . . . saw his beard. The dog got him. Don't know . . . how bad."

"Did they set out together."

"No. Split up. Uhhn! I'm sorry. Forgive . . . me."

Brother Martin planned and organized the search with the counsel of Brother Conrad and of Brother Anthony, who had hunted men in jungles in the military. The party was ready in half an hour, with dawn still more than an hour away. The monks knelt in the moonlight. The abbot blessed them and bade them Godspeed.

Brother Wilfred had judged Cap, the dog who'd been with Brother Edward, still fit to work, though with a diminished capacity. The animal was listless and withdrawn, but responded well to the stimulant Brother Wilfred administered. Cap and Lucky took their respective scents from Hauptmann and Alvarado's sleeping boards.

Brother Thomas and Brother Abner set off with Lucky on Hauptmann's track. The presumption was that Hauptmann had Brother Edward's gun; certainly, armed or not, he was the most dangerous of the three. Brother Thomas, at the end of Lucky's twenty-foot tracking lead, had a scoped rifle slung over his shoulder. Brother Abner carried a 12-gauge riot gun.

Brother Wilfred handled Cap himself, since he was the most finely attuned to the animal. He wore an automatic holstered at his side. Brother Louis, who went with him, carried a Winchester .270.

A party of ten struck out to the east following the blood spoor Kennedy had left. Brother Anthony expected that Kennedy would be able to bind the wound and stanch the flow of blood. When that happened, the party was to split itself into five two-man teams. Kennedy would leave signs of passage somewhere: an overturned stone, broken twigs, a snippet of fabric. The monks sent after him were those among the company most familiar with the wilderness.

Brother Martin watched them move out toward the tree line, flashlights bobbing in the night. When they disappeared into the woods he turned back to the monastery. He closed and locked the gate behind him. The razor wire was bowed where Michael's weight had pressed down upon it. It was stained dark, and on the ground beneath was a great pool of congealing blood.

Led by Brother Cooper, the monks the abbot had dispatched immediately after the escape was discovered had run down the access road to the highway with their flashlights playing into the woods on either side. They found, as expected, nothing. Brother Cooper lifted his walkie-talkie when they reached the highway.

In the monastery, Brother Martin walked into his office as Brother Anthony was radioing instructions to Brother Cooper. The abbot had put Brother Anthony in charge of the search and told him to use the office as a command post. Brother Anthony had taped large topographical maps to the walls. There were half a dozen Geodesic Survey maps arranged across the desk. Next to them lay an unholstered automatic, its presence an unconscious habit from Brother Anthony's former life. Brother Martin didn't comment; he would not trespass upon whatever idiosyncrasies Brother Anthony displayed now, he wanted the man to feel comfortable and natural.

"Spread your people along the highway at intervals of one hundred twenty-five yards," Brother Anthony said. "Only one man south of the road, the rest north. If possible, any monk who spots him should get help before trying to take him, but not—I repeat, not—at the risk of losing him. Give him half a second to comply. If he doesn't—" He looked up in question at Brother Martin. "—Kill him."

The abbot nodded curtly.

"He's too dangerous to take a chance with," Brother Anthony said. "Out." He set the walkie-talkie down.

"Why north?" Brother Martin asked.

"Actually I don't think they'll see him at all. I think he'll come out much further up. Here, look." He placed a finger on the map. "There's high ground to either side of the road, but it's a steeper climb to the south, with some sheer cliff faces. The north is much easier going. And there are ravines and stream beds. It's more wooded too, which gives him better cover, though I think he'll take to bald stone for a while."

"Why?"

"It doesn't hold scent as well as earth. He can't be sure the dog they hit is out of action or that we don't have another one. He'll walk a stream for a while too, trying to throw it off."

"Can he?"

"I don't know dogs that well, but I don't think so. Brother Wilfred says no."

"Keep me informed," Brother Martin said.

Brother Henry appeared.

The oblate Michael was dead.

Brother Martin went to the chapel.

The center was not holding.

Brother Peter came upon the first sign, a thread snagged on a brier, only inches above the ground. Brother Peter had hunted deer in the mountains of Pennsylvania in his youth. He held it up between his thumb and forefinger.

"Yeah. He's wearing pieces of Brother Hilliard's robe on his feet."

Brother Peter was paired with Brother William. The blood trail had thinned out and then vanished, as expected. It was an hour after dawn now.

The two monks separated themselves by twenty yards, then began to search in widening concentric circles. Brother William found the next trace a quarter-hour later, a pinch of stiff black horsehair. They stepped off from that point and repeated their circling maneuver. Brother William found the third sign too, a small splash of blood on a waxy leaf. Again they circled out.

"Brother William!"

Brother William, carrying the single weapon they had, a shotgun, went crashing through the brush toward Brother Peter. He found him standing sideways behind a large tree seventy yards off; they didn't think Kennedy was armed, but they couldn't be certain.

"That big clump of brush straight ahead," Brother Peter said.

"Kennedy!" Brother William shouted. "It's all over! Crawl out of there!"

There was silence.

Brother William worked the slide of the shotgun, chambering a shell with a loud metallic *k-lack*.

"Get the fuck out of there or I'm going to blow it up!"

There was a rustle in the brush, then Kennedy appeared holding a thick branch with both hands. He raised it like a club.

"Drop it," Brother William said.

"Fuck, you're going to waste me anyway. I might as well go out with balls."

Brother William shouldered the weapon. "Your choice. You got two seconds."

Kennedy stared down the bore.

He dropped the club.

Brother Stewart brought Orson into the short southern hall on the first floor. "I'll be back for you in an hour," he said, leaving Orson standing in front of a door. "Knock."

Orson was confused and uncertain. It was midmorning. Late last night a monk had entered his room and shined a flashlight in his face, which woke him. "Go back to sleep," the monk said, and left. Orson had heard low urgent voices in the hall, but couldn't make out many words. Something had gone wrong, but he didn't know what. For a while there was the rustle of monks' robes, the scrape of metal buckets against the floor, the sound of splashing water and the rasp of stiff brushes. It was all over in less than an hour, then there was silence again. Food had been brought to his room this morning. He hadn't been summoned out till now. He saw no other penitents about.

Hesitantly, he knocked.

"Come in."

He was stunned. It was a woman's voice.

He entered in trepidation.

She stood with her back to him looking out the window to the sunlit cloister. She was darkhaired and wore a long evanescent white gown which was scooped down from her neck, exposing a graceful and delicately curved back. Her shoulders were small and fineboned.

The sunlight limned her against the gown. She was naked beneath it.

She turned. She smiled. "Close the door."

Her décolletage dropped nearly to her waist, which was girdled with a braided cord. Half-mounds of her breasts were exposed; her nipples were hazily visible beneath the fabric of the gown, as was a shadowy triangle at the junction of her thighs.

He averted his eyes.

"Close the door," she said pleasantly.

He did.

She came to him and placed her hands lightly on his shoulders. She raised herself up and touched her lips to his. They were incredibly soft. Her perfume entered him like rain into parched earth. He cringed.

Hail Mary, he prayed, full of Grace. The Lord is with thee . . .

"What's wrong?" she asked with concern.

Blessed art thou amongst women and blessed is the fruit of thy womb, Jesus.

"Come." She led him to the bed. She lay down, crooking

one leg up, the line of her thigh and calf visible through the gown, graceful as a swan's neck. She patted the bed beside her. "Sit."

Holy Mary, Mother of God, pray for us sinners . . .

"I'd like you to," she said.

He lowered himself to the mattress. He was tense.

. . . now and at the hour of our death. Amen.

She took his hand. Her own was cool and smooth.

He looked to the door.

"Don't be afraid. We have privacy for an hour. No one will surprise us."

That was not what he feared. He was looking for rescue. He wanted his salvation to walk through the door and take him from here.

Hail Mary, full of Grace. The Lord is with thee.

"Talk to me," she said.

Blessed art thou amongst women and blessed is—

"Please."

Her voice was similar in timbre to that of Mary Tedesco, the girl he had beaten and humiliated last . . . month? A lifetime ago.

—the fruit of thy womb, Jesus.

"Tell me about yourself."

He couldn't think.

"Please, Orson," she said gently.

"I . . ."

"Yes," she said.

"I . . . I'm sinful. I've done great wrong."

He hunched over and covered his face with his hands.

"Tell me," she said.

Brother Stewart came an hour later.

Lily said, "You are a good man, Orson."

His heart leapt up. He knew a joy he had never known before.

* * *

In her room half an hour later, Lily said to Brother Martin, "I didn't state it in so many words, but the invitation was quite explicit."

The abbot nodded.

"I didn't push or provoke him. I would have if I'd thought he was holding back because he was afraid of reprisal, or that he was struggling against something he *truly* wanted."

"He wasn't in conflict at all?" Brother Martin asked with surprise.

"Some. But my sense was that he was desperate to find what was the *good* to do, what was right for its own sake. He spent most of the time vilifying himself. Quite strongly."

Brother Martin was both relieved and gratified. He'd hoped for this, and had needed it more than he'd permitted himself to admit: there had been too many defeats.

Lily had never been in any real jeopardy, of course. Brother Stewart had been just outside the door through the hour, ready to intervene in an instant.

Brother Andrew took Oakley Brown down into the basement. The monk tied a blindfold around Oakley's head and guided him across the floor.

"Stop here a moment."

Oakley wasn't afraid. He was weary and fatalistic. He didn't care much anymore.

"We're going down again. Put your hand on the wall to orient yourself."

The wall was cool to his touch. This stairwell was narrower, the steps not quite as high. The coolness was a relief to his chafed and sweating body.

They reached the bottom. The monk guided him a short distance, then stopped again. There was the sound of a key turning in a lock. A brush of air as a door was pulled open. A ballooning encompassing stench. Oakley gagged. A hand on his shoulder, Brother Andrew directed him forward, deeper into the stench. There was a soundlessness, a feeling of compression.

The monk put something in Oakley's hand. "That's a candle and a pack of matches," he said. "Think about eternity."

Then he was gone. Oakley heard the door close, the lock click. He stood still a moment, threatened by nausea in the stink. When he was in control of his stomach he removed the blindfold. It was totally black. He couldn't see anything at all. He felt dread. He didn't want to strike a light, but he couldn't *not* do it.

The match ignited.

He screamed and threw himself backward. The match flew from his hand and died in flight. He came up hard against the wall.

It was black again.

But Oakley saw the tableau in his mind as visibly as he had in the bright flare of the match. There, only a few feet before him, sat a naked and rotting dead man who was half skeleton. To the right of him, bloated up but still recognizable, was the man Oakley had known as Brother Richard. Slumped over on the left was the penitent Joel Ableman, mouth open and jaw hanging.

Oakley whimpered. He edged away from them along the wall. He found the door with his fingers. He turned to it in terror and beat his fists on it, begging to be let out.

He saw the dead men rising to embrace him.

He screamed and beat upon the door. But no one answered. No one came.

Brother Wilfred was afraid that Cap would burn himself out. The injury combined with the stimulant Brother Wilfred had administered had to be hard on the dog. But when he'd tried to stop and rest the animal it had grown so distressed at being pulled off the track that the monk had decided its frustration would only increase the strain and so he let the dog have its head. Cap worked eagerly, nose close to the ground, intent and focused.

At intervals, when they hit a clearing or gained high ground, Brother Louis would shoulder the Winchester and scan the surrounding terrain through the scope. He was doing so now, sweeping a deer trail that led straight up the slope. Cap had put them on this trail ten minutes ago, and the dog's excitement had mounted steadily.

"Got him!" Brother Louis said.

"Where?"

"About three hundred yards. He just ducked into the brush. I think he spotted us."

"It doesn't matter. He won't get away from Cap."

They climbed, the dog pulling at the lead, tail high and thrashing with excitement now. Brother Louis carried the rifle at the ready, a shell in the chamber, the safety off, his eyes searching the undergrowth.

Cap began to bark. He lunged against the lead.

"Alvarado!" Brother Wilfred called. "Come out."

"Don't shoot. Don't shoot." Alvarado stepped into view. His hands were high over his head. He looked ruefully at the barking dog.

Brother Louis's voice was tinny through the receiver on Brother Martin's desk.

"This is party three to base. Come in, base."

Brother Anthony was alone in the abbot's office, studying one of the big maps on the wall. He picked up the mike and depressed the stud. "Base here, over."

"We found the South American book and recovered it without any problem. Everything's secure. Over."

"What's your location? Over."

"About a third of a mile up Balsam Mountain, maybe a quarter-mile west of the big spar. Over."

Brother Anthony glanced down at one of the Geodesic maps

on the desk. He nodded with satisfaction. More or less where he'd thought the man would be. As had been Kennedy.

"Good. Bring it in. Out."

He replaced the mike. He picked up a second map. He traced the tip of his finger over a section that represented an area approximately half a mile square. Somewhere in there. Or very close. That's where they'd find Hauptmann.

Brother Cooper brought Caparelli to the abbot, who was in the library. He said, "Caparelli has determined a penance he thinks would be appropriate for himself."

Brother Martin placed a marker in his book and closed it. He leaned back in his chair. He studied the penitent's face. Caparelli's progress had been good. "Tell me," he said.

"It's something I saw in Mexico. It made me sick. I couldn't understand it then."

The abbot waited.

"I think I should . . . whip myself."

Brother Martin felt a sense of failure.

"I think," Caparelli said, "I should do it every day. For a month. With . . . with that whip you have with all the thongs." He looked out the window. His voice was distant. "And each day, when I'm done, then I think one of the brothers should whip me."

The abbot knew exhilaration. It was done. He was theirs. He forced constraint upon himself. "How many strokes do you propose?"

"As many as I can give myself. Until I can't do it anymore."

"And then?"

"The brother will give me more."

"How many more?"

"Five? Ten?"

"You tell me."

"Fifteen," Caparelli said.

"When do you propose to begin?"

"Today."

Brother Martin steepled his fingers and put them under his chin. "Your penance is accepted. You will appear with Brother Cooper in the cloister in forty-five minutes to begin."

At the appointed time, a good portion of the company and most of the penitents had been assembled in the cloister. Brother Martin informed them what was happening.

He extended the cat-o'-nine-tails to Caparelli. "When you are ready."

Caparelli removed his tunic. His skin was mottled with irritation. He took the cat strongly in his right hand and looked up to the sky a moment. Then he swung the whip hard up over his left shoulder.

Sw-wack.

He swung it over his right shoulder.

Sw-wack.

Left shoulder.

He went, "Gha!"

Right shoulder.

"Gha!"

He beat himself until his skin separated and blood flowed from his back, until he glistened with sweat and his legs trembled, until he was glassy-eyed and until he could raise his arm no longer and it hung dead at his side, the cat dangling from his hand.

Brother Cooper took the whip from his hand.

"Prepare yourself," the abbot said.

Caparelli stared straight ahead, blood running from his back down his buttocks and legs. "'Fifteen," he whispered. "Fifteen . . . fifteen . . . fifteen." It was a chant.

Brother Martin raised three fingers to Brother Cooper.

Brother Cooper slashed the cat forward.

"Unnhh!" Caparelli reeled.

The second blow drove him to his knees.

Brother Cooper struck him again.

He fell forward onto his hands. "Fifteen," he breathed. "Fifteen . . ."

"No," Brother Martin said. "That is enough."

The abbot instructed Brother Cooper to help him back to his room.

An hour after Caparelli's scourging, Brother Phelan came to Jaretzki and told him to go to the chapel.

The dim chapel was empty. Jaretzki didn't know what to do. He sat down in a pew. He became aware, gradually, of . . . a presence. He looked about and saw nothing.

Still, the sense persisted.

His neck hairs began to prickle. He turned slowly and peered into the dark recess that contained the side altar to his right. He squinted. It could not be. His mind was playing tricks on him. He stood and walked over.

It was. Upon the altar. A darkhaired woman in a lucent white gown. She lay on her back. Her lips parted in a slow smile. She lifted a hand with long tapered fingers. He took it. It was cool and delicate to his touch. She withdrew it and lowered it, letting it come to rest on her hip.

He moved his eyes with deliberate care from her finefeatured face down the length of her body to her sculpted feet, then back. Her even white teeth opened slightly.

His cock became rigid.

He laid the tip of his index finger against her cheek.

He drew it across, to the rise of her upper lip, to her teeth, down to the tip of her tongue. The woman drew in breath. He hesitated, his cock now throbbing, then lay his next finger alongside the first and slowly inserted them deep into her mouth.

She closed her lips around them. She sucked them. Her tongue caressed them.

He eased them out.

He rested their tips, wetly, upon her pursed lips.

He exhaled in an explosive burst. He turned away, against all desire, in rebellion against himself, in response only to discipline, which hold over him was tenuous, with neither thought nor hesitation, else he would not have been able to do it, and he walked with long strides down the length of the chapel and out through the doors and straight for the stairs that would take him back up to his room.

He didn't even notice Brother Phelan, who was standing off to the side of the chapel entrance in precautionary vigil.

Brother Martin had established a temporary office in the conference room while Brother Anthony occupied his, monitoring the hunt for Hauptmann. The abbot had sealed off his anxiety, but he was not fully free of it. It was like a ringing in the ears, sometimes forgotten in the focus of a moment, but always there.

At his request, Brother Gilbert brought Pretty Boy to him. "It's time to hear what penance you've decided for yourself, Johnson."

The black man's eye was puffy and swollen shut. He stood crabbed in pain from a beating yesterday.

"Well?"

Pretty Boy licked his lips.

"I'm waiting, Johnson."

Pretty Boy forced himself to it. "I think I should be branded."

"Oh? How, and where?"

"With a *P*," he said with some bitterness. "For pimp. One on my chest. Another one on my back."

"I'll consider it," Brother Martin said. He bent back down over his notes.

It was still early afternoon when he went to Lily's room.

She seemed disquieted. She walked back and forth as she described her encounter with Jaretzki.

"He *wanted* me," she said when she finished. "Very much. It was palpable. I don't think it would have taken much to push him over the line. It was quite close."

Brother Martin didn't think so either, which confirmed his

earlier reservations. Jaretzki's intensity and passion, his response to the theatrical, his ability to *live* a role had been useful and constructive thus far, but they could, in the end, be the very things that might undermine his conversion, abruptly catch him up someday two or three years in the future and cause him simply to walk away. If the order was to ensure his salvation, they had to cut him off from that possibility and fix him in this time.

The abbot came out of his musings and realized that Lily had finally sat down. But she was running a hand over her mouth and looking out to the cloister in abstraction.

"Is anything troubling you?" he asked.

"No," she said. "Everything's fine." She smiled. "I didn't sleep well last night, that's all. I think a nap might help."

"You're sure."

"Yes. Thank you for asking."

Thinking about Jaretzki, he left her to rest.

In the chapter room, Rios stood first at the lectern. Then Sawyer. The abbot was satisfied. Neither equivocated; there was no self-justification in what they said. The Retreat *was* bearing fruit, it *was* more than the sum of its failures.

He called up Orson.

Orson stood silent several moments. "There is one final thing I have held back. I wish now to confess it before you all." His eyes sought out Caparelli.

Brother Raphael had attended Caparelli earlier in his cell, salving and bandaging his back. He'd been given permission to replace his tunic with his original penitent's robe. He sat blunted and hunched over on the front bench, a dozen feet from the lectern.

"I don't know how to say this. It was not only a sin against God, but also a betrayal of someone who always loved and trusted me and was never anything but generous to me. Many years ago, when I was eighteen, I was friends with a very sweet, quiet and devout girl who was my blood relative. We grew up together. As we reached our teens, I sort of became her chaperon and protector. I was the one who took her places she wanted to go when her father didn't want her there alone."

Caparelli bunched up his brow. He worked to focus on what Orson was saying.

"She was two years younger than I. She was sixteen when it happened. There was a dance at a church. Her date got sick, and she didn't want to go by herself—she was very pretty and boys used to bother her a lot. So she asked me to go with her. I smoked a lot of grass. I had a pint bottle of Scotch. She wouldn't smoke or drink, but I did talk her into going for a walk with me down by the docks. She was gorgeous, like a painting by Titian. I was high. I planned it. I knew where there was a warehouse I could get into. And I knew I could get away with it because she'd be too ashamed to tell anyone. Anyone. I wanted her more than I ever wanted anything. I *had* to have her. So I did it. I took her. I raped her."

Tears slicked his cheeks. He looked directly into Caparelli's eyes. "I'm sorry, Uncle. I raped Maria. I raped your daughter. Please forgive me."

As Orson's words sunk into Caparelli's dulled mind with increasing clarity, horror had begun to grow within him, and that horror had begun to rouse the beast in his soul, the beast the monks had beaten down and which now lay stuporous and dying; the words blew breath into its nostrils, the images vitalized its expiring heart. Savage blood pumped through its veins, filling it with all the old power and madness.

Caparelli's lips pulled back from his teeth. His hands opened and reached. He surged off the bench with a guttural roar. He knocked over the lectern and grabbed at Orson. His momentum carried them both to the floor. His meaty hands clamped around his nephew's head and his blunt thumbs struck for their targets.

Brother Martin sprang from his chair and threw himself on

Caparelli. He jerked at the man's forearms trying to break his grip. A second monk rushed forward to help, and a third.

The beast had usurped a piece of Caparelli's mind for an instant—his cunning, the part that knew it would have only a moment or two at the most. An instant decision to go for the only thing possible.

Orson was screaming.

Brother Martin strained at Caparelli's arms. Brother Henry was hammering at his head with balled fists. Brother George had him by the ankles and was trying to drag him off; but Caparelli held tight and pulled Orson along the floor with him. Brother Martin locked his own hands and smashed them against Caparelli's inner elbows, jarring the man's grip loose.

"Aiiiiyyahhhh!" Caparelli shouted in triumph.

Orson was shrieking. He rolled across the floor with his hands clapped to his face, trailing blood. Other monks pinned and held him down. He twisted under their hands and beat his heels on the floor.

Brother Martin went to his side. Brother Raphael was already there. Together they pried his hands from his face.

The eye sockets were filled with bloody yellowish jelly.

The sun was low in the afternoon sky. Lucky was hard on the scent again and pulling against his tracking harness. Brother Thomas and Brother Abner were struggling after him up a steep incline of rock which was spotted with wind-bent pines and clumps of straggly brush. This part of the lower mountain was piebald with large patches of rock that were cut with ravines in which stands of trees grew. Elsewhere, on the plateaus, such as the one Lucky was leading them up to now, and where the grade was gentler, the blue-green woods were dense.

Hauptmann had used the barren rock and the streams well. Lucky had lost the trail three times already, but he'd found it again, eventually, and had been driving hard for the last quarter-hour. Brother Thomas was focused entirely on the dog, trying to follow the instructions Brother Wilfred had given him, seeking just the right balance between inhibiting the animal and reinforcing it, maintaining its edge. Brother Abner kept a few paces behind him, scrutinizing the terrain carefully. He carried the shotgun with a shell in the chamber and his thumb on the safety.

The climb became more difficult as they neared the edge of the plateau. Lucky's nails scratched against the rock and dislodged small stones as he scrambled upward, damp nose nearly touching the stone, pulling the scent in quick rapid snorts. His ears were clicked forward and his tail high with concentration and excitement. He gained the plateau and strained against the lead impatiently as the monks pulled themselves up and over the edge. They stood a moment breathing heavily and wiping the sweat from their faces.

The shelf was some two hundred yards wide and three hundred yards deep. There were trees, some boulders.

Lucky pulled hard to the left, barking.

Brother Thomas tensed. "I think—"

Hauptmann sprang from behind a pile of rock directly in front of the dog. He fired twice with Brother Gilbert's automatic.

The dog went down and twisted on the stone.

"You fucking bastard!" Brother Thomas dropped the lead and charged.

Hauptmann fired twice again.

The slugs punched into Brother Thomas's chest. Twin puffs of dust rose from his robe. He didn't falter. His bony-knuckled hands were open.

Brother Abner dropped to one knee and threw the shotgun to his shoulder. "Down, Thomas! Get down!"

Hauptmann fired in rapid succession. Brother Thomas was hit three times more. He staggered the last few feet, seized Hauptmann by the throat and wrist and slammed the German's arm down against his knee—the gun went clattering across the stone. He lifted Hauptmann and hit him once, twice, in the face. Then he threw him backward.

Hauptmann struck against a tree and fell to the ground. He gained his hands and knees, shaking his head. Brother Abner advanced with the shotgun leveled. "Get back, Thomas!"

Brother Thomas stared at Hauptmann. Lopsided circles of blood were spreading over the front of the monk's robe. A trickle of it ran from the corner of his mouth. He made a sound of dumb rage and took an unsteady step toward the penitent.

"No," Brother Abner said.

Brother Thomas stopped. Puzzlement came over his face. He rocked on his feet. Then he toppled over backward with his arms flung out.

Hauptmann looked to the fallen pistol.

Brother Abner sighted down the barrel of the shotgun. "Give me a reason. I'll turn you into chop-meat. Please, I'm begging you. Any tiny reason at all."

Carefully, Hauptmann raised his hands and locked them behind his head.

Brother Abner knelt by Brother Thomas. He held the shotgun leveled with one hand and didn't take his eyes from Hauptmann. He found Brother Thomas's shoulder with his other hand.

Brother Thomas coughed, spraying out blood.

"It's going to be all right," Brother Abner said.

"Bless . . . me."

Brother Thomas shuddered, then lay still.

Brother Abner felt his throat for a pulse. There was none. He tried the wrist. Brother Thomas was dead.

Brother Abner retrieved the pistol. One slug had shattered Lucky's jaw, the other had struck him in the chest. The dog lay breathing in wet gasps, paws twitching. Brother Abner fired a shot from the automatic into its skull. The animal jerked. It went limp.

Brother Abner walked slowly to Hauptmann. He put the

shotgun to his shoulder and centered the muzzle on Hauptmann's face. He stood utterly quiet several moments. Then he stepped back and lowered the weapon.

He said, "Get on your hands and knees and crawl, you sonofabitch."

Chapter 20

A monk summoned Brother Martin shortly after the bells of Compline. "They're coming," he said.

There had been only one curt message from Brother Abner, several hours ago: "I have the German book. The cost was large. I am returning alone with it. Out." He hadn't responded to Brother Anthony's repeated calls.

From the open door the abbot saw two figures approaching from the far tree line. One was on its hands and knees. The second, walking behind, carried a shotgun.

Brother Martin went down the steps, through the gate and across the field to meet them.

Hauptmann, his head hanging, grimed and soaked with sweat, trembling with exhaustion, came to a stop when he encountered the abbot and raised his face. It was drawn with pain. There were two spotty trails of blood in the grass leading back to the trees.

"Stand up," Brother Martin said.

Brother Abner said, "Brother Thomas is dead. The dog is dead."

Hauptmann couldn't rise by himself.

Brother Martin took the shotgun from Brother Abner. "Help him."

Brother Harold was waiting in the entrance hall. He stared at Hauptmann through puffy redrimmed eyes. His mouth was tight. The abbot had not been able to comfort him much over the death of the oblate Michael. Brother Harold's hands were opening and closing. He clenched them into fists and moved toward Hauptmann.

Sharply, the abbot said, "Brother Harold. You have duties. Attend to them."

The monk hesitated.

"Brother Harold," the abbot repeated.

Brother Harold wrenched himself around and left.

Brother Gabriel, on post, closed the door, shutting out the soft evening light, and threw home the bolts.

Hauptmann blinked in the dim hall. His face was haggard but without expression. "So?"

"See him to the infirmary and have Brother Raphael attend to his hands and knees," Brother Martin told Brother Abner. "Then come to my office." He handed the shotgun to Brother Gabriel. "Have this returned to the armory."

He went to the office and waited for Brother Abner, who arrived a few minutes later. "What happened out there?"

Brother Abner recounted the story.

"You were told to bring him in," the abbot said. "Nothing more. It was not within your authority to administer punishment."

"I stand before you in guilt."

"What was your motivation?"

"Anger. Revenge."

"You have sinned."

"Yes, my abbot."

"Did you take pleasure in his pain?"

"No."

"Did you seek pleasure in it?"

"I wanted to cause him pain, but I didn't look for pleasure in it."

"That is something, at least. But the sin you did commit cannot go unpunished."

"No, my abbot."

"Find Brother Cooper. Inform him that it is my order that

you be chastised with ten lashes. You will spend the next three nights in sleepless vigil in the chapel. You will partake of nothing but water and bread through the next fourteen days."

Brother Abner went to one knee and kissed the abbot's ring. "I am obedient to your will."

He left to find Brother Cooper.

Brother Martin, with Brother Conrad, went first to Kennedy's room. Kennedy was pensive and distanced. He told them his version of the escape simply and in a flat tone. It seemed plausible. Brother Martin made no comment. His only interest in it now was to find where the order had erred, so they would not repeat it.

"I presume," the abbot said, "that you have considered a penance other than the one you initially proposed."

Kennedy was looking out the narrow window. "You know what you're going to do with me."

"Do we?"

"You're going to kill me." Kennedy turned from the window to look into the abbot's eyes. "And it doesn't make any difference."

"We want to save your soul."

"So did I once."

"That's your final word?"

"Yes."

"All right."

The abbot and Brother Conrad left.

Alvarado's story didn't vary much from Kennedy's. But he told it with an undertone of indignation, as if they were responsible for having driven him to such extremity.

"What penance do you suggest for yourself?" Brother Martin asked.

"I have done nothing wrong."

"As you fear God, I ask you to reconsider."

"I tell you that I have done nothing wrong," Alvarado said, but his voice was less certain.

Hauptmann lay on his sleeping board with his hands and knees swathed in bandaging. He said only, "I escaped. I was caught."

"Cite a penance for yourself."

"I refuse."

"Then you will accept ours."

"You have no authority," Hauptmann said.

"We have every responsibility," Brother Martin replied.

Hauptmann ignored him.

"You have until midnight to change your mind," Brother Martin said.

The light was fading. The monastery was preparing to shut down for the night. Brother Lawrence and Brother Andrew came for Pretty Boy.

"Your penance is unacceptable," Brother Lawrence said.

"What do you mean?" Pretty Boy cried. "What are you gonna do?"

Brother Lawrence pinned him. Brother Andrew dropped a rope over him and cinched his arms tight to his sides. They led him down the stairs and out of the monastery.

"Where you takin' me?" he wailed.

Brother Andrew unlocked the gate, closed it behind them.

"I said I'd be branded. It's my *penance*. Don't do nothin' else to me!"

They took him to the livestock barn. The air inside was sweet and heavy with the odor of straw, grain, healthy animals. They walked him down its length to the back and opened the wide swinging doors. The barn gave directly onto a small gully. It was here that all the shoveled droppings from the cattle and horse stalls were brought in wheelbarrows and dumped.

A sprawling heap of manure rose up from the floor of the

gully almost to a level with the barn. Its top was the consistency of soft watery clay. It stank. A swarm of blowflies were feeding upon it. Big awkward dung beetles crawled over it and burrowed into its interior.

A pair of wide planks had been set across the top. Two shovels stood near them, blades partly sunk into the pile. A pit had been dug in the center, a little less than a yard wide and of a depth nearly equal the height of a man.

Pretty Boy jerked against their hands. "No!"

They dragged him out onto the planks, their combined weight forcing the boards deeper into the ordure, which oozed up and curled over the edges.

Pretty Boy struggled and screamed as they lowered him into the pit. His bare feet touched the bottom, then sank in past his ankles. He threw himself from side to side, which only caused him to sink farther. He stilled himself. He grew goggle-eyed. The monks shoveled manure in around him. It fell on him in heavy wet clumps.

He vomited.

He began to whimper.

The stench was a thick pall around him.

He gagged.

They buried him to his shoulders. A warm wet pressure that held him like a great hand.

He was weeping.

Brother Lawrence and Brother Andrew left.

The flies had lifted from the pile and buzzed about in agitation during the interment. Now they began to settle back again. One landed on his temple above his left eye. Another walked across the back of his neck.

Sawyer knelt in his cell before Brother Martin with his hands clasped and his head bowed.

"I was trusted to aid and succor the helpless," he said in a quavering voice. "And I did just the opposite. I've done evil. I'm sick in my soul. I'd give anything to undo what I've done."

"What penance do you propose for yourself?"

"Chain me someplace in the forest. Or bar me into a cave in the rock. I'll have nothing, only a single blanket for warmth. I'll live on bread and water. I'll stay until . . . until I'm at the very edge of death." He looked up with a teary face. "Or until the end if you think God demands that. I want only my salvation. I want only to earn God's forgiveness."

Brother Martin burst into laughter.

Sawyer was bewildered.

Brother Martin slapped his thigh. "You dumb asshole!"

"I—I don't understand."

"Salvation? For you? God isn't a fool. Do you think you can plunder your way through life and spit in His face and then when things get a little rough say, 'Oh gee, I'm sorry,' and that's it, everything's all right?

"God isn't a simpering spongyhearted dupe. He doesn't come with the dove and olive branch. He comes with fire and sword. He doesn't forgive, Sawyer—he *judges*.

"Salvation, for you? That's a joke. God despises you. Your soul is forfeit to His anger. For ever, Sawyer, for ever."

"No. That can't be. You told us— You brought us here to . . ."

"To begin the work that He will finish in eternity."

"No!" Sawyer clutched the abbot's robe. "Please. That can't be true!"

Brother Martin pried his hands loose. "You're damned, Sawyer. God *hates* you." He went out of the cell.

Sawyer rushed into the hall a moment later. Brother Martin was already descending the stairs, in the company of Brother Conrad.

"Brother Phelan!" Sawyer screamed. "Brother Stefan! Where are you? For the love of God, help me!"

On the stairs, the abbot said to Brother Conrad, "Have all of the company been informed?"

"Yes. They'll respond to him consistently."

"Who have you assigned to watch him?"

"Brother Henry."

"He understands the importance?"

"Yes. There won't be any . . ." Brother Conrad trailed off.

"Any repetition of Bates," the abbot finished. "Good. Thank you."

Bates's suicide hung heavily on him. He had pushed the man too far. This final movement was necessary in the overall orchestration of Sawyer's Retreat, but Brother Martin had had to force himself through his own apprehension and he would not be easy about it until it was done.

Moving down the east hall, Brother Anthony stopped abruptly. A small figure covered head to foot in a gray cloak, face obscured by the raised hood, was approaching from the opposite end, washed in the golden light of the ending day that spilled through the windows.

He said, "Lily."

She caught herself up, took an involuntary step back.

"Lily," he said again, softly.

He went to her. She remained still. Her eyes were cast down. "We're not supposed to see each other."

"Just a moment or two. There can't be any offense in an accident." It was and was not an accident. He hadn't allowed the thought into his consciousness, but still, this was the third time he'd found excuse to be in this corridor where her room was since Hauptmann had been brought in and he was freed from that responsibility.

He said, "Where are . . . I mean . . ."

"I'm coming from the chapel," she said. "I've been praying for strength."

"Has it"—he looked away—"been difficult?"

Not in the way he meant. She spread her hands ambiguously.

"Aha," he said, equally as meaningful and meaningless.

She reached for his hand, but then stopped herself. "There is one thing, Anthony, that perhaps it would be good for you to know." This was the understanding she believed she had come to while in prayer. It had comforted her and filled her with joy.

"And that is?"

Now she did take his hand, so lightly and spiritually loving that he was scarcely aware.

"Beyond the terrible times, beyond your affliction of violence, Anthony, and the sins we shared in bed, there was an intense and deep eroticism between us. With you in me, while your fingers . . . your mouth . . . what happened many times was a delirium, a consummation as if by a glorious fire. It was this, which I learned from, you, Anthony, that has allowed me to give myself to Christ." Unknowingly, her other hand rose and she lightly stroked his wrist with her fingers. "To open to Him without reserve. To surrender, to be annihilated in Him. To let Him *fill* me until I am nothing but His rapture."

Her hands dropped away. She looked down again.

"You gave me a way to God, Anthony."

He nodded slowly. "Thank you for telling me," he said. Without understanding why, he knew that he would spend the night in prayer. "I will meditate upon this."

She smiled radiantly, slipped past and was gone.

Jaretzki was brought to the abbot's office. Brother Martin asked him, "'What penance have you decided upon for yourself?"

"A lifetime of abasement and service. I will take upon myself all the duties and tasks of the monastery that are the most humble and unpleasant. Everything that is loathsome and noxious shall become my responsibility. And I will offer each moment of it up to God and pray that someday He will see fit to grant me the grace of His love and forgiveness."

The man was fervent, and Brother Martin didn't doubt his sincerity. Which made what he had to do all the more difficult. He said, "I'll take this under advisement."

* * *

Brother James and Brother Vergil took Kennedy from the monastery at twilight. They paused outside the fence to tie his hands behind his back.

"So it's now, is it?" Kennedy said without emotion.

They led him away without answering.

"It's just as well," he said. "It's time to be quit of all this."

They took him to the pond.

He stared at the water. He grew edgy.

They directed him forward.

"No! Jesus, not this way!" He tore free and bolted. With his hands tied behind him, he ran with a clumsy lumbering gait. They caught him and dragged him back. He kicked and threw himself about between them. "Oh Christ, don't do it! Any way but this!"

His feet sank into the silty bottom. The water reached his knees, his thighs.

He threw his head back. "For the love of God, *no!*"

They pulled him waist-deep. Then Brother James seized his shoulders, hooked a leg behind his and pushed him down and under.

Scream, God he wanted to scream when the water closed over his head. But he clamped his jaw instead and tried to twist free of the monk's hands. He couldn't. He could find no leverage to work against, nothing solid, only the horrifying suspension of the non-world.

Jesus! Jesus! *Mercy!*

He managed to get his legs beneath him. He shoved his feet down through the mud to the hard underlying base. He tried to piston himself up, but there was no give in Brother James's arms and he couldn't.

He turned his face up toward the shimmering gray light that was agonizingly so near. He could see Brother James's bare wrists and the fabric of his loose sleeves, insanely billowing in the water as if in some slow and gentle fantasy. Farther up, past the surface and distorted by the water, he could see the bearded face of the monk.

Kennedy's lungs were afire. His body cried for him to give it air. He tried to drive himself up with short hard slams against the monk's rigid arms.

No!

He ground his teeth to keep from opening his mouth.

Yes, his lungs screamed.

No!

His head pounded. Talons of pain tore at the muscles of his jaw.

Yes!

NO!

His mouth jerked open with a release of bubbles and he couldn't stop himself from gasping for breath—sucking mud-roiled water into his lungs.

He choked it out, only to pull in more again. His stomach convulsed. He shuddered and twisted under Brother James's hands. Shuddered, twisted...

Brother Phelan was worried about Caparelli. He asked the abbot to speak with him. Caparelli was lying stomach-down on his sleeping board with his face turned to the wall. He didn't turn his head to see who had entered.

"Caparelli," Brother Martin said.

There was no answer.

The abbot hunkered down next to him and touched his shoulder. "Dominic."

There was a stifled choking sound.

"Dominic. Look at me."

Slowly, Caparelli shifted. His face was stricken, his eyes filled with tears. "I'm a monster," he said. "There's no hope for me."

"You sinned, and grievously, but you are *not* a monster. You're a man. You are God's child. And God stands always ready to forgive and embrace his children anew."

"No. Not me. I thought it was gone. But it isn't. It's still inside me, the evil."

"We are none of us perfect. Not you, not I, not any living person on this earth. That is why Christ died on the Cross. To gain salvation for us. With His help, we can overcome our evil and our human imperfection."

"It's too late for me. God doesn't love me. I know it."

Brother Martin took his shoulders and raised him up to a sitting position. "That isn't true, Dominic," he said forcefully. "Did you confess to Brother Stewart?"

"Yes."

"Did you repent your sin?"

"Yes."

"Did he grant you absolution?"

"Yes."

"He did that not as a man, but as God's agent. It was *God* who absolved you. *He* forgave you, not his priest."

"No," Caparelli said dully. "I'm evil. I can't be forgiven."

The abbot pressed his fingers into the penitent's flesh. "Listen to me. Of all the sins, Despair is the greatest—because it denies that God is loving and that God is good. If there *is* a single sin that can't be forgiven, which I doubt, then that sin is Despair. You have renounced sin, you do not wish to sin, you have begun your penance. So I beg of you, Dominic, do not commit yet another. Do not despair!"

"I . . . I don't know."

"I do. You are my beloved brother in Christ, and I swear it to you on all that I hold sacred."

A glimmer of doubtful hope appeared in Caparelli's face.

"It is *true,*" Brother Martin said. "Allow God's love to flow into you, that's all that He asks. Come. Let us say the Act of Contrition together." He helped Caparelli to his knees, and knelt beside him.

When he left he was mostly satisfied that he'd stopped Caparelli's slow spiral down, but he told Brother Phelan to stay with the man until the close of the day and continue to draw him out.

Now, to Kennedy.

Kennedy was sitting in a corner of his room with his back against the wall. His hair tunic was gone, he was in his gray penitent's robe. Brother James had given him a woolen blanket, which he now had wrapped around him like a shawl. He'd been given soup, cheese and bread. He held a mug of steaming coffee to his mouth. He was ashen.

He and the abbot looked at each other in silence. After several moments he asked, "Why did you do that to me?"

"As punishment, and to save your soul, and in the hope that you will eventually join us here as a brother."

"But that . . . of all things. You can't understand the horror of it for me. Anything else. I'd rather be torn apart. Literally."

"I can understand. We do understand. It's in your profile. You almost drowned as a child and you're terrified of water. That is *precisely* the reason we chose it."

Kennedy closed his eyes and grimaced with the memory.

"It was the only way," the abbot said. "And the best way. You know that. It may have been the moment of your rebirth. I hope it was."

"What do I have to face next?"

"Nothing, Tom. For you, the Retreat is over. Tomorrow you will become a postulant."

"Which means?"

"Tomorrow," Brother Martin said, and left.

Brother Harold brought Wycisowicz to Lily's door. "Knock," he said. "I'll be back in an hour."

The monk walked down the hall, turned the corner and was gone.

Wycisowicz looked about suspiciously. He'd felt beaten to the edge of death by the drug-induced convulsions and had been weak and disoriented for two days after. But he was a strong man in good condition and was almost fully recovered now. He'd tried to present himself as shaken at some core level, slowed, reflective. So far, they seemed to be buying it; they'd left him pretty much alone.

But now this, whatever it was. Well, he didn't have any choice, did he? He knocked.

"Come in."

A woman?

He stepped in.

She was standing at the opposite end of the room, before a shuttered window. Beautiful, and wearing a gown a woman would put on only for one reason. He got hard instantly.

"Close the door," she said, with a little movement of her head.

He wanted to lick her.

He shut the door without taking his eyes from her.

What was this?

"We have an hour to ourselves." She crossed to the bed and sat. "Come. Here, beside me."

A reward?

A test?

Well, tough shit, motherfuckers. I'm going to flunk your goddamn test.

He went to the bed and stood above her, looking down. "Who are you?"

"Does it make any difference?"

"No, I guess not."

"But *you're* important."

"Yeah? To you?"

She smiled enigmatically.

"I'm going to be," he said. "For the next hour anyway."

He raised her to her feet. He grinned and pulled the straps of her gown down off her shoulders. Her breasts, large for her slender rib cage, swung free. He grabbed one, cupped her buttocks with his other hand and pulled her into his swollen groin. He clamped his mouth down on hers.

Her perfume almost made him come.

He worked her mouth open. She resisted, but he thrust his tongue in anyway. She tried to push off from him.

He pulled his head back. "You're fucking terrific. Sorry I

didn't have time to pick up flowers." He kneaded her breast roughly, squeezed her buttock.

Her eyes flicked to the door. She pulled in breath and opened her mouth.

His hand shot from her breast to cover her mouth. He grabbed the back of her neck. "A setup!" he said, low and angrily.

He'd worked enough himself to recognize when one was being run on him. He stared at the door. Then he looked back to her. Her eyes were fearful above his hand.

"Uh-huh," he said.

He pulled her to the door, cocked his head and listened. He didn't hear anything, but that was meaningless. He peered at the doorknob. It could be locked, but there was no button, it required a key. He brought her back to the far side of the room.

"Where's the key," he whispered into her ear.

She shook her head.

He dug his fingers into her flesh.

"The key."

The color drained from her face. Her eyes slitted with pain. She shook her head again.

He twisted his fingers into her hair and placed his thumb over her eye. "You make any kind of sound, I'm going to pop this out. Now where's the goddamn key?" He lifted his hand from her mouth, ready to clamp it down again.

"I don't have it," she said. "The abbot does. Please. I don't. Believe me."

He covered her mouth. "Well," he whispered. "All right. They're going to do whatever they're going to do to me anyway. But I'm going to get me a nice piece of their pussy before they do it."

He forced her onto the bed. She struggled, but she was much smaller than he, and he was powerful. He pinned her with a knee in her midriff, tore pieces from her gown.

"Don't worry, pretty baby. It's not going to hurt. Not a whole lot anyway. And you'll like it, even that part."

He balled one of the pieces into a wad and stuffed it into

her mouth, secured it in place with a second piece and tied her hands behind her back with a third.

Her gown was shredded to her waist. He bobbled her breasts. *"Nice,"* he said.

He pulled off his tunic and dropped it to the floor. His cock was thick and gorged, shot its length with a large blue vein. He hefted it.

"A beauty, huh? It's a cryin' shame we can't use your mouth. It truly is."

He straddled her on his hands and knees, ducked his head and pulled as much as he could of her breast into his mouth. He sucked hard on it, ran the tip of his tongue around her nipple. "Oh, that is sweet," he said.

Lily lay atop her bound arms with her head turned to the side and her eyes squeezed shut. There were tears on her cheeks.

"Come on, li'l darlin'. Get yourself into it. No sense you not havin' a good time too. Tell you what."

He pulled up the bottom of her gown and bunched it around her waist, exposing her loins.

"You'll like this a whole lot better. Ain't no mama's child can resist ol' Witz's golden tongue. Why, that's just the prettiest and most ladylike li'l bush I ever did see."

Lily's sob was muffled. She pressed her legs tightly together.

Wycisowicz pried them open. He knelt between them, then went down on his stomach. He took her thighs in his hands. He spread her, canted her pelvis.

"That's a purely beautiful thing," he said. "Just like a little cheerleader's. Oh, I'll bet you taste scrumptious. Yes!" He lowered his mouth to her.

She rolled suddenly and swung her leg up over him. She threw herself from the bed, lunging to strike the end table. It rocked over on two legs, balanced a moment, then toppled. The water crock and bowl crashed to the floor.

Wycisowicz was on his feet instantly. He stared down at her in rage.

There was a moment of stillness.

Then the door banged open. Brother Harold stood in the frame. He looked at them in bewilderment. But only for a moment. "Wycisowicz!"

Wycisowicz was already moving. He aimed a kick at the monk's groin. Brother Harold pivoted. Wycisowicz recovered and chopped with a stiff hand for the monk's throat. But even as he did he saw Brother Harold swinging a spring-loaded sap and knew that he wasn't going to make it. Brother Harold pulled his head back—the edge of Wycisowicz's hand grazed his neck harmlessly—and ticked the lead sap against the penitent's temple. The monk was skillful; a hard crack would have broken the skull.

Wycisowicz didn't feel any pain. Simply a heaviness. He couldn't see properly. He couldn't think. His legs wouldn't hold him up. He fell against the jamb and slumped to the floor.

Brother Harold took him by the arms and started to pull him into the hall.

Lily went, "Mhhmm!" She was naked and vulnerable on the floor.

Brother Harold snapped his gaze up to her eyes, which were pleading and wide with fear, but even though he focused it there, the image of her body, in the fractional moment he saw it, had seared itself into his mind. He went to her wardrobe, took out her cloak and laid it over her, careful to keep his eyes from her body.

"I'll—I'll be right back to free you. Don't worry. It's all right now. I'll only be gone a minute."

He closed the door behind him so she would not have to be seen like that if anyone happened down the hall.

Wycisowicz was dazed but not unconscious. The monk half carried him down the hall. Brother Allen and the oblate Gregory were working in the cloister gardens. They stared. Only now did it occur to Brother Harold that Wycisowicz was naked.

"Some trouble," he said. "It's over now. Bring this man to his room and see that he doesn't leave it."

Gregory took Wycisowicz by the shoulder and twisted his arm up behind his back.

Brother Harold hurried back to Lily's room. He closed the door for her privacy. He knelt and loosened the gag. "I'm so sorry," he said. "I didn't hear anything. I didn't know."

She began to cry.

"Please," he said. "Please don't. It's all right now. You're safe."

"My wrists," she said. She shifted so he could reach them.

He looked away from her back. He fumbled for her bound wrists. The accidental touch of her skin, at the beginning curve of her buttocks, the warmth and astonishing smoothness and softness, struck him with the force of a blow. His breath caught. His ears burned as he worked the knot. He stared fixedly at the wall.

"There," he said. "I'll send the abbot. I—"

"No!" She sat up suddenly, threw her arms around him and buried her face in his chest. "Don't leave me yet. Please. Please! I don't want to be alone."

"I . . ."

"Please!" She gave way to sobs, jerking against him.

His hands circled in confusion. They came to rest on her back, leaped off as if they had touched fire. Tentatively, he patted her hair.

"It's all right," he said with difficulty. "No one's going to hurt you."

Her warmth and the smell of her skin made him lightheaded. Her sobs reached within him to the great raw wound that was the oblate Michael. His own eyes filled with tears. They ran slowly down his face. They fell upon her forehead. She raised her face and looked at him.

"I . . ." he said. "I lost a . . . a son. Yes, he was that, he was like a child to me. He . . . trusted me. I wasn't there. They killed him."

His tears ran freely now.

She lifted a hand to his cheek. She brushed his tears with her fingertips.

At her touch he went, "Ohhh."

She rose to her knees. The cloak fell away from her. She took his face in her hands and looked into his eyes.

He felt the strength rush out of him, leaving him weak and scarcely able to move.

"I . . . lost a child once too. A beautiful child who trusted me. A . . . golden little boy."

She guided his head down to her breast, encircled him with her arms.

He groaned.

"So . . . much loss," she whispered. "And so long, so long a time."

She rocked him and began to croon to him.

He cried against her breast. He held himself to her.

She turned his face up and looked into his eyes. She touched her lips to his, simply touched. Her hair swung forward. It enshrouded his face and lay delicately on his cheeks.

She opened her lips just enough for the tip of her tongue to slip out. She pressed it to his lips, withdrew it, pressed again. Hesitantly, his own lips opened. She touched his teeth, which remained a barrier some moments, then separated, but not much; enough, only, for the tips of their tongues to meet and to move slowly back and forth against each other.

She placed his hands on her breasts.

He moaned.

Her tongue entered his mouth. She slipped her hands into the loose collar of his robe, moved them slowly over his shoulders, down to his chest.

He kissed her.

She stood, raising him up with her, their mouths still together. She pressed softly into him, felt the warmth and hardness of him. She ended their kiss. She stroked his cheeks with her fingers. His eyes were closed. He breathed shallowly. She looked at him with gentleness, grief and love.

She went to her dressing table, lifted a box of powder and took something from beneath it. She crossed to the door.

Brother Harold opened his eyes at the sound: *cl-lick*. She was at the door, with her hand on a key, which was in the lock. She moved away, loosed the braided cord at the waist of her torn gown and let the remnants of it fall down her legs to her ankles. She stepped out of it and came to him.

She put her hands on his shoulders. "Please," she said.

He trembled.

"Please. For all that is good and sweet."

He gazed upon her in wonder. A slow exaltation and a tenderness beyond any he had ever known grew within him and he reached to draw her in. She helped him to disrobe, dreamily, ceremonially.

They lay beside each other on the bed. They touched, they kissed softly, and in time she opened herself to him, like fog parting before a rising sun, and he entered her as quietly and lightly as the slip of a deer into a glade.

They moved together, temperately, for a long and merciful time. When finally they came, they did so with each other without frenzy or detonation, but rather a slow melting into a deepening reservoir of rapture in which they ceased to be themselves and became, for a time that could not be measured, a corporate unity that was its own definition.

From there they gradually withdrew, as they must, and began to form separately again, but within each other's arms, and only dimly aware of the process, because the awareness was softened by languor and finally a sleep that overtook them before it was done.

They slept holding each other.

They were awakened—both startled and neither knowing how much time later—by a knock upon the door.

"Lily?" It was the abbot.

Brother Harold tensed.

Lily put her hands to his face and laid her lips upon his.

Brother Martin's footsteps drew away down the hall.

Brother Harold and Lily touched each other's cheeks, kissed each other's fingers.

They rose. They dressed in silence.

"I, I am sorry I led you into sin," Brother Harold said.

"It was not you who led." She took his hands. "And it was sin only in its prohibition. Not of itself. It couldn't be. You know that in your heart. Confess the violation of your vows, as I will mine, but offer thanksgiving to God for the joy with which He blessed us."

"Yes, I do thank Him."

"And I, you."

"And you."

They held each other tightly.

"Good-bye, my sister in Christ."

"Good-bye, my brother."

It was not easy for either of them to step back.

Brother Harold tore himself around, unlocked the door and went into the hall.

Brother Martin said to Alvarado, "Your penance is this. You will write every day, over and over, the Act of Contrition. And as you do you will meditate upon each word."

The abbot removed something from the folds of his robe and unfolded it.

"This is the square of skin Brother Raphael took from you. It has been tanned. Imperfect contrition is that which results from a fear of punishment. *Perfect* contrition is a deep sorrow for and renunciation of sin which rises, unsullied by any other consideration, from a pure love of God. When you are able to write a perfect Act of Contrition, then you will inscribe it upon your own skin, which you will carry with you for the remainder of your life here in the monastery."

Alvarado waited. "That is all? There is nothing more you are not telling me about?"

"That's all. But be aware that it must be a *Perfect* Act. If it is not, we will know. This skin will be profaned, and you will once again be sent to the pyre. Only this time the wood will be dry and the flames will not be extinguished."

Orson lay on his back in the infirmary. The large bandages over his eyes were held in place by a winding of gauze around his head. His arms were slack at his sides. Save for the slow rise and fall of his chest, he was perfectly still. Brother Raphael had sedated him, but said that his mind would still be functional if he were awake.

Softly, Brother Martin said, "Orson?"

"Yes."

"It's Brother Martin."

"Yes."

"I'm sorry for this."

Orson said nothing.

"Brother Raphael has told you. Nothing can be done."

"I know."

"Are you in much pain?"

"It hurts. But I would have thought there'd be more."

"What is in your heart?"

"Bitterness. Fear."

"Fear?"

"I thought I felt God. I thought I knew what he wanted from me. Now I don't. And I'm afraid."

The abbot rested his hand on Orson's shoulder. "God is mysterious. But He isn't to be feared."

"Did I deserve to be blinded? Tell me, did I?"

"Pray that He may grant you understanding."

"I will pray. Although I'm not going to find it easy."

The abbot was gratified; he would have mistrusted anything else.

"This darkness is sufficient penance. Don't you think so,

Brother Martin?" It was not a question, and his voice was hard and edged.

"Yes, I do think so. And I think that . . ." The abbot was humbled. He believed that eventually Orson would be not only a monk of the Order, but one of the finer among them. But he didn't say that, because, though it was true, the desire to state it was born mostly from his need to soften the knowledge that many among the penitents would go no further than postulant, and because such awareness now could endanger the man's spiritual progress. So instead, he said only, "I think that all will be well."

It was late. Hauptmann was awake. The painkillers Brother Raphael had given him blocked only a portion of the throbbing in his bandaged knees and hands. Though he was exhausted, he couldn't sleep. He wasn't thinking; rather simply letting his mind drift wherever it would. That was often an effective way to approach a problem when critical analysis failed. Idle meandering would sometimes deliver up the overlooked detail. There was a way out. There always was. He would find it.

Thus was he occupied when Brother Martin entered his room.

The abbot said, "It is midnight."

"And?"

"As I told you earlier, it is time for you to cite a penance for yourself."

Hauptmann turned away.

Brother Martin waited, then said, "So be it. Gunther Hauptmann, you are offered two choices. The first—which, since you have forced us to this position, I implore you to take—is to become an oblate of this order. If you do, you shall become our responsibility and will live out the remainder of your natural life in peace and well-being with us."

"Oblate?"

"Generally, an oblate is a lay person who has not taken

vows or been formally received into an order, but who lives with the order and dedicates himself to a spiritual life. With us, because of our special mission, the condition is by necessity somewhat different. Michael, the man you threw atop the wire, was an oblate. Gregory is an oblate. These were once men like you. We could not save them. They chose to become oblate: they underwent prefrontal lobotomy."

"You're joking."

"I have not joked in many years."

Hauptmann reflected upon the two men the abbot had named. It seemed plausible.

"Are you familiar with lobotomy?" Brother Martin asked.

"To a degree."

"It is surgical destruction of the frontal lobes of the brain. There is no significant pain involved. The results are not always fully predictable. Much depends upon the individual personality. But they are always satisfactory for our purposes. There is no longing afterward for the previous life. You simply become . . . something else. Benign. No longer a threat to God's world, and still capable of salvation."

Hauptmann looked at the abbot with contempt. "Do you think that any sane man would consent to having his mind destroyed?"

"Some have."

"And the alternative?"

"We will deliver you into the hands of God."

"You mean kill me."

"With deep regret, and with our prayers for your reunion with God in Heaven."

"I don't believe you."

"Please do."

Hauptmann looked deep into the abbot's eyes.

It was possible.

There was no choice, really. If he had any chance at all, it was to call what might, marginally, be the abbot's bluff.

"I prefer to end it here."

Hauptmann thought he saw, for a moment, sadness play over the monk's face.

"As you wish. There will be no pain. Vengeance is not involved. You have half an hour. I hope you will use it to make your peace with God."

Hauptmann waited a few minutes after the abbot left, listening. He went to his door and opened it.

Brother Anthony stood across the hall. Brother Anthony had a gun in his hand. He said nothing. He simply raised the gun and pointed it at Hauptmann's chest.

Hauptmann closed the door.

It was possible.

He lay down on his sleeping board.

His mind drifted in no particular direction. He wasn't afraid. He had experienced urgency and tension in his life, but he didn't think he had ever truly known fear. He was not afraid of death. Maybe that was why it had been so easy for him to kill. He didn't know. Nor could he *know* that he actually was going to die now.

There was no point in thinking about it.

Brother Anthony entered his room with Brother Cooper some half an hour later.

"Come," Brother Anthony said.

They took him out and down the hall to the stairs. He could vaguely hear the massed voices of the monks lifted in song, in chant actually, monophonic and melodious, a Gregorian chant. It grew louder as they neared the chapel, swelled full and strong when Brother Cooper opened the doors.

The chapel was illuminated with wavering light from ranks of tall candles. The company was assembled within, their cowls raised and their faces in shadow. Brother Cooper closed the doors. The chant continued, soft and undulating. There was a joy in it, a tenderness.

Brother Raphael was standing just inside the door. He pushed up the sleeve of Hauptmann's tunic and tied his arm off with a piece of rubber tubing.

"Make a fist," he said. He held a syringe in his hand.

Hauptmann did. Brother Raphael waited until the vein grew prominent.

"This is quick," Brother Raphael said. "You won't feel anything. You'll simply go to sleep." He slipped the needle into the vein and depressed the plunger. "May God bless you," he said, and removed the needle.

A sense of relaxation began in Hauptmann. He listened to the chant, he looked at the flickering candles. It was quite beautiful.

He felt somewhat lightheaded. He swayed on his feet.

Brother Cooper caught him as he began to go over backward. Brother Anthony stepped forward, and two other monks joined them. They lifted Hauptmann up to their shoulders and bore him down the aisle toward the altar, as the rest of the company sang.

It was lovely to be carried thus, surrounded and encapsulated so warmly by those clear voices. Hauptmann smiled. He heard somewhere, with pleasure, the crackling of gunfire, the dull *wumph!* of explosives he had set. All was well. He was functioning cleanly. His smile widened as he watched the rolling orange fireball that was his craft and pride.

And then, then there was a kind of quiet suspension and he was far above the earth and its concerns, and he was looking down at the rolls of billowing white clouds, so utterly beautiful and peaceful.

Gunther Hauptmann died.

The four monks carrying him gained the altar and laid his body gently upon it.

Brother Stewart, wearing the purple stole around his neck, anointed the dead man's forehead, cheeks and lips with oil and spoke over him the words of Conditional Absolution.

He said, "Rest with God, my troubled son."

Then he turned to face the company, made in the air with a broad gesture the sign of the cross, and lifted his voice with his brothers to join in celebration.

Chapter 21

The monks remained in chapel after Hauptmann was removed.

The abbot sent Brother Stefan for Sawyer. In the hall outside Sawyer's room, Brother Lawrence sat on a stool keeping watch on him. Sawyer was not asleep. He had gone from monk to monk throughout the day pleading for salvation. He was mocked, reviled and turned away without hope. He had prayed frenziedly in the unanswering chapel, wandered about the monastery alternately stupefied and wailing. An hour ago when he'd tried to pray again, Brother Lawrence had laughed at him. He'd flung himself down and wept. His eyes were empty now as he looked up at Brother Stefan.

"Come," the monk said.

Sawyer rose and followed him mechanically, without will, as if *he* had disappeared, and all that was left were a living mannequin. In the chapel he followed Brother Stefan up to the altar and stood motionless before it looking down at his feet, arms limp at his sides.

Brother Martin said, "Philip Sawyer, we have summoned you here before the Lord God as the final act of your Retreat. The penance you proposed for yourself was judged sincere, but neither relevant nor beneficial to you. We therefore instituted our own. You have now known not only the physical torment you inflicted upon others but the utter hopelessness and despair you caused them. There is nothing more horrible one can do to another person.

"I ask you once again, do you renounce forever your sins against God and His children?"

Sawyer lifted his eyes. "But you said..."

The abbot's voice softened. "Philip, it was my duty before God to tell you what I did. My painful duty. Hear me, and know that it cannot be otherwise: God is endlessly merciful. He can no more withhold His forgiveness and love than fire can quench or water burn. He is perfect love, and He cannot be other than what He is. Do you renounce your sins?"

Sawyer was bewildered. Then comprehension began to suffuse his face, and was followed by joy. He sank to his knees. "Yes! Oh yes!"

"Do you do so out of pure love of God and a true abhorrence of sin?"

"Yes!"

"Are you resolved never to sin again?"

"Yes!"

"Are you prepared to dedicate your life to His service and glorification?"

"I am!"

"Then say with me the Act of Contrition and cleanse your soul so that you may receive the Body and Blood of Christ."

Sawyer clasped his hands and prayed with fervor.

Brother Stewart stepped forward holding a ciborium. He brought forth from it a consecrated Host.

Sawyer tilted his head and opened his mouth. Brother Stewart laid the Host upon his tongue.

The abbot said, "Your time as a penitent is over. Tonight you shall become a postulant of the Order of Saint Hector."

Sawyer's eyes were closed. The Body and Blood of his God dissolved within his mouth, and beatitude spread within him.

The company lifted their voices in thanksgiving.

Brother Lawrence and Brother Andrew dug Pretty Boy out of the rotting manure at dawn.

He stared off to the woods while they worked. There was dried vomit and crusted bile around his mouth and on his chin.

His head and shoulders were blistered with insect bites. The monks took him out through the barn and back to the monastery, to the showers. He stood filthy and stinking and silent and didn't move.

"Clean yourself up," Brother Lawrence said.

He didn't respond.

Brother Lawrence turned the shower on and pressed a bar of soap into his hand. "Wash."

The water coursed down over him loosening the rotten dung. He lifted the soap. He washed. He let the soap fall to the floor. He stood motionless beneath the beating water.

Brother Lawrence turned the shower off and handed him a towel. "Dry yourself."

They gave him a gray penitent's robe to put on and took him to the abbot's office.

Brother Martin said, "The Retreat is over for you, Floyd. You can go to your room."

Pretty Boy remained slumpshouldered and silent.

"I said it's over now."

Pretty Boy's eyes filled with tears. The tears dropped to the floor. He turned and walked out of the office.

In the midmorning, Caparelli asked to see his nephew. The abbot consented. Brother Conrad brought him to the infirmary.

Orson turned his head on the pillow. "Who's there?"

Caparelli looked down at him, stricken with grief and unable to speak.

"Someone is," Orson said. "I heard you come in."

"It's me, Orson. Dominic." Caparelli went to his knees and pressed Orson's hand to his cheek. "I'm sorry. I'd do anything to change it. Anything. Forgive me!"

Orson was quiet.

"Please," Caparelli choked. "You must."

Orson pulled his hand from Caparelli's. He laid it on the man's head and stroked the thick graying hair.

"I forgive you, Uncle."

"Oh God!" Caparelli clawed at his own face. "I'm not worthy! I'm coming to you, Orson," he screamed. "I give you my own eyes as penance!"

"No!" Brother Conrad lunged around the bed. "Caparelli, don't!"

Caparelli shrieked as the monk grappled with him.

Brother Raphael rushed in.

Orson sat up. "What's happening? Uncle, stop!"

The monks wrestled Caparelli to the floor. There was blood on his face and hands. Brother Conrad pinned him while Brother Raphael loaded a syringe and injected him with a sedative. The penitent twisted and groaned. Slowly, he loosened. He rolled his head ponderously from side to side.

He went: "Hnnnnh. Hnnnnh."

"Help me get him onto a bed," Brother Raphael said.

"What's happened?" Orson said.

"He's hurt himself," Brother Conrad said.

Brother Raphael went out.

"How bad?"

"I don't know."

Brother Raphael returned. "Hold his head steady." The monk flicked on the light of an ophthalmoscope and peered through the conical viewer into each of Caparelli's eyes. He swabbed blood away and carefully pulled the lids up. "Get Brother Walter. Tell him I need him for surgery."

"Is it as serious as it looks?"

"The left one is lacerated but it'll be all right. I'll try to save the right one. I'm not optimistic."

Brother Conrad left.

Sitting in his bed, braced up on one arm, Orson's face was turned sightlessly to Caparelli's bed. "Uncle," he said softly.

Caparelli couldn't hear him.

"Why? I forgave you."

* * *

The morning was sunny and pleasant. Brother Martin held Lily's elbow as he escorted her to the car in which Brother George waited to take her back into Scanandaga. The cloak of her hood was up, hiding her face.

The abbot was deeply abstracted.

He had failed to see the possibility of Wycisowicz's assault against Lily, which now seemed apparent to him.

He should have realized the magnitude of Caparelli's despair, and how dangerous to him it was.

He feared the harsh, final actions of the Retreat, which lay ahead of him today.

But he let none of this show. He owed Lily a leave-taking of grace and reassurance.

They reached the car. "I thank you," he said. "Your help was valuable to us and to the penitents. God is grateful, and so are we. We will remember you in our prayers."

"Do," she said. "I'm in need of the Lord's strength. I . . ." She didn't finish.

She'd been composed after the attack, but he sensed her agitation nonetheless and had done what he could to dispel it and soothe her. In the end, her calmness had made him believe in her.

"You're still troubled," he said.

She examined his face. "Less than you."

He was appalled that she had seen through to his various distresses. "Only with concern for you."

"That's unnecessary," she said. "I'm quite all right. But please do remember me in your prayers."

"We will."

Her eyes grew mysteriously sad. "So, Brother Martin. It is done. I am grateful that God allowed me to serve as an instrument of His will in your behalf. God be with you."

"And with you."

The abbot opened the door for her. She turned to enter, paused and looked over the roof of the car to the monastery.

Brother Martin followed her eyes.

Brother Harold was standing at the entrance gazing out at them. He disappeared in an instant.

After an infinitesimal pause, Lily slipped into the car and closed the door behind her. She sat straight, with her hands in her lap, looking directly ahead through the windshield.

Brother George started the engine.

"Good-bye," Brother Martin said through the open window.

"Good-bye." She kept her eyes fixed forward.

Brother George pulled the vehicle away. Brother Martin looked after it, at Lily's stiff figure. He pictured Brother Harold, tried to recall the expression on the monk's face. He became thoughtful.

It had been decided to undertake the work in Ballantine's room instead of the surgery, where his cries would have disturbed DiPalo and Caparelli. Brother Raphael brought Brother Louis and Brother William with him.

With some sorrow, he said to the penitent, "You failed to suggest a penance for yourself."

Ballantine was indignant. "Nor do I intend to."

"The option is no longer yours."

Ballantine saw the instrument in the infirmarer's blue-veined hand. He recognized it instantly and backed up against the wall, his breath catching.

Brother Louis and Brother William seized him and forced him to the floor.

He twisted under their hands. "You're mad! Don't! Don't do it!"

"It will be easier on you if you don't struggle." Brother Raphael lubricated the slender flexible rod.

"Stop! You don't know what you can do with that!"

"I know very well what I can do with it, what I'm going to do." The infirmarer took Ballantine's limp penis in his hand, positioned the rod.

Ballantine rolled his hips, kicked out with his legs.

"Be still," Brother Raphael counseled. "You know there will be damage I don't intend if you struggle."

Ballantine tensed. Sweat broke onto his skin. Consciously, he loosened his body. He stared hard at the ceiling. "No anesthetic?"

"No."

"How bad?"

"That's a value judgment. There will be permanent damage, but nothing will be destroyed."

A tic pulled at Ballantine's mouth.

Brother Raphael inserted the rod, worked it slowly up the urethra.

Ballantine's breath was rapid and shallow.

The infirmarer stopped and reached for the base of the instrument, where there was a small knurled knob. He turned it.

At the end of the rod, within Ballantine, six tiny surgical blades lifted from their slots. In deft hands, the instrument could clear blockages and remove scar tissue. In equally deft hands, with the blades roughened slightly, it could accomplish precisely the opposite.

Rotating it as he went, Brother Raphael drew the instrument back down through the length of Ballantine's penis.

Ballantine groaned. His eyes widened, his lips drew back. He trembled. But he didn't move; he was afraid to.

He went, "Ghhhaaaa!" as the monk pulled the rod free.

It was stained crimson.

Brother Louis and Brother William released him. With a cry, he doubled in on himself like a recoiling spring. His hands went to his genitals. He was gasping. He glistened with sweat.

"The Retreat, for you, is over," Brother Raphael said.

When they left, Ballantine was clutching himself and rocking back and forth.

Brother Raphael reported to the abbot.

"It went well?"

"Yes. The pain will be intense and he'll urinate blood for the next day or so. Once the scar tissue is fully formed, he'll experience low-level pain each time he urinates. For the rest of his life."

"And you're certain about infection."

The infirmarer nodded. "He'll contract bladder infections periodically because of urine retention. They'll be painful, but we can knock it out with drugs. It won't get out of hand and it isn't life-threatening."

"Fine. Thank you. You may go."

"I..."

"Yes?"

"Nothing."

Brother Martin studied him. "I know this is difficult for you. It is a sacrifice. I give you my blessing and my gratitude. Do not be harsh on yourself; you serve God's will."

They were not enough, the abbot's words, but they were of some help and Brother Raphael was thankful for them. He left to pray.

Brother Harold appeared at the office shortly before noon. He brushed his hair back with an agitated sweep of his hand. He stood before the desk pulling at the cloth of his robe.

The abbot waited.

The young monk opened his mouth, closed it, looked away, looked back.

"Yes?" Brother Martin said.

"My abbot, I—I wish to be released from my vows!" He dropped to his knees and buried his face in his hands. "I'm sorry," he choked. "I have sinned. I have . . . I must be released. I must."

Brother Martin watched him cry. "Stand up, Brother Harold."

The monk got to his feet. His cheeks were wet with tears. The abbot spoke evenly, but there was fear in his heart.

"There is no release from the Order of Saint Hector. You know that."

"Please," Brother Harold whispered.

"What have you done?" The monk told him. "And why do you now wish release from your vows?"

"I . . . am in love with her. I want to marry her."

Brother Martin was relieved. There was an easy way, then. The fundamental responsibility of an abbot was to see that no monk ever left the order. None. Ever. It was to be prevented through any means necessary. He saw now that he could accomplish this without drastic measure, for which he was grateful.

"How does she feel?" he asked.

"I don't know."

"Didn't she tell you?"

"I didn't raise it with her. But I know from what happened that she could. That she would. I'm certain."

"You can't marry her."

Brother Harold lifted his hands. "I'm begging you."

"I do not tell you that as your abbot. It is not my law. It is the law of the Church. It is the law of God, against which there is no appeal. She is already joined in the sacrament of Holy Matrimony. If you had declared yourself, she would have told you."

Brother Harold was stricken. "But . . . that can't be. She's a nun, a sister of the Blessed Bernadine."

"She lives and works with the sisters, but she is not one of them. She is married. And her husband is a monk. Of the Order of Saint Hector. Her husband is Brother Anthony."

Brother Harold shook his head. "No," he said quietly. "No."

"Yes. Theirs has become a marriage in Christ now, but it is still a marriage, sanctified by the Church, and cannot be put asunder. You are bound by that as much as they."

A sob tore from the young monk.

"So you see that she is not free to marry. But even if she

were, I could not permit you to leave. Only one thing can free any of us from the Order. You know that well: death."

Brother Harold was crying without sound.

"Prostrate yourself," the abbot said. Brother Harold went to the floor. "You have seriously violated your vows. Your sin is grievous. Do you repent it?"

"I repent the violation of my vows."

"That is only one part. Do you repent the act, which was itself sin?"

"I . . . am sorry for whatever sin there might have been within it."

Brother Martin rubbed his forehead with the tip of his index finger. Brother Harold had been a devout and exemplary monk. He was still young. The woman was beautiful. The oblate Michael's death had shaken him deeply. Still, there was sin here. And still, Brother Harold was in jeopardy.

"You will inform Brother Conrad that you are to receive ten lashes, after which you will retire to your cell. The shutter will be closed to seal out the light. You will be shackled and you will remain thus thirty days, taking only bread and water. We will review this at the end of that period."

Brother Harold cried out. The abbot did not think it a response to the punishment, but rather an expression of loss—of Lily, of Michael, perhaps even of a long-ago innocence. He felt compassion, but was careful not to let it show when he dismissed him.

He sat alone several minutes, tension building, then summoned the oblate Gregory, spoke a few words to him and dispatched him.

He waited, pacing slowly back and forth.

Gregory was back ten minutes later. Brother Harold had indeed reported to Brother Conrad. The flogging was under way. Brother Louis was bringing manacles from the workshop.

The abbot sighed. He'd thought himself right, but he hadn't *known* himself right; the possibility of a confused and distraught monk in flight through the woods had frightened him.

* * *

There was the question of Rauscher. He had postponed it as long as he could. It was time.

Rauscher.

Free will was everything. Without free will there was no volition. Without volition there was no salvation.

The position of oblate was new to the order. It had been instituted only half a century ago, shortly after Dr. Angelo Lombretti had pioneered the surgical procedure that made it possible. The order had welcomed it as a humane option. Brother Martin had searched the records carefully, and it was as he had feared: lobotomy had been offered to a penitent when the situation warranted, but it had never been *forced* upon one. The surgery—especially in the extent that was customary to the order—did indeed destroy much, if not all, of the oblate's free will. But—and this was vital, this made possible the option—the penitent was allowed full exercise of his unimpaired will in making the decision. In the last act for which he could be held morally responsible, he *chose* salvation.

The order had erred with Rauscher. He, the abbot, had erred, since the ultimate decision and thus the responsibility rested in him alone. Rauscher was mentally defective, not truly capable of ethical choice. Which meant, no matter how violent or destructive he was, that he was not a proper candidate for a Retreat. His soul was already beloved of God, Who had afflicted him thus for His own mysterious reasons. But they couldn't set him free. Once he had entered into the monastery that first day, their commitment was irrevocable.

There wasn't anything else to do.

He summoned Brother Conrad. "Max Rauscher is to go oblate. Instruct Brother Raphael to do it this afternoon."

Rauscher would be the Order's responsibility for the rest of his life, would be Brother Martin's responsibility.

He spoke over the telephone with Bob Turner, the field agent, and a relatively new one, who'd recommended Rauscher, and went over with him again the criteria he was to use in considering candidates. He didn't tell him that his next referral would come under the most exacting scrutiny and that if the candidate was not prime that he, Turner, would be discarded as an agent. Which was a simple matter of notifying him that the monastery was no longer engaged in the program.

Program.

That's all it was to the handful of agents scattered about the country. A program. They knew there was something out of the ordinary about it; the need for strict secrecy and the fact that they never again saw the man they referred made that inescapable. They were told simply that it was a rehabilitative program and that from the monastery a retreatant was placed into another environment, much the same way an addict was by social agencies, which greatly enhanced his chance of permanent cure. It was inevitable that in time some of the agents would come to understand that something much larger was happening. But by then the order would have winnowed out over the years those who might have raised difficult questions. All of their agents, like Hill in Chicago, Hawthorne in New York and Eyler in Atlanta, were men of deep character, spirituality and moral sensitivity, and all of them had in some way been wounded and hurt by society's inability to control many of life's human monsters.

Agents were recruited with painstaking care. Preferably, and most often, by other agents already seasoned through years of service. At times, by select monks of the order. If there was a need, the abbot would send a monk into the outside world in search of men fit to serve as agents. This was always perilous. Only a monk of great spiritual strength would be dispatched, and the safeguards were multiple, the conditions strict. Time in the world at large was limited, the daily regimen of prayer and devotion severe, and the monk was required to report to the abbot each evening by telephone. In former times, they had been sent out in pairs so they could strengthen, support and watch each other, and that was still done if the abbot was not fully confident. Brother Martin felt that he himself would never send a man out on his own.

If a monk in the field failed to make contact even for a single evening, the prior was ordered out after him immediately. Most often there would be a simple explanation. But if the monk was in difficulty, wavering in faith or dedication, the prior would bring him back. Rarely did a monk turn rogue. But no matter how remote, that was always a possibility.

In such a case the prior's duty was clear.

He hunted down and killed the apostate.

Brother Cooper and Brother Gabriel took Wycisowicz into the kitchen and through the door that connected it with the ice house. The ice house was built of wood. It was tall, windowless. Brother Cooper lit a lantern, which cast a corona of yellow light about them. There was a deep spongy layer of sawdust beneath their feet. The ice blocks, big two-foot cubes that were cut in winter from the top of a lake and hauled out on horse-drawn sleds, were ranked in ascending steps against the far wall to a height twice that of a man. They were covered with a thick layer of insulating sawdust.

"What you got for me now?" Wycisowicz said.

Wordlessly, Brother Cooper took up a hoe-like instrument with a wide wooden blade and began scraping sawdust off the top of the first step. He exposed two of the big blocks. He dragged them out a few feet with a pair of heavy tongs and positioned them butt to butt, then drove spikes into them, near the bottom, with a hand sledge. He removed a long coil of rope from a peg on the wall and dropped it near the ice.

The monks stripped off Wycisowicz's tunic and walked him forward.

"You want me to beg? Is that what you want?"

They didn't answer. They stretched him facedown across the ice and wound the rope from spike to spike, crosshatching it across his body, pinning him tightly.

"Well, I'm not going to, you freaks."

The monks bound his wrists and ankles to the spikes. Brother Cooper picked up the lantern.

The ice was like fire against Wycisowicz's naked skin. He shuddered. He tensed involuntarily, trying to draw away from it.

The door closed, plunging him into blackness. He shouted, "You hear me? I'm not going to! I'm not going to give you nothin'!"

The abbot went with Brother Anthony to Marcus's cell. The huge man's cheeks were stubbled, his slack gray skin mottled with rashes. He was sitting slumpshouldered in the corner. His hands were limp in his lap.

"What penance have you decided upon for yourself?" Brother Martin asked.

Marcus looked up slowly. His voice was flat. "Kill me."

"Death?"

"It makes no difference."

Brother Anthony drew a gun from his robe. He chambered a shell and aimed at Marcus's head.

Marcus looked at him without expression.

The abbot placed his hand atop the gun. He said, "The Retreat is over for you."

Brother Anthony put the weapon back into his robe and followed the abbot out into the hall.

Marcus lowered his head. He stared into his lap, without seeing anything.

In the hall, the abbot dismissed Brother Anthony, then walked to Oakley Brown's door. Brother Stewart was inside keeping watch on the penitent.

Brown had been hysterical when they'd removed him from the Chamber of Mortal Meditation. He'd gibbered and twisted as they wrestled him up to his cell, long strings of saliva mixed with blood from his chewed lips dripping from his jaw. Brother Raphael had injected him with a sedative, from which effect he'd emerged some half an hour ago.

Brother Stewart was hunkered down, leaning against a wall. Brown stood at the end of the cell hugging himself. His face twitched, as if afflicted with a nervous disorder, and he was grinding his teeth.

"Brown," the abbot said.

Brown paid him no attention. "Gonna die. Gonna die and rot. Uh-huh." He nodded vigorously to himself. "Gonna rot. Gonna look like that. Gonna burn in Hell fo'ever. Mah Daddy tol' me. Gonna burn!"

"God is merciful," Brother Martin said with some softness. "He forgives. But penance must be done to earn his love."

"Uh-huh. Penance." He looked at Brother Martin. "Yes. Penance!"

"What penance do you propose for yourself?"

"Ennythin'. Please, just save me." Brown went to his knees before the abbot and grasped his robe. "Ennythin'. Jus' don' let me burn! *Ah don' want t' go t' Hell!*"

"Your sins are great. The penance must match them."

Brown lifted his hands to the abbot. "Ennythin'!" he cried.

"It is for you to name."

Brown looked at his hands. He turned the palms toward his eyes, then the backs again. He gazed at them several moments. "These," he said. "That's what Ah done all the evil with. That's what Ah sinned with. . . . Cut 'em off!"

"You wish us to cut your hands off as your penance?"

"Yes. Then mah sins be washed away. Then I won't never sin again, and Ah can be saved."

"You're sure of this."

Brown stared at his hands. He nodded. "Yes."

Brother Martin made the sign of the cross over him. *"In Nomine Patri, et Filii et Spiritu Sancti.* Oakley Brown, your contrition is judged sincere. You have done penance enough. God does not want your hands." He helped the man to his feet.

"But . . . but mah sins won't be forgiven less you cut 'em off."

"They can, and will. Rest now. For you, the Retreat is over."

* * *

At his desk later in the afternoon, Brother Martin made the final entries on Marcus and Brown in the log, then turned to the pages on Rauscher. The last entry was a terse paragraph explaining his decision.

He skipped a line and wrote: *Procedure completed successfully. Extensive destruction of prefrontal lobes. Brother Raphael states the oblate will require weeks, perhaps months of retraining before he can care for himself without help. He will always require direction, but will be able to perform basic tasks adequately.*

He set down his pen, closed his eyes and rubbed the bridge of his nose with his thumb and forefinger. Brother Raphael was now working on Jaretzki, who was the last to be dealt with. It would all be over in a matter of hours.

Had any abbot in the history of the order ever been as relieved as he would be to see a Retreat come to its end?

Probably yes. He was just now coming to understand that no man could direct a Retreat and hope to emerge unscathed.

It occurred to him suddenly, and with shock, that the burden could only become heavier, the decisions more tortured as the years went by.

He recoiled from the thought. He was empty. There were no resources left. He could not face it now.

There was a knock. "Brother Martin?" It was Brother Stefan's voice, tense.

"Yes."

Brother Stefan opened the door. "It's Rios. He's hurt himself."

"Badly?" Brother Martin came from around his desk.

"It's a question of whether major blood vessels are cut."

Rios was in the chapel on the floor before the altar. There were three monks with him working on his hands and feet. They were working with bloodsoaked towels.

Brother Martin knelt. "Let me see."

They opened the towels. Rios's hands and feet were raggedly pierced through, flesh savaged, bone and gristle visible, dark blood pulsing out. A bloody ice hammer, tapered to a sharp chiseled end, lay nearby.

Brother Martin said, "Close the towels. Reapply pressure." He sent Brother Stefan to the surgery. He asked, "Why, Rios?"

Rios smiled up at him radiantly. "I bleed with Christ. I take on His suffering with Him. I *love* Him."

Brother Walter arrived. Only one serious blood vessel had been cut, and he was able to tie that off without much difficulty. He cauterized and closed the wounds. While he worked, Rios smiled dreamily up at the vaulted ceiling.

"Rios," the abbot said. "Listen to me. God wants nothing more like this from you. He knows you did it for His sake— but He needs you to be healthy and whole. You cannot serve as He wants if you hurt yourself again. Do you understand?"

Rios smiled.

"Do you understand that?"

"Yes, Brother Martin," he said absently.

Brother Martin had him taken to the infirmary.

The abbot was troubled. Self-mutilation was fanaticism, not faith, a passion that could easily escalate into a raging religious mania, which was antithetical to true spirituality. But there was nothing that could be done now.

They would have to see what happened during the leavening process of his postulancy.

Jaretzki's surgery was fairly simple, and he wasn't under anesthetic very long. The recovery period was short. He was returned to his cell when he was clearminded and could walk again without difficulty.

Brother Martin visited him there.

The right side of the penitent's face sagged like a limp cloth; it was as if there were two faces; as if a photograph had been split in half vertically and then rejoined in misalignment; as if the right side of his face were dead, and the grave were calling.

Which was not entirely removed from the truth.

The several incisions were small. Each had required only a few stitches and was covered over with a piece of taped gauze the size of a thumbnail.

Jaretzki was sitting on his sleeping board, wrists balanced on his upraised knees. "Did you bring a mirror?"

"Yes." Brother Martin gave him a small hand mirror. He wasn't surprised that the man knew.

Jaretzki looked into the mirror. "I'm hideous," he said without emotion. "Why did you do this to me?"

"Hideous is in the eye of the beholder."

Jaretzki was silent a moment. "The outside world, the real world, they are the beholders."

"Are *they* the real world?"

Jaretzki looked at his reflection. "This wasn't necessary."

"It was. Your 'conversion,' if you will, is real enough, but only to an extent. The rest is no more than aesthetic fascination, which will wane soon enough, leaving you with a desire for the outside world again. This will mitigate that desire."

Jaretzki touched himself. "There's no feeling in parts. Did you sever nerves as well as muscle?"

"Muscle can be rejoined. Nerves are far less certain."

Jaretzki nodded.

"But it was not done for pragmatic reasons alone. It is also your penance, and when you come not simply to accept but to embrace it, then will you have found true contrition."

"That will not be easy."

"The road to God never is."

"Is there more?"

"You have finished your Retreat. Tonight you shall become a postulant."

"Which means?"

"Tonight, Vitek." The abbot left.

Wycisowicz was shaking uncontrollably and uttering rhythmic sounds of mindless pain when Brother Cooper came for him. The ice had frozen great patches of his chest, stomach, loins and thighs into numbness. His body temperature had dropped. The flesh all around the numbed sections felt pricked by thousands of tiny needles. His teeth chattered.

Brother Cooper loosed his bonds.

Wycisowicz didn't move. He went: "Uh-uh-uh-uh."

"You can get up."

Wycisowicz swiveled his eyes up and looked at the monk with little comprehension.

"You can get up," Brother Cooper repeated.

"Hunnh?"

"You're free now."

Wycisowicz blinked. He tried to rise, but collapsed back down, shaking. Brother Cooper helped him. He swayed on his feet, trembling, eyes wide and staring. He was wet. His body had melted its contours into the ice; there was a thin layer of water in the depression.

Brother Cooper wrapped a woolen blanket around him. "Come, Wycisowicz. I'll take you to your room. The Retreat is over."

Chapter 22

"Tonight," Brother Martin told the penitents in the refectory, "you will take places at table alongside us and break bread with us in celebration, for the Retreat is over."

At the lectern, Brother Stefan stood with his hands to either side of the closed Bible. He smiled lovingly. "My friends in Christ," he said. "We have no lengthy lesson this evening. I say to you only the words of Luke: 'Look up, and lift up your heads; for your redemption draweth nigh.'"

Brother Martin gave the blessing.

The meal was taken in silence. There was fried chicken in abundance, boiled potatoes and spinach, strong hot coffee. Most of the penitents ate with appetite, but a few did nothing more than pick at their food. Brother Abner fed Orson.

When the meal ended, Brother Martin rose. He looked each of the penitents in the eye. "You will come with me now."

In file, monks and penitents alternating, Brother Martin led them out of the refectory and down the long western hall. A temperate breeze blew in through the open windows, carrying the scent of fresh-mown grass and savory pungencies from the herbarium in the cloister. The sinking sun threw golden shafts of light across the dark stone floor. Without, birds were in full song.

They descended to the basement, where the abbot stood waiting while Brother Conrad opened the concealed entrance to the vault that lay below. The abbot led them down.

Of the twenty oaken doors set in the walls, twelve stood

open, revealing dark enclosures a little smaller than the cells in which the monks slept.

The penitents—twelve of them; Rauscher was absent—were positioned into a line facing the abbot.

He gazed solemnly at them. "At this moment you cease to be penitents. You have become postulants of the Order of Saint Hector. You are about to enter these cells. Here, alone, in the dark, you will spend the entire period of your postulancy. You will spend this time in prayer and in meditation upon your relationship with God."

Kennedy said, "How—"

"There are no questions! There is only what I tell you."

Kennedy looked down in submission.

"There is a small panel at the bottom of each door. Each morning and evening that panel will be opened briefly. You will be given food through it—the same fare that we take—and your chamber pots will be exchanged. You will keep your silence when the panel is open. Should you have a medical or spiritual problem, you may state it and you will receive help. If the problem is false or if you attempt to speak of anything else, you will be punished. Those of you who require medical care now will receive it daily until your need is over. But you will keep your silence while you are being ministered to.

"The period of postulancy will vary with each of you. When you are thought ready, a brother will begin to visit with you in your cell to engage in discourse and offer counsel. At the appropriate time, you will be removed from here and initiated into the general community as a novitiate. You will then live, pray and work with us until such day that it is fitting that you take your vows and be embraced by us as a full brother in the Order of Saint Hector."

He searched their faces. There was peace in some, hope in others; but he saw also doubt, slyness. Which, though expected, still saddened him.

"We are speaking," he said, "of weeks, of months, of years. I pray that someday we may welcome each and every one of you among us. Toward that end, and to whet your desire and strengthen your resolve, I will tell you that though my heart and soul cry out for this, my knowledge of the ways of men and the world, and the unbroken history of the order, which now approaches a thousand years, tell me that this will probably not be so.

"Some of you will not pass from your postulancy to your novitiate. Others will fail even in the nurturing life of the novice. And some will become brothers, even as I did, even as every monk of the order has done since the time of our beginning. But none of you will ever leave here. Your souls may—as did those of Joel Ableman, Peter Bates and Gunther Hauptmann—but you shall not. Not in the form in which you now exist, not in the fleshly bodies you inhabit.

"It is time now. I exhort you to prayer and communion with God. Nothing less than the fate of your soul is at stake. May God bless you."

He paused. "Philip Sawyer."

Brother Leopold put his hand on Sawyer's shoulder. He guided him to the first cell. Sawyer stepped in, then turned to look out at them. Brother Leopold closed the door, sealing him from view.

It fell into its jamb with a heavy *Chunk*.

Brother Leopold turned the key in the iron lock. *Cl-ank*.

"Gregorio Rios."

Brother Conrad directed Rios to a cell.

Chunk.

Cl-ank.

"Norman Marcus."

Chunk.

Cl-ank.

As the abbot named them, they were shut into their cells one by one.

"Vitek Jaretzki," Brother Martin said. The last.

Jaretzki went to his cell and stood looking out at Brother Martin with his ruined face. His eyes were sad. The left corner of his mouth raised slightly in a smile, and then he turned away.

Brother James closed the door. *Chunk. Cl-ank.*

The abbot signaled Brother Conrad. Brother Conrad withdrew the company, leaving him alone.

The stillness of the chamber was nearly a physical presence. Brother Martin felt it pressing in around him. He became weary. He felt old and enfeebled.

They were gone now, all of them. Some he would never see again. He looked at the thick wooden doors. The names fell from his mind, the faces. He saw only the blank doors. A single tear rolled down his cheek. He walked to the stairs and began to climb.

In the white and gold vestments of joy and resurrection, Brother Stewart offered up a Mass of thanksgiving.

Brother Martin prayed fervently. He had been weighed, and he prayed that God had not found him wanting in the balance. Panic seized him when he knelt to take the sacrament. He closed his eyes as much in dread as in reverence and he had to force himself to tilt back his head and open his mouth.

The body and blood of Christ came to rest lightly upon his tongue. Slowly, ever so slowly, comfort began to spread within him.

Brother Stewart completed the Mass save for the final words. These, as was the custom of the order at such moments, were reserved for the abbot.

Brother Martin rose and turned to face the company. He raised his hand in blessing.

"*Ite,*" he said, "*missa est.*"

Go, it is done.

Within his small cell, atop his pallet of rough ticking filled with straw, Brother Martin lay in tranquil sleep. Without, crickets were chirping and there was a distant har-umph from a bullfrog in the pond. The faintest of breezes slipped in through the narrow window, caressing him gently.

His body knew the time, and he began to wake. Even as he opened his eyes, he heard the rustle of robes beyond his door, the slip of sandaled feet.

There was a small knock. "It is the new day," Brother Phelan said softly.

"Praised be God," Brother Martin replied.

From somewhere near the livestock barn came the call of a great horned owl: *Hoooo, hoooo.*

It was hunting.

But Brother Martin didn't hear it.

The Retreat was over.

It was the new day.

Praised be God.

SHOCKINGLY
FRIGHTENING